VAMPIRE WAR TRILOGY

THE SAGA OF DARREN SHAN

THE DEMONATA

THE SAGA OF DARREN SHAN

*Also available in audio

DARREN SHAN

VAMPIRE WAR TRILOGY

THE SAGA OF DARREN SHAN

HUNTERS OF THE DUSK
ALLIES OF THE NIGHT
KILLERS OF THE DAWN

HarperCollins *Children's Books*

Hunt for Darren Shan
on the web at
www.darrenshan.com

Hunters of the Dusk first published in Great Britain by HarperCollins*Publishers* 2002
Allies of the Night first published in Great Britain by HarperCollins*Publishers* 2002
Killers of the Dawn first published in Great Britain by HarperCollins*Publishers* 2003

First published in this three-in-one edition by HarperCollins *Children's Books* 2005

HarperCollins *Children's Books* is a division of HarperCollins*Publishers* Ltd
77-85 Fulham Palace Road, Hammersmith
London W6 8JB

The HarperCollins *Children's Books* website address is:
www.harpercollins.co.uk

12

Text copyright © Darren Shan 2002, 2003

ISBN-13: 978 0 00 717958 9

The author asserts the moral right to
be identified as the author of the work.

Printed and bound in England by
Clays Ltd, St Ives plc

DARREN SHAN

HUNTERS OF THE DUSK

THE SAGA OF DARREN SHAN
BOOK 7

For:

Shirley & Derek — "Beauty and the Beast"

Sparring partners:
Gillie Russell & Zoë Clarke

Ringside crew:
The Christopher Little clan

OBEs (Order of the Bloody Entrails) to:
Kerri "carve yer guts up" Goddard-Kinch
"la femme fatale" Christine Colinet

PROLOGUE

IT WAS an age of tragic mistakes. For me, the tragedy began fourteen years earlier when, mesmerized by a vampire's amazing performing tarantula, I stole it from him. After an initially successful theft, everything went to hell, and I paid for my crime with my humanity. Faking my own death, I left my family and home, and travelled the world with the Cirque Du Freak, as the assistant to a blood-drinking creature of the night.

My name's Darren Shan. I'm a half-vampire.

I'm also — through a series of events so astounding I still have trouble believing they really happened — a Vampire Prince. The Princes are the leaders of the vampire clan, respected and obeyed by all. There are only five of them — the others are Paris Skyle, Mika Ver Leth, Arrow and Vancha March.

I'd been a Prince for six years, living within the Halls of Vampire Mountain (the stronghold of the clan), learning the customs and traditions of my people, and how to be a vampire of good standing. I'd also been learning the ways of warfare, and how to use weapons. The rules of battle were essential components of any vampire's education, but now more so than ever — because we were at war.

Our opponents were the vampaneze, our purple-skinned blood-cousins. They're a lot like vampires in many ways, but alien to us in one key area — they kill whenever they drink blood. Vampires don't harm those they feed from – we simply take a small amount of blood from each human we target – but vampaneze believe it's shameful to feed without draining their victims dry.

Though there was no love lost between the vampires and vampaneze, for hundreds of years an uneasy truce had existed between the two clans. That changed six years ago when a group of vampaneze – aided by a vampire traitor called Kurda Smahlt – stormed Vampire Mountain in an attempt to seize control of the Hall of Princes. We defeated them (thanks largely to my discovery of the plot prior to their assault), then interrogated the survivors, baffled by why they should choose to attack.

Unlike vampires, vampaneze had no leaders – they were entirely democratic – but when they split from the vampires six hundred years ago, a mysterious, powerful magician known as Mr Tiny paid them a visit and placed the Coffin of Fire in their possession. This coffin burnt alive anyone who lay within it — but Mr Tiny said that one night a man would lie down in it and step out unharmed, and that man would lead them into a victorious war with the vampires, establishing the vampaneze as the unopposed rulers of the night.

During the interrogation, we learnt to our horror that the Lord of the Vampaneze had finally arisen, and vampaneze across the world were preparing for the violent, bloody war to come.

Once our assailants had been put to a painful death, word spread from Vampire Mountain like wildfire: "We're at war with the vampaneze!" And we'd been locked in combat with them ever since, fighting grimly, desperate to disprove Mr Tiny's dark prophecy — that we were destined to lose the war and be wiped from the face of the earth...

CHAPTER ONE

IT WAS another long, tiring night in the Hall of Princes. A Vampire General called Staffen Irve was reporting to me and Paris Skyle. Paris was the oldest living vampire, with more than eight hundred years under his belt. He had flowing white hair, a long, grey beard, and had lost his right ear in a fight many decades ago.

Staffen Irve had been active in the field for three years, and had been giving us a quick rundown of his experiences in the War of the Scars, as it had come to be known (a reference to the scars on our fingertips, the common mark of a vampire or vampaneze). It was a strange war. There were no big battles and neither side used missile-firing weapons — vampires and vampaneze fight only with hand to hand weapons like swords, clubs and spears. The war was a series of isolated skirmishes, three or four vampires at a time pitting themselves against a similar number of vampaneze, fighting to the death.

"There was four of us 'gainst three of them," Staffen Irve said, telling us about one of his more recent encounters. "But my lads was dry behind the tonsils, while the vampaneze was battle-hardy. I killed one of 'em but the others got away, leaving two of my lads dead and the third with a useless arm."

"Have any of the vampaneze spoken of their Lord?" Paris asked.

"No, Sire. Those I take alive only laugh at my questions, even under torture."

In the six years that we'd been hunting for their Lord, there'd been no sign of him. We knew he hadn't been blooded – various vampaneze had told us that he was learning their ways before becoming one of them – and the general opinion was that if we were to have any chance of thwarting Mr Tiny's predictions, we had to find and kill their Lord before he assumed full control of the clan.

A cluster of Generals was waiting to speak with Paris. They moved forward as Staffen Irve departed, but I signalled them back. Picking up a mug of warm blood, I passed it to the one-eared Prince. He smiled and drank deeply, then wiped red stains from around his mouth with the back of a trembling hand — the responsibility of running the war council was taking its toll on the ancient vampire.

"Do you want to call it a night?" I asked, worried about Paris's health.

He shook his head. "The night is young," he muttered.

"But you are not," said a familiar voice behind me — Mr Crepsley. The vampire in the red cloak spent most of his time by my side, advising and encouraging me. He was in a peculiar position. As an ordinary vampire, he held no recognizable rank, and could be commanded by the lowliest of Generals. Yet as my guardian he wielded the unofficial powers of a Prince (since I followed his advice practically all the time). The reality was that Mr Crepsley was second in charge only to Paris Skyle, yet nobody openly acknowledged this. Vampire protocol — go figure!

"You should rest," Mr Crepsley said to Paris, laying a hand on the Prince's shoulder. "This war will run a long time. You must not exhaust yourself too early. We will have need of you later."

"Rot!" Paris laughed. "You and Darren are the future. I am the past, Larten. I will not live to see the end of this war if it drags on as long as we fear. If I do not make my mark now, I never will."

Mr Crepsley started to object, but Paris silenced him with the crooking of a finger. "An old owl hates to be told how young and virile he is. I am on my last legs, and anyone who says otherwise is a fool, a liar, or both."

Mr Crepsley tilted his head obediently. "Very well. I will not argue with you."

"I should hope not," Paris sniffed, then shifted tiredly on his throne. "But this *has* been a taxing night. I will talk with these Generals, then crawl off to my coffin to sleep. Will Darren be able to manage without me?"

"Darren will manage," Mr Crepsley said confidently, and stood slightly behind me as the Generals advanced, ready to advise when required.

Paris didn't make his coffin by dawn. The Generals had much to argue about – by studying reports on the movements of the vampaneze they were trying to pinpoint the possible hiding place of their Lord – and it was close to midday before the ancient Prince slipped away.

I treated myself to a short break, grabbed some food, then heard from three of the Mountain's fighting tutors, who were training the latest batch of Generals. After that I had to send two new Generals out into the field for their first taste of combat. I quickly went through the small ceremony – I had to daub their foreheads with vampire blood and mutter an ancient war prayer over them – then wished them luck and sent them off to kill vampaneze — or die.

Then it was time for vampires to approach me with a wide range of problems and queries. As a Prince I was expected to deal with every sort of subject under the moon. I was only a young, inexperienced half-vampire, who'd become a Prince more by default than merit, but the members of the clan placed their trust completely in their Princes, and I was afforded the same degree of respect as Paris or any of the others.

When the last vampire had departed, I snatched about three hours of sleep, in a hammock which I'd strung up at the rear of the Hall. When I woke, I ate some half-cooked, salted boar meat, washed down with water and followed by a small mug of blood. Then it was back to my throne for more planning, plotting and reports.

CHAPTER TWO

I SNAPPED out of sleep to the sound of screaming.

Jerking awake, I fell out of my hammock, on to the hard, cold floor of my rocky cell. My hand automatically darted for the short sword which I kept strapped by my side at all times. Then the fog of sleep cleared and I realized it was only Harkat, having a nightmare.

Harkat Mulds was a Little Person, a short creature who wore blue robes and worked for Mr Tiny. He'd been human once, though he didn't remember who he used to be, or when or where he lived. When he died, his soul remained trapped on Earth, until Mr Tiny brought him back to life in a new, stunted body.

"Harkat," I mumbled, shaking him roughly. "Wake up. You're dreaming again."

Harkat had no eyelids, but his large green eyes dimmed when he was asleep. Now the light in them flared and he moaned loudly, rolling out of his hammock, as I had moments before. "Dragons!" he screamed, voice muffled by the mask he always wore — he wasn't able to breathe normal air for more than ten or twelve hours, and without the mask he'd die. "Dragons!"

"No," I sighed. "You've been dreaming."

Harkat stared at me with his unnatural green eyes, then relaxed and tugged his mask down, revealing a wide, grey, jagged gash of a mouth. "Sorry, Darren. Did I wake ... you?"

"No," I lied. "I was up already."

I swung back on to my hammock and sat gazing at Harkat. There was no denying he was an ugly build of a creature. Short and squat, with dead, grey skin, no visible ears or a nose — he had ears stitched beneath the skin of his scalp, but was without a sense of smell or taste. He'd no hair, round, green eyes, sharp little teeth and a dark grey tongue. His face had been stitched together, like Frankenstein's monster.

Of course, I was no model myself — few vampires were! My face, body and limbs were laced with scars and burn marks, many picked up during my Trials of Initiation (which I'd passed at my second attempt, two years ago). I was also as bald as a baby, as a result of my first set of Trials, when I'd been badly burnt.

Harkat was one of my closest friends. He'd saved my life twice, when I was attacked by a wild bear on the trail to Vampire Mountain, then in a fight with savage boars during my first, failed Trials of Initiation. It bothered me to see him so disturbed by the nightmares which had been plaguing him for the last few years.

"Was this nightmare the same as the others?" I asked.

"Yes," he nodded. "I was wandering in a vast wasteland. The sky was red. I was searching for something but I didn't ... know what. There were pits full of stakes. A dragon attacked. I fought it off but ... another appeared. Then another. Then..." He sighed miserably.

Harkat's speech had improved greatly since he'd first started speaking. In the beginning he'd had to pause for breath after every two or three words, but he'd learnt to control his breathing technique and now only stalled during long sentences.

"Were the shadow men there?" I asked. Sometimes he dreamt of shadowy figures who chased and tormented him.

"Not this time," he said, "though I think they'd have appeared if you ... hadn't woken me up." Harkat was sweating — his sweat was a pale green colour — and his shoulders shook slightly. He suffered greatly in his sleep, and stayed awake as long as he could, only sleeping four or five hours out of every seventy-two.

"Want something to eat or drink?" I asked.

"No," he said. "Not hungry." He stood and stretched his burly arms. He was only wearing a cloth around his waist, so I could see his smooth stomach and chest — Harkat had no nipples or belly button.

"It's good to see you," he said, pulling on his blue robes, which he'd never grown out of the habit of wearing. "It's been ages since ... we got together."

"I know," I groaned. "This war business is killing me, but I can't leave Paris to deal with it alone. He needs me."

"How is Sire Skyle?" Harkat asked.

"Bearing up. But it's hard. So many decisions to make, so many troops to organize, so many vampires to send to their death."

We were silent a while, thinking about the War of the Scars and the vampires – including some very good friends of ours – who'd perished in it.

"How've you been?" I asked Harkat, shrugging off the morbid thoughts.

"Busy," he said. "Seba's working me harder all the time." After a few months of milling around Vampire Mountain, Harkat had gone to work for the quartermaster – Seba Nile – who was in charge of stocking and maintaining the Mountain's stores of food, clothes and weapons. Harkat started out moving crates and sacks around, but he'd learnt quickly about supplies and how to keep up with the needs of the vampires, and now served as Seba's senior assistant.

"Do you have to return to the Hall of Princes soon?" Harkat asked. "Seba would like to see you. He wants to show you ... some spiders." The mountain was home to thousands of arachnids, known as Ba'Halen's spiders.

"I have to go back," I said regretfully, "but I'll try to drop by soon."

"Do," Harkat said seriously. "You look exhausted. Paris is not the only one who ... needs rest."

Harkat had to leave shortly afterwards to prepare for the arrival of a group of Generals. I lay in my hammock and stared at the dark rock ceiling, unable to get back to sleep. This was the cell Harkat and me had first shared when we came to Vampire Mountain. I liked this tiny cubbyhole — it was the closest thing I had to a bedroom — but rarely got to see much of it. Most of my nights were spent in the Hall of Princes, and the few free hours I had by day were normally passed eating or exercising.

I ran a hand over my bald head while I was resting and thought back over my Trials of Initiation. I'd sailed through them the second time. I didn't have to take them — as a Prince, I was under no obligation — but I wouldn't have felt right if I hadn't. By passing the Trials, I'd proved myself worthy of being a vampire.

Apart from the scars and burns, I hadn't changed much in the last six years. As a half-vampire, I only aged one year for every five that passed. I was a bit taller than when I left the Cirque Du Freak with Mr Crepsley, and my features had thickened and matured slightly. But I wasn't a full-vampire and wouldn't change vastly until I became one. As a full-vampire I'd be much stronger. I'd also be able to heal cuts with my spit, breathe out a gas which could knock people unconscious, and communicate telepathically with other vampires. Plus I'd be able to flit, which is a super-fast speed vampires can attain. On the down side, I'd be vulnerable to sunlight and couldn't move about during the day.

But all that lay far ahead. Mr Crepsley hadn't said anything about when I'd be fully blooded, but I gathered it wouldn't happen until I was an adult. That was ten or fifteen years away — my body was still that of a teenager — so I had loads of time to enjoy (or endure) my extended childhood.

I lay relaxing for another half hour, then got up and dressed. I'd taken to wearing light blue clothes, trousers and a tunic, covered by a long, regal-looking robe. My right thumb snagged on the arm of the tunic as I was pulling it on, as it often did — I'd broken the thumb six years ago and it still stuck out at an awkward angle.

Taking care not to rip the fabric on my extra tough nails — which could gouge holes in soft rock — I freed my thumb and finished dressing. I pulled on a pair of light shoes and ran a hand over my head to make sure I hadn't been bitten by ticks. They'd popped up all over the mountain recently, annoying everyone. Then I made my way back to the Hall of Princes for another long night of tactics and debate.

CHAPTER THREE

THE DOORS to the Hall of Princes could only be opened by a Prince, by laying a hand on the doors or touching a panel on the thrones inside the Hall. Nothing could breach the walls of the Hall, which had been built by Mr Tiny and his Little People centuries before.

The Stone of Blood was housed in the Hall, and was of vital importance. It was a magical artefact. Any vampire who came to the mountain (most of the three thousand vampires in the world had made the trek at least once) laid their hands on the Stone and let it absorb some of their blood. The Stone could then be used to track that vampire down. So, if Mr Crepsley wanted to know where Arrow was, he had only to lay his hands on the Stone and think about him, and within seconds he'd have a fix on the Prince. Or, if he thought of an area, the Stone would tell him how many vampires were there.

I couldn't use the Stone of Blood to search for others — only full-vampires were able to do that — but I could be traced through it, since it had taken blood from me when I became a Prince.

If the Stone ever fell into the hands of the vampaneze, they could use it to track down all the vampires who'd bonded with it. Hiding from them would be impossible. They'd annihilate us. Because of this danger, some vampires wanted to destroy the Stone of Blood — but there was a legend that it could save us in our hour of greatest need.

I was thinking about all this while Paris used the Stone of Blood to manoeuvre troops in the field. As reports reached us of vampaneze positions, Paris used the Stone to check where his Generals were, then communicated telepathically with them, giving them orders to move from place to place. It was this which drained him so deeply. Others could have used the Stone, but as a Prince, Paris's word was law, and it was quicker for him to deliver the orders himself.

While Paris focused on the Stone, Mr Crepsley and me spent much of our time putting field reports together and building up a clear picture of the movements of the vampaneze. Many other Generals were also doing this, but it was our job to take their findings, sort through them, pick out the more important nuggets, and make suggestions to Paris. We had loads of maps, with pins stuck in to mark the positions of vampires and vampaneze.

Mr Crepsley had been intently studying a map for ten minutes, and he looked worried. "Have you seen this?" he asked eventually, summoning me over.

I stared at the map. There were three yellow flags and two red flags stuck close together around a city. We used five main colours to keep track of things. Blue flags for vampires. Yellow for vampaneze. Green for vampaneze strongholds — cities and towns which they defended like bases. White flags were stuck in places where we'd won fights. Red flags where we'd lost.

"What am I looking for?" I asked, staring at the yellow and red flags. My eyes were bleary from lack of sleep and too much concentrating on maps and poorly scrawled reports.

"The name of the city," Mr Crepsley said, running a fingernail over it.

The name meant nothing to me at first. Then my head cleared. "That's your original home," I muttered. It was the city where Mr Crepsley had lived when he was human. Twelve years ago, he'd returned, taking me and Evra Von — a snake-boy from the Cirque Du Freak — with him, to stop a mad vampaneze called Murlough, who'd gone on a killing spree.

"Find the reports," Mr Crepsley said. There was a number on each flag, linking it to reports in our files, so we knew exactly what each flag represented. After a few minutes, I found the relevant sheets of paper and quickly scanned them.

"Of the vampaneze seen there," I muttered, "two were heading into the city. The other was leaving. The first red flag's from a year ago — four Generals were killed in a large clash with several vampaneze."

"And the second red flag marks the spot where Staffen Irve lost two of his men," Mr Crepsley said. "It was when I was adding this flag to the map that I noticed the degree of activity around the city."

"Do you think it means anything?" I asked. It was unusual for so many vampaneze to be sighted in one location.

"I am not sure," he said. "The vampaneze may have made a base there, but I do not see why — it is out of the way of their other strongholds."

"We could send someone to check," I suggested.

He considered that, then shook his head. "We have already lost too many Generals there. It is not a strategically important site. Best to leave it alone."

Mr Crepsley rubbed the long scar which divided the flesh on the left side of his face and went on staring at the map. He'd cut his orange crop of hair tighter than usual – most vampires were cutting their hair short, because of the ticks – and he looked almost bald in the strong light of the Hall.

"It bothers you, doesn't it?" I noted.

He nodded. "If they *have* set up a base, they must be feeding on the humans. I still consider it home, and I do not like to think of my spiritual neighbours and relations suffering at the hands of the vampaneze."

"We could send in a team to flush them out."

He sighed. "That would not be fitting. I would be putting personal considerations before the welfare of the clan. If I ever get out in the field, I shall check on the situation myself, but there is no need to send others."

"What are the odds on you and me ever getting out of here?" I asked wryly. I didn't enjoy fighting, but after six years cooped up inside the mountain, I'd have given my fingernails for a few nights out in the open, even if it meant taking on a dozen vampaneze single-handed.

"The way things stand — poor," Mr Crepsley admitted. "I think we will be stuck here until the end of the war. If one of the other Princes suffers a serious injury and withdraws from battle, we might have to replace him. Otherwise..." He drummed his fingers on the map and grimaced.

"*You* don't have to stay," I said quietly. "There are plenty of others who could guide me."

He barked a laugh. "There are plenty who would steer you," he agreed, "but how many would clip you around the ear if you made an error?"

"Not many," I chuckled.

"They think of you as a Prince," he said, "whereas I still think of you first and foremost as a meddlesome little brat with a *penchant* for stealing spiders."

"Charming!" I huffed. I knew he was kidding – Mr Crepsley always treated me with the respect my position deserved – but there was some truth to his teasing. There was a special bond between Mr Crepsley and me, like between a father and son. He could say things to me that no other vampire would dare. I'd be lost without him.

Placing the map of Mr Crepsley's former home to one side, we returned to the more important business of the night, little dreaming of the events which would eventually lead us back to the city of Mr Crepsley's youth, or the awful confrontation with evil that awaited us there.

CHAPTER FOUR

THE HALLS and tunnels of Vampire Mountain were buzzing with excitement — Mika Ver Leth had returned after an absence of five years, and the rumour was that he had news of the Vampaneze Lord! I was in my cell, resting, when word broke. Wasting no time, I pulled on my clothes and hurried to the Hall of Princes at the top of the mountain, to check if the stories were true.

Mika was talking with Paris and Mr Crepsley when I arrived, surrounded by a pack of Generals eager for news. He was clad entirely in black, as was his custom, and his hawk-like eyes seemed darker and grimmer than ever. He raised one gloved hand in salute when he saw me pushing my way forward. I stood to attention and saluted back. "How's the cub Prince?" he asked with a quick, tight grin.

"Not bad," I replied, studying him for signs of injury — many who returned to Vampire Mountain carried the scars of battle. But although Mika looked tired, he hadn't been visibly wounded. "What about the Vampaneze Lord?" I asked directly. "According to the gossip, you know where he is."

Mika grimaced. "If only!" Looking around, he said, "Shall we assemble? I *have* news, but I'd rather announce it to the Hall in general." Everyone present made straight for their seats. Mika settled on his throne and sighed contentedly. "It's good to be back," he said, patting the arms of the hard chair. "Has Seba been taking good care of my coffin?"

"To the vampaneze with your coffin!" a General shouted, momentarily forgetting his place. "What news of the Vampaneze Lord?"

Mika ran a hand through his jet-black hair. "First, let's make it clear — I don't know where he is." A groan spread through the Hall. "But I've had word of him," Mika added, and all ears pricked up at that.

"Before I begin," Mika said, "do you know about the latest vampaneze recruits?" Everybody looked blank. "The vampaneze have been adding to their ranks since the start of the war, blooding more humans than usual, to drive their numbers up."

"This is old news," Paris murmured. "There are far fewer vampaneze than vampires in the world. We expected them to blood recklessly. It is nothing to worry about — we still outnumber them greatly."

"Yes," Mika said. "But now they're also using unblooded humans. They call them 'vampets'. Apparently the Vampaneze

Lord himself came up with the name. Like him, they're learning the rules of vampaneze life and warfare as humans, before being blooded. He plans to build an army of human helpers."

"We can deal with humans," a General snarled, and there were shouts of agreement.

"Normally," Mika agreed. "But we must be wary of these vampets. While they lack the powers of the vampaneze, they're learning to fight like them. Also, since they aren't blooded, they don't have to abide by the more restrictive vampaneze laws. They aren't honour bound to tell the truth, they don't have to follow ancient customs — and they don't have to limit themselves to hand to hand weapons."

Angry mutters swept through the Hall.

"The vampaneze are using *guns*?" Paris asked, shocked. The vampaneze were even stricter than vampires where weapons were involved. We could use boomerangs and spears, but most vampaneze wouldn't touch them.

"The vampets aren't vampaneze," Mika grunted. "There's no reason why a non-blooded vampet shouldn't use a gun. I don't think all their masters approve, but under orders from their Lord, they allow it.

"But the vampets are a problem for another night," Mika continued. "I only mention them now because it's relevant to how I found out about their Lord. A vampaneze would die screaming before betraying his clan, but the vampets aren't so hardened. I captured one a few months ago and squeezed some interesting details out of him.

Foremost of which is — the Vampaneze Lord doesn't have a base. He's travelling the world with a small band of guards, moving among the various fighting units, keeping up morale."

The Generals received the news with great excitement — if the Vampaneze Lord was mobile and lightly protected, he was more vulnerable to attack.

"Did this *vampet* know where the Vampaneze Lord was?" Mr Crepsley asked.

"No," Mika said. "He'd seen him, but that had been more than a year ago. Only those who accompany him know of his travel patterns."

"What else did he tell you?" Paris enquired.

"That their Lord still hasn't been blooded. And that despite his efforts, morale is low. Vampaneze losses are high, and many don't believe they can win the war. There has been talk of a peace treaty — even outright surrender."

Loud cheering broke out. Some Generals were so elated by Mika's words that a group swept forward, picked him up, and carried him from the Hall. They could be heard singing and shouting as they headed for the crates of ale and wine stored below. The other, more sober-headed Generals looked to Paris for guidance.

"Go on," the elderly Prince smiled. "It would be impolite to let Mika and his over-eager companions drink alone."

The remaining Generals applauded the announcement and hurried away, leaving only a few Hall attendants, myself, Mr Crepsley and Paris behind.

"This is foolish," Mr Crepsley grumbled. "If the vampaneze are truly considering surrender, we should push hard after them, not waste time—"

"Larten," Paris interrupted. "Follow the others, find the largest barrel of ale you can, and get good and steaming drunk."

Mr Crepsley stared at the Prince, his mouth wide open. "Paris!" he gasped.

"You have been caged in here too long," Paris said. "Go and unwind, and do not return without a hangover."

"But—" Mr Crepsley began.

"That is an order, Larten," Paris growled.

Mr Crepsley looked as though he'd swallowed a live eel, but he was never one to disobey an order from a superior, so he clicked his heels together, muttered, "Aye, Sire," and stormed off to the store-rooms in a huff.

"I've never seen Mr Crepsley with a hangover," I laughed. "What's he like?"

"Like a … what do the humans say? A gorilla with a sore head?" Paris coughed into a fist – he'd been coughing a lot lately – then smiled. "But it will do him good. Larten takes life too seriously sometimes."

"What about you?" I asked. "Do you want to go?"

Paris pulled a sour face. "A mug of ale would prove the end of me. I shall take advantage of the break by lying in my coffin at the back of the Hall and getting a full day's sleep."

"Are you sure? I can stay if you want."

"No. Go and enjoy yourself. I will be fine."

"OK." I hopped off my throne and made for the door.

"Darren," Paris called me back. "An excessive amount of alcohol is as bad for the young as for the old. If you are wise, you will drink in moderation."

"Remember what you told me about wisdom a few years ago, Paris?" I replied.

"What?"

"You said the only way to get wise was to get experienced." Winking, I rushed out of the Hall and was soon sharing a barrel of ale with a grumpy, orange-haired vampire. Mr Crepsley gradually cheered up as the night progressed, and was singing loudly by the time he reeled back to his coffin late the following morning.

CHAPTER FIVE

I COULDN'T understand why there were two moons in the sky when I awoke, or why they were green. Groaning, I rubbed the back of a hand over my eyes, then looked again. I realized I was lying on the floor, staring up at the green eyes of a chuckling Harkat Mulds. "Have fun last night?" he asked.

"I've been poisoned," I moaned, rolling over on to my stomach, feeling as though I was on the deck of a ship during a fierce storm.

"You won't be wanting boar guts and ... bat broth then?"

"Don't!" I winced, weak at the very thought of food.

"You and the others must have drained ... half the mountain's supply of ale last night," Harkat remarked, helping me to my feet.

"Is there an earthquake?" I asked as he let go of me.

"No," he said, puzzled.

"Then why's the floor shaking?"

He laughed and steered me to my hammock. I'd been sleeping inside the door of our cell. I had vague memories of falling off the hammock every time I tried to get on. "I'll just sit on the floor a while," I said.

"As you wish," Harkat chortled. "Would you like some ale?"

"Go away or I'll hit you," I growled.

"Is ale no longer to your liking?"

"No!"

"That's funny. You were singing about how much you … loved it earlier. 'Ale, ale, I drink like a whale, I am the … Prince, the Prince of ale'."

"I could have you tortured," I warned him.

"Never mind," Harkat said. "The whole clan went crazy … last night. It takes a lot to get a vampire drunk, but … most managed. I've seen some wandering the tunnels, looking lik—"

"Please," I begged, "don't describe them." Harkat laughed again, pulled me to my feet and led me out of the cell, into the maze of tunnels. "Where are we going?" I asked.

"The Hall of Perta Vin Grahl. I asked Seba about cures … for hangovers – I had a feeling you'd have one – and he said … a shower usually did the trick."

"No!" I moaned. "Not the showers! Have mercy!"

Harkat took no notice of my pleas, and soon he was shoving me under the icy cold waters of the internal waterfalls in the Hall of Perta Vin Grahl. I thought my head was going to explode when the water first struck, but after a few minutes the worst of my headache had passed and my stomach had settled. By the time I was towelling myself dry, I felt a hundred times better.

We passed a green-faced Mr Crepsley on our way back to our cell. I bid him a good evening, but he only snarled in reply.

"I'll never understand the appeal of … alcohol," Harkat said as I was dressing.

"Haven't you ever got drunk?" I replied.

"Perhaps in my past life, but not since … becoming a Little Person. I don't have taste buds, and alcohol doesn't … affect me."

"Lucky you," I muttered sourly.

Once I'd dressed, we strolled up to the Hall of Princes to see if Paris needed me, but it was largely deserted and Paris was still in his coffin.

"Let's go on a tour of the tunnels … beneath the Halls," Harkat suggested. We'd done a lot of exploring when we first came to the mountain, but it had been two or three years since we'd last gone off on an adventure.

"Don't you have work to do?" I asked.

"Yes, but…" He frowned. It took a while to get used to Harkat's expressions – it was hard to know whether someone without eyelids and a nose was frowning or grinning – but I'd learnt to read them. "It will hold. I feel strange. I need to be on the move."

"OK," I said. "Let's go walkabout."

We started in the Hall of Corza Jarn, where trainee Generals were taught how to fight. I'd spent many hours here, mastering the use of swords, knives, axes and spears. Most of the weapons were designed for adults, and were too large and cumbersome for me to master, but I'd picked up the basics.

The highest ranking tutor was a blind vampire called Vanez Blane. He'd been my Trials Master during both my Trials of Initiation. He'd lost his left eye in a fight with a lion many decades before, and lost the second six years ago in a fight with the vampaneze.

Vanez was wrestling with three young Generals. Though he was blind, he'd lost none of his sharpness, and the trio ended up flat on their backs in short order at the hands of the ginger-haired games master. "You'll have to learn to do better than that," he told them. Then, with his back to us, he said, "Hello, Darren. Greetings, Harkat Mulds."

"Hi, Vanez," we replied, not surprised that he knew who we were — vampires have very keen senses of smell and hearing.

"I heard you singing last night, Darren," Vanez said, leaving his three students to recover and regroup.

"No!" I gasped, crestfallen. I'd thought Harkat was joking about that.

"Very enlightening," Vanez smiled.

"I didn't!" I groaned. "Tell me I didn't!"

Vanez's smile spread. "I shouldn't worry. Plenty of others made asses of themselves too."

"Ale should be banned," I growled.

"Nothing wrong with ale," Vanez disagreed. "It's the ale-*drinkers* who need to be controlled."

We told Vanez we were going on a tour of the lower tunnels and asked if he'd like to tag along. "Not much point," he said. "I can't see anything. Besides…" Lowering his voice, he told us the three Generals he was training were due to be sent into action soon. "Between ourselves, they're as poor a trio as I've ever passed fit for duty," he sighed. Many vampires were being rushed into the field, to replace casualties in the War of the Scars. It was a contentious point among the clan – it usually took a minimum of twenty years to be declared a General of good standing – but Paris said that desperate times called for desperate measures.

Leaving Vanez, we made for the store-rooms to see Mr Crepsley's old mentor, Seba Nile. At seven hundred, Seba was the second oldest vampire. He dressed in red like Mr Crepsley, and spoke in the same precise way. He was wrinkled and shrunken with age, and limped badly – like Harkat – from a wound to his left leg gained in the same fight that had claimed Vanez's eye.

Seba was delighted to see us. When he heard we were going exploring, he insisted on coming with us. "There is something I wish to show you," he said.

As we left the Halls and entered the vast warren of lower connecting tunnels, I scratched my bald head with my fingernails.

"Ticks?" Seba asked.

"No," I said. "My head's been itching like mad lately. My arms and legs too, and my armpits. I think I have an allergy."

"Allergies are rare among vampires," Seba said. "Let me examine you." Luminous lichen grew along many of the walls and he was able to study me by the light of a thick patch. "Hmmm." He smiled briefly, then released me.

"What is it?" I asked.

"You are coming of age, Master Shan."

"What's that got to do with itching?"

"You will find out," he said mysteriously.

Seba kept stopping at webs to check on spiders. The old quartermaster was uncommonly fond of the eight-legged predators. He didn't keep them as pets, but he spent a lot of time studying their habits and patterns. He was able to communicate with them using his thoughts. Mr Crepsley could too, and so could I.

"Ah!" he said eventually, stopping at a large cobweb. "Here we are." Putting his lips together, he whistled softly, and moments later a big grey spider with curious green spots scuttled down the cobweb and on to Seba's upturned hand.

"Where did that come from?" I asked, stepping forward for a closer look. It was larger than the normal mountain spiders, and different in colour.

"Do you like it?" Seba asked. "I call them Ba'Shan's spiders. I hope you do not object — the name seemed appropriate."

"Ba'Shan's spiders?" I repeated. "Why would–"

I stopped. Fourteen years ago, I'd stolen a poisonous spider from Mr Crepsley — Madam Octa. Eight years later, I'd released her — on Seba's advice — to make a new home with the mountain spiders. Seba said she wouldn't be able to mate with the others. I hadn't seen her since I set her free, and had almost forgotten about her. But now the memory snapped into place, and I knew where this new spider had come from.

"It's one of Madam Octa's, isn't it?" I groaned.

"Yes," Seba said. "She mated with Ba'Halen's spiders. I noticed this new strain three years ago, although it is only this last year that they have multiplied. They are taking over. I think they will become the dominant mountain spider, perhaps within ten or fifteen years."

"Seba!" I snapped. "I only released Madam Octa because you told me she couldn't have offspring. Are they poisonous?"

The quartermaster shrugged. "Yes, but not as deadly as their mother. If four or five attacked together, they could kill, but not one by itself."

"What if they go on a rampage?" I yelled.

"They will not," Seba said stiffly.

"How do you know?"

"I have asked them not to. They are incredibly intelligent, like Madam Octa. They have almost the same mental abilities as rats. I am thinking of training them."

"To do *what*?" I laughed.

"Fight," he said darkly. "Imagine if we could send armies of trained spiders out into the world, with orders to find vampaneze and kill them."

I turned appealingly to Harkat. "Tell him he's crazy. Make him see sense."

Harkat smiled. "It sounds like a good idea … to me," he said.

"Ridiculous!" I snorted. "I'll tell Mika. He hates spiders. He'll send troops down here to stamp them out."

"Please do not," Seba said quietly. "Even if they cannot be trained, I enjoy watching them develop. Please do not rid me of one of my few remaining pleasures."

I sighed and cast my eyes to the ceiling. "OK. I won't tell Mika."

"Nor the others," he pressed. "I would be highly unpopular if word leaked."

"What do you mean?"

Seba cleared his throat guiltily. "The ticks," he muttered. "The new spiders have been feeding on ticks, so they have moved upwards to escape."

"Oh," I said, thinking of all the vampires who'd had to cut their hair and beards and shave under their arms because of the deluge of ticks. I grinned.

"Eventually the spiders will pursue the ticks to the top of the mountain and the epidemic will pass," Seba continued, "but until then I would rather nobody knew what was causing it."

I laughed. "You'd be strung up if this got out!"

"I know," he grimaced.

I promised to keep word of the spiders to myself. Then Seba headed back for the Halls – the short trip had tired him

— and Harkat and me continued down the tunnels. The further we progressed, the quieter Harkat got. He seemed uneasy, but when I asked him what was wrong, he said he didn't know.

Eventually we found a tunnel which led outside. We followed it to where it opened on to the steep mountain face, and sat staring up at the evening sky. It had been months since I'd stuck my head out in the open, and more than two years since I'd slept outdoors. The air tasted fresh and welcome, but strange.

"It's cold," I noted, rubbing my hands up and down my bare arms.

"Is it?" Harkat asked. His dead grey skin only registered extreme degrees of heat or cold.

"It must be late autumn or early winter." It was hard keeping track of the seasons when you lived inside a mountain.

Harkat wasn't listening. He was scanning the forests and valleys below, as if he expected to find someone there.

I walked a short bit down the mountain. Harkat followed, then overtook me and picked up speed. "Careful," I called, but he paid no attention. Soon he was running, and I was left behind, wondering what he was playing at. "Harkat!" I yelled. "You'll trip and crack your skull if you—"

I stopped. He hadn't heard a word. Cursing, I slipped off my shoes, flexed my toes, then started after him. I tried to control my speed, but that wasn't an option on such a steep decline, and soon I was hurtling down the mountain, sending pebbles and dust scattering, yelling at the top of my lungs with excitement and terror.

Somehow we kept on our feet and reached the bottom of the mountain intact. Harkat kept running until he came to a small circle of trees, where he finally stopped and stood as though frozen. I jogged after him and came to a halt. "What ... was that ... about?" I gasped.

Raising his left hand, Harkat pointed towards the trees.

"What?" I asked, seeing nothing but trunks, branches and leaves.

"He's coming," Harkat hissed.

"Who?"

"The dragon master."

I stared at Harkat oddly. He looked as though he was awake, but perhaps he'd dozed off and was sleepwalking. "I think we should get you back inside," I said, taking his outstretched arm. "We'll find a fire and–"

"Hello, boys!" somebody yelled from within the circle of trees. "Are you the welcoming committee?"

Letting go of Harkat's arm, I stood beside him – now as stiff as he was – and stared again into the cluster of trees. I thought I recognized that voice — though I hoped I was wrong!

Moments later, three figures emerged from the gloom. Two were Little People, who looked almost exactly like Harkat, except they had their hoods up and moved with a stiffness which Harkat had worked out of his system during his years among the vampires. The third was a small, smiling, white-haired man, who struck more fear in me than a band of marauding vampaneze.

Mr Tiny!

After more than six hundred years, Desmond Tiny had returned to Vampire Mountain, and I knew as he strode towards us, beaming like a rat-catcher in league with the Pied Piper of Hamlin, that his reappearance heralded nothing but trouble.

CHAPTER SIX

MR TINY paused briefly when he reached us. The short, plump man was wearing a shabby yellow suit — a thin jacket, no overcoat — with childish-looking green wellington boots and a chunky pair of glasses. The heart-shaped watch he always carried hung by a chain from the front of his jacket. Some said Mr Tiny was an agent of fate — his first name was Desmond, and if you shortened it and put the two names together, you got *Mr Destiny*.

"You've grown, young Shan," he said, running an eye over me. "And you, Harkat…" He smiled at the Little Person, whose green eyes seemed wider and rounder than ever. "*You* have changed beyond recognition. Wearing your hood down, working for vampires — and talking!"

"You knew … I could talk," Harkat muttered, slipping back into his old broken speech habits. "You always … knew."

Mr Tiny nodded, then started forward. "Enough of the chit-chat, boys. I have work to do and I must be quick. Time is precious. A volcano's due to erupt on a small tropical island tomorrow. Everybody within a ten-kilometre radius will be roasted alive. I want to be there — it sounds like great fun."

He wasn't joking. That's why everyone feared him — he took pleasure in tragedies which left anyone halfway human shaken to their very core.

We followed Mr Tiny up the mountain, trailed by the two Little People. Harkat looked back often at his 'brothers'. I think he was communicating with them — the Little People can read each other's thoughts — but he said nothing to me about it.

Mr Tiny entered the mountain by a different tunnel to the one we'd used. It was a tunnel I'd never been in, higher, wider and drier than most. There were no twists or side tunnels leading off it. It rose straight and steady up the spine of the mountain. Mr Tiny spotted me staring at the walls of the unfamiliar tunnel. "This is one of my short cuts," he said. "I've short cuts all over the world, in places you wouldn't dream of. Saves time."

As we progressed, we passed groups of very pale-skinned humans in rags, lining the sides of the tunnel, bowing low to Mr Tiny. These were the Guardians of the Blood, people who lived within Vampire Mountain and donated their blood to the vampires. In return, they were allowed to extract a vampire's internal organs and brain when he died — which they ate at special ceremonies!

I felt nervous walking past the ranks of Guardians – I'd never seen so many of them gathered together before – but Mr Tiny only smiled and waved at them, and didn't stop to exchange any words.

Within a quarter of an hour we were at the gate which opened on to the Halls of Vampire Mountain. The guard on duty swung the door wide open when we knocked but stopped when he saw Mr Tiny and half closed it again. "Who are you?" he snapped defensively, hand snaking to the sword on his belt.

"You know who I am, Perlat Cheil," Mr Tiny said, brushing past the startled guard.

"How do you know my–?" Perlat Cheil began, then stopped and gazed after the departing figure. He was trembling and his hand had fallen away from his sword. "Is that who I think it is?" he asked as I passed with Harkat and the Little People.

"Yes," I said simply.

"Charna's guts!" he gasped, and made the death's touch sign by pressing the middle finger of his right hand to his forehead, and the two fingers next to that over his eyelids. It was a sign vampires made when they thought death was close.

Through the tunnels we marched, silencing conversations and causing jaws to drop. Even those who'd never met Mr Tiny recognized him, stopped what they were doing and fell in behind us, following wordlessly, as though trailing a hearse.

There was only one tunnel leading to the Hall of Princes – I'd found another six years ago, but that had since been blocked off – and it was protected by the Mountain's finest guards. They were supposed to stop and search anyone seeking entry to the Hall, but when Mr Tiny approached, they gawped at him, lowered their weapons, then let him – and the rest of the procession – pass unobstructed.

Mr Tiny finally stopped at the doors of the Hall and glanced at the domed building which he'd built six centuries earlier. "It's stood the test of time quite well, hasn't it?" he remarked to no one in particular. Then, laying a hand on the doors, he opened them and entered. Only Princes were supposed to be able to open the doors, but it didn't surprise me that Mr Tiny had the power to control them too.

Mika and Paris were within the Hall, discussing the war with a gaggle of Generals. There were a lot of sore heads and bleary eyes, but everyone snapped to attention when they saw Mr Tiny striding in.

"By the teeth of the gods!" Paris gasped, his face whitening. He cringed as Mr Tiny set foot on the platform of thrones, then drew himself straight and forced a tight smile. "Desmond," he said, "it is good to see you."

"You too, Paris," Mr Tiny responded.

"To what do we owe this unexpected pleasure?" Paris enquired with strained politeness.

"Wait a minute and I'll tell you," Mr Tiny replied, then plopped himself down on a throne – *mine!* – crossed his legs and made himself comfortable. "Get the gang in," he said, crooking a finger at Mika. "I've something to say and it's for everybody's ears."

Within a few minutes, almost every vampire in the mountain had crowded into the Hall of Princes, and stood nervously by the walls — as far away from Mr Tiny as possible — waiting for the mysterious visitor to speak.

Mr Tiny had been checking his nails and rubbing them up and down the front of his jacket. The Little People were standing behind the throne. Harkat stood to their left, looking uncertain. I sensed he didn't know whether to stand with his brothers-of-nature or with his brothers-of-choice — the vampires.

"All present and correct?" Mr Tiny asked. He got to his feet and waddled to the front of the platform. "Then I'll come straight to the point. The Lord of the Vampaneze has been blooded." He paused, anticipating gasps, groans and cries of terror. But we all just stared at him, too shocked to react. "Six hundred years ago," he continued, "I told your forebears that the Vampaneze Lord would lead the vampaneze into a war against you and wipe you out. That was *a* truth — but not *the* truth. The future is both open and closed. There's only one 'will be' but there are often hundreds of 'can be's'. Which means the Vampaneze Lord and his followers *can* be defeated."

Breath caught in every vampire's throat and you could feel hope forming in the air around us, like a cloud.

"The Vampaneze Lord is only a half-vampaneze at the moment," Mr Tiny said. "If you find and kill him before he's fully blooded, victory will be yours."

At that, a huge roar went up, and suddenly vampires were

clapping each other on the back and cheering. A few didn't join in the hooting and hollering. Those with first-hand knowledge of Mr Tiny – myself, Paris, Mr Crepsley – sensed he hadn't finished, and guessed there must be a catch. Mr Tiny wasn't the kind to smile broadly when delivering good news. He only grinned like that when he knew there was going to be suffering and misery.

When the wave of excitement had died down, Mr Tiny raised his right hand. He clutched his heart-shaped watch with his left hand. The watch glowed a dark red colour, and suddenly his right hand glowed as well. All eyes settled on the five crimson fingers and the Hall went eerily quiet.

"When the Vampaneze Lord was discovered seven years ago," Mr Tiny said, his face illuminated by the glow of his fingers, "I studied the strings connecting the present to the future, and saw that there were five chances to avert the course of destiny. One of those has already come and gone."

The red glow faded from his thumb, which he tucked down into his palm. "That chance was Kurda Smahlt," he said. Kurda was the vampire who led the vampaneze against us, in a bid to seize control of the Stone of Blood. "If Kurda had succeeded, most vampires would have been absorbed by the vampaneze and the War of the Scars – as you've termed it – would have been averted.

"But you killed him, destroying what was probably your best hope of survival in the process." He shook his head and tutted. "That was silly."

"Kurda Smahlt was a traitor," Mika growled. "Nothing good comes of treachery. I'd rather die honourably than owe my life to a turncoat."

"More fool you," Mr Tiny chortled, then wiggled his glowing little finger. "This represents your last chance, if all others fail. It will not fall for some time yet – if at all – so we shall ignore it." He tucked the glowing finger down, leaving the three middle fingers standing.

"Which brings us to my reason for coming. If I left you to your own devices, these chances would slip by unnoticed. You'd carry on as you have been, the windows of opportunity would pass, and before you knew it..." He made a soft popping sound.

"Within the next twelve months," he said softly but clearly, "there may be three encounters between certain vampires and the Vampaneze Lord — assuming you heed my advice. Three times he will be at your mercy. If you seize one of these chances and kill him, the war will be yours. If you fail, there'll be one final, all-deciding confrontation, upon which the fate of every living vampire will hang." He paused teasingly. "To be honest, I hope it goes down to the wire — I love big, dramatic conclusions!"

He turned his back on the Hall and one of his Little People handed him a flask, from which he drank deeply. Furious whispers and conversations swept through the assembled vampires while he was drinking, and when he next faced the crowd, Paris Skyle was waiting. "You have been very generous with your information, Desmond," he said. "On behalf of all here, I thank you."

"Don't mention it," Mr Tiny said. His fingers had stopped glowing, he'd let go of his watch, and his hands now rested in his lap.

"Will you extend your generosity and tell us which vampires are destined to encounter the Vampaneze Lord?" Paris asked.

"I will," Mr Tiny said smugly. "But let me make one thing clear — the encounters will only occur if the vampires *choose* to hunt the Lord of the Vampaneze. The three I name don't have to accept the challenge of hunting him down, or take responsibility for the future of the vampire clan. But if they don't, you're doomed, for in these three alone lies the ability to change that which is destined to be."

He slowly looked around the Hall, meeting the eyes of every vampire present, searching for signs of weakness and fear. Not one of us looked away or wilted in the face of such a dire charge. "Very well," he grunted. "One of the hunters is absent, so I'll not name him. If the other two head for the cave of Lady Evanna, they'll probably run into him along the way. If not, his chance to play an active part in the future will pass, and it will boil down to that lone pair."

"And they are…?" Paris asked tensely.

Mr Tiny glanced over at me, and with a horrible sinking feeling in my gut, I guessed what was coming next. "The hunters must be Larten Crepsley and his assistant, Darren Shan," Mr Tiny said simply, and as all eyes in the Hall turned to seek us out, I had the sense of invisible tumblers clicking into place, and knew my years of quiet security inside Vampire Mountain had come to an end.

CHAPTER SEVEN

THE POSSIBILITY of refusing the challenge never entered my thoughts. Six years of living among vampires had filled me with their values and beliefs. Any vampire would lay down his life for the good of the clan. Of course, this wasn't as simple as giving one's life – I had a mission to fulfil, and if I failed, all would suffer – but the principle was the same. I'd been chosen, and a vampire who's been chosen does not say 'no'.

There was a short debate, in which Paris told Mr Crepsley and me that this was not official duty and we didn't have to agree to represent the clan — no shame would befall us if we refused to co-operate with Mr Tiny. At the end of the debate, Mr Crepsley stepped forward, red cloak snapping behind him like wings, and said, "I relish the chance to hunt down the Vampaneze Lord."

I stepped up after him, sorry I wasn't wearing my

impressive blue cloak, and said in what I hoped was a brave tone, "Me too."

"The boy knows how to keep it short," Mr Tiny murmured, winking at Harkat.

"What about the rest of us?" Mika asked. "I've spent five years hunting for that accursed Lord. I wish to accompany them."

"Aye! Me too!" a General in the crowd shouted, and soon everyone was bellowing at Mr Tiny, seeking permission to join us in the hunt.

Mr Tiny shook his head. "Three hunters must seek — no more, no less. Non-vampires may assist them, but if any of their kinsmen tag along, they shall fail."

Angry mutters greeted that statement.

"Why should we believe you?" Mika asked. "Surely ten stand a better chance than three, and twenty more than ten, and thirty—"

Mr Tiny clicked his fingers. There was a sharp, snapping sound and dust fell from overhead. Looking up, I saw long jagged cracks appear in the ceiling of the Hall of Princes. Other vampires saw them too and cried out, alarmed.

"Would you, who has not seen three centuries, dare to tell me, who measures time in continental drifts, about the mechanisms of fate?" Mr Tiny asked menacingly. He clicked his fingers again and the cracks spread. Chunks of the ceiling crumbled inwards. "A thousand vampaneze couldn't chip the walls of this Hall, yet I, by clicking my fingers, can bring it tumbling down." He lifted his fingers to click them again.

"No!" Mika shouted. "I apologize! I didn't mean to offend you!"

Mr Tiny lowered his hand. "Think of this before crossing me again, Mika Ver Leth," he growled, then nodded at the Little People he'd brought with him, who headed for the doors of the Hall. "They'll patch the roof up before we leave," Mr Tiny said. "But next time you anger me, I'll reduce this Hall to rubble, leaving you and your precious Stone of Blood to the whim of the vampaneze."

Blowing dust off his heart-shaped watch, Mr Tiny beamed around the Hall again. "I take it we're decided — three it shall be?"

"Three," Paris agreed.

"Three," Mika muttered bleakly.

"As I said, non-vampires may — indeed, *must* — play a part, but for the next year no vampire should seek out any of the hunters, unless for reasons which have nothing to do with the search for the Vampaneze Lord. Alone they must stand and alone they must succeed or fail."

With that, he brought the meeting to a close. Dismissing Paris and Mika with an arrogant wave of his hand, he beckoned Mr Crepsley and me forward, and grinned at us as he lay back on my throne. He kicked off one of his wellies while he was talking. He wasn't wearing socks, and I was shocked to see he had no toes — his feet were webbed at the ends, with six tiny claws jutting out like a cat's.

"Frightened, Master Shan?" he asked, eyes twinkling mischievously.

"Yes," I said, "but I'm proud to be able to help."

"What if you *aren't* any help?" he jeered. "What if you fail and damn the vampires to extinction?"

I shrugged. "What comes, we take," I said, echoing a saying which was common among the creatures of the night.

Mr Tiny's smile faded. "I preferred you when you were less clever," he grumbled, then looked to Mr Crepsley. "What about you? Scared by the weight of your responsibilities?"

"Yes," Mr Crepsley answered.

"Think you might break beneath it?"

"I might," Mr Crepsley said evenly.

Mr Tiny pulled a face. "You two are no fun. It's impossible to get a rise out of you. Harkat!" he bellowed. Harkat approached automatically. "What do you think of this? Does the fate of the vampires bother you?"

"Yes," Harkat replied. "It does."

"You care for them?" Harkat nodded. "Hmmm." Mr Tiny rubbed his watch, which glowed briefly, then touched the left side of Harkat's head. Harkat gasped and fell to his knees. "You've been having nightmares," Mr Tiny noted, fingers still at Harkat's temple.

"Yes!" Harkat groaned.

"You want them to stop?"

"Yes."

Mr Tiny let go of Harkat, who cried out, then gritted his sharp teeth and stood up straight. Small green tears of pain trickled from the corners of his eyes.

"It's time for you to learn the truth about yourself," Mr Tiny said. "If you come with me, I'll reveal it and the nightmares will stop. If you don't, they'll continue and worsen, and within a year you'll be a screaming wreck."

Harkat trembled at that, but didn't rush to Mr Tiny's side. "If I wait," he said, "will I have … another chance to learn … the truth?"

"Yes," Mr Tiny said, "but you'll suffer much in the meantime, and I can't guarantee your safety. If you die before learning who you really are, your soul will be lost forever."

Harkat frowned uncertainly. "I have a feeling," he mumbled. "Something whispers to me— " he touched the left side of his chest "—here. I feel that I should go with Darren … and Larten."

"If you do, it will improve their chances of defeating the Vampaneze Lord," Mr Tiny said. "Your participation isn't instrumental, but it could be important."

"Harkat," I said softly, "you don't owe us. You've already saved my life twice. Go with Mr Tiny and learn the truth about yourself."

Harkat frowned. "I think that if I … leave you to learn the truth, the person I was … won't like what I've done." The Little Person spent a few more difficult seconds brooding about it, then squared up to Mr Tiny. "I'll go with them. Right or wrong, I feel my place is … with the vampires. All else must wait."

"So be it," Mr Tiny sniffed. "If you survive, our paths will cross again. If not…" His smile was withering.

"What of our search?" Mr Crepsley asked. "You mentioned Lady Evanna. Do we start with her?"

"If you wish," Mr Tiny said. "I can't and won't direct you, but that's where *I* would start. After that, follow your heart. Forget about the quest and go where you feel you belong. Fate will direct you as it pleases."

That was the end of our conversation. Mr Tiny slipped away without a farewell, taking his Little People (they'd completed their repair work while he was talking), no doubt anxious to make that fatal volcano of his the next day.

Vampire Mountain was in uproar that night. Mr Tiny's visit and prophecy were debated and dissected at length. The vampires agreed that Mr Crepsley and me had to leave on our own, to link up with the third hunter – whoever he might be – but were divided as to what the rest of them should do. Some thought that since the clan's future rested with three lone hunters, they should forget the war with the vampaneze, since it no longer seemed to serve any purpose. Most disagreed and said it would be crazy to stop fighting.

Mr Crepsley led Harkat and me from the Hall shortly before dawn, leaving the arguing Princes and Generals behind, saying we needed to get a good day's rest. It was hard to sleep with Mr Tiny's words echoing round my brain, but I managed to squeeze in a few hours.

We woke about three hours before sunset, ate a short meal and packed our meagre belongings (I took a spare set of clothes, some bottles of blood, and my diary). We said private goodbyes to Vanez and Seba – the old quartermaster was especially sad to see us go – then met Paris Skyle at the gate leading out of the Halls. He told us Mika was staying on to assist with the night-to-night running of the war. He looked very poorly as I shook his hand, and I had a feeling that he hadn't many years left — if our search kept us away from Vampire Mountain for a long period, this might be the last time I saw him.

"I'll miss you, Paris," I said, hugging him roughly after we'd shaken hands.

"I will miss you too, young Prince," he said, then squeezed me tight and hissed in my ear: "Find and kill him, Darren. There is a cold chill in my bones, and it is not the chill of old age. Mr Tiny has spoken the truth — if the Vampaneze Lord comes into his full powers, I am sure we all shall perish."

"I'll find him," I vowed, locking gazes with the ancient Prince. "And if the chance falls to me to kill him, my aim will be true."

"Then may the luck of the vampires be with you," he said.

I joined Mr Crepsley and Harkat. We saluted to those who'd gathered to see us off, then faced down the tunnels and set off. We moved quickly and surely, and within two hours had left the mountain and were jogging over open ground, beneath a clear night sky.

Our hunt for the Lord of the Vampaneze had begun!

CHAPTER EIGHT

IT WAS great to be back on the road. We might be walking into the heart of an inferno, and our companions would suffer immeasurably if we failed, but those were worries for the future. In those first few weeks all I could think about was how refreshing it was to stretch my legs and breathe clean air, not caged in with dozens of sweaty, smelly vampires.

I was in high spirits as we cut a path through the mountains by night. Harkat was very quiet and spent a lot of time mulling over what Mr Tiny had said. Mr Crepsley seemed as glum as ever, though I knew that underneath the gloomy façade he was as pleased to be out in the open as I was.

We struck a firm pace and kept to it, covering many kilometres over the course of each night, sleeping deeply by day beneath trees and bushes, or in caves. The cold was fierce when we set off, but as we wound our way down through the mountain range, the biting chill lessened. By the time we reached the lowlands we were as comfortable as a human would have been on a blustery autumn day.

We carried spare bottles of human blood, and fed on wild animals. It had been a long time since I hunted, and I was rusty to begin with, but I soon got back into the swing of it.

"This is the life, isn't it?" I noted one morning as we chewed on the roasted carcass of a deer. We didn't light a fire most days — we ate our meat raw — but it was nice to relax around a mound of blazing logs every once in a while.

"It is," Mr Crepsley agreed.

"I wish we could go on like this forever."

The vampire smiled. "You are not in a hurry to return to Vampire Mountain?"

I pulled a face. "Being a Prince is a great honour, but it's not much fun."

"You have had a rough initiation," he said sympathetically. "Were we not at war, there would have been time for adventure. Most Princes wander the world for decades before settling down to royal duty. Your timing was unfortunate."

"Still, I can't complain," I said cheerfully. "I'm free now."

Harkat stirred up the fire and edged closer towards us. He hadn't said a lot since leaving Vampire Mountain, but now he lowered his mask and spoke. "I loved Vampire Mountain. It felt like home. I never felt so at ease before, even when I …

was with the Cirque Du Freak. When this is over, if I have … the choice, I'll return."

"There is vampire blood in you," Mr Crepsley said. He was joking, but Harkat took the statement seriously.

"There might be," he said. "I've often wondered if I was a vampire in … my previous life. That might explain why I was sent to Vampire Mountain … and why I fitted in so well. It could also explain the stakes … in my dreams."

Harkat's dreams often involved stakes. The ground would give way in his nightmares and he'd fall into a pit of stakes, or be chased by shadow men who carried stakes and drove them through his heart.

"Any fresh clues as to who you might have been?" I asked. "Did meeting Mr Tiny jog your memory?"

Harkat shook his chunky, neckless head. "No further insights," he sighed.

"Why did Mr Tiny not tell you the truth about yourself if it was time for you to learn?" Mr Crepsley asked.

"I don't think it's as … simple as that," Harkat said. "I have to earn the truth. It's part of the … deal we made."

"Wouldn't it be weird if Harkat *had* been a vampire?" I remarked. "What if he'd been a Prince — would he still be able to open the doors of the Hall of Princes?"

"I don't think I was a Prince," Harkat chuckled, the corners of his wide mouth lifting in a gaping smile.

"Hey," I said, "if *I* can become a Prince, anyone can."

"True," Mr Crepsley muttered, then ducked swiftly as I tossed a leg of deer at him.

Once clear of the mountains, we headed south-east and soon reached the outskirts of civilization. It was strange to see electric lights, cars and planes again. I felt as though I'd been living in the past and had stepped out of a time machine.

"It's so noisy," I commented one night as we passed through a busy town. We'd entered it to draw blood from humans, slicing them in their sleep with our nails, taking a small amount of blood, closing the cuts with Mr Crepsley's healing spit, leaving them oblivious to the fact that they'd been fed upon. "So much music and laughter and shouting." My ears were ringing from the noise.

"Humans always chatter like monkeys," Mr Crepsley said. "It is their way."

I used to object when he said things like that, but not any more. When I became Mr Crepsley's assistant, I'd clung to the hope of returning to my old life. I'd dreamt of regaining my humanity and going home to my family and friends. No longer. My years in Vampire Mountain had rid me of my human desires. I was a creature of the night now — and content to be so.

The itching was getting worse. Before leaving town, I found a pharmacy and bought several anti-itching powders and lotions, which I rubbed into my flesh. The powders and lotions brought no relief. Nothing stopped the itching, and I scratched myself irritably as we journeyed to the cave of Lady Evanna.

Mr Crepsley wouldn't say much about the woman we were

going to meet, where she lived, whether she was a vampire or human, and why we were going to see her.

"You should tell me these things," I grumbled one morning as we made camp. "What if something happens to you? How would Harkat and me find her?"

Mr Crepsley stroked the long scar running down the left side of his face — after all our years together, I still didn't know how he got it — and nodded thoughtfully. "You are right. I will draw a map before nightfall."

"And tell us who she is?"

He hesitated. "That is harder to explain. It might be best coming from her own lips. Evanna tells different people different things. She might not object to you knowing the truth — but then again, she might."

"Is she an inventor?" I pressed. Mr Crepsley owned a collection of pots and pans which folded up into tiny bundles, making them easier to carry. He'd told me that Evanna had made them.

"She sometimes invents," he said. "She is a woman of many talents. Much of her time is spent breeding frogs."

"Excuse me?" I blinked.

"It is her hobby. Some people breed horses, dogs or cats. Evanna breeds frogs."

"How can she breed frogs?" I snorted sceptically.

"You will find out." Then he leant forward and tapped my knee. "Whatever you say, do not call her a witch."

"Why would I call her a witch?" I asked.

"Because she is one — sort of."

"We're going to meet a *witch*?" Harkat snapped worriedly.

"That troubles you?" Mr Crepsley asked.

"Sometimes in my dreams ... there's a witch. I've never seen her face — not clearly — and I'm not sure ... if she's good or bad. There are times when I run to her for help, and times ... when I run away, afraid."

"You haven't mentioned that before," I said.

Harkat's smile was shaky. "With all the dragons, stakes and shadow men ... what's one little witch?"

The mention of dragons reminded me of something he'd said when we met Mr Tiny. He'd called him 'the dragon master'. I asked Harkat about this but he couldn't remember saying it. "Although," he mused, "I sometimes see Mr Tiny in my dreams, riding the ... backs of dragons. Once he tore the brain out of one and ... tossed it at me. I reached to catch it but ... woke before I could."

We thought about that image a long time. Vampires place a lot of importance on dreams. Many believe that dreams act as links to the past or future, and that much can be learnt from them. But Harkat's dreams didn't seem to have any bearing on reality, and in the end Mr Crepsley and me dismissed them, rolled over and slept. Harkat didn't — he stayed awake, green eyes glowing faintly, putting off sleep as long as he could, avoiding the dragons, stakes, witches and other perils of his troubled nightmares.

CHAPTER NINE

ONE DUSK I awoke with a feeling of absolute comfort. As I stared up at a red, darkening sky, I tried putting my finger on why I felt so good. Then I realized — the itching had stopped. I lay still a few minutes, afraid it would return if I moved, but when I finally got to my feet, there wasn't the slightest prickling sensation. Grinning, I headed for a small pond we'd camped by, to wet my throat.

I lowered my face into the cool, clear water of the pond and drank deeply. As I was rising, I noticed an unfamiliar face in the reflecting surface of the water — a long-haired, bearded man. It was directly in front of me, which meant he must be standing right behind me — but I hadn't heard anyone approach.

Swivelling swiftly, my hand shot to the sword which I'd brought from Vampire Mountain. I had it halfway out of its scabbard before stopping, confused.

There was no one there.

I looked around for the shabby, bearded man, but he was nowhere to be seen. There were no nearby trees or rocks he could have ducked behind, and not even a vampire could have moved quickly enough to disappear so swiftly.

I turned back towards the pond and looked into the water again. There he was! As clear and hairy as before, scowling up at me.

I gave a yelp and jumped back from the water's edge. Was the bearded man *in* the pond? If so, how was he breathing?

Stepping forward, I locked gazes with the hairy man – he looked like a caveman – for the third time and smiled. He smiled back. "Hello," I said. His lips moved when mine did, but silently. "My name's Darren Shan." Again his lips moved in time with mine. I was getting annoyed – was he mocking me? – when realization struck — it was *me!*

I could see my eyes and the shape of my mouth now that I looked closely, and the small triangular scar just above my right eye, which had become as much a part of me as my nose or ears. It was my face, no doubt about that — but where had all the hair come from?

I felt around my chin and discovered a thick bushy beard. Running my right hand over my head – which should have been smooth – I was stunned to feel long, thick locks of hair. My thumb, which stuck out at an angle, caught in several of the strands, and I winced as I tugged it free, pulling some hair out with it.

What in Khledon Lurt's name had happened to me?

I checked further. Ripping off my T-shirt revealed a chest and stomach covered in hair. Huge balls of hair had also formed under my armpits and over my shoulders. I was hairy all over!

"*Charna's guts!*" I roared, then ran to wake my friends.

Mr Crepsley and Harkat were breaking camp when I rushed up, panting and shouting. The vampire took one look at my hairy figure, whipped out a knife and roared at me to stop. Harkat stepped up beside him, a grim expression on his face. As I halted, gasping for breath, I saw they didn't recognize me. Raising my hands to show they were empty, I croaked, "Don't ... attack! It's ... me!"

Mr Crepsley's eyes widened. "*Darren?*"

"It can't be," Harkat growled. "This is an impostor."

"No!" I moaned. "I woke up, went to the pond to drink, and found ... found..." I shook my hairy arms at them.

Mr Crepsley stepped forward, sheathed his knife, and studied my face incredulously. Then he groaned. "The *purge!*" he muttered.

"The *what?*" I shouted.

"Sit down, Darren," Mr Crepsley said seriously. "We have a lot of talking to do. Harkat — go fill our canteens and fix a new fire."

When Mr Crepsley had gathered his thoughts, he explained to Harkat and me what was happening. "You know that half-vampires become full-vampires when more vampire blood is pumped into them. What we have never discussed —

since I did not anticipate it so soon – is the other way in which one's blood can turn.

"Basically, if one remains a half-vampire for an extremely long period of time – the average is forty years – one's vampire cells eventually attack the human cells and convert them, resulting in full-vampirism. We call this the purge."

"You mean I've become a full-vampire?" I asked quietly, both intrigued and frightened by the notion. Intrigued because it would mean extra strength, the ability to flit and communicate telepathically. Frightened because it would also mean a total retreat from daylight and the world of humanity.

"Not yet," Mr Crepsley said. "The hair is simply the first stage. We shall shave it off presently, and though it will grow back, it will stop after a month or so. You will undergo other changes during that time – you will grow, and experience headaches and sharp bursts of energy – but these too will cease. At the end of the changes, your vampiric blood may have replaced your human blood entirely, but it probably will not, and you will return to normal — for a few months or a couple of years. But sometime within the next few years, your blood *will* turn completely. You have entered the final stages of half-vampirism. There is no turning back."

We spent most of the rest of the night discussing the purge. Mr Crepsley said it was rare for a half-vampire to undergo the purge after less than twenty years, but it was probably linked to when I'd become a Vampire Prince — more vampiric blood had been added to my veins during the ceremony, and that must have speeded up the process.

I recalled Seba studying me in the tunnels of Vampire Mountain, and told Mr Crepsley about it. "He must have known about the purge," I said. "Why didn't he warn me?"

"It was not his place," Mr Crepsley said. "As your mentor, I am responsible for informing you. I am sure he would have told me about it, so that I could have sat down with you and explained it, but there was no time — Mr Tiny arrived and we had to leave the Mountain."

"You said Darren would grow during … the purge," Harkat said. "How much?"

"There is no telling," Mr Crepsley said. "Potentially, he could mature to adulthood in the space of a few months — but that is unlikely. He shall age a few years, but probably no more."

"You mean I'll finally hit my teens?" I asked.

"I would imagine so."

I thought about that for a while, then grinned. "Cool!"

But the purge was far from cool — it was a curse! Shaving off all the hair was bad enough – Mr Crepsley used a long, sharp blade, which scraped my skin raw – but the changes my body was undergoing were much worse. Bones were lengthening and fusing. My nails and teeth grew – I had to bite my nails and grind my teeth together while I walked at night to keep them in shape – and my feet and hands got longer. Within weeks I was five centimetres taller, aching all over from growth pains.

My senses were in a state of disarray. Slight sounds were magnified — the snapping of a twig was like a house collapsing. The dullest of smells set my nose tingling. My sense of taste deserted me completely. Everything tasted like cardboard. I began to understand what life must be like for Harkat and made a resolution never to tease him about his lack of taste buds again.

Even dim lights were blinding to my ultra-sensitive eye. The moon was like a fierce spotlight in the sky, and if I opened my eyes during the day, I might as well have been sticking two fiery pins into them — the inside of my head would flare with a metallic pain.

"Is this what sunlight is like for full-vampires?" I asked Mr Crepsley one day, as I shivered beneath a thick blanket, eyes shut tight against the painful rays of the sun.

"Yes," he said. "That is why we avoid even short periods of exposure to daylight. The pain of sunburn is not especially great – not for the first ten or fifteen minutes – but the glare of the sun is instantly unbearable."

I suffered with immense headaches during the purge, a result of my out-of-control senses. There were times when I thought my head was going to explode, and I'd weep helplessly from the pain.

Mr Crepsley helped me fight the dizzying effects. He bound light strips of cloth across my eyes – I could still see pretty well – and stuffed balls of grass into my ears and up my nostrils. That was uncomfortable, and I felt ridiculous – Harkat's howls of laughter didn't help – but the headaches lessened.

Another side-effect was a fierce surge of energy. I felt as if I was operating on batteries. I had to run ahead of Mr

Crepsley and Harkat at night, then double back to meet them, just to tire myself out. I exercised like crazy every time we stopped — push-ups, pull-ups, sit-ups — and usually woke long before Mr Crepsley, unable to sleep more than a couple of hours at a time. I climbed trees and cliffs, and swam across rivers and lakes, all in an effort to use up my unnatural store of energy. I'd have wrestled an elephant if I'd found one!

Finally, after six weeks, the turmoil ceased. I stopped growing. I didn't have to shave any more (though the hair on my head remained — I was no longer bald!). I removed the cloth and grass balls, and my taste returned, although patchily to begin with.

I was about seven centimetres taller than I'd been when the purge hit me, and noticeably broader. The skin on my face had hardened, giving me a slightly older appearance — I looked like a fifteen- or sixteen-year-old now.

Most importantly — I was still a half-vampire. The purge hadn't eliminated my human blood cells. The downside of that was I'd have to undergo the discomfort of the purge again in the future. On the plus side I could continue to enjoy sunlight for the time being, before having to abandon it forever in favour of the night.

Although I was keen to become a full-vampire, I'd miss the daytime world. Once my blood turned, there was no going back. I accepted that, but I'd be lying if I said I wasn't nervous. This way, I had months — perhaps a year or two — to prepare myself for the change.

I'd outgrown my clothes and shoes, so I had to stock up at a small human outpost (we were leaving civilization behind again). In an army surplus shop, I chose gear similar to my old stuff, adding a couple of purple shirts to my blue ones, and a dark green pair of trousers. As I was paying for the clothes, a tall, lean man entered. He was wearing a brown shirt, black trousers and a baseball cap. "I need supplies," he grunted at the man serving behind the counter, tossing a list at him.

"You'll need a licence for the guns," the shopkeeper said, running an eye over the scrap of paper.

"I've got one." The man was reaching into a shirt pocket when he caught sight of my hands and stiffened. I was holding my new clothes across my chest, and the scars on my fingertips – where I'd been blooded by Mr Crepsley – were clear.

The man relaxed instantly and turned away — but I was sure he'd recognized the scars and knew what I was. Hurrying from the shop, I found Mr Crepsley and Harkat on the edge of town and told them what had happened.

"Was he nervous?" Mr Crepsley asked. "Did he follow when you left?"

"No. He just went stiff when he saw the marks, then acted as though he hadn't seen them. But he knew what the marks meant — I'm certain of it."

Mr Crepsley rubbed his scar thoughtfully. "Humans who know the truth about vampire marks are uncommon, but some exist. In all probability he is an ordinary person who has simply heard tales of vampires and their fingertips."

"But he *might* be a vampire hunter," I said quietly.

"Vampire hunters are rare — but real." Mr Crepsley thought it over, then decided. "We will proceed as planned, but keep our eyes open, and you or Harkat will remain on watch by day. If an attack comes, we shall be ready." He smiled tightly and touched the handle of his knife. "And waiting!"

CHAPTER TEN

BY DAWN we knew we had a fight on our hands. We were being followed, not just by one person, but three or four. They'd picked up our trail a few kilometres outside the town and had been tracking us ever since. They moved with admirable stealth, and if we hadn't been anticipating trouble, we might not have known anything was amiss. But when a vampire is alert to danger, not even the most fleet-footed human can sneak up on him.

"What's the plan?" Harkat asked as we were making camp in the middle of a small forest, sheltered from the sun beneath the intertwining branches and leaves.

"They will wait for full daylight to attack," Mr Crepsley said, keeping his voice low. "We will act as though all is normal and pretend to sleep. When they come, we deal with them."

"Will you be OK in the sun?" I asked. Though we were

sheltered where we were, a battle might draw us out of the shade.

"The rays will not harm me during the short time it will take to deal with this threat," Mr Crepsley replied. "And I will protect my eyes with cloth, as you did during your purge."

Making beds amid the moss and leaves on the ground, we wrapped ourselves in our cloaks and settled down. "Of course, they might just be curious," Harkat muttered. "They could simply want to see … what a real-life vampire looks like."

"They move too keenly for that," Mr Crepsley disagreed. "They are here on business."

"I just remembered," I hissed. "The guy in the shop was buying *guns!*"

"Most vampire hunters come properly armed," Mr Crepsley grunted. "Gone are the nights when the fools toted only a hammer and wooden stake."

There was no more talk after that. We lay still, eyes closed (except for Harkat, who covered his lidless eyes with his cloak), breathing evenly, feigning sleep.

Seconds passed slowly, taking an age to become minutes, and an eternity to become hours. It had been six years since my last taste of vicious combat. My limbs felt unnaturally cold, and stiff, icy snakes of fear coiled and uncoiled inside the walls of my stomach. I kept flexing my fingers beneath the folds of my cloak, never far from my sword, ready to draw.

Shortly after midday — when the sun would be most harmful to a vampire — the humans moved in for the kill. There were three of them, spread out in a semicircle. At first I could only hear the rustling of leaves as they approached, and the occasional snap of a twig. But as they closed upon us, I became aware of their heavy breathing, the creak of their tense bones, the pacy, panicked pounding of their hearts.

They came to a standstill ten or twelve metres away, tucked behind trees, preparing themselves to attack. There was a long, nervous pause — then the sound of a gun being slowly cocked.

"*Now!*" Mr Crepsley roared, springing to his feet, launching himself at the human nearest him.

While Mr Crepsley closed in on his assailant at incredible speed, Harkat and me targeted the others. The one I'd set my sights on cursed loudly, stepped out from behind his tree, brought his rifle up and got a snap shot off. A bullet whizzed past, missing me by several centimetres. Before he could fire again, I was upon him.

I wrenched the rifle from the human's hands and tossed it away. A gun went off behind me, but there was no time to check on my friends. The man in front of me had already drawn a long hunting knife, so I quickly slid my sword out.

The man's eyes widened when he saw the sword — he'd painted the area around his eyes with red circles of what looked like blood — then narrowed. "You're just a kid," he snarled, slashing at me with his knife.

"No," I disagreed, stepping out of range of his knife, jabbing at him with my sword. "I'm much more."

As the human slashed at me again, I brought my sword up and out in a smooth arcing slice, through the flesh, muscles and bones of his right hand, severing three of his fingers, disarming him in an instant.

The human cried out in agony and fell away from me. I took advantage of the moment to see how Mr Crepsley and Harkat were faring. Mr Crepsley had already despatched his human, and was striding towards Harkat, who was wrestling with his opponent. Harkat appeared to have the advantage of his foe, but Mr Crepsley was moving into place to back him up should the battle take a turn for the worse.

Satisfied that all was going in our favour, I switched my attention back to the man on the ground, psyching myself up for the unpleasant task of making an end of him. To my surprise, I found him grinning horribly at me.

"You should have taken my other hand too!" he growled.

My eyes fixed on the man's left hand and my breath caught in my throat — he was clutching a hand grenade close to his chest!

"Don't move!" he shouted as I lurched towards him. He half-pressed down on the detonator with his thumb. "If this goes off, it takes you with me!"

"Easy," I sighed, backing off slightly, gazing fearfully at the primed grenade.

"I'll take it easy in hell," he chuckled sadistically. He'd shaved his head bald and there was a dark 'V' tattooed into either side of his skull, just above his ears. "Now, tell your foul vampire partner and that grey-skinned monster to let my companion go, or I'll—"

There was a sharp whistling sound from the trees to my left. Something struck the grenade and sent it flying from the human's hand. He yelled and grabbed for another grenade (he had a string of them strapped around his chest). There was a second whistling sound and a glinting, multi-pointed object buried itself in the middle of the man's head.

The man slumped backwards with a grunt, shook crazily, then lay still. I stared at him, bewildered, automatically bending closer for a clearer look. The object in his head was a gold throwing star. Neither Mr Crepsley nor Harkat carried such a weapon — so who'd thrown it?

In answer to my unvoiced question, someone jumped from a nearby tree and strode towards me. "Only ever turn your back on a corpse!" the stranger snapped as I whirled towards him. "Didn't Vanez Blane teach you that?"

"I ... forgot," I wheezed, too taken aback to say anything else. The vampire – he had to be one of us – was a burly man of medium height, with reddish skin and dyed green hair, dressed in purple animal hides which had been stitched together crudely. He had huge eyes – almost as large as Harkat's – and a surprisingly small mouth. Unlike Mr Crepsley, his eyes were uncovered, though he was squinting painfully in the sunlight. He wore no shoes and carried no weapons other than dozens of throwing stars strapped to several belts looped around his torso.

"I'll have my shuriken back, thank you," the vampire said to the dead human, prying the throwing star loose, wiping it clean of blood, and reattaching it to one of the belts. He turned the man's head left and right, taking in the shaved skull, tattoos and red circles around the eyes. "A vampet!" he snorted. "I've clashed with them before. Miserable curs." He spat on the dead man, then used his bare foot to roll him over, so he was lying face down.

When the vampire turned to address me, I knew who he was — I'd heard him described many times — and greeted him with the respect he deserved. "Vancha March," I said, bowing my head. "It's an honour to meet you, Sire."

"Likewise," he replied blithely.

Vancha March was the Vampire Prince I'd never met, the wildest and most traditional of all the Princes.

"Vancha!" Mr Crepsley boomed, tearing the cloth away from around his eyes, crossing the space between us and clasping the Prince's shoulders. "What are you doing here, Sire? I thought you were further north."

"I was," Vancha sniffed, freeing his hands and wiping the knuckles of his left hand across his nose, then flicking something green and slimy away. "But there was nothing happening, so I cut south. I'm heading for Lady Evanna's."

"We are too," I said.

"I figured as much. I've been trailing you for the last couple of nights."

"You should have introduced yourself sooner, Sire," Mr Crepsley said.

"This is the first time I've seen the new Prince," Vancha replied. "I wanted to observe him from afar for a while." He studied me sternly. "On the basis of this fight, I have to say I'm not overly impressed!"

"I erred, Sire," I said stiffly. "I was worried about my friends and I made the mistake of pausing when I should have pushed ahead. I accept full responsibility, and I apologize most humbly."

"At least he knows how to make a good apology," Vancha laughed, clapping me on the back.

Vancha March was covered in grime and dirt and smelt like a wolf. It was his standard appearance. Vancha was a true being of the wilds. Even among vampires, he was considered an extremist. He only wore clothes that he'd made himself from wild animal skins, and he never ate cooked meat or drank anything other than fresh water, milk and blood.

As Harkat limped towards us – having finished off his attacker – Vancha sat and crossed his legs. Lifting his left foot, he lowered his head to it and started biting the nails!

"So this is the Little Person who talks," Vancha mumbled, eyeing Harkat over the nail of his left big toe. "Harkat Mulds, isn't it?"

"It is, Sire," Harkat replied, lowering his mask.

"I might as well tell you straight up, Mulds — I don't trust Desmond Tiny or any of his stumpy disciples."

"And I don't trust vampires who … chew their toenails," Harkat threw back at him, then paused and added slyly, "*Sire*."

Vancha laughed at that and spat out a chunk of nail. "I think we're going to get along fine, Mulds!"

"Hard trek, Sire?" Mr Crepsley asked, sitting down beside the Prince, covering his eyes with cloth again.

"Not bad," Vancha grunted, uncrossing his legs. He then started in on his right toenails. "Yourselves?"

"The travelling has been good."

"Any news from Vampire Mountain?" Vancha asked.

"Lots," Mr Crepsley said.

"Save it for tonight." Vancha let go of his foot and lay back. He took off his purple cloak and draped it over himself. "Wake me when it's dusk," he yawned, rolled over, fell straight asleep and started to snore.

I stared, goggle-eyed, at the sleeping Prince, then at the nails he'd chewed off and spat out, then at his ragged clothes and dirty green hair, then at Harkat and Mr Crepsley. "*He's* a Vampire Prince?" I whispered.

"He is," Mr Crepsley smiled.

"But he looks like…" Harkat muttered uncertainly. "He acts like…"

"Do not be fooled by appearances," Mr Crepsley said. "Vancha chooses to live roughly, but he is the finest of vampires."

"If you say so," I responded dubiously, and spent most of the day lying on my back, staring up at the cloudy sky, kept awake by the loud snoring of Vancha March.

CHAPTER ELEVEN

WE LEFT the vampets lying where we'd killed them (Vancha said they weren't worthy of burial) and set off at dusk. As we marched, Mr Crepsley told the Prince of Mr Tiny's visit to Vampire Mountain, and what he'd predicted. Vancha said little while Mr Crepsley was talking, and brooded upon his words in silence for a long time after he finished.

"I don't think it takes a genius to surmise that I'm the third hunter," he said in the end.

"I would be most surprised if you were not," Mr Crepsley agreed.

Vancha had been picking between his teeth with the tip of a sharp twig. Now he tossed it aside and spat into the dust of the trail. Vancha was a master spitter — his spit was thick, globular and green, and he could hit an ant at twenty paces. "I don't trust that evil meddler, Tiny," he snapped. "I've run into him a couple of times, and I've made a habit of doing the opposite of anything he says."

Mr Crepsley nodded. "Generally speaking, I would agree with you. But these are dangerous times, Sire, and—"

"Larten!" the Prince interrupted. "It's 'Vancha', 'March' or 'Hey, ugly!' while we're on the trail. I won't have you kowtowing to me."

"Very well—" Mr Crepsley grinned "—*ugly.*" He grew serious again. "These are dangerous times, Vancha. The future of our race is at stake. Dare we ignore Mr Tiny's prophecy? If there is hope, we must seize it."

Vancha let out a long, unhappy sigh. "For hundreds of years, Tiny's let us think we were doomed to lose the war when the Vampaneze Lord arose. Why does he tell us now, after all this time, that it *isn't* cut and dried, but we can *only* prevent it if we follow his instructions?" The Prince scratched the back of his neck and spat into the bush to our left. "It sounds like a load of guano to me!"

"Maybe Evanna can shed light on the subject," Mr Crepsley said. "She shares some of Mr Tiny's powers and can sense the paths of the future. She might be able to confirm or dismiss his predictions."

"If so, I'll believe her," Vancha said. "Evanna guards her tongue closely, but when she speaks, she speaks the truth. If she says our destiny lies on the road, I'll gladly pitch in with you. If not..." He shrugged and let the matter rest.

Vancha March was *weird* — and that was putting it mildly! I'd never met anyone like him. He had a code all of his own.

As I already knew, he wouldn't eat cooked meat or drink anything but fresh water, milk and blood, and he made his clothes from the hides of animals he hunted. But I learnt much more about him during the six nights it took us to reach Lady Evanna's.

He followed the old ways of the vampires. Long ago, vampires believed that we were descended from wolves. If we lived good lives and stayed true to our beliefs, we'd become wolves again when we died and roam the wilds of Paradise as spirit creatures of the eternal night. To that end, they lived more like wolves than humans, avoiding civilization except when they had to drink blood, making their own clothes, following the laws of the wild.

Vancha wouldn't sleep in a coffin — he said they were too comfortable! He thought a vampire should sleep on open ground, covering himself with no more than his cloak. He respected vampires who used coffins but had a very low opinion of those who slept in beds. I didn't dare tell him about my preference for hammocks!

He had a great interest in dreams, and often ate wild mushrooms which led to vibrant dreams and visions. He believed the future was mapped out in our dreams, and if we learnt to decipher them, we could control our destinies. He was fascinated by Harkat's nightmares and spent many long hours discussing them with the Little Person.

The only weapons he used were his shurikens (the throwing stars), which he carved himself from various metals and stones. He thought hand to hand combat should be exactly that — fought with one's hands. He'd no time for swords, spears or axes and refused to touch them.

"But how can you fight someone who has a sword?" I asked one evening as we were getting ready to break camp. "Do you run?"

"I run from nothing!" he replied sharply. "Here — let me show you." Rubbing his hands together, he stood opposite me and told me to draw my sword. When I hesitated, he slapped my left shoulder and jeered. "Afraid?"

"Of course not," I snapped. "I just don't want to hurt you."

He laughed out loud. "There's not much fear of that, is there, Larten?"

"I would not be so sure," Mr Crepsley demurred. "Darren is only a half-vampire but he is sharp. He could test you, Vancha."

"Good," the Prince said. "I relish worthy opponents."

I looked pleadingly at Mr Crepsley. "I don't want to draw on an unarmed man."

"*Unarmed?*" Vancha shouted. "I have *two* arms!" He waved them at me.

"Go ahead," Mr Crepsley said. "Vancha knows what he is doing."

Pulling out my sword, I faced Vancha and made a half-hearted lunge. He didn't move. Simply watched as I pulled the tip of my sword up short.

"Pathetic," he sniffed.

"This is stupid," I told him. "I'm not–"

Before I could say anything else, he darted forward, seized me by the throat and made a small, painful cut across my neck with his nails.

"Ow!" I yelled, stumbling away from him.

"Next time I'll cut your nose off," he said pleasantly.

"No you won't!" I growled and swung at him with my sword, properly this time.

Vancha ducked clear of the arc of the blade. "Good," he grinned. "That's more like it."

He circled me, eyes on mine, fingers flexing slowly. I kept the tip of my sword low, until he came to a halt, then moved towards him and jabbed. I expected him to shift aside, but instead he brought the palm of his right hand up and swiped the blade away, as he would a flat stick. As I struggled to bring it back around, he stepped in, caught hold of my hand above the wrist, gave a sharp twist which caused me to release the sword — and I was weaponless.

"See?" he smiled, stepping back and raising his hands to show the fight was at an end. "If this was for real, your ass would be grass." Vancha had a foul mouth — that was one of his tamest insults!

"Big deal," I sulked, rubbing my sore wrist. "You beat a half-vampire. You couldn't win against a full-vampire or a vampaneze."

"I can and have," he insisted. "Weapons are tools of fear, used by those who are afraid. One who learns to fight with his hands always has the advantage over those who rely on swords and knives. Know why?"

"Why?"

"Because *they* expect to win," he beamed. "Weapons are false – they're not of nature – and inspire false confidence. When I fight, I expect to die. Even now, when I sparred with you, I anticipated death and resigned myself to it. Death is the worst this world can throw at you, Darren — if you accept it, it has no power over you."

Picking up my sword, he handed it to me and watched to see what I'd do. I had the feeling he wanted me to cast it aside — and I was tempted to, to earn his respect. But I'd have felt naked without it, so I slid it back into its sheath and glanced down at the ground, slightly ashamed.

Vancha clasped the back of my neck and squeezed amiably. "Don't let it bother you," he said. "You're young. You have loads of time to learn." His eyes creased as he thought about Mr Tiny and the Lord of the Vampaneze, and he added gloomily, "I hope."

I asked Vancha to teach me how to fight bare-handed. I'd studied unarmed combat in Vampire Mountain, but that had been against opponents who were also unarmed. Apart from a few lessons regarding what to do if I lost my weapon during battle, I'd never been taught how to take on a fully armed foe using only my hands. Vancha said it would take years to master, and I could expect lots of nicks and bruises while learning. I waved away such concerns — I loved the thought of being able to best an armed vampaneze with my bare hands.

Training couldn't start on the trail, but Vancha talked me through a few basic blocking tactics when we rested by day, and promised to give me a real work out when we got to Evanna's.

The Prince would tell me no more about the witch than Mr Crepsley had, though he did say she was both the fairest and least attractive of women — which made no sense at all!

I thought Vancha would be strongly anti-vampaneze – the vampires who despised vampaneze the most were normally those steeped in the old ways – but to my surprise he had nothing against them. "Vampaneze are noble and true," he said a couple of nights before we reached Evanna's. "I don't agree with their feeding habits – there's no need to kill when we drink – but otherwise I admire them."

"Vancha nominated Kurda Smahlt to become a Prince," Mr Crepsley remarked.

"I admired Kurda," Vancha said. "He was known for his brains, but he also had guts. He was a remarkable vampire."

"Don't you..." I coughed and trailed off into silence.

"Say what's on your mind," Vancha told me.

"Don't you feel bad for nominating him, after what he did, leading the vampaneze against us?"

"No," Vancha said bluntly. "I don't approve of his actions, and if I'd been at Council, I wouldn't have spoken up on his behalf. But he was following his heart. He acted for the good of the clan. Misguided as he was, I don't think Kurda was a real traitor. He acted poorly, but his motives were pure."

"I agree," Harkat said, joining the conversation. "I think Kurda's been poorly treated. It was right that he was killed when he … was captured, but it's wrong to say he was a villain, and not mention his name … in the Hall of Princes."

I didn't respond to that. I'd liked Kurda immensely, and knew he'd done his best to spare the vampires the wrath of the Vampaneze Lord. But he'd killed one of my other friends – Gavner Purl – and brought about the death of more, including Arra Sails, a female vampire who'd once been Mr Crepsley's mate.

I learnt the identity of Vancha's *real* enemy the day before we came to the end of the first leg of our journey. I'd been sleeping, but my face was itchy – an after-effect of the purge – and I awoke before midday. I sat up, scratching under my chin, and spotted Vancha at the edge of camp, his clothes tossed aside – except for a strip of bear hide tied around his waist – rubbing spit into his skin.

"Vancha?" I asked quietly. "What are you doing?"

"I'm going walking," he said, and continued rubbing spit into the flesh of his shoulders and arms.

I stared up at the sky. It was a bright day and hardly any clouds were around to block out the sun. "Vancha, it's *daytime*," I said.

"Really?" he replied sarcastically. "I'd never have guessed."

"Vampires burn in sunlight," I said, wondering if he'd bumped his head and forgotten what he was.

"Not immediately," he said, then looked at me sharply. "Have you ever wondered *why* vampires burn in the sun?"

"Well, no, not exactly…"

"There's no logical reason," Vancha said. "According to the stories humans tell, it's because we're evil, and evil beings can't face the sun. But that's nonsense — we're not evil, and even if we were, we should still be able to move about during the day.

"Look at wolves," he continued. "We're supposed to be descended from them, but they can endure the sunlight. Even true nocturnal creatures like bats and owls can survive by day. Sunlight might confuse them, but it doesn't kill them. *So why does it kill vampires?*"

I shook my head uncertainly. "I don't know. Why?"

Vancha barked a laugh. "Damned if I know! Nobody does. Some claim we were cursed by a witch or sorcerer, but I doubt that — the world's full of servants of the dark arts, but none with the power to make such a lethal curse. My hunch is Desmond Tiny."

"What's Mr Tiny got to do with it?" I asked.

"According to ancient legends – forgotten by most – Tiny created the first vampires. They say he experimented on wolves and mixed their blood with that of humans, resulting in…" He tapped his chest.

"That's ridiculous," I snorted.

"Perhaps. But if those legends are true, our sun-related weakness is also Tiny's work. They say he was afraid we'd grow too powerful and take over the world, so he tainted our blood and made us slaves of the night." He stopped rubbing spit in and gazed upwards, eyes scrunched up against the disorientating rays of sunlight. "Nothing's as awful as slavery," he said quietly. "If the stories are true, and we're night slaves because of Tiny's meddling, there's only one way to win back our freedom — *fight!* We have to take on the enemy, look it full in the face and spit in its eye."

"You mean fight Mr Tiny?"

"Not directly. He's too slippery a customer to pin down."

"Then who?"

"We have to fight his manservant," he said. When I looked blank, he elaborated: "The sun."

"The *sun?*" I laughed, then stopped when I saw he was serious. "How can you fight the sun?"

"Simple," Vancha said. "You face it, take its blows, and keep coming back for more. For years I've been subjecting myself to the rays of the sun. Every few weeks I walk about for an hour by day, letting the sun burn me, toughening my skin and eyes to it, testing it, seeing how long I can survive."

"You're crazy!" I chortled. "Do you really think you can get the better of the sun?"

"I don't see why not," he said. "A foe's a foe. If it can be engaged, it can be defeated."

"Have you made any progress?" I asked.

"Not really," he sighed. "It's much the same as when I began. The light half-blinds me — it takes almost a full day for my vision to return to normal and the headaches to fade. The rays cause a reddening within ten or fifteen minutes, and it gets painful soon after. I've managed to endure it for close to eighty minutes a couple of times, but I'm badly burnt by the end, and it takes five or six nights of total rest to recover."

"When did this war of yours begin?"

"Let's see," he mused. "I was about two hundred when I started—" Most vampires weren't sure of their exact age; when you lived as long as they did, birthdays ceased to mean very much "—and I'm more than three hundred now, so I guess it's been the best part of a century."

"A hundred years!" I gasped. "Have you ever heard the phrase, 'banging your head against a brick wall'?"

"Of course," he smirked, "but you forget, Darren — vampires can break walls with their heads!"

With that, he winked and walked off into the sunlight, whistling loudly, to engage in his crazy battle with a huge ball of burning gas hanging millions and millions of kilometres away in the sky.

CHAPTER TWELVE

A FULL moon was shining when we arrived at Lady Evanna's. Even so, I'd have missed the clearing if Mr Crepsley hadn't nudged me and said, "We are here." I later learnt that Evanna had cast a masking spell over the place, so unless you knew where to look, your eyes would skim over her home and not register it.

I stared straight ahead, but for a few seconds could see nothing but trees. Then the power of the spell faded, the imaginary trees 'vanished' and I found myself gazing down upon a crystal-clear pond, glowing a faint white colour from the light of the moon. There was a hill on the opposite side of the pond, and I could see the dark, arched entrance of a huge cave in it.

As we strolled down the gentle slope to the pond, the night air filled with the sound of croaking. I stopped, alarmed, but Vancha smiled and said, "Frogs. They're alerting Evanna. They'll stop once she tells them it's safe."

Moments later the frog chorus ceased and we walked in silence again. We skirted the edge of the pond, Mr Crepsley and Vancha warning Harkat and me not to step on any frogs, thousands of which were at rest by or in the cool water.

"The frogs are creepy," Harkat whispered. "I feel like they're ... watching us."

"They are," Vancha said. "They guard the pond and cave, protecting Evanna from intruders."

"What could a bunch of frogs do against intruders?" I laughed.

Vancha stooped and grabbed a frog. Holding it up to the moonlight, he gently squeezed its sides. Its mouth opened and a long tongue darted out. Vancha caught the tongue with the index finger and thumb of his right hand, careful not to touch the edges. "See the tiny sacs along the sides?" he asked.

"Those yellow-red bulges?" I said. "What about them?"

"Filled with poison. If this frog wrapped its tongue around your arm or the calf of your leg, the sacs would pop and the poison would seep in through your flesh." He shook his head grimly. "Death in thirty seconds."

Vancha laid the frog down on the damp grass and let go of its tongue. It hopped away about its business. Harkat and me walked with extreme care after that!

When we reached the mouth of the cave, we stopped. Mr Crepsley and Vancha sat down and laid aside their packs. Vancha took out a bone he'd been chewing on for the last couple of nights and got to work on it, pausing only to spit at the occasional frog which wandered too close to us.

"Aren't we going in?" I asked.

"Not without being invited," Mr Crepsley replied. "Evanna does not take kindly to intruders."

"Isn't there a bell we can ring?"

"Evanna has no need of bells," he said. "She knows we are here and will come to greet us in her own time."

"Evanna's not a lady to be rushed," Vancha agreed. "A friend of mine thought he'd enter the cave on the quiet once, to surprise her." He munched cheerfully on his bone. "She gave him huge warts all over. He looked like ... like..." Vancha frowned. "It's hard to say, because I've never seen anything quite like it — and I've seen most everything in my time!"

"Should we be here if she's that dangerous?" I asked worriedly.

"Evanna will not harm us," Mr Crepsley assured me. "She has a quick temper, and it's best not to rile her, but she would never kill one with vampire blood, unless provoked."

"Just make sure you don't call her a witch," Vancha warned, for what must have been the hundredth time.

Half an hour after we'd settled by the cave, dozens of frogs — larger than those surrounding the pond — came hopping out. They formed a circle around us and sat, blinking slowly, hemming us in. I started to get to my feet, but Mr Crepsley told me to stay seated. Moments later, a woman emerged from the cave. She was the ugliest, most unkempt woman I'd ever seen. She was short — barely taller than the squat Harkat Mulds — with long, dark, untidy hair.

She had rippling muscles and thick, strong legs. Her ears were sharply pointed, her nose was tiny – it looked like there were just two holes above her upper lip – and her eyes were narrow. When she got closer, I saw that one eye was brown and the other green. What was even stranger was that the colours switched — one minute her left eye would be brown, the next her right.

She was extraordinarily hairy. Her arms and legs were covered with black hair; her eyebrows were two large caterpillars; bushy hair grew out of her ears and nostrils; she had a fairly full beard, and her moustache would have put Otto von Bismarck to shame.

Her fingers were surprisingly stubby. As a witch, I'd expected her to have bony claws, though I guess that's an image I got from books and comics I read when I was a child. Her nails were cut short, except for on the two little fingers, where they grew long and sharp.

She didn't wear traditional clothes, or animal hides like Vancha. Instead she dressed in *ropes*. Long, thickly woven, yellow ropes, wrapped around her chest and lower body, leaving her arms, legs and stomach free.

I'd have found it hard to imagine a more fearsome, off-putting woman, and my insides gurgled uneasily as she shuffled towards us.

"Vampires!" she snorted, stepping through the ranks of frogs, which parted as she advanced. "Always ugly bloody vampires! Why don't handsome humans ever come a-calling?"

"They're probably afraid you'd eat them," Vancha laughed in reply, then stood and hugged her. She hugged back, hard, and lifted the Vampire Prince off his feet.

"My little Vancha," she cooed, as though cuddling a baby. "You've put on some weight, Sire."

"And you're uglier than ever, Lady," he grunted, gasping for breath.

"You're only saying that to please me," she giggled, then dropped him and turned to Mr Crepsley. "Larten," she nodded politely.

"Evanna," he replied, standing and bowing. Then, without warning, he kicked out at her. But, swift as he was, the witch was swifter. She grabbed his leg and twisted. He rolled over and collapsed flat on the ground. Before he could react, Evanna jumped on his back, grabbed his chin and pulled his head up sharply.

"Surrender?" she yelled.

"Yes!" he wheezed, face reddening — not with shame, but pain.

"Wise boy," she laughed, and kissed his forehead quickly.

Then she stood and studied Harkat and me, running a curious green eye over Harkat and a brown one over me.

"Lady Evanna," I said as warmly as I could, trying not to let my teeth chatter.

"It is good to meet you, Darren Shan," she replied. "You are welcome."

"Lady," Harkat said, bowing politely. He wasn't as nervous as me.

"Hello, Harkat," she said, returning Harkat's bow. "You are also welcome — as you were before."

"*Before?*" he echoed.

"This is not your first visit," she said. "You have changed in many ways, within and without, but I recognize you. I'm gifted that way. Appearances don't deceive me for long."

"You mean … you know who I was … before I became a Little Person?" Harkat asked, astonished. When Evanna nodded, he leant forward eagerly. "Who was I?"

The witch shook her head. "Can't say. That's for you to find out."

Harkat wanted to push the matter, but before he could, she fixed her gaze on me and stepped forward to cup my chin between several cold, rough fingers. "So this is the boy Prince," she murmured, turning my head left, then right. "I thought you would be younger."

"He was struck by the purge as we travelled here," Mr Crepsley informed her.

"That explains it." She hadn't let go of my face and still her eyes scanned me, as though probing for weakness.

"So," I said, feeling as though I should speak, saying the first thing that popped into my head, "you're a witch, are you?"

Mr Crepsley and Vancha groaned.

Evanna's nostrils flared and her head shot forward so our faces were millimetres apart. "*What* did you call me?" she hissed.

"Um. Nothing. Sorry. I didn't mean it. I—"

"You two are to blame!" she roared, spinning away from me to face a wincing Mr Crepsley and Vancha March. "You told him I was a witch!"

"No, Evanna," Vancha said quickly.

"We told him *not* to call you that," Mr Crepsley assured her.

"I should gut the pair of you," Evanna growled, cocking the little finger of her right hand at them. "I would, too, if Darren wasn't here — but I'd hate to make a bad first impression." Glowering hotly, she relaxed her little finger. Mr Crepsley and Vancha relaxed too. I could barely believe it. I'd seen Mr Crepsley face fully armed vampaneze without flinching, and was sure Vancha was every bit as composed in the face of great danger. Yet here they stood, trembling before a short, ugly woman with nothing more threatening than a couple of long fingernails!

I started to laugh at the vampires, but then Evanna whirled around and the laughter died on my lips. Her face had changed and she now looked more like an animal than a human, with a huge mouth and long fangs. I took a frightened step back. "Mind the frogs!" Harkat shouted, grabbing my arm to stop me stepping on one of the poisonous guards.

I glanced down to make sure I hadn't trodden on any frogs. When I looked up again, Evanna's face was back to normal. She was smiling. "Appearances, Darren," she said. "Never let them fool you." The air around her shimmered. When it cleared, she was tall, lithe and beautiful, with golden hair and a flowing white gown. My jaw dropped and I stared at her rudely, astonished by how pretty she was.

She clicked her fingers and was her original self again. "I'm a sorceress," she said. "A wyrd sister. An enchantress. A priestess of the arcane. I am not—" she added, shooting a piercing look at Mr Crepsley and Vancha, "—a *witch*. I'm a creature of many magical talents. These allow me to take any shape I choose — at least in the minds of those who see me."

"Then why..." I started to say, before remembering my manners.

"...do I choose this ugly form?" she finished for me. Blushing, I nodded. "I feel comfortable this way. Beauty means nothing to me. Looks are the least important thing in my world. This is the shape I assumed when I first took human form, so it is the shape I return to most often."

"I prefer you when you're beautiful," Vancha muttered, then coughed gruffly when he realized he'd spoken aloud.

"Be careful, Vancha," Evanna chuckled, "or I'll take my hand to you as I did to Larten all those years ago." She cocked an eyebrow at me. "Did he ever tell you how he got that scar?"

I looked at the long scar running down the left side of Mr Crepsley's face, and shook my head. The vampire was blushing a deep crimson colour. "Please, Lady," he pleaded. "Do not speak of it. I was young and foolish."

"You most certainly were," Evanna agreed, and nudged me wickedly in the ribs. "I was wearing one of my beautiful faces. Larten got tipsy on wine and tried to kiss me. I gave him a little scratch to teach him some manners."

I was stunned. I'd always thought he picked up the scar fighting vampaneze or some fierce animal of the wilds!

"You are cruel, Evanna," Mr Crepsley moped, stroking his scar miserably.

Vancha was laughing so hard that snot was streaming from his nose. "Larten!" he howled. "Wait till I tell the others! I always wondered why you were so coy about that scar. Normally vampires boast about their wounds, but you—"

"Shut up!" Mr Crepsley snapped with uncharacteristic bluntness.

"I could have healed it," Evanna said. "If it had been stitched immediately, it wouldn't be half as noticeable as it is. But he took off like a kicked dog and didn't return for thirty years."

"I did not feel wanted," Mr Crepsley said softly.

"Poor Larten," she smirked. "You thought you were a real ladies' man when you were a young vampire, but..." She pulled a face and cursed. "I knew I'd forgotten something. I meant to have them set up when you arrived, but I got distracted." Muttering to herself, she turned to the frogs and made low, croaking noises.

"What's she doing?" I asked Vancha.

"Talking to the frogs," he said. He was still grinning about Mr Crepsley's scar.

Harkat gasped and dropped to his knees. "Darren!" he called, pointing to a frog. Crouching beside him, I saw that on the back of the frog was an eerily accurate image of Paris Skyle, done in dark green and black.

"Weird," I said, and gently touched the image, ready to whip my hand back if the frog opened its mouth. I frowned and traced the lines more firmly. "Hey," I said, "this isn't paint. I think it's a birthmark"

"It can't be," Harkat said. "No birthmark could look that ... much like a person, especially not one we— Hey! There's another!"

I turned and looked where he was pointing. "That's not Paris," I said.

"No," Harkat agreed, "but it's a face. And there's a third." He pointed to a different frog.

"And a fourth," I noted, standing and gazing around.

"They *must* be painted on," Harkat said.

"They're not," Vancha said. Bending, he picked up a frog and held it out for us to examine. This close to it, aided by the strong light of the moon, we could see that the marks were actually underneath the frog's uppermost layer of skin.

"I told you Evanna bred frogs," Mr Crepsley reminded us. He took the frog from Vancha and traced the shape of the face, which was burly and bearded. "It is a mix of nature and magic. She finds frogs with strong natural markings, magically enhances them, and breeds them, producing faces. She is the only one in the world who can do it."

"Here we are," Evanna said, pushing Vancha and me aside, leading nine frogs over to Mr Crepsley. "I feel guilty for lumbering you with that scar, Larten. I shouldn't have cut so deeply."

"It is forgotten, Lady," he smiled gently. "The scar is part of me now. I am proud of it—" he glared at Vancha "—even if others can only mock."

"Still," she said, "it irks me. I've presented you with gifts over the years — such as the collapsible pots and pans — but they haven't satisfied me."

"There is no need—" Mr Crepsley began.

"Shut up and let me finish!" she growled. "I think at last I have a gift which will restore amends. It's not something you can take, just a little ... token."

Mr Crepsley looked down at the frogs. "I hope you do not mean to give the frogs to me."

"Not exactly." She croaked an order to the frogs and they rearranged themselves. "I know Arra Sails was killed in the fighting with the vampaneze six years ago," she said. Mr Crepsley's face dropped at the mention of Arra's name. He'd been very close to her and had taken her death hard.

"She died valiantly," he said.

"I don't suppose you kept anything of hers, did you?"

"Such as?"

"A lock of hair, a knife which was dear to her, a scrap of her clothes?"

"Vampires do not indulge in such foolishness," he said gruffly.

"They should," Evanna sighed. The frogs stopped moving, she looked down at them, nodded and stepped aside.

"What are—" Mr Crepsley began, then fell silent as his eyes took in the frogs and the huge face spread across their backs.

It was the face of Arra Sails, a section on each frog's back. The face was perfect in every detail and boasted more colour than the faces on the other frogs — Evanna had worked in yellows, blues and reds, bringing life to its eyes, cheeks, lips and hair. Vampires can't be photographed — their atoms bounce around in a bizarre way, impossible to capture on film — but this was as close to a photo of Arra Sails as was imaginable.

Mr Crepsley hadn't moved. His mouth was a tight line across the lower half of his face, but his eyes were filled with warmth, sadness and … love.

"Thank you, Evanna," he whispered.

"No need," she smiled softly, then looked around at the rest of us. "I think we should leave him alone a while. Come into the cave."

Wordlessly we followed her in. Even the normally raucous Vancha March was quiet, pausing only to clasp Mr Crepsley's left shoulder and squeeze comfortingly. The frogs hopped along after us, except the nine with Arra's features plastered across their backs. They stayed, held their shape and kept Mr Crepsley company as he gazed sorrowfully at the face of his one-time mate and dwelt at length upon the painful past.

CHAPTER THIRTEEN

EVANNA HAD prepared a feast for us, but it was all vegetables and fruit — she was a vegetarian and wouldn't allow anyone to eat meat in her cave. Vancha teased her about it — "Still on the cow-food, Lady?" — but ate his share along with Harkat and me, though he only chose food which hadn't been cooked.

"How can you eat that?" I asked, revolted, as he tucked into a raw turnip.

"All in the conditioning," he winked, biting deeply into it. "Yum — a worm!"

Mr Crepsley joined us as we were finishing. He was in a sombre mood for the rest of the night, saying little, staring off into space.

The cave was far more luxurious than the caverns of Vampire Mountain. Evanna had made a real home of it, with soft feather beds, wonderful paintings on the walls and huge candle-lit lamps which cast a rosy glow over everything. There were couches to lie on, fans to cool us, exotic fruit and wine. After so many years of rough living, it seemed like a palace.

As we relaxed and digested the meal, Vancha cleared his throat and broached our reason for being here. "Evanna, we've come to discuss—"

She silenced him with a quick wave of a hand. "We'll have none of that tonight," she insisted. "Official business can wait until tomorrow. This is a time for friendship and rest."

"Very well, Lady. This is your domain and I bow to your wishes." Lying back, Vancha burped loudly, then looked for somewhere to spit. Evanna tossed a small silver pot at him. "Ah!" he beamed. "A spittoon." He leant over and spat forcefully into it. There was a slight 'ping' and Vancha grunted happily.

"I was cleaning up for days the last time he visited," Evanna remarked to Harkat and me. "Pools of spit everywhere. Hopefully the spittoon will keep him in order. Now if only there was something for him to flick his nose-pickings into..."

"Are you complaining about me?" Vancha asked.

"Of course not, Sire," she replied sarcastically. "What woman could object to a man invading her home and covering the floor with mucus?"

"I don't think of you as a woman, Evanna," he laughed.

"Oh?" There was ice in her tone. "What *do* you think of me as?"

"A witch," he said innocently, then leapt from the couch and raced out of the cave before she cast a spell on him.

Later, when Evanna had regained her sense of humour, Vancha snuck back in to his couch, fluffed up a cushion, stretched out and chewed at a wart on his left palm.

"I thought you only slept on the floor," I remarked.

"Ordinarily," he agreed, "but it'd be impolite to refuse another's hospitality, especially when your host is the Lady of the Wilds."

I sat up curiously. "Why do you call her a Lady? Is she a princess?"

Vancha's laughter echoed through the cave. "Do you hear that, Lady? The boy thinks you're a princess!"

"What's so strange about that?" she asked, stroking her moustache. "Don't all princesses look like this?"

"Beneath Paradise, perhaps," Vancha chuckled. Vampires believe that the souls of good vampires go beyond the stars to Paradise when they die. There isn't such a thing as hell in vampire mythology – most believe the souls of bad vampires stay trapped on Earth – but occasionally one would refer to a 'beneath Paradise'.

"No," Vancha said seriously. "Evanna's far more important and regal than any mere princess."

"Why, Vancha," she cooed, "that was almost flattering."

"I can flatter when I want," he said, then broke wind loudly. "And flutter too!"

"Disgusting," Evanna sneered, but she had a hard time hiding a smile.

"Darren was asking about you on the way here," Vancha said to Evanna. "We told him nothing of your past. Would you care to fill him in?"

Evanna shook her head. "You tell it, Vancha. I'm not in the mood for story-telling. But keep it short," she added, as he opened his mouth to begin.

"I will," he promised.

"And don't be rude."

"Lady Evanna!" he gasped. "Am I ever?" Grinning, he ran a hand through his green hair, thought a while, then began in a soft voice which I hadn't heard him use before. "Heed, children," he said, then cocked an eyebrow and said in his own voice, "That's the way to begin a story. Humans start with 'Once upon a time', but what do humans know about—"

"Vancha," Evanna interrupted. "I said keep it short."

Vancha grimaced, then started over, again in his soft voice. "Heed, children — we creatures of the night were not made to beget heirs. Our women can't give birth and our men can't sire children. This is the way it's been since the first vampire walked by the light of the moon, and the way we thought it would always be.

"But seventeen hundred years ago, there lived a vampire by the name of Corza Jarn. He was ordinary in all respects, making his way in the world, until he fell in love and mated with a vampiress called Sarfa Grall. They were happy, hunting and fighting side by side, and when the first term of their mating agreement elapsed, they agreed to mate again."

That's how vampire 'marriages' work. Vampires don't agree to stay with one another for life, only for ten, fifteen or twenty years. Once that time is up, they can agree to another decade or two together, or go their separate ways.

"Midway through their second term," Vancha continued, "Corza grew restless. He wished to have a baby with Sarfa and raise a child of his own. He refused to accept their natural limitations and went looking for the cure to vampire sterility. For decades he searched in vain, the loyal Sarfa by his side. A hundred years came and went. Two hundred. Sarfa died during the quest but this didn't put Corza off — if anything, it made him search even harder for a solution. Finally, fourteen hundred years ago, his search led him to that meddler with the watch — Desmond Tiny.

"Now," Vancha said gruffly, "it's not known exactly how much power Mr Tiny wields over vampires. Some say he created us, others that he once was one of us, others still that he's simply an interested observer. Corza Jarn knew no more about Tiny's true self than the rest, but he believed the magician could help, and followed him around the world, begging him to put an end to the barren curse of the vampire clan.

"For two centuries Mr Tiny laughed at Corza Jarn and waved his pleas away. He told the vampire – now old and feeble, close to death – to stop worrying. He said children weren't meant for vampires. Corza wouldn't accept this. He pestered Tiny and begged him to give the vampires hope. He offered his soul in exchange for a solution, but Mr Tiny sneered and said if he wanted Corza's soul, he would simply take it."

"I haven't heard that part of the story before," Evanna cut in.

Vancha shrugged. "Legends are flexible. I think it's good to remind people of Tiny's cruel nature, so I do, every chance I get.

"Eventually," he returned to the story, "for reasons of his own, Tiny relented. He said he'd create a woman capable of bearing a vampire's child, but added a catch — the woman and her children would either make the clan more powerful than ever ... or destroy us completely!

"Corza was troubled by Tiny's words, but he'd sought too long and hard to be dissuaded by the threat. He agreed to Tiny's terms, and let him take some of his blood. Tiny mixed Corza's blood with that of a pregnant wolf and worked strange charms on her. The wolf gave birth to four cubs. Two were stillborn and normal in shape, but the others were alive — and human in appearance! One was a boy, the other a *girl*."

Vancha paused and looked at Evanna. Harkat and me looked too, our eyes wide. The witch grimaced, then stood and took a bow. "Yes," she said, "*I* was that hairy little she-cub."

"The children grew quickly," Vancha went on. "Within a year they were adults and left their mother and Corza, to seek out their destiny in the wilds. The boy went first, without saying anything, and nobody knows what became of him.

"Before the girl left, she gave Corza a message to take to the clan. He was to tell them what had happened, and say that she took her duties very seriously. He was also to tell them that she was not ready for motherhood, and that no vampire should seek her out as a mate. She said there was much she had to consider, and it would be centuries — perhaps longer — before she made her choice.

"That was the last any vampire saw of her for four hundred years."

He stopped, looked thoughtful for a moment, then picked up a banana and began to eat it, skin and all. "The end," he mumbled.

"The *end*?" I shouted. "It can't end there! What happened next? What did she do for those four centuries? Did she choose a mate when she came back?"

"She chose no mate," Vancha said. "Still hasn't. As for what she got up to…" He smiled. "Maybe you should ask her yourselves."

Harkat and me turned to Evanna. "*Well*?" we asked together.

Evanna pursed her lips. "I chose a name," she said.

I laughed. "You can't have spent four hundred years picking a name!"

"That wasn't all I got up to," she agreed, "but I devoted much of that time to the choice. Names are vital to beings of destiny. I have a role to play in the future, not just of the vampire clan, but of every creature in the world. The name I chose would have a bearing on that role. I settled in the end for Evanna." She paused. "I *think* it was a good choice."

Rising, Evanna croaked something at her frogs, who set off for the mouth of the cave. "I must go," she said. "We have spoken enough of the past. I will be absent most of the day. When I return, we shall discuss your quest and the part I am to take in it." She departed after the frogs, and moments later had disappeared into the ripening rays of the dawn.

Harkat and me stared after her. Then Harkat asked Vancha if the legend he'd told was true. "As true as any legend can be," Vancha replied cheerfully.

"What does that mean?" Harkat asked.

"Legends change in the telling," Vancha said. "Seventeen hundred years is a long time, even by vampire standards. Did Corza Jarn really drag around the world after Desmond Tiny? Did that agent of chaos agree to help? Could Evanna and the boy have been born of a she-wolf?" He scratched an armpit, sniffed his fingers and sighed. "Only three people in the world know the truth — Desmond Tiny, the boy – if he still lives – and Lady Evanna."

"Have you ever asked Evanna if it's true?" Harkat enquired.

Vancha shook his head. "I've always preferred a stirring good legend to boring old facts." With that, the Prince rolled over and dropped off to sleep, leaving Harkat and me to discuss the story quietly and wonder.

CHAPTER FOURTEEN

I AROSE with Vancha a couple of hours after midday and commenced my training in the shade near the cave entrance. Harkat watched us with interest, as did Mr Crepsley when he woke early that afternoon. Vancha started me off with a stick, saying it would be months before he tried me with real weapons. I spent the afternoon watching him flick and stab the stick at me. I didn't have to do anything else, just observe the movements of the stick and learn to identify and anticipate the various ways an attacker had of using it.

We practised until Evanna returned, half an hour shy of sunset. She said nothing of where she'd been or what she'd been up to, and nobody enquired.

"Having fun?" she asked, entering the cave with her entourage of frogs.

"Heaps," Vancha replied, throwing the stick away. "The boy wants to learn to fight with his hands."

"Are swords too heavy for him?"

Vancha pulled a face. "Very funny."

Evanna's laughter brightened the cave. "I'm sorry. But fighting with hands – or swords – seems so childish. People should battle with their brains."

I frowned. "How?"

Evanna glanced at me, and all of a sudden the strength went from my legs and I fell to the floor. "What's happening?" I squealed, flopping about like a dying fish. "What's wrong with me?"

"Nothing," Evanna said, and to my relief my legs returned to normal. "*That's* how you fight with your brain," she said as I gathered myself together. "Every part of the body connects to the brain. Nothing functions without it. Attack with your brain, and victory is all but assured."

"Could I learn to do that?" I asked eagerly.

"Yes," Evanna said. "But it would take a few hundred years and you would have to leave the vampires and become my assistant." She smiled. "What do you think, Darren? Would it be worth it?"

"I'm not sure," I muttered. I liked the idea of learning magic, but living with Evanna wasn't appealing — with her quick temper, I doubted she'd make an understanding or forgiving teacher!

"Let me know if you change your mind," she said. "It's been a long time since I had an assistant, and none ever completed their studies — they all ran off after a few years, though I can't imagine why." Evanna brushed past us into the cave. Moments later she called us, and when we entered, we found another feast waiting.

"Did you use magic to get it ready so quickly?" I asked, sitting down to eat.

"No," she replied. "I simply moved a little faster than normal. I can work at quite a speed when I wish."

We ate a big dinner, then sat around a fire and discussed Mr Tiny's visit to Vampire Mountain. Evanna seemed to know about it already, but let us tell the story and said nothing until we had finished. "The three hunters," she mused once we'd brought her up to date. "I have been waiting for you for many centuries."

"You have?" Mr Crepsley asked, startled.

"I lack Desmond's clear insight into the future," she said, "but I see some of what is to come — or what *might* come. I knew three hunters would emerge to face the Vampaneze Lord, but I didn't know who they'd be."

"Do you know if we'll be successful?" Vancha asked, observing her keenly.

"I doubt if even Desmond knows that," she said. "Two strong futures lie ahead, each as possible as the other. It's rare for fate to boil down to two such evenly matched eventualities. Normally the paths of the future are many. When two exist like this, chance decides which the world will take."

"What about the Lord of the Vampaneze?" Mr Crepsley asked. "Have you any idea where he is?"

"Yes." Evanna smiled.

Mr Crepsley's breath caught in his throat.

"But you won't tell us, will you?" Vancha snorted in disgust.

"No," she said, her smile spreading. Her teeth were long, jagged and yellow like a wolf's.

"Will you tell us how we are to find him?" Mr Crepsley asked. "And when?"

"I cannot," Evanna said. "If I told, I would change the course of the future, and that's not allowed. You must search for him yourselves. I will accompany you on the next leg of your journey, but I cannot—"

"You're coming with us?" Vancha exploded in astonishment.

"Yes. But only as a travelling companion. I'll play no part in the quest to find the Vampaneze Lord."

Vancha and Mr Crepsley exchanged uneasy looks.

"You have never travelled with vampires before, Lady," Mr Crepsley said.

Evanna laughed. "I know how important I am to your people, and for that reason I've avoided too much contact with the children of the night — I tire of vampires pleading with me to mate with them and have their babies."

"Then why come with us now?" Vancha asked bluntly.

"There's someone I wish to meet," she answered. "I could seek him alone, but I prefer not to. My reasons will become clear in time."

"Witches are so bloody secretive," Vancha grumbled, but Evanna didn't rise to the bait.

"If you prefer to travel without me, you may," she said. "I will not impose my presence upon you."

"We would be honoured to have you as an escort, Lady Evanna," Mr Crepsley assured her. "And please do not take offence if we appear suspicious or unwelcoming — these are troublesome, confusing times, and we bark where sometimes we should whisper."

"Well put, Larten," she smiled. "If that's settled, I'll pack my things and we'll take to the road."

"So soon?" Mr Crepsley blinked.

"Now is as good a time as ever."

"I hope the frogs aren't coming," Vancha huffed.

"I wasn't going to bring them," Evanna said, "but now that you mention it..." She laughed at his expression. "Don't worry — my frogs will stay and keep things tidy for when I return." She started to leave, paused, turned slowly and squatted. "One more thing," she said, and by her serious expression we knew something bad was coming. "Desmond should have told you this, but he obviously chose not to — playing mind games, no doubt."

"What is it, Lady?" Vancha asked when she paused.

"It concerns the hunt for the Vampaneze Lord. I don't know whether you'll succeed or fail, but I have seen into the future of each possible outcome and gleaned some facts of what lies in store.

"I will not speak of the future where you succeed — it is not for me to comment on that — but if you fail..." Again she stalled. Reaching out, she took both of Vancha's hands in her left — it seemed to have grown incredibly large — and Mr Crepsley's in her right. While she held hands with them, she locked gazes with me, and spoke. "I tell you this because I think you should know. I don't say it to frighten you, but to prepare you, should matters come to the worst.

"Four times your paths are fated to cross with that of the Vampaneze Lord. If they do cross, on each occasion you will have it within your power to make an end of him. If you fail, the vampaneze are destined to win the War of the Scars. This you already know.

"But what Desmond didn't tell you is — by the end of the hunt, if you have faced the Vampaneze Lord four times and failed to kill him, only one of you will be alive to witness the fall of the vampire clan." Lowering her gaze and removing her hands from Mr Crepsley's and Vancha's, she said in something less than a whisper, "The other two will be *dead*."

CHAPTER FIFTEEN

WE SOLEMNLY filed out of Evanna's cave and circled the pond, each of us brooding about the witch's prophecy. We'd known from the start that this would be a peril-filled quest, with death never far from our heels. But it's one thing to anticipate your possible end, quite another to be told it's a certainty if you fail.

We followed no particular direction that first night, only walked aimlessly through the darkness, saying nothing, barely taking note of our surroundings. Harkat hadn't been included in Evanna's prophecy – he wasn't one of the hunters – but was as disturbed as the rest of us.

Towards dawn, as we were making camp, Vancha suddenly burst out laughing. "Look at us!" he hooted, as we stared at him uncertainly. "We've been moping all night like four sad souls at a funeral. What idiots we've been!"

"You think it amusing to have a death sentence imposed on us, Sire?" Mr Crepsley asked archly.

"Charna's guts!" Vancha cursed. "The sentence has been there since the start — all that's changed is that we know about it!"

"A little knowledge is a ... dangerous thing," Harkat muttered.

"That's a human way of thinking," Vancha chided him. "I'd rather know what lies ahead, good or bad. Evanna has done us a favour by telling us."

"How do you figure that?" I asked.

"She confirmed that we'll have four chances to kill the Vampaneze Lord. Think about it — four times his life will be ours to take. Four times we'll face him and do battle. He might get the better of us once. Perhaps twice. But do you really think he'll evade us four times in a row?"

"He will not be alone," Mr Crepsley said. "He travels with guards, and all vampaneze in the area will rush to his aid."

"What makes you think that?" Vancha challenged him.

"He is their Lord. They will sacrifice their lives to protect him."

"Will our fellow vampires back us up if *we* run into trouble?" Vancha responded.

"No, but that is because..." Mr Crepsley stopped.

"...Mr Tiny's told them not to," Vancha grinned. "And if he's picked just three vampires to go head to head with the Vampaneze Lord, maybe—"

"—he has only picked three vampaneze to help their Lord!" Mr Crepsley finished, excited.

"Right," Vancha beamed. "So the odds against us besting him are, in my view, better than even. Do you agree?" All three of us nodded thoughtfully. "Now," he continued, "let's say we make a pig's ear of it. We face him four times, we blow it, and our chance to defeat him passes. What happens then?"

"He leads the vampaneze into war against the vampires and wins," I said.

"Exactly." Vancha's smile faded. "By the way, I don't believe that. I don't care how powerful their Lord is, or what Des Tiny says — in a war with the vampaneze, I'm certain we'll win. But if we don't, I'd rather die beforehand, fighting for our future, than be there to watch the walls of our world come crashing down."

"Brave words," I grunted sourly.

"The truth," Vancha insisted. "Would you prefer to die at the hands of the Vampaneze Lord, when hope is still on our side, or survive and bear witness to the downfall of the clan?" I didn't reply, so Vancha went on. "If the predictions are true, and we fail, I don't want to be around for the end. It would be a terrible tragedy, and would madden anyone who saw it.

"Believe me," Vancha said, "the two who die in that eventuality will be fortunate. We shouldn't worry about dying — it's *living* we have to fear if we fail!"

I didn't get much sleep that day, thinking about what Vancha had said. I doubt if any of us slept much, except Evanna, who snored even louder than the Prince.

Vancha was right. If we failed, the one who survived would have the worst time of all. He'd have to watch the vampires perish, and bear the burden of blame. If we were to fail, death along the way was the best any of us could hope for.

Our spirits had lifted when we rose that evening. We were no longer afraid of what lay ahead, and instead of talking negatively, we discussed our route. "Mr Tiny said to follow our hearts," Mr Crepsley reminded us. "He said fate would lead us if we placed ourselves in its hands."

"You don't think we should try tracking down the Vampaneze Lord?" Vancha asked.

"Our people have spent six years seeking him, without success," Mr Crepsley said. "Of course we must keep our eyes peeled, but otherwise I believe we should go about our business as if he did not exist."

"I don't like it," Vancha grumbled. "Fate's a cruel mistress. What if destiny doesn't lead us to him? Do you want to report back in a year and say, 'Sorry, we didn't run into the blighter, bad luck, what?'"

"Mr Tiny said to follow our hearts," Mr Crepsley repeated stubbornly.

Vancha threw his hands into the air. "OK — we'll do it your way. But you two will have to pick the course — as many women have attested, I'm a boundless cad who doesn't have a heart."

Mr Crepsley smiled thinly. "Darren? Where do you want to go?"

I started to say I didn't care, then stopped as an image flashed through my thoughts — a picture of a snake-boy sticking an extra long tongue up his nose. "I'd like to see how Evra's doing," I said.

Mr Crepsley nodded approvingly. "Good. Just last night I was wondering what my old friend Hibernius Tall was up to. Harkat?"

"Sounds good to me," Harkat agreed.

"So be it." Facing Vancha, Mr Crepsley said in as imperious a tone as he could muster, "Sire, we head for the Cirque Du Freak."

And so our direction was decided and the dice of destiny were cast.

CHAPTER SIXTEEN

MR CREPSLEY was able to tap into Mr Tall's thoughts and pinpoint the position of the Cirque Du Freak. The travelling circus was relatively near, and it would take us only three weeks to link up with it if we forced the pace.

After a week, we hit civilization again. As we passed a small town one night, I asked Mr Crepsley why we didn't hop on a bus or train, which would get us to the Cirque Du Freak much quicker. "Vancha does not approve of human modes of transport," he said. "He has never been in a car or on a train."

"*Never?*" I asked the barefooted Prince.

"I wouldn't even spit on a car," he said. "Awful things. The shape, the noise, the smell." He shivered.

"What about planes?"

"If the gods of the vampires meant for us to fly," he said, "they'd have given us wings."

"What about you, Evanna?" Harkat asked. "Have you ever flown?"

"Only on a broomstick," she said. I didn't know if she was joking or not.

"And you, Larten?" Harkat asked.

"Once, long ago, when the Wright brothers were just getting going." He paused. "It crashed. Luckily, it had not been flying very high, so I was not seriously injured. But these new contraptions, which soar above the clouds … I think not."

"Afraid?" I smirked.

"Once bitten, twice shy," he replied.

We were a strange group, no doubt about it. We had almost nothing in common with humans. They were creatures of the technological age, but we belonged to the past — vampires knew nothing of computers, satellite dishes, microwave ovens, or any other modern conveniences; we travelled by foot most of the time, had simple tastes and pleasures, and hunted as animals. Where humans sent aeroplanes to wage their wars and fought by pressing buttons, we battled with swords and our hands. Vampires and humans might share the same planet, but we lived in different worlds.

I awoke one afternoon to the sound of Harkat's moans. He was having another nightmare and was tossing feverishly about on the grassy bank where he'd fallen asleep. I leant over to wake him. "Hold," Evanna said. The witch was in the lower branches of a tree, observing Harkat with unseemly interest. A squirrel was exploring her head of long hair, and another was chewing on the ropes she used as clothes.

"He's having a nightmare," I said.

"He has them often?"

"Almost every time he sleeps. I'm supposed to wake him if I hear him having one." I bent to shake him awake.

"Hold," Evanna said again, jumping down. She shuffled over and touched the three middle fingers of her right hand to Harkat's forehead. She closed her eyes and crouched there a minute, then opened them and let go. "Dragons," she said. "Bad dreams. His time of insight is upon him. Did Desmond say nothing about revealing who Harkat was in his previous life?"

"Yes, but Harkat chose to come with us, to search for the Vampaneze Lord."

"Noble but foolish," she mused.

"If you told him who he was, would that ease his nightmares?"

"No. He must learn the truth himself. I'd make things worse if I meddled. But there is a way to temporarily ease his pain."

"How?" I asked.

"One who speaks the language of the dragons could help."

"Where will we find someone like that?" I snorted, then paused. "Can you...?" I left the question hanging.

"Not I," she said. "I can talk to many animals, but not dragons. Only those who have bonded with the flying reptiles can speak their language." She stood. "*You* could help."

"Me?" I frowned. "I haven't bonded with a dragon. I've never even seen one. I thought they were imaginary."

"In this time and place, they are," Evanna agreed. "But there are other times and places, and bonds can be formed unknown."

That didn't make sense, but if I could somehow help Harkat, I would. "Tell me what I have to do," I said.

Evanna smiled approvingly, then told me to lay my hands on Harkat's head and close my eyes. "Focus," she said. "We need to find an image for you to fix upon. How about the Stone of Blood? Can you picture it, red and throbbing, the blood of the vampires flowing through its mysterious veins?"

"Yes," I said, bringing the stone effortlessly to mind.

"Keep thinking of it. In a few minutes you'll experience unpleasant sensations, and maybe catch glimpses of Harkat's nightmares. Ignore them and stay focused on the Stone. I will do the rest."

I did as she said. At first it was easy, but then I began to feel strange. The air around me seemed to get hotter and it became harder to breathe. I heard the beating of immense wings, then caught a glimpse of something dropping from a blood-red sky. I cringed, almost let go of Harkat, but remembered Evanna's advice and forced myself to focus on the image of the Stone of Blood.

I sensed something huge land behind me, and felt hot eyes boring into my back, but I didn't turn or shrink away. I reminded myself that this was a dream, an illusion, and thought about the Stone.

Harkat appeared before me in the vision, stretched upon a bed of stakes, which impaled him all over. He was alive but in incredible pain. He couldn't see me — the tips of two stakes poked out of the sockets where his eyes should have been.

"His pain is nothing to what *you* will feel," someone said, and looking up I saw a figure of shadows, elusive and dark, hovering close by.

"Who are you?" I gasped, momentarily forgetting about the Stone.

"I am the Lord of the Crimson Night," he replied mockingly.

"The Lord of the Vampaneze?" I asked.

"Of them and all others," the shadow man jeered. "I have been waiting for you, Prince of the Damned. Now I have you — and I won't let go!" The shadow man darted forward, his fingers ten long claws of dark menace. Red eyes glowed in the black pit that was his face. For a terrifying moment I thought he was going to grab and devour me. Then a tiny voice — Evanna's — whispered, "It's just a dream. He can't hurt you, not yet, not if you focus on the Stone."

Shutting my eyes within the dream, I ignored the charge of the shadow man and concentrated on the pulsing Stone of Blood. There was a hissing scream and I felt as though a wave of frothing madness had broken over me. Then the nightmare faded and I was back in the real world.

"You can open your eyes now," Evanna said. My eyes snapped open. I let go of Harkat and wiped my hands over my face, reacting as though I'd been touched by something dirty. "You did well," Evanna congratulated me.

"That ... *thing*," I gasped. "What was it?"

"The Lord of Destruction," she said. "The Master of Shadows. The would-be ruler of the eternal night."

"He was so powerful, so evil."

She nodded. "He will be."

"*Will be?*" I echoed.

"What you saw was a shade of the future. The Lord of the Shadows has not yet come into his own, but he will, eventually. This cannot be avoided, and you should not worry about it. All that matters for the time being is that your friend will sleep untroubled now."

I glanced down at Harkat, who was resting peacefully. "He's OK?"

"He will be, for a time," Evanna said. "The nightmares will return, and when they do he'll have to face his past and learn who he was, or succumb to madness. But for now he can sleep soundly, unafraid."

She headed back to her tree.

"Evanna," I stopped her with a soft call. "This Lord of the Shadows... There was something familiar about him. I couldn't make out his face, but I felt I knew him."

"So you should," she whispered in reply. She hesitated, pondering how much to tell me. "What I say now is between you and me," she warned. "It must go no further. You can tell no one, not even Larten or Vancha."

"I won't," I promised.

Keeping her back to me, she said, "The future is dark, Darren. There are two paths, and both are winding and troubled, paved with the souls of the dead. In one of the possible futures, the Vampaneze Lord has become the Master of Shadows and ruler of the dark. In the other..."

She paused, and her head tilted backwards, as though she was staring up at the sky for an answer. "In the other, the Lord of the Shadows is *you*."

And she departed, leaving me confused and shaken, dearly wishing that Harkat's moans hadn't woken me up.

A couple of nights later, we hooked up with the Cirque Du Freak.

Mr Tall and his band of magical performers were playing outside a small village, in an abandoned church. The show was drawing to a close when we arrived, so we slipped inside and watched the finale from the back. Sive and Seersa — the twisting twins — were onstage, twirling around each other and performing incredible acrobatic stunts. Mr Tall came on after them, dressed in a dark suit, with his customary red hat and gloves, and said the show was over. People began to leave, many muttering about the weak finish, when two snakes slid down from the rafters, sending waves of fear rippling through the crowd.

I grinned when I saw the snakes. This was how most of the shows drew to a close. People were tricked into thinking the show was over, then the snakes appeared and gave the crowd one last scare. Before the serpents could do any damage, Evra Von — their master — would step in and calm them down.

Sure enough, as the snakes were about to slither on to the floor, Evra stepped forward. But he wasn't alone — there was a small child with him, who went to one of the snakes and controlled it as Evra controlled the other. The kid was a new addition. I assumed Mr Tall had picked him up on his travels.

After Evra and the boy had wrapped the snakes around themselves, Mr Tall came on again and said the show was over for real. We kept to the shadows while the crowd streamed past, chattering with excitement. Then, as Evra and the child unwound and brushed themselves down, I moved. "Evra Von!" I roared.

Evra whirled around, startled. "Who's there?" I didn't answer, but walked forward briskly. His eyes widened with astonished delight. *"Darren!"* he yelled, and threw his arms around me. I hugged him tightly, ignoring the feel of his slippery scales, delighted to see him after so many years. "Where have you been?" he cried when we let go of one another. There were tears of happiness in his eyes — mine were wet too.

"Vampire Mountain," I said lightly. "How about you?"

"All over the world." He studied me curiously. "You've grown."

"Only recently. And not as much as you." Evra was a man now. He was only a few years older than me, and we'd looked much the same age when I first joined the Cirque Du Freak, but now he could have passed for my father.

"Good evening, Evra Von," Mr Crepsley said, stepping forward to shake hands.

"Larten," Evra nodded. "It's been a long time. I'm glad to see you."

Mr Crepsley stood to one side and introduced our companions. "I would like you to meet Vancha March, Lady Evanna, and Harkat Mulds, whom I believe you already know."

"Hello," Vancha grunted.

"Greetings," Evanna smiled.

"Hi, Evra," Harkat said.

Evra blinked. "It spoke!" he gasped.

"Harkat speaks a lot these nights," I grinned.

"It has a name?"

"It has," Harkat said. "And 'it' would like very much ... to be called 'he'."

Evra didn't know what to say. When I'd lived with him, we'd spent a lot of our time gathering food for the Little People, and never once had one of them said a word. We thought they couldn't speak. Now here I was with a Little Person – the limping one, whom we'd nicknamed Lefty – acting as if his being able to talk was no big deal.

"Welcome back to the Cirque Du Freak, Darren," somebody said, and looking up I found myself face to belly button with Mr Tall. I'd forgotten how quickly and silently the owner of the Cirque could move.

"Mr Tall," I replied, nodding politely (he didn't like to shake hands).

He greeted the others by name, including Harkat. When Harkat returned the greeting, Mr Tall didn't look in the least surprised. "Would you care to eat?" he asked us.

"That would be delightful," Evanna answered. "And I would have a word or two with you afterwards, Hibernius. There are things we must discuss."

"Yes," he agreed without batting an eyelid. "There are."

As we filed out of the church, I fell in step with Evra to discuss old times. He was carrying his snake over his shoulders. The boy who'd performed with Evra caught up with us as we exited, dragging the other snake behind him like a toy. "Darren," Evra said, "I'd like you to meet Shancus."

"Hello, Shancus," I said, shaking the boy's hand.

"'Lo," he replied. He had the same yellow, green hair, narrow eyes, and multicoloured scales as Evra. "Are you the Darren Shan I was named after?" he asked.

I glanced sideways at Evra. "Am I?"

"Yes," he laughed. "Shancus was my first-born. I thought it would be—"

"*First-born?*" I interrupted. "He's *yours?* You're his *father?*"

"I certainly hope so," Evra grinned.

"But he's so big! So old!"

Shancus preened proudly at the remark.

"He'll be five soon," Evra said. "He's large for his age. I started him out in the act a couple of months ago. He's a natural."

This was bizarre! Of course, Evra was old enough to be married with kids, and there was no reason for me to be surprised by the news — but it seemed like only a few months since we'd been hanging out together as teenagers, wondering what life would be like when we grew up.

"You've got other children?" I asked.

"A couple," he said. "Urcha – three – and Lilia, who'll be two next month."

"Are they all snake-children?"

"Urcha isn't. He's upset – he wants scales too – but we try to make him feel as loved and extraordinary as the others."

"*We* being. . .?"

"Me and Merla. You don't know her. She joined the show shortly after you left — ours was a whirlwind romance. She can detach her ears and use them as mini-boomerangs. You'll like her."

Laughing, I said I was sure I would, then followed Evra and Shancus after the others, to dinner.

It was wonderful to be back with the Cirque Du Freak. I'd been edgy and moody for the last week and a half, thinking about what Evanna had said, but my fears faded within an hour of returning to the circus fold. I met many old friends — Hans Hands, Rhamus Twobellies, Sive and Seersa, Cormac Limbs and Gertha Teeth. I also saw the Wolf Man, but he wasn't quite as welcome a sight as the others, and I kept clear of him as much as possible.

Truska — who could grow a beard at will, then suck the hairs back inside her face — was there too, and delighted to see me. She greeted me in broken English. She hadn't been able to speak the language six years ago, but Evra had been teaching her and she was making good progress. "It is hard," she said as we mingled with the others in a large, run-down school which was serving as the Cirque's base. "I not good at language. But Evra is patient and I slowly learning. I make mistakes still, but—"

"We all make mistakes, gorgeous," Vancha interrupted, popping up beside us. "And yours was not making an honest vampire of me when you had the chance!" He wrapped his arms around Truska and kissed her. She laughed when he let go and waved a finger at him.

"Naughty!" she giggled.

"You two know each other, I take it," I commented dryly.

"Oh, yes," Vancha leered. "We're old friends. Many's the night we went skinny-dipping together in oceans deep and blue, eh, Truska?"

"Vancha," she tutted. "You promised not of that to mention!"

"So I did," he chuckled, then began talking with her in her native tongue. They sounded like a pair of seals barking at each other.

Evra introduced me to Merla, who was very pleasant and pretty. He made her show me her detachable ears. I agreed that they were fabulous, but I declined her offer to let me have a go throwing them.

Mr Crepsley was as pleased to be back as I was. As a dutiful vampire, he'd devoted most of his life to the Generals and their cause, but I suspect his heart lay secretly with the

Cirque Du Freak. He loved to perform and I think he missed being on the stage. Many people asked him if he was back to stay, and expressed disappointment when he said he wasn't. He made light of it, but I think he was genuinely touched by their interest and would have stayed if he could.

There were Little People with the Cirque Du Freak, as usual, but Harkat kept away from them. I tried getting him involved in conversation with others, but people felt nervous around him — they weren't accustomed to a Little Person who could talk. He spent most of the night alone, or in a corner with Shancus, who was fascinated by him and kept asking impolite questions (most to do with whether he was a man or a woman — in fact, like all the Little People, he was neither).

Evanna was known by many people at the Cirque Du Freak, although very few of them had met her before — their parents, grandparents or great-grandparents had told them about her. She spent a few hours mingling and catching up on the past – she had an impressive memory for names and faces – then said her farewells for the night and departed with Mr Tall, to discuss matters strange, portentous and arcane (or else to chat about frogs and magic tricks!).

We retired with the coming of the dawn. We bid goodnight to those still awake, then Evra guided us to our tents. Mr Tall had kept Mr Crepsley's coffin ready for him and the vampire climbed into it with a look of sheer contentment — vampires love their coffins in a way no human can ever understand.

Harkat and me strung up a couple of hammocks and slept in a tent next to Evra and Merla's. Evanna moved into a van adjoining Mr Tall's. And Vancha... Well, when we met him that evening, he swore blind he'd stayed with Truska, and bragged about what a hit he was with the ladies. But by all the leaves and grass stuck to his hair and animal hides, I think it more likely he passed the day by himself under a bush!

CHAPTER SEVENTEEN

HARKAT AND me got up an hour or so before sunset and walked around the camp with Evra and Shancus. I was chuffed that Evra had named his first-born after me and promised to send the boy birthday presents in future, if I could. He wanted me to give him a spider – Evra had told him all about Madam Octa – but I had no intention of sending him one of the poisonous arachnids from Vampire Mountain — I knew from painful experience the trouble a tarantula could cause!

The Cirque Du Freak was much the same as ever. A few new acts had joined, and one or two had parted company with the show, but mostly it was as it had been. Though the circus hadn't changed, *I* had. I sensed that after a while, as we strolled from one caravan or tent to another, pausing to chat with the performers and stagehands. When I lived at the Cirque, I was young – in appearance at least – and people treated me as a child. They didn't any more. While I didn't look that much older, there must have been something different about me, because they no longer spoke down to me.

Although I'd been acting as an adult for years, this was the first time I really thought about how much I'd changed and how I could never return to the lighter days of my youth. Mr Crepsley had been telling me for ages — usually when I complained about how slowly I was maturing — that a night would come when I'd wish I could be young again. Now I realized he was right. My childhood had been a long, drawn-out affair, but within a year or two the purge would rid me of both my human blood and youth, and after that there could be no going back.

"You look pensive," Evra noted.

"I'm thinking about how much things have changed," I sighed. "You married and with kids. Me with worries of my own. Life used to be much simpler."

"It always is for the young," Evra agreed. "I keep telling Shancus that, but he doesn't believe me, any more than we did when we were growing up."

"We're getting old, Evra."

"No we aren't," he said. "We're getting *older*. It'll be decades before I hit old age — centuries for you."

That was true, but I couldn't shake the feeling that I'd somehow grown ancient overnight. For more than twenty-five years I'd lived and thought as a child — Darren Shan, the boy Prince! — but now I didn't feel I was a child any longer.

Mr Crepsley tracked us down as we were devouring hot sausages around a camp fire. Truska had cooked them and was handing them out. The vampire took one, thanked her, and swallowed it in two quick bites. "Savoury," he said, licking his lips, then turned to me with a gleam in his eye. "Would you care to take to the stage tonight? Hibernius has said we may perform."

"What would we do?" I asked. "We don't have Madam Octa any longer."

"I can perform magic tricks, as I did when I first joined the Cirque Du Freak, and you can be my assistant. With our vampiric speed and strength, we can pull off some truly remarkable conjuring feats."

"I dunno," I said. "It's been a long time. I might get stage fright."

"Nonsense. You are doing it. I will not take no for an answer."

"If you put it that way..." I grinned.

"You will need some grooming if we are to present ourselves to the public," Mr Crepsley said, eyeing me critically. "A haircut and manicure are in order."

"I take care of that," Truska said. "I also am having Darren's old pirate costume. I could fix up it to fit him again."

"You've still got that old thing?" I asked, remembering how cool I'd felt when Truska kitted me out as a pirate not long after I'd joined the Cirque Du Freak. I had to leave the fancy clothes behind when I left to travel to Vampire Mountain.

"I am a good holder-on to things," she smiled. "I fetch it and measure you. The suit might not be ready this tonight, but tomorrow I have it in shape. Come to me an hour now from, for measuring."

Vancha was jealous when he heard we were going to be performing. "What about me?" he grumbled. "I know a bit of magic. Why can't I go on too?"

Mr Crepsley stared at the green-haired Prince, with his bare feet, muddy legs and arms, his animal hides and shurikens. He sniffed the air — Vancha had showered in rainfall about six nights earlier, but hadn't washed since — and crinkled his nose. "You are not the essence of presentability, Sire," he remarked carefully.

"What's wrong with me?" Vancha asked, looking down, seeing nothing amiss.

"One must be elegant when one takes to the stage," Mr Crepsley said. "You lack a certain *je ne sais quoi*."

"I don't know about that," I said. "I think there's a perfect part for him in the show."

"There!" Vancha beamed. "The boy has a keen eye."

"He could go on at the start, with the Wolf Man," I said, only barely managing to keep a straight face. "We could pretend they were brothers."

Vancha glared at me as Mr Crepsley, Harkat, Evra and Shancus fell apart with laughter. "You're getting too smart by far!" he snapped, then stormed off to find someone to rant at.

At the appointed time I went to be measured and get my hair cut by Truska. Evra and Shancus also went to prepare for the show, while Harkat helped Mr Crepsley search for props to use in his act.

"Is life being good to you?" Truska asked, snipping my newly-grown fringe.

"It could be worse," I said.

"Vancha told me you now are being a Prince."

"He wasn't supposed to tell anyone," I complained.

"Do not fear. I keep news myself to. Vancha and me old friends. He knows I can a secret keep." She lowered the pair of scissors and looked at me oddly. "Have you seen anything of Mr Tiny since leaving?" she asked.

"That's a strange question," I replied warily.

"He here was, many months ago. Came see Hibernius."

"Oh?" That must have been before his trip to Vampire Mountain.

"Hibernius was troubled after visit. He told me dark times are out in front of us. He said I might be wanting to think of going home to my people. Said I might be safer there."

"Did he say anything about—" I lowered my voice "—the Lord of the Vampaneze or a Master of Shadows?"

She shook her head. "He said only that we was all in for rough nights, and that there much fighting and dying would be before it became over." Then she started clipping again, and after that she measured me for the suit.

I was thinking hard about our conversation when I left Truska's van and went in search of Mr Crepsley. It might be that, prompted by my concerns, my feet led me on purpose to Mr Tall's van, or maybe it was accidental. Either way, I found myself hovering outside a few minutes later, pondering the situation and whether I should ask him about it.

As I stood, deliberating, the door opened and Mr Tall and Evanna emerged. The witch was clad in a black cloak, almost invisible in the darkness of the cloudy night.

"I wish you would not do this," Mr Tall said. "The vampires have been good friends to us. We should help them."

"We cannot take sides, Hibernius," Evanna replied. "It is not our place to decide the twists of fate."

"Still," he muttered, his long face creased, "to embrace these others and parlay with them ... I don't like it."

"We must remain neutral," she insisted. "We have neither allies nor foes among the creatures of the night. If you or I took sides, we could destroy everything. As far as we're concerned, both must be equal, neither good nor bad."

"You are correct," he sighed. "I have spent too long with Larten. I'm letting my friendship for him cloud my judgement."

"There's nothing wrong with befriending these beings," Evanna said. "But we must not get personally involved, not until the future unravels and we have to."

With that, she kissed Mr Tall on the cheek — I don't know how one so short reached all the way up to one so tall, but she did — and slipped away out of camp. Mr Tall watched her go, an unhappy look on his face, then closed the door and went about his business.

I remained where I was a moment, replaying the strange conversation. I wasn't entirely sure what was going on, but I gathered that Evanna was about to do something which Mr Tall didn't like — something that seemed to bode ill for vampires.

As a Prince, I should have waited for Evanna to come back and challenged her openly about the conversation. It wasn't proper for one of my standing to eavesdrop, and it would be positively rude to sneak out of camp after her. But politeness and good manners had never been high on my list of priorities. I'd rather have Evanna think less of me – even punish me for my insolence – and know what she was up to, than let her slip away and face a nasty surprise further down the line.

Kicking off my shoes, I hurried out of camp, spotted the top of her hooded head vanishing behind a tree in the distance – she was moving fast – and set off after her as quickly and quietly as I could.

It was hard keeping up with Evanna. She was swift and sure-footed, leaving almost no trace of her passage. If the chase had endured, I'd have lost her, but she drew to a halt after three or four kilometres, stood breathing in the air a moment, then walked to a small copse of trees, whistled loudly, and entered.

I waited a few minutes to see if she'd emerge. When she didn't, I followed her to the edge of the copse and stood listening. When I heard nothing I slipped between the trees and advanced cautiously. The ground was damp and masked the sounds of my footsteps, but I took no chances: Evanna's sense of hearing was at least as sharp as a vampire's — one snapped twig would be enough to alert her to my presence.

As I progressed, the sound of soft talking reached me. There were several people up ahead, but they were speaking in hushed tones and I was too far away to hear what they were saying. With an increasing sense of unease I crept forward, and finally I was near enough to identify a group of shadowy figures at the heart of the copse.

I didn't move any closer, for fear I'd give myself away, but squatted, watched and listened. Their voices were muffled and only the occasional disconnected word or half-sentence came across. Their voices rose from time to time when they laughed, but even then they were careful not to laugh too loud.

My eyes gradually adjusted to the darkness and I was able to make some sense of the shapes. Apart from Evanna — whose shadow was impossible to mistake — I counted eight people, sitting, squatting or lying down. Seven were large and muscular. The eighth was slight, dressed in a hood and robes, serving drinks and food to the others. They all appeared to be men.

I could be no more certain than that, given the distance and darkness. Either I'd have to get a lot closer to learn more about them, or the moon would have to shine. Glancing up at the cloudy sky through the dense branches of the trees, I figured there wasn't much chance of that. Rising silently, I started to back away.

That's when the servant in the robes lit a candle.

"Put that out, fool!" one of the others barked, and a strong hand knocked the candle to the floor, where a foot roughly quenched it.

"Sorry," the servant squeaked. "I thought we were safe with Lady Evanna."

"We're never safe," the burly man snapped. "Remember that, and don't make such a mistake again."

The men fell back into conversation with Evanna, their voices low and impenetrable, but I was no longer interested in what they had to say. During the few seconds of candlelight, I'd glimpsed purple skin, red eyes and hair, and knew who and what the men were, and why Evanna had been so secretive — she'd come to meet with a group of *vampaneze!*

CHAPTER EIGHTEEN

RETREATING STEALTHILY, I cleared the copse. Seeing no guards, I rushed back to the Cirque Du Freak, pausing neither for breath nor thought. I reached the campsite ten minutes later, having raced as fast as my powers allowed.

The show had commenced and Mr Crepsley was standing in what used to be the church's vestry, watching Rhamus Twobellies eat a tyre. He looked very dashing in his red suit, and he'd rubbed blood along the scar down the left side of his face, drawing attention to it, making him look more mysterious than usual.

"Where have you been?" he snapped as I entered, panting. "I have looked all over for you. I thought I would have to perform alone. Truska has your pirate costume ready. If we hurry, we can—"

"Where's Vancha?" I gasped.

"Off sulking somewhere," Mr Crepsley chuckled. "He

still has not—"

"Larten," I interrupted. He stopped, alerted to the danger by my rare use of his first name. "Forget the show. We have to find Vancha. *Now!*"

He asked no questions. Telling a stagehand to inform Mr Tall of his withdrawal from the bill, he led me out to search for Vancha. We found him with Harkat in the tent I was sharing with the Little Person. He was teaching Harkat how to throw shurikens. Harkat was finding it difficult — his fingers were too large to easily grasp the small stars.

"Look who it is," Vancha jeered as we entered. "The king of the clowns and his head assistant. How's show business, boys?"

I pulled the flap of the tent closed and sunk to my haunches. Vancha saw the serious expression in my eyes and put his shurikens away. Quickly and calmly, I told them what had happened. There was a pause when I finished, broken by Vancha, who let fly with a barbed stream of curses.

"We shouldn't have trusted her," he snarled. "Witches are treacherous by nature. She's probably selling us out to the vampaneze even as we speak."

"I doubt that," Mr Crepsley said. "Evanna would hardly require the aid of the vampaneze if she meant to do us harm."

"You think she's gone over there to discuss frogs?" Vancha barked.

"I do not know what they are discussing, but I do not believe she is betraying us," Mr Crepsley said stubbornly.

"Maybe we should ask Mr Tall," Harkat suggested. "From what Darren says, he knows what Evanna ... is up to. Perhaps he would tell us."

Vancha looked at Mr Crepsley. "He's your friend. Should we try?"

Mr Crepsley shook his head. "If Hibernius knew we were in danger, and was capable of warning or aiding us, he would have."

"Very well," Vancha smiled grimly. "We'll have to take them on ourselves." He stood and checked his supply of shurikens.

"We're going to fight them?" I asked, insides tightening.

"We're hardly going to sit here and wait for them to attack!" Vancha replied. "The element of surprise is vital. While we have it, we must make use of it."

Mr Crepsley looked troubled. "Perhaps they do not mean to attack," he said. "We only arrived last night. They could not have known we were coming. Their being here might have nothing to do with us."

"Nonsense!" Vancha howled. "They're here to kill, and if we don't strike first, they'll be on us before—"

"I'm not so sure," I muttered. "Now that I think about it, they weren't on guard or nervous, as they would have been if they were preparing for a fight."

Vancha cursed some more, then sat down again. "OK. Let's say they aren't after us. Perhaps it's coincidence and they don't know we're here." He leant forward. "But they will when Evanna's finished filling them in!"

"You think she'll tell them about us?" I asked.

"We'd be fools to chance it." He cleared his throat. "In case you've forgotten, we're at war. I've nothing personal against our blood-cousins, but for the time being they're our enemies, and we must show them no mercy. Let's say these vampaneze and their servant have nothing to do with our being here. So what? It's our duty to engage them in battle and cut them down."

"That's murder, not self-defence," Harkat said softly.

"Aye," Vancha agreed. "But would you rather we let them go on to murder some of our own? Our quest to find the Vampaneze Lord takes precedence over all else, but when the chance to cull a few stray vampaneze drops our way, we'd be fools — traitors! — not to seize it."

Mr Crepsley sighed. "And Evanna? What if she takes the side of the vampaneze against us?"

"Then we fight her too," Vancha sniffed.

"You fancy your chances against her?" Mr Crepsley smiled thinly.

"No. But I know my duty." He stood, and this time there was a certainty to his stance. "I'm going to kill vampaneze. If you want to come, you can. If not..." He shrugged.

Mr Crepsley looked at me. "What do you say, Darren?"

"Vancha's right," I said slowly. "If we let them go, and they kill vampires later, we'd be to blame. Besides, there's something we're overlooking — the Lord of the Vampaneze." Mr Crepsley and Vancha stared at me. "We're destined to cross paths with him, but I think we have to chase that destiny. Maybe these vampaneze know where he is or will be. I doubt it's coincidence that we're here at the same time as them. This might be fate's way of leading us to him."

"A solid argument," Vancha said.

"Perhaps." Mr Crepsley didn't sound convinced.

"Remember Mr Tiny's words?" I said. "To follow our hearts? My heart says we should face these vampaneze."

"Mine too," Harkat said after a moment's hesitation.

"And mine," Vancha added.

"I thought you had no heart," Mr Crepsley muttered, then stood. "But my heart also demands confrontation, although my head disagrees. We will go."

Vancha grinned bloodthirstily and clapped Mr Crepsley on the back, then without further ado we stole away into the night.

At the copse we made our plans.

"We'll close on them from four different angles," Vancha said, taking charge. "That way we'll make them think there are more of us."

"There are nine of them in all," Mr Crepsley noted, "including Evanna. How do we divide them up?"

"Two vampaneze for you, two for me, two for Harkat. Darren takes the seventh and the servant — he's probably a half-vampaneze or vampet, so he shouldn't pose too much of a problem."

"And Evanna?" Mr Crepsley asked.

"We could all rush her at the end," Vancha suggested.

"No," Mr Crepsley decided. "I will handle her."

"You're sure?"

Mr Crepsley nodded.

"Then all that's left is to split up and move in. Get as close as you can. I'll start by launching a couple of shurikens. I'll aim for arms and legs. Once you hear screams and curses — hit them hard."

"Things would go much smoother if you aimed for throats and heads," I noted.

"I don't fight that way," Vancha growled. "Only cowards kill a foe without facing him. If I have to — as when killing the vampet with the hand grenade — I will, but I prefer to fight cleanly."

The four of us split up and circled the trees, entering the copse at different points. I felt vulnerable and small when I found myself alone in the woods, but quickly thrust such feelings aside and concentrated on my mission. "May the gods of the vampires guide and protect us," I muttered under my breath, before advancing, sword drawn.

The vampaneze and Evanna were still in the clearing at the heart of the copse, talking softly. The moon had broken through the clouds, and although the overhanging branches kept most of the light out, the area was brighter than it had been when I was here before.

Easing forward, I got as close to the vampaneze as I dared, then pulled up behind a thick trunk and waited. All was silent around me. I'd thought Harkat might alert them to our presence — he couldn't move as quietly as a vampire

— but the Little Person was taking great care and made no sound.

I started to count, silently, inside my head. I was up to ninety-six when there was a sharp whistling hiss to my far left, followed by a startled shriek. Less than a second later, another whistle and another scream. Gripping my sword tight, I swung around the tree and darted forward, roaring wildly.

The vampaneze were quick to react, and were on their feet, weapons in hand, by the time I reached them. Fast as they were, Mr Crepsley and Vancha were faster, and as I locked swords with a tall, muscular vampaneze, from whose left shin stuck a silver shuriken, I saw Mr Crepsley cut open the stomach and chest of one of our opponents, killing him instantly, while Vancha's thumb took out the left eye of another — he dropped to the ground, wailing.

I had just enough time to note that the man on the ground wasn't purple-skinned like the rest — a vampet! — then I had to concentrate on the vampaneze in front of me. He was at least two heads taller then me, broader and stronger. But size, as I'd been taught in Vampire Mountain, wasn't everything, and while he lashed out at me with savage strokes, I jabbed and feinted, nicking him here, poking him there, drawing blood, enraging him, spoiling his aim and rhythm, causing him to swing erratically.

As I parried one of his blows, someone stumbled into my back and I tumbled to the ground. Rolling over swiftly, I jumped to my feet and saw a bloody-faced vampaneze fall, gasping for breath. Harkat Mulds stood over him, a red-stained axe in his left hand, an injured right arm hanging limp by his side.

The vampaneze who'd been attacking me now focused on Harkat. With a bellow he swung at the Little Person's head. Harkat brought his axe up just in time, knocked the sword up high of its mark, then stepped back, tempting the vampaneze forward.

I looked around quickly, taking in the state of play. Three of our foes were down, although the vampet who'd lost his eye was scrabbling about for a sword and looked ready to rejoin the action. Mr Crepsley was battling a vampaneze who favoured knives, and the two were swinging around and slicing at each other like a pair of whirling dancers. Vancha had his hands full with a huge, axe-wielding brute. His axe was twice the size of Harkat's, yet he rolled it about between his immense fingers as if it weighed nothing. Vancha was sweating, and bleeding from a cut to his waist, but he wasn't conceding any ground.

Across from me, the seventh vampaneze – tall, slim, with a smooth face, long hair tied back, dressed in a light green suit – and the hooded servant were watching the fighting. Both clutched long swords and stood ready to flee if the battle seemed lost, or dive in and finish things off if they sensed victory. Such cynical tactics disgusted me, and drawing a knife, I sent it whizzing at the head of the servant, who wasn't much bigger than me.

The small man in the robes saw the knife and twitched his head out of the path of its flight. By his swiftness, I knew he must be a blooded creature of the night — no human could have moved so quickly.

The vampaneze next to the servant scowled as I drew another knife, paused a moment, then darted across the clearing before I could take aim. Dropping the knife, I raised my sword and turned his blow aside, but only barely managed to get it up in time to deflect his second strike. He was fast and well-trained in the ways of war. I was in trouble.

I backed away from the vampaneze, protecting myself as best I could. The tip of his sword became a blur as it struck, and though I defended myself ably, his blade soon bit. I felt a wound open on the top of my left arm ... a deep gash to my right thigh ... a jagged scratch across my chest.

I backed up against a tree and caught the sleeve of my right arm on a branch. The vampaneze thrust his sword at my face. I thought the end had come, but then my arm tore free and my sword came across to block his and drive it towards the ground. I pushed down with my sword, hoping to make my foe drop his weapon, but he was too strong and brought his sword up in a smooth reverse movement. His blade slid up the length of mine, giving birth to a shower of sparks. It was moving so fast, and there was so much force behind it, that instead of being routed away by the hilt of my sword when it got there, it cut clean through the gold casing — and clean through the flesh and bone of my sticking-out right thumb!

I screamed as my thumb shot away into the darkness. My sword dropped from my fingers and I fell, defenceless. The vampaneze glanced around casually, dismissing me as a threat. Mr Crepsley was winning the war of the knives — his opponent's face had been slashed to ribbons. Harkat had defied the handicap of his injured arm and buried the tip of his axe deep in his vampaneze's stomach — though the vampaneze bellowed valiantly and fought on, he was surely lost. Vancha was struggling with his opponent, but was holding his own, and when Mr Crepsley or Harkat came to his aid, their combined force would be enough to make an end of the giant. The vampet who'd lost an eye was on his feet, sword in hand, but was swaying unsteadily and wouldn't pose much of a problem.

While all this was happening, Evanna had remained seated on the ground, a neutral look on her face, taking no part in the fighting.

We were going to win and the vampaneze in the green suit knew it. Snarling, he swung once more at my head – aiming to cut it clean off at the neck – but I rolled out of his way, into a pile of leaves. Rather than duck after me to finish me off, he about-faced, ran to where the robed servant was standing, grabbed a spare sword from the ground, then hurried through the trees, pushing the servant ahead of him.

Getting to my feet, I moaned loudly from the pain, then gritted my teeth against it, picked up the knife I'd dropped earlier, and moved in to help Harkat finish off his vampaneze. It wasn't noble, sticking a knife into a warrior's back, but all I cared about was ending the battle, and I felt no pity for the vampaneze when he stiffened and collapsed, my blade buried deep between his shoulder blades.

Mr Crepsley had dispatched the vampaneze with the knives, and after taking care of the one-eyed vampet — a swift cut to his throat — he started forward to help Vancha. That's when Evanna stood and called to him. "Will you raise your blades to *me* too, Larten?"

Mr Crepsley hesitated, knives hovering in his hands, then dropped his guard and went on one knee before her. "Nay, Lady," he sighed. "I will not."

"Then I will not raise a hand to you," she said, and commenced walking from one dead vampaneze to another, kneeling beside them, making the death's touch, whispering, "Even in death may you be triumphant."

Mr Crepsley got to his feet and studied Vancha as he battled the largest of the vampaneze. "A close call, Sire," he noted dryly as the giant barely missed the top of Vancha's scalp with his huge war axe. Vancha honoured Mr Crepsley with one of his foulest curses in reply. "Would you be offended if I offered my assistance, Sire?" Mr Crepsley asked politely.

"Get over here quick!" Vancha snarled. "Two are getting away. We have to— *Charna's guts!*" he yelled, again only barely dodging the head of the axe.

"Harkat, stay with me," Mr Crepsley said, moving forward to intercept the giant. "Darren, go with Vancha after the others."

"Right," I said. I didn't mention the fact that I was missing a thumb — such considerations were nothing in the heat of life or death battle.

As Mr Crepsley and Harkat engaged the giant, Vancha swung away, paused for breath, then nodded for me to follow as he raced after the vampaneze and the servant. I kept close to him, sucking on the bloody stump where my thumb used to be, grabbing a knife from my belt with my left hand. As we broke from the trees, we saw the pair ahead. The servant was climbing on to the vampaneze's back — it was clear that they were planning to flit.

"No you don't!" Vancha growled, and sent a dark shuriken flying. It struck the servant high above the right shoulder blade. He cried out and toppled off the vampaneze's back. The vampaneze spun, stooped to pick up his fallen comrade, saw Vancha closing in, and jumped to his feet, pulling a sword and moving forward. I hung back, not wanting to get in Vancha's way, keeping an eye on the fallen servant, waiting to see how the fight progressed.

Vancha was almost within striking distance of the vampaneze when he drew up short, as though injured. I thought he must have been hit with something — a knife or arrow — but he didn't look hurt. He just stood, arms outstretched, staring at the vampaneze. The vampaneze was motionless too, his red eyes wide, his dark purple face incredulous. Then he lowered his sword, slid it into its scabbard, turned and picked up the servant.

Vancha did nothing to stop him.

Behind me I heard Mr Crepsley and Harkat break free of the trees. They raced forward, then stopped by my side when they saw the vampaneze escaping, Vancha standing by and watching.

"What the—" Mr Crepsley began, but then the vampaneze hit flitting speed and disappeared.

Vancha looked back at us, then sank to the ground. Mr Crepsley cursed — not quite as foul as Vancha's earlier outburst, but close — and sheathed his knives in disgust. "You let them escape!" he shouted. Striding forward, he stood over Vancha and regarded him with undisguised contempt. "*Why?*" he growled, hands bunched into fists.

"I couldn't stop him," Vancha whispered, eyes downcast.

"You did not even try!" Mr Crepsley roared.

"I couldn't fight him," Vancha said. "I always feared this night would come. I prayed it wouldn't, but part of me knew it would."

"You are not making sense!" Mr Crepsley snapped. "Who was that vampaneze? Why did you let him escape?"

"His name is Gannen Harst," Vancha said in a low, broken voice. He looked up and there were hard, glittering tears in his eyes. "He's my *brother*."

CHAPTER NINETEEN

FOR A long time nothing was said. Harkat, Mr Crepsley and me stared at Vancha, whose eyes were fixed on the ground. Overhead the moon had vanished behind thick banks of cloud. When they finally parted, Vancha began to talk, as though prompted by the moonbeams.

"My real name's Vancha Harst," he said. "I changed it when I became a vampire. Gannen's a year or two younger than me — or is it the other way round? It's been so long, I can't remember. We were very close growing up. We did everything together — including joining the vampaneze.

"The vampaneze who blooded us was an honest man and a good teacher. He told us exactly what our lives would be like. He explained their ways and beliefs, how they looked upon themselves as the guardians of history by keeping alive the memories of those they drank from." (If a vampire or vampaneze drains a person's blood, he absorbs part of their spirit and memories.) "He said vampaneze killed when they drank, but did it swiftly and painlessly."

"That makes it OK?" I snorted.

"To the vampaneze, yes," Vancha said.

"How can you—" I started to explode.

Mr Crepsley stopped me with a soft wave of his hand. "This is not the time for a moral debate. Let Vancha talk."

"There's not a whole lot more to tell," Vancha said. "Gannen and I were blooded as half-vampaneze. We served together for a few years as assistants. I couldn't accustom myself to the killing. So I quit."

"As simply as that?" Mr Crepsley asked sceptically.

"No," Vancha said. "The vampaneze normally don't permit assistants to live if they choose to part company with the clan. No vampaneze will kill one of his own, but that law doesn't apply to a half-vampaneze. My master should have killed me when I said I wanted out.

"Gannen saved me. He pleaded for my life. When that failed, he said our master would have to kill him also. In the end my life was spared, but I was warned to avoid all vampaneze in future, including Gannen, whom I never saw again until tonight.

"For several years I lived miserably. I tried feeding as vampires do, not killing those I fed upon, but vampaneze blood exerts a powerful hold. I'd lose control when I fed, and kill in spite of myself. In the end I made up my mind not to feed at all, and die. It was then that I met Paris Skyle, who took me under his wing."

"Paris blooded you?" Mr Crepsley asked.

"Yes."

"Even though he knew what you were?"

Vancha nodded.

"But how can you blood someone as a vampire if he's already been blooded as a vampaneze?" I asked.

"It is possible for those who are not fully blooded," Mr Crepsley said. "A half-vampire can become a vampaneze, and vice versa, but it is dangerous and rarely attempted. I know of only three other cases — and twice it ended in death, for both the blooder and the blooded."

"Paris knew the risks," Vancha said, "but didn't tell me about them until afterwards. I wouldn't have gone through with it if I'd known his life was in danger."

"What did he have to do?" Harkat asked.

"Take my blood and give me his, the same as any ordinary blooding," Vancha said. "The only difference was, half my blood was vampaneze, which is poisonous to vampires. Paris took my tainted blood, and his body's natural defences broke it down and rendered it harmless. But it could have easily killed him, just as his blood could have killed me. But the luck of the vampires was with us — we both survived, though our agonies were great.

"With my vampaneze blood transformed by Paris's blood, I was able to control my feeding urges. I studied under Paris and in time trained to be a General. My vampaneze links were revealed to no one except the other Princes."

"They approved of your blooding?" Mr Crepsley asked.

"After I'd proven myself many times — yes. They worried about Gannen — they were afraid my loyalties would be divided if I met him again, as they have been tonight — but they accepted me and vowed to keep my true history a secret."

"Why wasn't *I* told about you?" I asked.

"Had I come to Vampire Mountain while you were there, you would have been told. But it's impolite to speak of one when he's absent."

"This is damned frustrating," Mr Crepsley grunted. "I understand why you did not speak of it before, but if we had known, *I* could have gone after your brother and left you to take care of that giant in the trees."

"How was I to know?" Vancha smiled weakly. "I didn't see his face until I was moving in for the kill. He was the last person I expected to run into."

Behind us, Evanna emerged from between the trees. Her hands were red with the blood of dead vampaneze. She was carrying something. As she got closer, I realized it was my missing thumb. "Found this," she said, tossing it to me. "Thought you might like it back."

I caught the thumb, then looked down at the stump where it had been cut off. I hadn't been aware of the pain while listening to Vancha talk, but now the throbbing intensified. "Can we stitch it back on?" I winced.

"Possibly," Mr Crepsley said, examining the stump and thumb. "Lady Evanna — you have the power to connect it immediately and effortlessly, do you not?"

"I do," Evanna agreed, "but I won't. Snoops don't deserve special favours." She wagged a finger at me. "You should have been a spy, Darren." It was hard to tell whether she was annoyed or amused.

Vancha had string and a needle made from fish bone, and while Mr Crepsley held my thumb in place, the Prince stitched it back on, even though his thoughts were elsewhere. It hurt tremendously, but I just had to look away and grit my teeth. The stitching completed, the vampires rubbed their spit around the join, to quicken the healing process, strapped the thumb tight to my fingers so that the bones could fuse, then let me be.

"That is the best we can do," Mr Crepsley said. "If it gets infected, we will chop it off again and you will have to make do without."

"That's right," I growled. "Look on the bright side."

"It's my head you should be chopping off," Vancha said bitterly. "I should have put duty before kinship. I don't deserve to live."

"Nonsense!" Mr Crepsley huffed. "Any man who would strike a brother is no man at all. You did what any of us would have done. It is unfortunate that you ran into him now, but we have not been harmed by your slip, and I think—"

He stopped at a sudden burst of laughter from Evanna. The witch was giggling wildly, as if he'd cracked a great joke.

"Did I say something funny?" Mr Crepsley asked, bemused.

"Oh, Larten, if only you knew!" she squealed.

He raised an eyebrow at Vancha, Harkat and me. "What is she laughing at?"

None of us knew.

"Never mind why she's laughing," Vancha said, stepping forward to confront the witch. "*I* want to know what she was doing here in the first place, and why she was consorting with the enemy while pretending to be our ally."

Evanna stopped laughing and faced Vancha. She grew magically, until she was towering over him like a coiled cobra, but the Prince didn't flinch. Gradually the menace drained out of her and she resorted to her standard shape. "I never claimed to be your ally, Vancha," she said. "I travelled with you, and broke bread with you — but I never said I was on your side."

"Does that mean you're on *theirs?*" he snarled.

"I take nobody's side," she replied coolly. "The divide between vampires and vampaneze is of no interest to me. I look upon you as silly, warring boys, who will one night come to their senses and stop spitting angrily at one another."

"An interesting view," Mr Crepsley remarked ironically.

"I don't understand," I said. "If you aren't on their side, what were you doing with them?"

"Conversing," she said. "Taking their measure, as I did with you. I've sat with the hunters and studied them. Now I've done likewise with the hunted. Whichever way the War of the Scars goes, I'll have to deal with the victors. It's good to know in advance the calibre of those to whom your future is tied."

"Can anyone make sense of this?" Vancha asked.

Evanna smirked, delighted by our confusion. "Do you fine, fighting gentlemen read mystery novels?" she asked. We stared at her blankly. "If you did, you'd have guessed by now what's going on."

"Have you ever hit a woman?" Vancha asked Mr Crepsley.

"No," he said.

"*I* have," Vancha grunted.

"Temper," the witch giggled, then grew serious. "If you have something that is precious, and others are looking for it, where is the best place to hide it?"

"If this rubbish continues…" Vancha warned.

"It's not rubbish," Evanna said. "Even humans know the answer to this one."

We thought about it in silence. Then I raised a hand, as though in school, and said, "Out in the open, in front of everyone?"

"Exactly," Evanna applauded. "People searching – or hunting – rarely find what they seek if it's placed directly before them. It's common to overlook that which is most obvious."

"What does any of this have to do with–" Mr Crepsley began.

"The man in the robes … was no servant," Harkat interrupted grimly. Our heads turned questioningly. "That's what we overlooked … wasn't it?"

"Precisely," the witch said, and now there was a touch of sympathy to her tone. "By dressing and treating him as a servant — as they have since they took to the road — the vampaneze knew he'd be the last target anyone would focus on in the event of an attack." Holding up four fingers, Evanna slowly bent the index one over, and said, "Your brother didn't run because he was afraid, Vancha. He fled to save the life of the man he was protecting — the fake servant — the *Lord of the Vampaneze!*"

CHAPTER TWENTY

UNDER ORDERS from Evanna — she threatened to blind and deafen us if we disobeyed — we buried the dead vampaneze and vampet in the copse, digging deep graves and placing them on their backs, facing towards the sky and Paradise, before covering them over.

Vancha was inconsolable. On our return to the Cirque Du Freak, he demanded a bottle of brandy, then locked himself away in a small trailer and refused to answer our calls. He blamed himself for the escape of the Vampaneze Lord. If he'd tackled his brother, the Vampaneze Lord would have been at our mercy. It was the first of our four promised chances to kill him, and it was hard to imagine a simpler opportunity falling into our laps.

Mr Tall already knew what had happened. He'd been expecting the confrontation and told us that the vampaneze had been trailing the Cirque Du Freak for more than a month.

"They knew we were coming?" I asked.

"No," he said. "They were following us for other reasons."

"But *you* knew we were coming ... didn't you?" Harkat challenged him.

Mr Tall nodded sadly. "I'd have warned you, but the consequences would have been dire. Those with insight into the future are forbidden to influence it. Only Desmond Tiny can meddle directly in the affairs of time."

"Do you know where they have gone," Mr Crepsley asked, "or when we are due to clash with them again?"

"No," Mr Tall said. "I could find out, but I read the future as little as possible. What I *can* tell you is that Gannen Harst is prime protector of the Lord of the Vampaneze. The six you killed were normal guards who can be replaced. Harst is the key guardian. Where the Lord goes, he goes too. Had he been killed, the odds of future success would have weighed heavily on your side."

"If only I had gone after Harst instead of Vancha," Mr Crepsley sighed.

Evanna, who'd said nothing since we returned, shook her head. "Don't waste time regretting lost chances," she said. "You weren't destined to face Gannen Harst at this stage of the hunt. Vancha was. It was fate."

"Let's be positive," I said. "We now know who the Vampaneze Lord is travelling with. We can spread Gannen Harst's description and tell our people to look out for him. And they won't be able to pull that servant disguise again — next time we'll be ready and know who to look for."

"This is true," Mr Crepsley agreed. "Plus we have suffered no losses. We are as strong as we were at the start of our quest, we are wiser, and we still have three chances to kill him."

"Then why do we feel … so terrible?" Harkat asked glumly.

"Failure is always a bitter pill to swallow," Mr Crepsley said.

We saw to our wounds after that. Harkat's arm was badly cut but no bones were broken. We set it in a sling, and Mr Crepsley said it would be fine in a couple of nights. My right thumb was turning an ugly colour, but Mr Tall said it wasn't infected and would be OK if I rested it.

We were preparing for sleep when we heard angry bellows. Hurrying through the camp – Mr Crepsley with a heavy cloak tossed over his head to protect him from the morning sun – we found Vancha on the outskirts, tearing off his clothes, an empty bottle of brandy on the ground beside him, screaming at the sun. "Roast me!" he challenged it. "I don't care! Do your worst! See if I give a—"

"Vancha!" Mr Crepsley snapped. "What are you doing?"

Vancha whirled, snatched up the bottle and pointed it at Mr Crepsley as though it was a knife. "Stay away!" he hissed. "I'll kill you if you try to stop me!"

Mr Crepsley came to a halt. He knew better than to mess with a drunken vampire, especially one of Vancha's powers. "This is stupid, Sire," he said. "Come inside. We will find another bottle of brandy and help you drink—"

"—to the health of the Vampaneze Lord!" Vancha shrieked crazily.

"Sire, this is madness," Mr Crepsley said.

"Aye," Vancha agreed in a sadder, sober tone. "But this is a mad world, Larten. Because I spared the life of my brother — who once saved mine — our greatest enemy has escaped and our people face defeat. What sort of a world is it where evil is born of an act of goodness?"

Mr Crepsley had no answer for that.

"Dying will not help, Vancha," Harkat said. "*I* should know."

"It won't help," Vancha agreed, "but it will punish, and I deserve to be punished. How could I face my fellow Princes and Generals after this? My chance to kill the Lord of the Vampaneze has passed. Better I pass with it than linger and shame us all."

"So you plan on staying out here and letting the sun kill you?" I asked.

"Aye," he chuckled.

"You're a coward," I sneered.

His expression hardened. "Take heed, Darren Shan — I'm in the mood to crack a few skulls before I die!"

"And a fool," I pressed on, regardless. I stormed past Mr Crepsley and pointed accusingly at Vancha with my good left hand. "Who gave you the right to quit? What makes you think you can abandon the quest and damn us all?"

"What are you talking about?" he stammered, confused. "I'm no longer part of the quest. It's up to you and Larten now."

"Is it?" Turning, I searched for Evanna and Mr Tall. I found them together, behind the crowd of circus performers and assistants which had been attracted by the howls of the Prince. "Lady Evanna. Mr Tall. Answer if you may — does Vancha still have a part to play in the hunt for the Vampaneze Lord?"

Mr Tall shared an uneasy glance with Evanna. She hesitated, then said grudgingly, "He has the power to influence the quest."

"But I failed," Vancha said, bewildered.

"*Once*," I agreed. "But who's to say you won't have another chance? Nobody said we'd have one chance each. For all we know, all four opportunities are destined to fall to *you!*"

Vancha blinked, and his mouth slowly opened.

"Even if the chances are to be shared evenly," Mr Crepsley chipped in, "there are a further three to go, and Darren and I are only two — therefore one of us must be destined to face the Vampaneze Lord twice if it goes down to the final encounter."

Vancha wavered on his feet, considering our words, then dropped the bottle and stumbled towards me. I caught and steadied him. "I've been an idiot, haven't I?" he groaned.

"Yes," I agreed, smiling, then led him back into the shade, where he joined us in slumber until the darkening of night.

We arose with the sinking of the sun and gathered in Mr Tall's van. As dusk deepened, and Vancha drank mug after mug of steaming hot coffee to cure his hangover, we debated our next move and decided it would be for the best if we left the Cirque Du Freak. I would have liked to stay on longer, and so would Mr Crepsley, but our destiny lay elsewhere. Besides, Gannen Harst might return with an army of vampaneze, and we didn't want to find ourselves boxed in, or bring the wrath of our foes down upon the circus folk.

Evanna would not be travelling with us. The witch told us she was returning to her cave and frogs, to prepare for the tragedies to come. "And there *will* be tragedies," she said, a sparkle in her brown and green eyes. "Whether for the vampires or vampaneze, I don't yet know. But it must end in tears for one set, that much is certain."

I can't say I missed the short, hairy, ugly witch when she left — her dark predictions had brought nothing but gloom into our lives, and I thought we were better off without her.

Vancha would also be departing by himself. We'd agreed that he should return to Vampire Mountain and tell the others of our encounter with the Lord of the Vampaneze. They needed to know about Gannen Harst. Vancha would link up with us again later, by tracking Mr Crepsley's mental waves.

We bid short farewells to our friends at the Cirque Du Freak. Evra was sad that I had to leave so soon, but he knew my life was complicated. Shancus was even sadder — it would be his birthday soon and he'd been anticipating a wonderful present. I told the snake-boy I'd find something exciting on the road and send it to him – although I couldn't guarantee it would reach him in time for his birthday — and that cheered him up.

Truska asked if I wanted to take my newly tailored pirate costume with me. I told her to hang on to it — it would only get stained and torn during my travels. I swore I'd be back to try it out. She said I'd better, then treated me to a long goodbye kiss which had Vancha seething with jealousy.

Mr Tall met us at the edge of camp as we were about to leave. "Sorry I couldn't come earlier," he said. "Business to deal with. The show must go on."

"Take care, Hibernius," Mr Crepsley said, shaking the tall man's hand. For once Mr Tall didn't shirk away from the contact.

"You too, Larten," he replied, a grave expression on his face. Looking around at us, he said, "Dark times lie ahead, regardless of the outcome of your quest. I want you to know that there will always be a home for you — *all* of you — here at the Cirque Du Freak. I can't play as active a part in the deciding of the future as I wish, but I *can* offer sanctuary."

We thanked him for his offer, then watched as he walked away and was swallowed by the shadows of his beloved circus camp.

Facing each other, we hesitated, reluctant to part.

"Well!" Vancha boomed eventually. "Time I was off. It's a long trek to Vampire Mountain, even when flitting." Vampires weren't supposed to flit on the way to the mountain fortress, but the rules had been relaxed during wartime to allow for quicker communication between Generals and Princes.

Each of us shook Vancha's hand. I felt miserable at the thought of parting with the red-skinned, sun-fighting Prince. "Cheer up," he laughed at my gloomy expression. "I'll be back in time to lead the second charge against the Vampaneze Lord. You have my word, and Vancha March never broke..." He paused. "'March' or 'Harst'?" he mused aloud, then spat into the dirt at his feet. "Charna's guts! I've gone this long as Vancha March — I'll stick with it."

Saluting, he turned abruptly and jogged away. Soon he was running. Then, in a flash, he hit flitting speed and was lost to sight.

"And then there were three," Mr Crepsley muttered, gazing at Harkat and me.

"Back where we started six years ago," I said.

"But we had a destination then," Harkat noted. "Where are we going ... this time?"

I looked to Mr Crepsley for an answer.

He shrugged. "We can decide later. For now, let us simply walk."

Hoisting our bags on to our backs, we spared the Cirque Du Freak one last, lingering glimpse, then faced the cold, unwelcoming darkness and set forth, surrendering ourselves to the forces of destiny and future terrors of the night.

TO BE CONTINUED...

DARREN SHAN

ALLIES OF THE NIGHT

THE SAGA OF DARREN SHAN
BOOK 8

For:
Bas — my Debbie Hemlock

OBE
(Order of the Bloody Entrails) to:
Davina "bonnie" McKay

Quality Control:
Gillie Russell & Zoë Clarke

Party Animals:
The Christopher Little Clan

PROLOGUE

IT WAS an age of war. After six hundred years of peace, the vampires and vampaneze had taken up arms against each other in a brutal, bloody battle to the death. The War of the Scars began with the coming of the Lord of the Vampaneze. He was destined to lead his people to total, all-conquering victory — unless killed before he was fully blooded.

According to the mysterious and powerful Mr Tiny, only three vampires stood a chance of stopping the Vampaneze Lord. They were the Prince, Vancha March; the one-time General, Larten Crepsley; and a half-vampire, me — Darren Shan.

It was predicted by Mr Tiny that our path would cross four times with that of the Vampaneze Lord, and each time the destiny of the vampires would be ours for the making. If we killed him, we'd win the War of the Scars. If not, the vampaneze would cruise to savage victory and wipe our entire clan from the face of the earth.

Mr Tiny said we couldn't call upon other vampires for help during the quest, but we could accept the aid of non-vampires. Thus, when Mr Crepsley and me left Vampire Mountain (Vancha joined us later), the only one to come with us was Harkat Mulds, a stunted, grey-skinned Little Person.

Leaving the Mountain — our home for six years — we headed for the cave of Lady Evanna, a witch of great power. She could see into the future but would only reveal this much to us — if we failed to kill the Lord of the Vampaneze, by the end of our quest, two of us would be dead.

Later on, we linked up with the Cirque Du Freak, where I'd lived with Mr Crepsley when I originally became his assistant. Evanna travelled with us. At the Cirque, we ran into a group of vampaneze. A short fight ensued, during which most of the vampaneze were killed. Two escaped — a full-vampaneze by the name of Gannen Harst, and his servant, who we later learnt was the Lord of the Vampaneze, in disguise.

We were sickened when Evanna revealed the true identity of Gannen Harst's servant, but Vancha was especially miserable, because he had let them escape — Gannen Harst was Vancha's brother, and Vancha had let him go without challenging him, unaware that his brother was prime protector of the Vampaneze Lord.

But there was no time to sit around feeling sorry for ourselves. We still had three chances to find and kill our deadly foe, so our quest continued. Putting the lost chance behind us, we sharpened our blades, parted company with Evanna and our friends in the Cirque Du Freak, and took to the road again, more determined than ever to succeed...

CHAPTER ONE

YOUR DAILY POST, SEPTEMBER 15
BLOODY NIGHTS OF DEATH!!!

This once-sleepy city is under siege. In the space of six short months eleven people have been brutally murdered, their bodies drained of blood and dumped in various public places. Many more have vanished into the shadows of the night and might be lying beneath the streets, their lifeless bodies decomposing in the lonely dark.

Officials cannot account for the gruesome killing spree. They do not believe the murders to be the work of one man, but nor have they been able to link the crimes to any known criminals. In the largest single police operation in the city's history, most local gangs have been broken up, religious cult leaders arrested and the doors of secret orders and brotherhoods smashed down ... to no effect at all!

CUSTOMARY BLUNTNESS

Chief Inspector of police, Alice Burgess, when queried about the lack of results, responded with her own brand of customary bluntness. "We've been working like dogs," she snapped. "Everyone's on unpaid overtime. Nobody's shirking responsibility. We're patrolling the streets in force, arresting anyone who even *looks* suspicious. We've initiated a 7 pm curfew for children, and have advised adults to remain indoors too. If you find someone who can do a better job, give me a call and I'll gladly step aside."

Comforting words — but nobody here is taking comfort from them. The people of this city are tired of promises and pledges. Nobody doubts the honest, hard-working efforts of the local police – or the army who have been called in to assist in the operation – but faith in their ability to bring an end to the crisis has hit an all-time low. Many are moving out of the city, staying with relatives or in hotels, until the killings cease.

"I have kids," Michael Corbett, the forty-six-year-old owner of a second-hand bookshop told us. "Running away doesn't make me feel proud, and it'll ruin my business, but the lives of my wife and children come first. The police can do no more now than they did thirteen years ago. We've just got to wait for this to blow over, like it did before. When it does, I'll return. In the mean time, I think anyone who stays is crazy."

HISTORY OF DEATH

When Mr Corbett spoke of the past, he was referring to a time, nearly thirteen years ago, when horror similarly visited this city. On that occasion, nine bodies were discovered by a pair of teenagers, butchered and drained as the recent eleven victims have been.

But those bodies were carefully hidden, and only unearthed long after death had occurred. Today's murderers – rather, *tonight's*, since each victim has been taken after sunset – are not bothering to hide the evidence of their foul deeds. It's as though they are proud of their cruelty, leaving the bodies where they know they will be found.

Many locals believe the city is cursed and has a history of death. "I've been expecting these killings for fifty years," said Dr Kevin Beisty, a local historian and expert on the occult. "Vampires visited here more than one hundred and fifty years ago, and the thing about vampires is, once they find a place they like — they always come back!"

DEMONS OF THE NIGHT

Vampires. If Dr Beisty's was the only voice crying out against demons of the night, he could be dismissed as a crank. But many other people believe that we are suffering at the hands of vampires. They point to the fact that the attacks always occur at night, that the bodies have been drained of blood – seemingly without the aid of medical equipment – and, most tellingly, that although three of the victims were photographed by hidden security cameras when they were abducted, their attackers' faces *did not show up on film*!!

Chief Inspector Alice Burgess is dismissive of the vampire theory. "You think Count Dracula's on the rampage?" she laughed contemptuously. "Don't be ridiculous! This is the twenty-first century. Warped, sick humans are behind all this. Don't waste my time blaming bogeymen!"

When pushed, the Chief Inspector had this to add: "I don't believe in vampires, and I don't want idiots like you filling people's heads with such nonsense. But I'll tell you this: I'll do whatever it takes to stop these savages. If that means driving a stake through some madman's chest because he believes he's a vampire, I'll do it, even if it costs me my job and freedom. Nobody's walking away from this on an insanity plea. There's only one way to pay back the deaths of eleven good men and women — *extermination*!

"And I'll do it," Chief Inspector Burgess vowed, a fiery gleam in her pale eyes which would have done Professor Van Helsing proud. "Even if I have to track them to Transylvania and back. There'll be no escaping the sword of justice, be they humans or vampires.

"Tell your readers that I'll get their tormentors. They can bet on that. They can bet their *lives*..."

* * *

MR CREPSLEY pushed the manhole cover up and out of the way, while Harkat and me waited in the darkness below. After checking the street for signs of life, he whispered, "All clear," and we followed him up the ladder and out into fresh air.

"I hate those bloody tunnels," I groaned, slipping off my shoes, which were soaked through with water, mud and other things I didn't want to think about. I'd have to wash them out in the sink when we got back to the hotel and leave them on top of a radiator to dry, as I'd been doing at the end of every night for the past three months.

"I despise them too," Mr Crepsley agreed, gently prying the remains of a dead rat from the folds of his long red cloak.

"They're not so bad," Harkat chuckled. It was OK for him — he had no nose or sense of smell!

"At least the rain has held off," Mr Crepsley said.

"Give it another month," I replied sourly. "We'll be wading up to our hips down there by mid-October."

"We will have located and dealt with the vampaneze by then," Mr Crepsley said, without conviction.

"That's what you said two months ago," I reminded him.

"And last month," Harkat added.

"You wish to call off the search and leave these people to the vampaneze?" Mr Crepsley asked quietly.

Harkat and me looked at each other, then shook our heads. "Of course not," I sighed. "We're just tired and cranky. Let's get back to the hotel, dry ourselves off and get something warm to eat. We'll be fine after a good day's sleep."

Finding a nearby fire escape, we climbed to the roof of the building and set off across the skylight of the city, where there were no police or soldiers.

Six months had passed since the Lord of the Vampaneze escaped. Vancha had gone to Vampire Mountain to tell the Princes and Generals the news, and had not yet returned. For the first three months Mr Crepsley, Harkat and me had roamed without purpose, letting our feet take us where they wished. Then word reached us of the terror in Mr Crepsley's home city — people were being killed, their bodies drained of blood. Reports claimed vampires were to blame, but we knew better. Rumours had previously reached us of a vampaneze presence in the city, and this was all the confirmation we needed.

Mr Crepsley cared for these people. Those he'd known when he lived here as a human were long since dead and buried, but he looked upon their grandchildren and great-grandchildren as his spiritual kin. Thirteen years earlier, when a mad vampaneze by the name of Murlough was savaging the city, Mr Crepsley returned – with me and Evra Von, a snake-boy from the Cirque Du Freak – to stop him. Now that history was repeating itself, he felt compelled to intervene again.

"But maybe I should ignore my feelings," he'd mused three months earlier, as we discussed the situation. "We must focus on the hunt for the Vampaneze Lord. It would be wrong of me to drag us away from our quest."

"Not so," I'd disagreed. "Mr Tiny told us we'd have to follow our hearts if we were to find the Vampaneze Lord. Your heart's drawing you home, and my heart says I should stick by you. I think we should go."

Harkat Mulds, a grey-skinned Little Person who'd learned to talk, agreed, so we set off for the city where Mr Crepsley had been born, to evaluate the situation and help if we could. When we arrived, we soon found ourselves in the middle of a perplexing mystery. Vampaneze were definitely living here – at least three or four, if our estimate was correct – but were they part of the war force or rogue madmen? If they were warriors, they should be more careful about how they killed — sane vampaneze don't leave the bodies of their victims where humans can find them. But if they were mad, they shouldn't be capable of hiding so skilfully — after three months of searching, we hadn't found a trace of a single vampaneze in the tunnels beneath the city.

Back at the hotel, we entered via the window. We'd rented two rooms on the upper floor, and used the windows to get in and out at night, since we were too dirty and damp to use the lobby. Besides, the less we moved about on the ground, the better — the city was in uproar, with police and soldiers patrolling the streets, arresting anyone who looked out of place.

While Mr Crepsley and Harkat used the bathrooms, I undressed and waited for a free bath. We could have rented three rooms, so we'd each have a bath, but it was safer for

Harkat not to show himself — Mr Crepsley and me could pass for human, but the monstrous-looking, stitched-together Harkat couldn't.

I nearly fell asleep sitting on the end of the bed. The last three months had been long and arduous. Every night we roamed the roofs and tunnels of the city, searching for vampaneze, avoiding the police, soldiers and frightened humans, many of whom had taken to carrying guns and other weapons. It was taking its toll on all of us, but eleven people had died – that we knew of – and more would follow if we didn't stick to our task.

Standing, I walked around the room, trying to stay awake long enough to get into the bath. Sometimes I didn't, and would wake the following night stinking, sweaty and filthy, feeling like something a cat had coughed up.

I thought about my previous visit to this city. I'd been much younger, still learning what it meant to be a half-vampire. I'd met my first and only girlfriend here — Debbie Hemlock. She'd been dark-skinned, full-lipped and bright-eyed. I would have loved to get to know her better. But duty called, the mad vampaneze was killed, and the currents of life swept us apart.

I'd walked by the house where she'd lived with her parents several times since returning, half-hoping she still lived there. But new tenants had moved in and there was no sign of the Hemlocks. Just as well, really — as a half-vampire I aged at a fifth the human rate, so although nearly thirteen years had passed since I last kissed Debbie, I only looked a few years older. Debbie would be a grown woman now. It would have been confusing if we'd run into one another.

The door connecting the bedrooms opened and Harkat entered, drying himself with a huge hotel towel. "The bath's free," he said, wiping around the top of his bald, grey, scarred head with the towel, careful not to irritate his round green eyes, which had no eyelids to protect them.

"Cheers, ears," I grinned, slipping by him. That was an in-joke — Harkat, like all the Little People, had ears, but they were stitched under the skin at the sides of his head, so it looked as if he hadn't any.

Harkat had drained the bath, put the plug back in and turned on the hot tap, so it was almost full with fresh water when I arrived. I tested the temperature, added a dash of cold, turned off the taps and slid in — heavenly! I raised a hand to brush a lock of hair out of my eyes but my arm wouldn't lift all the way — I was too tired. Relaxing, I decided to just lie there a few minutes. I could wash my hair later. To simply lie in the bath and relax ... for a few minutes ... would be...

Without finishing the thought, I fell soundly asleep, and when I awoke it was night again, and I was blue all over from having spent the day in a bath of cold, grimy water.

CHAPTER TWO

WE RETURNED to the hotel at the end of another long, disappointing night. We'd stayed at the same hotel since coming to the city. We hadn't meant to – the plan had been to switch every couple of weeks – but the search for the vampaneze had left us so exhausted, we hadn't been able to muster the energy to go looking for fresh accommodation. Even the sturdy Harkat Mulds, who didn't need to sleep very much, was dozing off for four or five hours each day.

I felt better after a hot bath and flicked on the TV to see if there was any news about the killings. I learnt it was early Thursday morning – days melted into one another when you lived among vampires, and I rarely took any notice of them – and no new deaths had been reported. It had been almost two weeks since the last body was discovered. There was the slightest hint of hope in the air — many people thought the reign of terror had come to an end. I doubted we'd be that lucky, but I kept my fingers crossed as I turned the set off and headed for the welcome hotel bed.

Sometime later I was roughly shaken awake. A strong light was shining through the thin material of the curtains and I knew instantly that it was midday or early afternoon, which was way too soon to be even thinking about getting out of bed. Grunting, I sat up and found an anxious-looking Harkat leaning over me.

"Wassup?" I muttered, rubbing the grains of sleep from my eyes.

"Someone's knocking at ... your door," Harkat croaked.

"Tell them to please go away," I said — or words to that effect!

"I was going to, but..." He paused.

"Who is it?" I asked, sensing trouble.

"I don't know. I opened the door of *my* room a crack ... and checked. It's nobody connected with the hotel, although ... there's a staff member with him. He's a small man, carrying a big ... briefcase, and he's..." Again Harkat paused. "Come see for yourself."

I got up as there was a round of fresh knuckle raps. I hurried through to Harkat's room. Mr Crepsley was sleeping soundly in one of the twin beds. We tiptoed past him and opened the door ever so slightly. One of the figures in the corridor was familiar – the day manager of the hotel – but I'd never seen the other. He was small, as Harkat had said, and thin, with a huge black briefcase. He was wearing a dark grey suit, black shoes and an old-fashioned bowler hat. He was scowling and raising his knuckles to knock again as we closed the door.

"Think we should answer?" I asked Harkat.

"Yes," he said. "He doesn't look like the sort who'll ... go away if we ignore him."

"Who do you think he is?"

"I'm not sure, but there's something ... officious about him. He might be a police officer or in ... the army."

"You don't think they know about...?" I nodded at the sleeping vampire.

"They'd send more than one man ... if they did," Harkat replied.

I thought about it for a moment, then made up my mind. "I'll go see what he wants. But I won't let him in unless I have to — I don't want people snooping around in here while Mr Crepsley's resting."

"Shall I stay here?" Harkat asked.

"Yes, but keep close to the door and don't lock it — I'll call if I run into trouble."

Leaving Harkat to fetch his axe, I quickly pulled on a pair of trousers and a shirt and went to see what the man in the corridor wanted. Pausing by the door, not opening it, I cleared my throat and called out innocently, "Who is it?"

In immediate response, in a voice like a small dog's bark, the man with the briefcase said, "Mr Horston?"

"No," I replied, breathing a small sigh of relief. "You have the wrong room."

"Oh?" The man in the corridor sounded surprised. "This isn't Mr Vur Horston's room?"

"No, it's—" I winced. I'd forgotten the false names we'd given when registering! Mr Crepsley had signed in as Vur Horston and I'd said I was his son. (Harkat had crept in when no one was watching.) "I mean," I began again, "this is *my* room, not my dad's. I'm Darren Horston, his son."

"Ah." I could sense his smile through the door. "Excellent. You're the reason I'm here. Is your father with you?"

"He's..." I hesitated. "Why do you want to know? Who are you?"

"If you open the door and let me in, I'll explain."

"I'd like to know who you are first," I said. "These are dangerous times. I've been told not to open the door to strangers."

"Ah. Excellent," the little man said again. "I should of course not expect you to open the door to an unannounced visitor. Forgive me. My name is Mr Blaws."

"Blores?"

"*Blaws*," he said, and patiently spelt it out.

"What do you want, Mr Blaws?" I asked.

"I'm a school inspector," he replied. "I've come to find out why you aren't in school."

My jaw dropped about a thousand kilometres.

"May I come in, Darren?" Mr Blaws asked. When I didn't answer, he rapped on the door again and sung out, "Darrrrennn?"

"Um. Just a minute, please," I muttered, then turned my back to the door and leant weakly against it, wildly wondering what I should do.

If I turned the inspector away, he'd return with help, so in the end I opened the door and let him in. The hotel manager departed once he saw that everything was OK, leaving me alone with the serious-looking Mr Blaws. The little man set his briefcase down on the floor, then removed his bowler hat and held it in his left hand, behind his back, as he shook my hand with his right. He was studying me carefully. There was a light layer of bristle on my chin, my hair was long and scruffy, and my face still carried small scars and burn marks from my Trials of Initiation seven years before.

"You look quite old," Mr Blaws commented, sitting down without being asked. "Very mature for fifteen. Maybe it's the hair. You could do with a trim and a shave."

"I guess..." I didn't know why he thought I was fifteen, and I was too bewildered to correct him.

"So!" he boomed, laying his bowler hat aside and his huge briefcase across his lap. "Your father – Mr Horston – is he in?"

"Um ... yeah. He's ... sleeping." I was finding it hard to string words together.

"Oh, of course. I forgot he was on night shifts. Perhaps I should call back at a more convenient..." He trailed off, thumbed open his briefcase, dug out a sheet of paper and studied it as though it was an historical document. "Ah," he said. "Not possible to rearrange — I'm on a tight schedule. You'll have to wake him."

"Um. Right. I'll go ... see if he's..." I hurried through to where the vampire lay sleeping and anxiously shook him awake. Harkat stood back, saying nothing — he'd heard everything and was just as confused as I was.

Mr Crepsley opened one eye, saw that it was daytime, and shut it again. "Is the hotel on fire?" he groaned.

"No."

"Then go away and—"

"There's a man in my room. A school inspector. He knows our names — at least, the names we checked in under — and he thinks I'm fifteen. He wants to know why I'm not at school."

Mr Crepsley shot out of bed as though he'd been bitten. "How can this be?" he snapped. He rushed to the door, stopped, then retreated slowly. "How did he identify himself?"

"Just told me his name — Mr Blaws."

"It could be a cover story."

"I don't think so. The manager of the hotel was with him. He wouldn't have let him up if he wasn't on the level. Besides, he *looks* like a school inspector."

"Looks can be deceptive," Mr Crepsley noted.

"Not this time," I said. "You'd better get dressed and come meet him."

The vampire hesitated, then nodded sharply. I left him to prepare, and went to close the curtains in my room. Mr Blaws looked at me oddly. "My father's eyes are very sensitive," I said. "That's why he prefers to work at night."

"Ah," Mr Blaws said. "Excellent."

We said nothing more for the next few minutes, while we waited for my 'father' to make his entrance. I felt very uncomfortable, sitting in silence with this stranger, but he acted as though he felt perfectly at home. When Mr Crepsley finally entered, Mr Blaws stood and shook his hand, not letting go of the briefcase. "Mr Horston," the inspector beamed. "A pleasure, sir."

"Likewise." Mr Crepsley smiled briefly, then sat as far away from the curtains as he could and drew his red robes tightly around himself.

"So!" Mr Blaws boomed after a short silence. "What's wrong with our young trooper?"

"Wrong?" Mr Crepsley blinked. "Nothing is wrong."

"Then why isn't he at school with all the other boys and girls?"

"Darren does not go to school," Mr Crepsley said, as though speaking to an idiot. "Why should he?"

Mr Blaws was taken aback. "Why, to learn, Mr Horston, the same as any other fifteen year old."

"Darren is not..." Mr Crepsley stopped. "How do you know his age?" he asked cagily.

"From his birth certificate, of course," Mr Blaws laughed.

Mr Crepsley glanced at me for an answer, but I was as lost as he was, and could only shrug helplessly. "And how did you acquire that?" the vampire asked.

Mr Blaws looked at us strangely. "You included it with the rest of the relevant forms when you enrolled him at Mahler's," he said.

"*Mahler's?*" Mr Crepsley repeated.

"The school you chose to send Darren to."

Mr Crepsley sank back in his chair and brooded on that. Then he asked to see the birth certificate, along with the other 'relevant forms'. Mr Blaws reached into his briefcase again and fished out a folder. "There you go," he said. "Birth certificate, records from his previous school, medical certificates, the enrolment form you filled in. Everything present and correct."

Mr Crepsley opened the file, flicked through a few sheets, studied the signatures at the bottom of one form, then passed the file across to me. "Look through those papers," he said. "Check that the information is ... *correct*."

It wasn't correct, of course – I wasn't fifteen and hadn't been to school recently; nor had I visited a doctor since joining the ranks of the undead – but it was fully detailed. The files built up a complete picture of a fifteen-year-old boy called Darren Horston, who'd moved to this city during the summer with his father, a man who worked night shifts in a local abattoir and...

My breath caught in my throat — the abattoir was the one where we'd first encountered the mad vampaneze, Murlough, thirteen years ago! "Look at this!" I gasped, holding the form out to Mr Crepsley, but he waved it away.

"Is it *accurate*?" he asked.

"Of course it's accurate," Mr Blaws answered. "You filled in the forms yourself." His eyes narrowed. "Didn't you?"

"Of course he did," I said quickly, before Mr Crepsley

could reply. "Sorry to act so befuddled. It's been a hard week. Um. Family problems."

"Ah. That's why you haven't shown up at Mahler's?"

"Yes." I forced a shaky smile. "We should have rung and informed you. Sorry. Didn't think."

"No problem," Mr Blaws said, taking the papers back. "I'm glad that's all it was. We were afraid something bad had happened to you."

"No," I said, shooting Mr Crepsley a look that said, 'play ball'. "Nothing bad happened."

"Excellent. Then you'll be in on Monday?"

"Monday?"

"Hardly seems worth while coming in tomorrow, what with it being the end of the week. Come early Monday morning and we'll sort you out with a timetable and show you around. Ask for—"

"Excuse me," Mr Crepsley interrupted, "but Darren will not be going to your school on Monday or any other day."

"Oh?" Mr Blaws frowned and gently closed the lid of his briefcase. "Has he enrolled at another school?"

"No. Darren does not need to go to school. *I* educate him."

"Really? There was no mention in the forms of your being a qualified teacher."

"I am not a—"

"And of course," Blaws went on, "we both know that only a qualified teacher can educate a child at home." He smiled like a shark. "Don't we?"

Mr Crepsley didn't know what to say. He had no experience of the modern educational system. When he was a boy, parents could do what they liked with their children. I decided to take matters into my own hands.

"Mr Blaws?"

"Yes, Darren?"

"What would happen if I didn't turn up at Mahler's?"

He sniffed snootily. "If you enrol at a different school and pass on the paperwork to me, everything will be fine."

"And if – for the sake of argument – I didn't enrol at another school?"

Mr Blaws laughed. "Everyone has to go to school. Once you turn sixteen, your time is your own, but for the next..." He opened the briefcase again and checked his files "...seven months, you must go to school."

"So if I chose not to go...?"

"We'd send a social worker to see what the problem was."

"And if we asked you to tear up my enrolment form and forget about me – if we said we'd sent it to you by mistake – what then?"

Mr Blaws drummed his fingers on the top of his bowler hat. He wasn't used to such bizarre questions and didn't know what to make of us. "We can't go around tearing up official forms, Darren," he chuckled uneasily.

"But if we'd sent them by accident and wanted to withdraw them?"

He shook his head firmly. "We weren't aware of your existence before you contacted us, but now that we are, we're responsible for you. We'd have to chase you up if we thought you weren't getting a proper education."

"Meaning you'd send social workers after us?"

"Social workers first," he agreed, then looked at us with a glint in his eye. "Of course, if you gave them a hard time, we'd have to call in the police next, and who knows where it would end."

I took that information on board, nodded grimly, then faced Mr Crepsley. "You know what this means, don't you?" He stared back uncertainly. "You'll have to start making packed lunches for me!"

CHAPTER THREE

"MEDDLING, SMUG, stupid little..." Mr Crepsley snarled. He was pacing the hotel room, cursing the name of Mr Blaws. The school inspector had left and Harkat had rejoined us. He'd heard everything through the thin connecting door, but could make no more sense of it than us. "I will track him down tonight and bleed him dry," Mr Crepsley vowed. "That will teach him not to come poking his nose in!"

"Talk like that won't fix this," I sighed. "We have to use our heads."

"Who says it is talk?" Mr Crepsley retorted. "He gave us his telephone number in case we need to contact him. I will find his address and—"

"It's a mobile phone," I sighed. "You can't trace addresses through them. Besides, what good would killing him do? Somebody else would replace him. Our records are on file. He's only the messenger."

"We could move," Harkat suggested. "Find a new hotel."

"No," Mr Crepsley said. "He has seen our faces and would broadcast our descriptions. It would make matters more complicated than they already are."

"What I want to know is *how* our records were submitted," I said. "The signatures on the files weren't ours, but they were pretty damn close."

"I know," he grunted. "Not a great forgery, but adequate."

"Is it possible there's been ... a mix-up?" Harkat asked. "Perhaps a real Vur Horston and his son ... sent in the forms, and you've been confused with them."

"No," I said. "The address of this hotel was included and so were our room numbers. And..." I told them about the abattoir.

Mr Crepsley stopped pacing. "*Murlough!*" he hissed. "That was a period of history I thought I would never have to revisit."

"I don't understand," Harkat said. "How could this be connected to Murlough? Are you saying he's alive and has ... set you up?"

"No," Mr Crepsley said. "Murlough is definitely dead. But someone must know we killed him. And that someone is almost certainly responsible for the humans who have been killed recently." He sat down and rubbed the long scar that marked the left side of his face. "This is a trap."

There was a long, tense silence.

"It can't be," I said in the end. "How could the vampaneze have found out about Murlough?"

"Desmond Tiny," Mr Crepsley said bleakly. "*He* knew about our run in with Murlough, and must have told the vampaneze. But I cannot understand why they faked the birth certificate and school records. If they knew so much about us, and where we are, they should have killed us cleanly and honourably, as is the vampaneze way."

"That's true," I noted. "You don't punish a murderer by sending him to school. Although," I added, remembering my long-ago schooldays, "death *can* sometimes seem preferable to double science on a Thursday afternoon..."

Again a lengthy silence descended. Harkat broke it by clearing his throat. "This sounds crazy," the Little Person said, "but what if Mr Crepsley *did* ... submit the forms?"

"Come again?" I said.

"He might have done it in ... his sleep."

"You think he *sleep wrote* a birth cert and school records, then submitted them to a local school?" I didn't even bother to laugh.

"Things like this have happened before," Harkat mumbled. "Remember Pasta O'Malley at the ... Cirque Du Freak? He read books at night when he was asleep. He could never recall reading them, but if you asked ... him about them, he could answer all your questions."

"I'd forgotten about Pasta," I muttered, giving Harkat's proposal some thought.

"I could not have filled in those forms," Mr Crepsley said stiffly.

"It's unlikely," Harkat agreed, "but we do strange things ... when we sleep. Perhaps you—"

"No," Mr Crepsley interrupted. "You do not understand. I could not have done it because..." He looked away sheepishly. "I cannot read or write."

The vampire might have had two heads, the way Harkat and me gawped at him.

"Of course you can read and write!" I bellowed. "You signed your name when we checked in."

"Signing one's name is an easy feat," he replied quietly, with wounded dignity. "I can read numbers and recognize certain words – I am able to read maps quite accurately – but as for genuine reading and writing..." He shook his head.

"How can you not be able to read or write?" I asked ignorantly.

"Things were different when I was young. The world was simpler. It was not necessary to be a master of the written word. I was the fifth child of a poor family and went to work at the age of eight."

"But ... but..." I pointed a finger at him. "You told me you love Shakespeare's plays and poems!"

"I do," he said. "Evanna read all his works to me over the decades. Wordsworth, Keats, Joyce — many others. I often meant to learn to read for myself, but I never got around to it."

"This is ... I don't... Why didn't you tell me?" I snapped. "We've been together fifteen years, and this is the first time you've mentioned it!"

He shrugged. "I assumed you knew. Many vampires are illiterate. That is why so little of our history or laws is written down — most of us are incapable of reading."

Shaking my head, exasperated, I put aside the vampire's revelation and concentrated on the more immediate problem. "You didn't fill out the forms — that's settled. So who did and what are we going to do about it?"

Mr Crepsley had no answer to that, but Harkat had a suggestion. "It could have been Mr Tiny," he said. "He loves to stir things up. Perhaps this is his idea ... of a joke."

We mulled that one over.

"It has a whiff of him about it," I agreed. "I can't see why he'd want to send me back to school, but it's the sort of trick I can imagine him pulling."

"Mr Tiny would appear to be the most logical culprit," Mr Crepsley said. "Vampaneze are not known for their sense of humour. Nor do they go in for intricate plots — like vampires, they are simple and direct."

"Let's say he *is* behind it," I mused. "That still leaves us with the problem of what to do. Should I report for class Monday morning? Or do we ignore Mr Blaws' warning and carry on as before?"

"I would rather not send you," Mr Crepsley said. "There is strength in unity. At present, we are well prepared to defend ourselves should we come under attack. With you at school, we would not be there to help you if you ran into trouble, and you would not be able to help us if our foes struck here."

"But if I don't go," I noted, "we'll have school inspectors — and worse — dogging our heels."

"The other option is to leave," Harkat said. "Just pack our bags and go."

"That is worth considering," Mr Crepsley agreed. "I do not like the idea of leaving these people to suffer, but if this *is* a trap designed to divide us, perhaps the killings will stop if we leave."

"Or they might increase," I said, "to tempt us back."

We thought about it some more, weighing up the various options.

"I want to stay," Harkat said eventually. "Life is getting more dangerous, but perhaps ... that means we're meant to be here. Maybe this city is where we're destined ... to lock horns with the Vampaneze Lord again."

"I agree with Harkat," Mr Crepsley said, "but this is a matter for Darren to decide. As a Prince, he must make the decision."

"Thanks a lot," I said sarcastically.

Mr Crepsley smiled. "It is your decision, not only because you are a Prince, but because this concerns you the most — *you* will have to mix with human children and teachers, and *you* will be the most vulnerable to attack. Whether this is a vampaneze trap or a whim of Mr Tiny's, life will be hard for you if we stay."

He was right. Going back to school would be a nightmare. I'd no idea what fifteen year olds studied. Classes would be hard. Homework would drive me loopy. And having to answer to teachers, after six years of lording it over the vampires as a Prince... It could get very uncomfortable.

Yet part of me was drawn to the notion. To sit in a classroom again, to learn, make friends, show off my advanced physical skills in PE, maybe go out with a few girls...

"The hell with it," I grinned. "If it's a trap, let's call their bluff. If it's a joke, we'll show we know how to take it."

"That is the spirit," Mr Crepsley boomed.

"Besides," I chuckled weakly, "I've endured the Trials of Initiation twice, a terrifying journey through an underground stream, encounters with killers, a bear and wild boars. How bad can *school* be?"

CHAPTER FOUR

I ARRIVED at Mahler's an hour before classes began. I'd had a busy weekend. First there'd been my uniform to buy – a green jumper, light green shirt, green tie, grey trousers, black shoes – then books, notepaper and A4 writing pads, a ruler, pens and pencils, an eraser, set squares and a compass, as well as a scientific calculator, whose array of strange buttons – 'INV', 'SIN', 'COS', 'EE' – meant nothing to me. I'd also had to buy a homework report book, which I'd have to write all my homework assignments in — Mr Crepsley would have to sign the book each night, saying I'd done the work I was meant to.

I shopped by myself — Mr Crepsley couldn't move about during the day, and Harkat's strange appearance meant it was better for him to stay inside. I got back to the hotel with my bags late Saturday evening, after two days of non-stop shopping. Then I remembered that I'd need a schoolbag as well, so I rushed out on one last-gasp, lightning-fast expedition to the nearest supplier. I bought a simple black bag with plenty of space for my books, and picked up a plastic lunch box as well.

Mr Crepsley and Harkat got a great kick out of my uniform. The first time they saw me stuffed inside it, walking stiffly, they laughed for ten minutes. "Stop it!" I growled, tearing a shoe off and lobbing it at them.

I spent Sunday wearing in the uniform, walking about the hotel rooms fully dressed. I did a lot of scratching and twitching — it had been a long time since I'd had to wear anything so confining. That night I shaved carefully and let Mr Crepsley cut my hair. Afterwards he and Harkat left to hunt for the vampaneze. For the first night since coming to the city, I stayed behind — I had school in the morning, and needed to be fresh for it. As time progressed, I'd work out a schedule whereby I'd assist in the hunt for the killers, but the first few nights were bound to be difficult and we all agreed it would be for the best if I dropped out of the hunt for a while.

I got hardly any sleep. I was almost as nervous as I'd been seven years earlier, when awaiting the verdict of the Vampire Princes after I'd failed my Trials of Initiation. At least then I knew what the worst could be – death – but I'd no idea what to expect from this strange adventure.

Mr Crepsley and Harkat were awake in the morning to see me off. They ate breakfast with me and tried to act as though I'd nothing to worry about. "This is a wonderful opportunity," Mr Crepsley said. "You have often complained of the life you lost when you became a half-vampire. This is a chance to revisit your past. You can be human again, for a while. It will be fascinating."

"Why don't you go instead of me then?" I snapped.

"I would if I could," he deadpanned.

"It'll be fun," Harkat assured me. "Strange at first, but give it time and you'll fit in. And don't feel inferior: these kids will know ... a lot more about the school curriculum than you, but you are ... a man of the world and know things that they will ... never learn, no matter how old they live to be."

"You are a Prince," Mr Crepsley agreed, "far superior to any there."

Their efforts didn't really help, but I was glad they were supporting me instead of mocking me.

With breakfast out of the way, I made a few ham sandwiches, packed them in my bag along with a small jar of pickled onions and a bottle of orange juice, and then it was time to leave.

"Do you want me to walk you to school?" Mr Crepsley asked innocently. "There are many dangerous roads to cross. Or perhaps you could ask a lollypop lady to hold your hand and—"

"Stuff it," I grunted, and bolted out the door with my bag full of books.

Mahler's was a large, modern school, the buildings arranged in a square around an open-air, cement recreational area. The main doors were open when I arrived, so I entered and went looking for the headmaster's room. The halls and rooms were clearly signposted, and I found Mr Chivers' room within a couple of minutes, but there was no sign of the headmaster. Half an hour passed — no Mr Chivers. I wondered if Mr Blaws had forgotten to tell the headmaster of my early arrival, but then I recalled the little man with the huge briefcase, and knew he wasn't the sort who forgot things like that. Maybe Mr Chivers thought he was supposed to meet me by the main doors or the staffroom. I decided to check.

The staffroom could have held twenty-five or thirty teachers, but I saw only three when I knocked and entered in response to a cry of, "Come in." Two were middle-aged men, glued to thick chairs, reading enormous newspapers. The other was a burly woman, busy pinning sheets of printed paper to the walls.

"Help you?" the woman snapped without looking around.

"My name's Darren Horston. I'm looking for Mr Chivers."

"Mr Chivers isn't in yet. Have you an appointment?"

"Um. Yes. I think so."

"Then wait for him outside his office. This is the *staffroom*."

"Oh. OK."

Closing the door, I picked up my bag and returned to the headmaster's room. There was still no sign of him. I waited ten more minutes, then went searching for him again. This time I made for the school entrance, where I found a group of teenagers leaning against a wall, talking loudly, yawning, laughing, calling each other names and cursing pleasantly.

They were dressed in Mahler uniforms like me, but the clothes looked natural on them.

I approached a gang of five boys and two girls. They had their backs to me and were discussing some programme they'd seen on TV the night before. I cleared my throat to attract their attention, then smiled and stuck out a hand to the nearest boy when he turned. "Darren Horston," I grinned. "I'm new here. I'm looking for Mr Chivers. You haven't seen him, have you?"

The boy stared at my hand – he didn't shake it – then into my face.

"You wot?" he mumbled.

"My name's Darren Horston," I said again. "I'm looking for–"

"I 'eard you the first time," he interrupted, scratching his nose and studying me suspiciously.

"Shivers ain't in yet," a girl said, and giggled as though she'd said something funny.

"Shivers ain't ever in before ten past nine," one of the boys yawned.

"An' even later on a Monday," the girl said.

"*Everyone* knows *that*," the boy who'd first spoken added.

"Oh," I muttered. "Well, as I said, I'm new here, so I can't be expected to know things that everyone else knows, can I?" I smiled, pleased to have made such a clever point on my first day in school.

"Get stuffed, asswipe," the boy said in response, which wasn't exactly what I'd been expecting.

"Pardon?" I blinked.

"You 'eard." He squared up to me. He was about a head taller, dark-haired, with a nasty squint. I could knock the stuffing out of any human in the school, but I'd momentarily forgotten that, and backed away from him, unsure of why he was acting this way.

"Go on, Smickey," one of the other boys laughed. "Do 'im!"

"Nah," the boy called Smickey smirked. "He ain't worth it."

Turning his back on me, he resumed his conversation with the others as though nothing had interrupted it. Shaken and confused, I slouched away. As I turned the corner, out of human but not vampire hearing, I heard one of the girls say, "That guy's seriously weird!"

"See that bag he was carrying?" Smickey laughed. "It was the size of a cow! He must have half the books in the country in it!"

"He spoke weird," the girl said.

"And he looked even weirder," the other girl added. "Those scars and red patches of flesh. And did you see that awful haircut? He looked like somefing out of a zoo!"

"Too right," Smickey said. "He smelt like it too!"

The gang laughed, then talk turned to the TV programme again. Trudging up the stairs, clutching my bag to my chest, feeling very small and ashamed of my hair and appearance, I positioned myself by Mr Chivers' door, hung my head, and miserably waited for the headmaster to show.

It had been a discouraging start, and though I liked to think things could only get better, I had a nasty feeling in the pit of my belly that they were going to get a whole lot worse!

CHAPTER FIVE

MR CHIVERS arrived shortly after a quarter past nine, puffing and red-faced. (I later learnt that he cycled to school.) He hurried past me without saying anything, opened the door to his room, and stumbled to the window, where he stood staring down at the cement quad. Spotting someone, he slid open the window and roared, "Kevin O'Brien! Have you been kicked out of class already?"

"Wasn't my fault, sir," a young boy shouted back. "The top came off my pen in my bag, ruining my homework. Could have happened to anyone, sir. I don't think I should be kicked out for—"

"Report to my office during your next free period, O'Brien!" Mr Chivers interrupted. "I have a few floors for you to scrub."

"Aw, sir!"

Mr Chivers slammed the window shut. "You!" he said, beckoning me in. "What are you here for?"

"I'm—"

"You didn't break a window, did you?" he cut in. "Because if you did, there'll be hell and leather to pay!"

"I didn't break a window," I snapped. "I haven't had time to break anything. I've been stuck outside your door since eight, waiting. You're late!"

"Oh?" He sat down, surprised by my directness. "Sorry. A flat tyre. It's the little monster who lives two floors below. He..." Clearing his throat, he remembered who he was and adopted a scowl. "Never mind about me — who are you and why were you waiting?"

"My name's Darren Horston. I'm—"

"—the new boy!" he exclaimed. "Sorry — clean forgot you were coming." Getting up, he took my hand and pumped it. "I was away this weekend – orienteering – only got back last night. I jotted down a note and pinned it to the fridge on Friday, but I must have missed it this morning."

"No problem," I said, freeing my fingers from his sweaty hand. "You're here now. Better late than never."

He studied me curiously. "Is that how you addressed your previous headmaster?" he asked.

I remembered how I used to tremble when faced with the headmistress of my old school. "No," I chuckled.

"Good, because it's not how you'll address me either. I'm no tyrant, but I don't stand for backchat. Speak respectfully when you talk to me, and add a 'sir' at the end. Got that?"

I took a deep breath. "Yes." A pause. "Sir."

"Better," he grunted, then invited me to sit. Opening a drawer, he found a file and perused it in silence. "Good grades," he said after a couple of minutes, laying it aside. "If you can match those here, we won't complain."

"I'll do my best. Sir."

"That's all we ask." Mr Chivers was studying my face, fascinated by my scars and burn-marks. "You've had a rough ride, haven't you?" he remarked. "Must be horrible to be trapped in a burning building."

"Yes, sir." That was in the report Mr Blaws had shown me — according to the forms my 'father' submitted, I'd been badly burnt in a house fire when I was twelve.

"Still, all's well that ends well! You're alive and active, and anything else is a bonus." Standing, he put the file away, checked the front of his suit – there were traces of egg and toast crumbs on his tie and shirt, which he picked at – then made for the door, telling me to follow.

Mr Chivers led me on a quick tour of the school, pointing out the computer rooms, assembly hall, gymnasium and the main classrooms. The school used to be a music academy, hence its name (Mahler was a famous composer), but had closed down twenty years earlier, before reopening as a regular school.

"We still place a lot of emphasis on musical excellence," Mr Chivers told me as we checked out a large room with half a dozen pianos. "Do you play any instruments?"

"The flute," I said.

"A flautist! Superb! We haven't had a decent flautist since

Siobhan Toner graduated three — or was it four? — years ago. We'll have to try you out, see what you're made of, eh?"

"Yes, sir," I replied weakly. I figured we were talking at cross purposes — he was referring to real flutes, whereas all I knew how to play was a tin-whistle — but I didn't know whether it was the time for me to point this out. In the end I kept my mouth shut and hoped he'd forget about my supposed flute-playing talents.

He told me each lesson lasted forty minutes. There was a ten-minute break at eleven o'clock; fifty minutes for lunch at ten past one; school finished at four. "Detention runs from four-thirty to six," he informed me, "but hopefully that won't concern you, eh?"

"I hope not, sir," I replied meekly.

The tour concluded back at his office, where he furnished me with my timetable. It was a frightening list — English, history, geography, science, maths, mechanical drawing, two modern languages, computer studies. A double dose of PE on Wednesdays. I had three free periods, one on Monday, one on Tuesday, one on Thursday. Mr Chivers said these were for extra-curricular activities, such as music or extra languages, or they could be used as study classes.

He shook my hand again, wished me the best of luck and told me to call on him if I ran into difficulty. After warning me not to break any windows or give my teachers grief he showed me out into the corridor, where he left me. It was 9.40 A bell rang. Time for my first class of the day — geography.

The lesson went reasonably well. I'd spent the last six years poring over maps and keeping abreast of the War of the Scars, so I had a better idea of the shape of the world than most of my classmates. But I knew nothing about *human* geography – a lot of the lesson revolved around economies and culture, and how humans shaped their environments – and I was at a loss every time talk switched from mountain ranges and rivers to political systems and population statistics.

Even allowing for my limited knowledge of humans, geography was as easy a start as I could have wished for. The teacher was helpful, I was able to keep up with most of what was being discussed, and I thought I'd be able to catch up with the rest of the class within a few weeks.

Maths, which came next, was a different matter entirely. I knew after five minutes that I was in trouble. I'd covered only basic maths in school, and had forgotten most of the little I used to know. I could divide and multiply, but that was as far as my expertise stretched — which, I quickly discovered, wasn't nearly far enough.

"What do you mean, you've never done algebra?" my teacher, a fierce man by the name of Mr Smarts, snapped. "Of course you have! Don't take me for a fool, lad. I know you're new, but don't think that means you can get away with murder. Open that book to page sixteen and do the first set of problems. I'll collect your work at the end of class and see where you stand."

Where I stood was outside in the cold, a hundred kilometres distant. I couldn't even *read* the problems on page sixteen, never mind solve them! I looked through the earlier pages and tried copying the examples set there, but I hadn't a clue what I was doing. When Mr Smarts took my copy from me and said he'd check it during lunch and return it to me that afternoon in science – I had him for that as well – I was too downhearted to thank him for his promptness.

Break was no better. I spent the ten minutes wandering alone, being stared at by everyone in the yard. I tried making friends with some of the people I recognized from my first two classes, but they wanted nothing to do with me. I looked, smelt and acted weird, and there was something *not right* about me. The teachers hadn't sussed me out yet, but the kids had. They knew I didn't belong.

Even if my fellow students had tried making me feel welcome, I'd have struggled to adapt. I knew nothing of the films and TV shows they were discussing, or the rock stars or styles of music, or the books and comics. Their way of speaking was strange too — I couldn't understand a lot of their slang.

I had history after the break. That used to be one of my favourite subjects, but this syllabus was far more advanced than mine had been. The class was focusing on World War II, which was what I'd been studying during my last few months as a human. Back then I'd only had to learn the major events of the war, and the leaders of the various countries. But as a fifteen year old, who'd supposedly progressed through the system, I was expected to know the detailed ins and outs of battles, the names of generals, the wide-ranging social effects of the war, and so on.

I told my teacher I'd been concentrating on ancient history in my old school, and complimented myself on such a clever answer — but then she said there was a small class of ancient history students at Mahler's and she'd get me transferred first thing tomorrow.

Ai-yi-yi-yi-yi!

English next. I was dreading it. I could bluff my way through subjects like geography and history, by saying I'd been following a different syllabus. But how was I going to explain my shortcomings in English? I could pretend not to have read all the books and poems that the others had, but what would happen when my teacher asked what I'd read instead? I was doomed!

There was a free table close to the front of the class, where I had to sit. Our teacher was late — because of the size of the school, teachers and pupils often arrived slightly late for class. I spent a couple of minutes anxiously scanning the book of poetry I'd bought last Friday, desperately committing a few scraps of random poems to memory, in the hope that I could fob the teacher off with them.

The door to the classroom opened, the noise level dropped, and everyone stood up. "Sit down, sit down," the teacher said, making straight for her desk, where she laid her stack of books. Facing the class, she smiled and brushed her hair back. She was a young, pretty black woman. "I hear we've a new addition," she said, looking around the room for me. "Will you stand up please, so I can identify you?"

Standing, I raised a hand and smiled edgily. "Here," I said.

"Close to the front," she beamed. "A good sign. Now, I have your name and details written down somewhere. Just give me a minute and I'll..."

She was turning aside to look among her books and papers, when all of a sudden she stopped as though slapped, glanced sharply at me and took a step forward. Her face lit up and she exclaimed, "*Darren Shan?*"

"Um. Yes." I smiled nervously. I'd no idea who she was, and was scouring my memory banks — was she staying in the same hotel as me? — when something about the shape of her mouth and eyes jogged a switch inside my brain. Leaving my table, I took several steps towards her, until we were only a metre apart, then studied her face incredulously. "*Debbie?*" I gasped. "*Debbie Hemlock?*"

CHAPTER SIX

"DARREN!" DEBBIE squealed, throwing her arms around me.

"Debbie!" I whooped and hugged her hard.

My English teacher was Debbie Hemlock — my ex-girlfriend!

"You've barely changed!" Debbie gasped.

"You look so different!" I laughed.

"What happened to your face?"

"How did you become a teacher?"

Then, together: "What are you doing here?"

We stopped, wide-eyed, beaming madly. We were no longer hugging, but our hands were joined. Around us, my fellow students gawped as though they were witnessing the end of the universe.

"Where have..." Debbie started, then glanced around. Realizing we were the centre of attention, she let go of my hands and smiled sheepishly. "Darren and I are old friends," she explained to the class. "We haven't seen each other in..."

Again she stopped, this time with a frown. "Excuse us," she muttered, grabbing my right hand and roughly leading the way outside. Closing the door, she swung me up against a wall, checked to make sure we were alone in the hall, leant in close and hissed, "Where the hell have you been all these years?"

"Here and there," I smiled, eyes roving her face, stunned by how much she'd changed. She was taller too — even taller than me now.

"Why is your face the same?" she snapped. "You look almost exactly as I remember you. You've aged a year or two, but it's been *thirteen* years!"

"How time flies," I smirked, then stole a quick kiss. "Good to see you again, Miss Hemlock."

Debbie froze at the kiss, then took a step back. "Don't do that."

"Sorry. Just glad to see you."

"I'm glad to see you too. But if anyone sees me kissing a student..."

"Oh, Debbie, I'm not really a student. You know that. I'm old enough to be... Well, you know how old I am."

"I thought I did. But your face..." She traced the outline of my jaw, then my lips and nose, then the small triangular scar above my right eye. "You've been in the wars," she noted.

"You wouldn't believe it if I told you how right you are," I smiled.

"Darren Shan." She shook her head and repeated my name. "Darren Shan."

Then she slapped me!

"What's that for?" I yelped.

"For leaving without saying goodbye and ruining my Christmas," she growled.

"That was thirteen years ago. Surely you're not still upset about it."

"The Hemlocks can carry a grudge a long, long time," she said, but there was the glint of a smile in her eyes.

"I did leave you a going-away present," I said.

For a moment her face was blank. Then she remembered. "The tree!"

Mr Crepsley and me had killed the mad vampaneze — Murlough — in Debbie's house on Christmas Eve, after using her as bait to lure him out of his lair. Before leaving, I'd placed a small Christmas tree by her bedside and decorated it (I'd drugged Debbie and her parents earlier, so they were unconscious when Murlough attacked).

"I'd forgotten about the tree," she muttered. "Which brings us to another point — what happened back then? One moment we were sitting down to dinner, the next I woke up in bed and it was late Christmas Day. Mum and Dad woke in their beds too, with no idea of how they got there."

"How are Donna and Jesse?" I asked, trying to avoid her question.

"Fine. Dad's still travelling the world, going wherever his work takes him, and Mum's started a new... No," she said, prodding me in the chest. "Forget what's been going on with *me*. I want to know what's up with *you*. For thirteen years you've been a fond memory. I tried finding you a few times, but you'd vanished without a trace. Now you waltz back into my life, looking as though the years had been months. I want to know what gives."

"It's a long story," I sighed. "And complicated."

"I've got time," she sniffed.

"No, you haven't," I contradicted her, nodding at the closed classroom door.

"Damn. I forgot about them." She strode to the door and opened it. The kids inside had been talking loudly, but they stopped at the sight of their teacher. "Get out your books!" she snapped. "I'll be with you presently." Facing me again, she said, "You're right — we don't have time. And my schedule's full for the rest of the day — I've a teachers' meeting to attend during lunch. But we have to get together soon and talk."

"How about after school?" I suggested. "I'll go home, change clothes, and we can meet ... where?"

"My place," Debbie said. "I live on the third floor of an apartment block. 3c, Bungrove Drive. It's about a ten-minute walk from here."

"I'll find it."

"But give me a couple of hours to correct homework," she said. "Don't come before half-six."

"Sounds perfect."

"Darren Shan," she whispered, a small smile lifting the corners of her mouth. "Who'd have believed it?" She leant towards me, and I thought — hoped! — she was going to kiss me, but then she stopped, adopted a stern expression and pushed me back into class ahead of her.

The lesson passed in a blur. Debbie tried hard not to pay special attention to me, but our eyes kept meeting and we were unable to stop smiling. The others kids noted the remarkable bond between us and it was the talk of the school by lunchtime. If the students had been suspicious of me at the start of the day, now they were downright wary, and everyone gave me a wide berth.

I breezed through the later classes. It didn't bother me that I was out of my depth and ignorant of the subject matter. I no longer cared or tried to act clued up. Debbie was all I could think about. Even when Mr Smarts threw my maths copy at me in science and bawled furiously, I only smiled, nodded and tuned him out.

At the end of the day I rushed back to the hotel. I'd been given the key to a locker, where I was supposed to leave my books, but I was so excited I didn't bother with it, and carried the full bag of books home with me. Mr Crepsley was still in bed when I arrived, but Harkat was awake, and I hurriedly told him about my day and meeting Debbie.

"Isn't it wonderful?" I finished breathlessly. "Isn't it incredible? Isn't it the most..." I couldn't think of any way to describe it, so I simply threw my hands into the air and yelled, "Yahoo!"

"It's great," Harkat said, wide mouth spreading into a jagged smile, but he didn't sound happy.

"What's wrong?" I asked, reading the unease in his round green eyes.

"Nothing," he said. "It's great. Really. I'm thrilled for you."

"Don't lie to me, Harkat. Something's bugging you. What?"

He came out with it. "Doesn't this seem a bit ... *too* coincidental?"

"What do you mean?"

"Of all the schools you could have gone to ... all the teachers in the world ... you end up at the one where your ... old girlfriend's teaching? And in her class?"

"Life's like that, Harkat. Strange things happen all the time."

"Yes," the Little Person agreed. "And sometimes they happen ... by chance. But other times they're ... arranged."

I'd been unbuttoning my shirt, having slipped off my jumper and tie. Now I paused, fingers on the buttons, and studied him. "What are you saying?"

"Something smells rotten. If you'd run into Debbie in the street, that ... would be something else. But you're in her class at a school where ... you shouldn't be. Somebody set you up to go to Mahler's, someone who ... knows about Murlough, and about your past."

"You think the person who forged our signatures knew Debbie was working at Mahler's?" I asked.

"That's obvious," Harkat said. "And that in itself is cause for worry. But there's something else we ... must consider. What if the person who set you up didn't ... just *know* about Debbie — what if it *was* Debbie?"

CHAPTER SEVEN

I COULDN'T believe Debbie was in league with the vampaneze or Mr Tiny, or had played any part in setting me up to go to Mahler's. I told Harkat how stunned she'd been to see me, but he said she might have been acting. "If she went to all the trouble of getting ... you there, she'd hardly *not* act surprised," he noted.

I shook my head stubbornly. "She wouldn't do something like this."

"I don't know her, so I can't voice ... an opinion. But *you* don't really know her either. She was a child when you ... last saw her. People change as they grow."

"You don't think I should trust her?"

"I'm not saying that. Maybe she's genuine. Maybe she had nothing to do with faking the ... forms, or with you being there — it *could* be a ... huge coincidence. But caution is required. Go see her, but keep an eye ... on her. Be careful what you say. Put some probing questions to her. And take a weapon."

"I couldn't hurt her," I said quietly. "Even if she has plotted against us, there's no way I could kill her."

"Take one anyway," Harkat insisted. "If she's working with the vampaneze, it may not be ... *her* you have to use it on."

"You reckon the vampaneze could be lying in wait there?"

"Maybe. We couldn't understand why ... the vampaneze — if they're behind the fake forms — would send you ... to school. If they're working with Debbie — or using ... her — this might explain it."

"You mean they want to get me at Debbie's alone, so they can pick me off?"

"They might."

I nodded thoughtfully. I didn't believe Debbie was working with our foes, but it was possible that they were manipulating her to get to me. "How should we handle this?" I asked.

Harkat's green eyes betrayed his uncertainty. "I'm not sure. It would be foolish to walk into ... a trap. But sometimes risks must be taken. Perhaps this is our way to flush out ... those who would ensnare us."

Chewing my lower lip, I brooded upon it a while, then followed the most sensible course of action — I went and woke Mr Crepsley.

I rang the bell for 3c and waited. A moment later, Debbie's voice came over the intercom. "Darren?"

"The one and only."

"You're late." It was twenty past seven. The sun was setting.

"Got stuck doing homework. Blame my English teacher — she's a real dragon."

"Ha-flaming-ha."

There was a buzzing noise and the door opened. I paused before entering and looked across the street at the opposite block of apartments. I spotted a lurking shadow on the roof — Mr Crepsley. Harkat was behind Debbie's building. Both would rush to my rescue at the first sign of trouble. That was the plan we'd hatched. Mr Crepsley had suggested beating a hasty retreat – things were getting too complicated for his liking – but when I pulled rank, he'd agreed to make the most of the situation and attempt to turn the tables on our opponents — *if* they showed.

"If a fight develops," he warned me before setting out, "it may not be possible to choose targets. You are not prepared to raise a hand against your friend, but *I* am, if she is working with the enemy. Do not get in my way if that happens."

I nodded grimly. I wasn't sure I could stand by and let him harm Debbie, even if it turned out that she was conspiring against us — but I'd try.

Trotting up the stairs, I was painfully aware of the two knives I was carrying, strapped to my calves so as not to show. I hoped I wouldn't have to use them, but it was good to know they were there if needed.

The door to 3c was open, but I knocked before entering. "Come in," Debbie called. "I'm in the kitchen."

I closed the door but didn't lock it. Quickly scanned the apartment. Very tidy. Several bookcases, overflowing with books. A CD player and stand; lots of CDs. A portable TV set. A cover poster of *The Lord of the Rings* on one wall, a picture of Debbie with her parents on another.

Debbie stepped in from the kitchen. She was wearing a long red apron and there was flour in her hair. "I got bored waiting for you," she said, "so I started to make scones. Do you like yours with currants or without?"

"Without," I said and smiled as she ducked back into the kitchen — killers and their cohorts don't greet you with flour in their hair! Any half-doubts I had about Debbie quickly vanished and I knew I'd nothing to fear from her. But I didn't drop my guard — Debbie didn't pose a threat, but there might be vampaneze in the room next door or hovering on the fire escape.

"How did you enjoy your first day at school?" Debbie asked, as I wandered round the living room.

"It was strange. I haven't been inside a school since... Well, it's been a long time. So much has changed. When I was..." I stopped. The cover of a book had caught my eye: *The Three Musketeers*. "Is Donna still making you read this?"

Debbie poked her head through the doorway and looked at the book. "Oh," she laughed. "I was reading that when we first met, wasn't I?"

"Yep. You hated it."

"Really? That's odd — I love it now. It's one of my favourites. I recommend it to my pupils all the time."

Shaking my head wryly, I laid the book down and went to view the kitchen. It was small, but professionally organized. There was a lovely smell of fresh dough. "Donna taught you well," I remarked. Debbie's mum used to be a chef.

"She wouldn't let me leave home until I could run a good kitchen," Debbie smiled. "Graduating university was easier than passing the tests she set."

"You've been to university?" I asked.

"I'd hardly be teaching if I hadn't."

Laying a tray of unbaked scones into a petite oven, she switched off the light and motioned me back to the living room. As I flopped into one of the soft chairs she went to the CD stand and looked for something to play. "Any preferences?"

"Not really."

"I don't have much in the way of pop or rock. Jazz or classical?"

"I don't mind."

Choosing a CD, she took it out of its case, inserted it in the player and turned it on. She stood by the player a couple of minutes while flowing, lifting music filled the air. "Like it?" she asked.

"Not bad. What is it?"

"*The Titan.* Do you know who it's by?"

"Mahler?" I guessed.

"Right. I thought I'd play it for you, so you're familiar with it — Mr Chivers gets very upset if his students don't recognize Mahler." Taking the chair next to mine, Debbie studied my face in silence. I felt uncomfortable, but didn't turn away. "So," she sighed. "Want to tell me about it?"

I'd discussed what I should tell her with Mr Crepsley and Harkat, and quickly launched into the story we'd settled upon. I said I was the victim of an ageing disease, which meant I aged slower than normal people. I reminded her of the snake-boy, Evra Von, whom she'd met, and said the two of us were patients at a special clinic.

"You aren't brothers?" she asked.

"No. And the man we were with wasn't our father — he was a nurse at the hospital. That's why I never let you meet him — it was fun, having you think I was an ordinary person, and I didn't want him giving the game away."

"So how old *are* you?" she enquired.

"Not much older than you," I said. "The disease didn't set in until I was twelve. I wasn't very different to other children until then."

She considered that in her careful, thoughtful manner. "If that's true," she said, "what are you doing in school now? And why pick mine?"

"I didn't know you were working at Mahler's," I said. "That's a freak occurrence. I've returned to school because... It's hard to explain. I didn't get a proper education when I was growing up. I was rebellious and spent a lot of time off fishing or playing football when I should have been learning.

Lately I've been feeling like I missed out. A few weeks ago I met a man who forges papers — passports, birth certificates, stuff like that. I asked him to set me up with a fake ID, so I could pretend I was fifteen."

"Whatever for?" Debbie asked. "Why didn't you go to an adult night school?"

"Because, looks-wise, I'm *not* an adult." I pulled a sad face. "You don't know how miserable it gets, growing so slowly, explaining myself to strangers, knowing they're talking about me. I don't mingle much. I live alone and stay indoors most of the time. I felt this was an opportunity to pretend I was normal. I thought I could fit in with the people I most resemble — fifteen year olds. I hoped, if I dressed and talked like them, and went to school with them, maybe they'd accept me and I wouldn't feel so lonely." Lowering my gaze, I added mournfully, "I guess the pretence stops now."

There was a silent beat. Another. Then Debbie said, "Why should it?"

"Because you know about me. You'll tell Mr Chivers. I'll have to leave."

Debbie reached across and took my left hand in hers. "I think you're crazy," she said. "Practically everyone I know couldn't wait to leave school, and here you are, desperate to return. But I admire you for this. I think it's great that you want to learn. I think you're very brave, and I won't say anything about it."

"Really?"

"I think you'll be found out eventually – an act like this is impossible to sustain – but I won't blow the whistle on you."

"Thanks, Debbie. I..." Clearing my throat, I looked at our joined hands. "I'd like to kiss you – to thank you – but I don't know if you want me to."

Debbie frowned, and I could see what she was thinking — was it acceptable for a teacher to let one of her pupils kiss her? Then she chuckled and said, "OK — but just on my cheek."

Lifting my head, I leant over and brushed her cheek with my lips. I would have liked to kiss her properly, but knew I couldn't. Although we were of similar ages, in her eyes I was still a teenager. There was a line between us we couldn't step over — much as the adult within me hungered to cross it.

We talked for hours. I learnt all about Debbie's life, how she'd gone to university after school, studied English and sociology, graduated and went on to become a teacher. After a few part-time appointments elsewhere, she'd applied for a number of permanent positions here — she'd seen out her schooldays in this city, and felt it was the nearest place she had to a home. She ended up at Mahler's. She'd been there two years and loved it. There'd been men in her life – she'd been engaged at one stage! – but none at the moment. And she said – very pointedly – that she wasn't looking for any either!

She asked me about that night thirteen years ago and what had happened to her and her parents. I lied and said there'd been something wrong with the wine. "You all fell asleep at the table. I rang for the nurse who was looking after Evra and me. He came, checked, said you were OK and would be fine when you woke. We put the three of you to bed and I slipped away. I've never been good at saying farewell."

I told Debbie I was living alone. If she checked with Mr Blaws, she'd know that was a lie, but I didn't think ordinary teachers mixed much with inspectors.

"It's going to be bizarre having you in my class," she murmured. We were sitting on the couch. "We'll have to be careful. If anyone suspects there was ever anything between us, we must tell the truth. It'd mean my career if we didn't."

"Maybe it's a problem we won't have to worry about much longer," I said.

"What do you mean?"

"I don't think I'm cut out for school. I'm behind in all the subjects. In some – maths and science – I'm not even within sighting distance of everyone else. I think I'll have to drop out."

"That's quitting talk," she growled, "and I won't stand for it." She popped one of the scones – they were chestnut brown, smeared with butter and jam – into my mouth and made me munch on it. "Finish what you start or you'll regret it."

"Buh I cahn't duh iht," I mumbled, mouth full of scone.

"Of course you can," she insisted. "It won't be easy. You'll have to study hard, maybe get some private tuition..." She stopped and her face lit up. "That's it!"

"What?" I asked.

"You can come to *me* for lessons."

"What sort of lessons?"

She punched my arm. "School lessons, you ninny! You can come round for an hour or two after school every day. I'll help you with your homework and fill you in on stuff you've missed."

"You wouldn't mind?" I asked.

"Of course not," she smiled. "It will be a pleasure."

Enjoyable as the night was, it had to end eventually. I'd forgotten about the possible threat of the vampaneze, but when Debbie excused herself and went to the bathroom, I fell to thinking about them, and wondered if Mr Crepsley or Harkat had sighted any — I didn't want to come to Debbie's for lessons if it meant getting her mixed up in our dangerous affairs.

If I waited for her to return, I might forget about the threat again, so I composed a quick note – 'Have to go. Wonderful to see you. Meet you at school in the morning. Hope you won't mind if I don't do my homework!' – left it on the bare plate which had contained the scones, and ducked out as quietly as possible.

I trotted down the stairs, humming happily, paused outside the main door at the bottom and let rip with three long whistles — my signal to Mr Crepsley to let him know that I was leaving. Then I made my way round to the back of the building and found Harkat hiding behind a couple of large black rubbish bins. "Any trouble?" I asked.

"None," he replied. "Nobody's gone near the place."

Mr Crepsley arrived and crouched behind the bins with us. He looked more solemn than usual. "Spot any vampaneze?" I asked.

"No."

"Mr Tiny?"

"No."

"Things are looking good then," I smiled.

"What about Debbie?" Harkat asked. "Is she on the level?"

"Oh, yes." I gave them a quick account of my conversation with Debbie. Mr Crepsley said nothing, only grunted as I filled him in. He appeared very moody and distant.

"...so we've arranged to meet each evening after school," I finished. "We haven't set a time yet. I wanted to discuss it with you two first, to see if you want to shadow us when we meet. I don't think there's any need – I'm sure Debbie isn't part of a plot – but if you want, we can schedule the lessons for late at night."

Mr Crepsley sighed half-heartedly. "I do not think that will be necessary. I have scouted the area thoroughly. There is no evidence of the vampaneze. It would be preferable if you came in daylight, but not essential."

"Is that a seal of approval?"

"Yes." Again he sounded unusually downhearted.

"What's wrong?" I asked. "You're not still suspicious of Debbie, are you?"

"It has nothing to do with her. I..." He looked at us sadly. "I have bad news."

"Oh?" Harkat and me exchanged uncertain glances.

"Mika Ver Leth transmitted a short telepathic message to me while you were inside."

"Is this about the Lord of the Vampaneze?" I asked nervously.

"No. It is about our friend, your fellow Prince, Paris Skyle. He..." Mr Crepsley sighed again, then said dully, "Paris is dead."

CHAPTER EIGHT

THE DEATH of the ancient Prince should have come as no great surprise — he was the wrong side of eight hundred, the War of the Scars had taken its toll on him, and I remembered thinking when I left Vampire Mountain how poorly he looked — but I hadn't expected him to go this quickly, and the news knocked the wind out of me.

As far as Mr Crepsley knew, the Prince had died of natural causes. He wouldn't be sure until he got to Vampire Mountain — vampires could only send basic telepathic messages — but there'd been no hint of foul play in Mika's message.

I wanted to go with him to the funeral — it would be a huge affair, which almost every vampire in the world would attend — but Mr Crepsley asked me not to. "One Prince must always remain absent from Vampire Mountain," he reminded me, "in case anything happens to the others. I know you were

246

fond of Paris, but Mika, Arrow and Vancha knew him far longer than you. It would be unfair to ask one of them to give up their place."

I was disappointed, but bowed to his wishes — it would have been selfish of me to put myself before the elder Princes. "Tell them to be careful," I warned him. "I don't want to be the only Prince left — if they all perished together, and I had to lead the clan by myself, it would be a disaster!"

"You can say that again," Harkat laughed, but there was no merriment in his voice. "Can I come with you?" he asked Mr Crepsley. "I'd like to pay ... my respects."

"I would rather you remained with Darren," Mr Crepsley said. "I do not like the idea of leaving him on his own."

Harkat nodded immediately. "You're right. I'll stay."

"Thanks," I said softly.

"Now," Mr Crepsley mused, "that leaves us with the question of whether you hold camp here or locate elsewhere."

"We'll stay, of course," I said rather quickly.

Morose as he was, the vampire managed a wry smile. "I thought you would say that. I glimpsed you through the window as you kissed your teacher's cheek."

"You were spying on me!" I huffed.

"That was the general idea, was it not?" he replied. I sputtered indignantly, but of course that *had* been the plan. "You and Harkat should withdraw while I am away," Mr Crepsley continued. "If you come under attack, you will be hard-pushed to defend yourselves."

"I'm ready to risk it if Harkat is," I said.

Harkat shrugged. "The thought of staying doesn't ... frighten me."

"Very well," Mr Crepsley sighed. "But promise me you will abandon the search for the killers while I am absent, and do nothing to endanger yourselves."

"You've no fear on that score," I told him. "Chasing killers is the last thing on my mind. I've something far more terrifying to deal with — homework!"

Mr Crepsley wished us well, then hurried back to the hotel to gather his belongings and depart. He was gone when we got there, probably already at the edge of the city, getting ready to flit. It felt lonely without him, and a little bit scary, but we weren't too worried. He should only be gone a few weeks at most. What could possibly go wrong in so short a time?

The next fortnight was tough. With Mr Crepsley out of the city, the hunt for the vampaneze suspended, and the death count stable (nobody new had been killed recently), I was able to concentrate on school — which was just as well, given the amount of work I had to put into it.

Debbie pulled some strings to lighten my load. Guided by her, I played up the effects of the imaginary fire I'd been trapped in and said I'd missed a lot of school. I explained the good marks by saying my father had been best friends with the headmaster of my old school. Mr Chivers was decidedly unimpressed when he heard that, but Debbie convinced him not to take matters further.

I opted out of modern languages and dropped back a couple of years in maths and science. I felt more peculiar than ever sitting amidst a bunch of thirteen year olds, but at least I was able to follow what they were doing. I still had Mr Smarts for science, but he was more understanding now that he knew I hadn't been faking ignorance, and spent a lot of time helping me catch up.

I faced difficulties in English, history and geography, but with the extra free periods I had instead of languages, I was able to focus on them and was gradually pulling even with the others in my class.

I enjoyed mechanical drawing and computer studies. My Dad had taught me the basics of MD when I was a kid – he'd hoped I'd go into draughtsmanship when I grew up – and I quickly picked up on what I'd missed. To my surprise, I took to computers like a vampire to blood, aided by my super-fast fingers, which could speed about a keyboard faster than any human typist's.

I had to keep a close watch on my powers. I was finding it hard to make friends – my classmates were still suspicious of me – but I knew I could become popular if I took part in the lunchtime sporting activities. I could shine in any game – football, basketball, handball – and everyone likes a winner. The temptation to show off, and earn a few friends in the process, was strong.

But I resisted. The risk was too great. It wasn't just the possibility that I'd do something superhuman – like leap higher than a professional basketball player – which might tip people off to my powers, but the fear that I might injure somebody. If someone dug me in the ribs while playing football, I might lose my temper and take a punch at him, and my punches could put a human in hospital, or worse — a morgue!

PE was therefore a frustrating class — I had to deliberately mask my strength behind a clumsy, pathetic façade. English, oddly enough, was a pain too. It was great to be with Debbie, but when we were in class we had to act like an ordinary teacher and student. There could be no undue familiarity. We maintained a cool, distant air, which made the forty minutes — eighty on Wednesdays and Fridays, when I had double English — pass with agonizing slowness.

After school and at weekends, when I went round to her apartment for private tuition, it was different. There we could relax and discuss whatever we wanted; we could curl up on the couch with a bottle of wine and watch an old film on the TV, or listen to music and chat about the past.

I ate at Debbie's most nights. She loved cooking, and we experimented with a variety of culinary feasts. I soon put on weight, and had to go jogging late at night to keep myself trim.

But it wasn't all relaxation and good food with Debbie. She was determined to educate me to a satisfactory level and spent two or three hours every evening working on my subjects with me. It wasn't easy for her — apart from being tired after her day at work, she didn't know a lot about maths, science and geography — but she stuck with it and set an example which I felt compelled to follow.

"Your grammar's shaky," she said one night, reading through an essay I'd written. "Your English is good but you have some bad habits you need to break."

"Such as?"

"This sentence, for instance: 'John and me went to the store to buy a magazine.' What's wrong with that?"

I thought about it. "We went to buy newspapers?" I suggested innocently.

Debbie threw the copy at me. "Seriously," she giggled.

I picked up the copy and studied the sentence. "It should be 'John and I'?" I guessed.

"Yes," she nodded. "You use 'and me' all the time. It's not grammatically correct. You'll have to rise out of it."

"I know," I sighed. "But it'll be tough. I keep a diary, and I've always used 'and me' — it just seems more natural."

"Nobody ever said English was natural," Debbie scolded me, then cocked an eyebrow and added, "I didn't know you kept a diary."

"I've kept one since I was nine years old. All my secrets are in it."

"I hope you don't write about *me*. If it fell into the wrong hands..."

"Hmm," I smirked. "I could blackmail you if I wanted, couldn't I?"

"Just try it," she growled. Then, earnestly, "I really don't think you should write about us, Darren. Or if you do, use a code, or invent a name for me. Diaries *can* be misplaced, and if word of our friendship leaked, I'd have a hard time setting things straight."

"OK. I haven't included any new entries lately – I've been too busy – but when I do, I'll exercise due discretion." That was one of Debbie's pet phrases.

"And make sure when you're describing us that it's 'Miss X and *I*', not 'Miss X and *me*'," she said pompously, then screeched as I pounced across the room and set about tickling her until her face turned red!

CHAPTER NINE

ON MY third Tuesday at school, I made a friend. Richard Montrose was a small, mousey-haired boy, whom I recognized from my English and history classes. He was a year younger than most of the others. He didn't say very much, but was always being complimented by the teachers. Which of course made him the perfect target for bullies.

Since I didn't take part in games on the quad, I spent most of my lunch breaks strolling around, or in the computer room on the third floor of the building at the rear of the school. That's where I was when I heard sounds of a scuffle outside and went to investigate. I found Richard pinned to the wall by Smickey Martin — the guy who'd called me an asswipe on my first day at school — and three of his pals. Smickey was rooting through the younger boy's pockets. "You know you have to pay, Monty," he laughed. "If we don't take yer money, someone else will. Better the devil you know than the devil you don't."

"Please, Smickey," Richard sobbed. "Not this week. I have to buy a new atlas."

"Should have taken more care of your old one," Smickey snickered.

"*You're* the one who ripped it up, you..." Richard was on the point of calling Smickey something awful, but drew up short.

Smickey paused threateningly. "Wot was you gonna call me, Monty?"

"Nothing," Richard gasped, truly frightened now.

"Yes, you was," Smickey snarled. "Hold him, boys. I'm gonna teach him a—"

"You'll teach him nothing," I said quietly from behind.

Smickey turned swiftly. When he saw me, he laughed. "Little Darrsy Horston," he chuckled. "Wot are you doing here?" I didn't answer, only stared coldly at him. "Better run along, Horsty," Smickey said. "We ain't come after you for money yet — but that's not to say we won't!"

"You won't get anything from me," I told him. "And you won't get anything from Richard in future either. Or anyone else."

"Oh?" His eyes narrowed. "Them's awful big words, Horsty. If you take 'em back quick, I might forget you said 'em."

I stepped forward calmly, relishing the chance to put this bully in his place. Smickey frowned — he hadn't been expecting an open challenge — then grinned, grabbed Richard's left arm and swung him towards me. I stepped aside as Richard cried out — I was fully focused on Smickey — but then I heard him collide with something hard. Glancing back, I saw that he'd slammed into the banisters of the stairs and was toppling over — about to fall head first to the floor three storeys below!

I threw myself backwards and snatched for Richard's feet. I missed his left foot but got a couple of fingers on his right ankle just before he disappeared over the side of the handrail. Gripping the fabric of his school trousers hard, I grunted as the weight of his body jerked me roughly against the banisters. There was a ripping sound, and I feared his trousers would tear and I'd lose him. But the material held, and as he hung over the railings, whimpering, I hauled him back up and set him on his feet.

When Richard was safe, I turned to deal with Smickey Martin and the rest, but they'd scattered like the cowards they were. "So much for that lot," I muttered, then asked Richard if he was OK. He nodded feebly but said nothing. I left him where he was and returned to the soft hum of the computer room.

Moments later, Richard appeared in the doorway. He was still shaking, but he was smiling also. "You saved my life," he said. I shrugged and stared at the screen as though immersed in it. Richard waited a few seconds, then said, "Thanks."

"No problem." I glanced up at him. "Three floors isn't that big a fall. You'd probably only have broken a few bones."

"I don't think so," Richard said. "I was going nose-down, like a plane." He sat beside me and studied the screen. "Creating a screen saver?"

"Yes."

"I know where to find some really good scenes from sci-fi and horror movies. Want me to show you?"

I nodded. "That'd be cool."

Smiling, his fingers flew over the keyboard and soon we were discussing school and homework and computers, and the rest of the lunch break whizzed by.

Richard swapped seats in English and history in order to sit beside me, and let me copy from his notes — he had his own shorthand system which allowed him to jot down everything that was said in class. He also started spending most of his breaks and lunches with me. He pulled me out of the computer room and introduced me to other friends of his. They didn't exactly welcome me with open arms, but at least I had a few people to talk to now.

It was fun hanging out, discussing TV, comics, music, books and (of course!) girls. Harkat and me — Harkat and *I* — had TV sets in our rooms at the hotel, and I started watching a few programmes at night. Most of the stuff my new friends enjoyed was formulaic and tedious, but I pretended to enthuse about it like they did.

The week passed swiftly and before I knew it I was facing another weekend. For the first time I was mildly disappointed to have two free days on my hands – Richard would be away at his grandparents' – but cheered up at the thought of spending them with Debbie.

I'd been thinking a lot about Debbie, and the bond between us. We'd been very close as teenagers, and I now felt closer to her than ever. I knew there were obstacles — especially my appearance — but having spent so much time with her, I now believed we could overcome those obstacles and pick up where we'd left off thirteen years before.

That Friday night, I summoned all my courage as we were sitting together on the couch, leant over and tried to kiss Debbie. She looked surprised, and pushed me away lightly, laughing uneasily. When I tried to kiss her again, her surprise turned to icy anger and she shoved me away firmly. "No!" she snapped.

"Why not?" I retorted, upset.

"I'm your teacher," Debbie said, standing. "You're my student. It wouldn't be right."

"I don't want to be your student," I growled, standing up beside her. "I want to be your boyfriend."

I leant forward to kiss her again, but before I could, she slapped me hard. I blinked and stared at her, stunned. She slapped me again, softer this time. She was trembling and there were tears in her eyes.

"Debbie," I groaned, "I didn't mean to—"

"I want you to leave now," Debbie said. I took a couple of steps back, then halted. I opened my mouth to protest. "No," Debbie said. "Don't say anything. Just go, please."

Nodding miserably, I turned my back on her and walked to the door. I paused with my fingers on the handle and spoke to her without looking back. "I only wanted to be closer to you. I didn't mean any harm."

After short silence Debbie sighed and said, "I know."

I risked a quick look back — Debbie had her arms crossed over her chest and was gazing down at the floor. She was close to crying. "Does this change things between us?" I asked.

"I don't know," she answered honestly. She glanced up at me and I could see confusion mingled in her eyes with the tears. "Let's leave it for a couple of days. We'll talk about this on Monday. I need to think it over."

"OK." I opened the door, took a step out, then said very quickly, "You might not want to hear this, but I love you, Debbie. I love you more than anybody else in the world." Before she could reply, I shut the door and slunk away down the stairs like a downtrodden rat.

CHAPTER TEN

I PACED the streets as though walking fast could rid me of my problems, thinking of things I might have said to Debbie to make her accept me. I was sure she felt the same way about me that I felt about her. But my looks were confusing her. I had to find a way to get her to view me as an adult, not a child. What if I told her the truth? I imagined breaking the news to her:

"Debbie, prepare yourself for a shock — I'm a vampire."

"That's nice, dear."

"You're not upset?"

"Should I be?"

"I drink blood! I creep around in the dead of night, find sleeping humans, and open up their veins!"

"Well ... nobody's perfect."

The imaginary conversation brought a fleeting smile to my lips. Actually, I had no idea how Debbie would react. I'd never broken the news to a human before. I didn't know where or how to start, or what a person would say in response. *I* knew vampires weren't the murderous, emotionless monsters of horror movies and books — but how would I convince others?

"Bloody humans!" I grumbled, kicking a postbox in anger. "Bloody vampires! We should all be turtles or something!"

On that ridiculous thought, I looked around and realized I'd no idea which part of city I was in. I scouted for a familiar street name, so I could chart a course for home. The streets were largely deserted. Now that the mystery killers had stopped or moved on, the soldiers had withdrawn, and although local police still patrolled the streets, the barricades had come down and you could walk unheeded. Even so, the curfew was still in effect, and most people were happy to respect it.

I relished the dark, quiet streets. Walking alone down narrow, twisting alleys, I could have been winding my way through the tunnels of Vampire Mountain. It was comforting to imagine myself back with Seba Nile, Vanez Blane and the others, no love life, school or fate-fuelled quests to trouble me.

Thinking about Vampire Mountain set me thinking about Paris Skyle. I'd been so busy with school and Debbie, I hadn't had time to brood on the death of the Prince. I'd miss the old vampire who'd taught me so much. We'd shared laughter as well. As I stepped over a pile of rubbish strewn across the ground of a particularly dark alley, I recalled the time a few years ago when he leant too close to a candle and set his beard on fire. He'd hopped around the Hall of Princes like a clown, shrieking and slapping at the flames until—

Something struck the back of my head, hard, and I went toppling into the rubbish. I cried out as I fell, my recollections of Paris shattering, then rolled away defensively, clutching my head between my hands. As I rolled, a silver object came crashing down on the ground where my head had been, and sparks flew.

Ignoring my wounded head, I scrambled to my knees and looked for something to defend myself with. The plastic top of a dustbin lay nearby. It wouldn't be much good but it was all I could find. Stooping swiftly, I snatched it up and held it in front of me like a shield, turning to meet the charge of my assailant, who was streaking towards me at a speed no human could have matched.

Something gold flashed and swung down upon my makeshift shield, cutting the dustbin lid in half. Somebody chuckled, and it was the sound of pure, insane evil.

For a dreadful moment I thought it was Murlough's ghost, come to wreak revenge. But that was silly. I believed in ghosts — Harkat used to be one, before Mr Tiny brought him back from the dead — but this guy was far too solid to be a spirit.

"I'll cut you to pieces!" my attacker boasted, circling me warily. There was something familiar about his voice, but try as I might, I couldn't place it.

I studied his outline as he circled around me. He was wearing dark clothes and his face was masked by a balaclava. The ends of a beard jutted out from underneath it. He was large and chunky – but not as fat as Murlough had been – and I could see two blood-red eyes glinting above his snarling teeth. He had no hands, just two metallic attachments – one gold, the other silver – attached to the ends of his elbows. There were three hooks on each attachment, sharp, curved and deadly.

The vampaneze – the eyes and speed were the giveaway – struck. He was fast, but I avoided the killer hooks, which dug into the wall behind me and gouged out a sizeable crater when he pulled free. It took less than a second for my attacker to free his hand, but I used that time to strike, kicking him in the chest. But he'd been expecting it and brought his other arm down upon my shin, cruelly knocking my leg aside.

I yelped as pain shot up the length of my leg. Hopping madly, I threw the two halves of the useless dustbin lid at the vampaneze. He ducked out of the way, laughing. I tried to run — no good. My injured leg wouldn't support me, and after a couple of strides I collapsed to the floor, helpless.

I whirled over on to my back and stared up at the hook-handed vampaneze as he took his time approaching. He swung his arms back and forth as he got closer, the hooks making horrible screeching noises as they scraped together. "Going to cut you," the vampaneze hissed. "Slow and painful. I'll start on your fingers. Slice them off, one at a time. Then your hands. Then your toes. Then–"

There was a sharp clicking noise, followed by the hiss of parted air. Something shot by the vampaneze's head, only narrowly missing. It struck the wall and embedded itself — a short, thick, steel-tipped arrow. The vampaneze cursed and crouched, hiding in the shadows of the alley.

Moments ticked by like spiders scuttling up my spine. The vampaneze's angry breath and my gasping sobs filled the air. There was no sight or sound of the person who'd fired the arrow. Shuffling backwards, the vampaneze locked gazes with me and bared his teeth. "I'll get you later," he vowed. "You'll die slowly, in great agony. I'll cut you. Fingers first. One at a time." Then he turned and sprinted. A second arrow was fired after him, but he ducked low and again it missed, burying itself in a large bag of rubbish. The vampaneze exploded out of the end of the alley and vanished quickly into the night.

There was a lengthy pause. Then footsteps. A man of medium height appeared out of the gloom. He was dressed in black, with a long scarf looped around his neck, and gloves covering his hands. He had grey hair – though he wasn't old – and there was a stern set to his features. He was holding a gun-shaped weapon, out of the end of which jutted a steel-tipped arrow. Another of the arrow-firing guns was slung over his left shoulder.

I sat up, grunting, and tried to rub some life back into my right leg. "Thanks," I said as the man got closer. He didn't answer, just proceeded to the end of the alley, where he scanned the area beyond for signs of the vampaneze.

Turning, the grey-haired man came back and stopped a couple of metres away. He was holding the arrow gun in his right hand, but it wasn't pointed harmlessly down at the ground — it was pointing at *me*.

"Mind lowering that?" I asked, forcing a sheepish smile. "You just saved my life. Be a shame if that went off by accident and killed me."

He didn't reply immediately. Nor did he lower the gun. There was no warmth in his expression. "Does it surprise you that I spared your life?" he asked. As with the vampaneze, there was something familiar about this man's voice, but again I couldn't place it.

"I ... guess," I said weakly, nervously eyeing the arrow gun.

"Do you know why I saved you?"

I gulped. "Out of the goodness of your heart?"

"Maybe." He took a step closer. The tip of the gun was now aimed directly at my heart. If he fired, he'd create a hole the size of a football in my chest. "Or maybe I was saving you for myself!" he hissed.

"Who are you?" I croaked, desperately pressing back against the wall.

"You don't recognize me?"

I shook my head. I was certain I'd seen his face before, but I couldn't put a name to it.

The man breathed out through his nose. "Strange. I never thought you'd forget. Then again, it's been a long time, and the years haven't been as kind to me as they've been to you. Perhaps you'll remember *this*." He held out his left hand. The

264

palm of the glove had been cut away, exposing the flesh beneath. It was an ordinary hand in all respects save one — in the centre, a rough cross had been carved into the flesh.

As I stared at the cross, pink and tender-looking, the years evaporated and I was back in a cemetery on my first night as a vampire's assistant, facing a boy whose life I'd saved, a boy who was jealous of me, who thought I'd conspired with Mr Crepsley and betrayed him.

"*Steve!*" I gasped, staring from the cross to his cold, hard eyes. "*Steve Leopard!*"

"Yes," he nodded grimly.

Steve Leopard, my one-time best friend. The angry, mixed-up boy who'd sworn to become a vampire hunter when he grew up, so that he could track me down — and kill me!

CHAPTER ELEVEN

HE WAS close enough for me to lunge at the gun barrel and maybe redirect it. But I couldn't move. I was stunned beyond anything but passive observation. Debbie Hemlock walking into my English class had left me gobsmacked — but Steve Leopard (his real name was Leonard) turning up out of the blue like this was ten times as shocking.

After a handful of anxious seconds, Steve lowered the arrow gun, then jammed it through a belt behind his back. He extended his hands, took my left arm above the elbow, and hauled me to my feet. I rose obediently, a puppet in his hands.

"Had you going for a minute, didn't I?" he said — and smiled.

"You're not going to kill me?" I wheezed.

"Hardly!" He took my right hand and shook it awkwardly. "Hello, Darren. Good to see you again, old friend."

I stared at our clasped hands, then at his face. Then I threw my arms around him and hugged him for dear life. "Steve!" I sobbed into his shoulder.

"Stop that," he muttered and I could hear the sound of his own voice breaking. "You'll have *me* in tears if you keep it up." Pushing me away, he wiped around his eyes and grinned.

I dried my cheeks and beamed. "It's really you!"

"Of course. You don't think two people could be born this handsome, do you?"

"Modest as ever," I noted wryly.

"Nothing to be modest about," he sniffed, then laughed. "You able to walk?"

"I think a hobble's the best I can manage," I said.

"Then lean on me. I don't want to hang around. Hooky might come back with his friends."

"*Hooky*? Oh, you mean the vampa—" I stopped, wondering how much Steve knew about the creatures of the night.

"The vampaneze," he finished, nodding soberly.

"You know about them?"

"Obviously."

"Is the hook-handed guy the one who's been killing people?"

"Yes. But he isn't alone. We'll discuss it later. Let's get you out of here and cleaned up first." Letting me lean on him, Steve led me back the way I'd come, and as we walked I couldn't help wondering if I'd been knocked unconscious in the alley. If not for the pain in my leg – which was all too real – I'd have been seriously tempted to think this was nothing but a wishful dream.

Steve took me to the fifth floor of a run-down apartment block. Many of the doors we passed along the landing were boarded-over or broken down. "Nice neighbourhood," I commented sarcastically.

"It's a condemned building," he said. "A few apartments are occupied – mostly by old folk with nowhere else to go – but the majority are empty. I prefer places like this to boarding houses and hotels. The space and quiet suit my purposes."

Steve stopped at a battered brown door kept shut by an extra thick padlock and chain. Rooting through his pockets, he found a key, unlocked the padlock, removed the chain and pushed the door open. The air inside was stale, but he took no notice as he bundled me inside and closed the door. The darkness within held until he lit a candle. "No electricity," he said. "The lower apartments are still connected, but it went off up here last week."

He helped me into a cluttered living room and laid me down on a couch that had seen better days — it was threadbare, and wiry springs stuck out through several holes. "Try not to impale yourself," Steve laughed.

"Is your interior decorator on strike?" I asked.

"Don't complain," Steve scolded me. "It's a good base to work from. If we had to report back to some swanky hotel, we'd have to explain your leg and why we're covered in filth.

As for accounting for *these*..." He shrugged off the pair of arrow guns and laid them down.

"Care to tell me what's going on, Steve?" I asked quietly. "How you were in that alley and why you're carrying those?"

"Later," he said, "after we've tended to your wounds. And after you've—" he produced a mobile phone and tossed it to me "—made a call."

"Who am I supposed to ring?" I asked, staring at the phone suspiciously.

"Hooky followed you from your friend's house — the dark-skinned lady."

My face whitened. "He knows where Debbie lives?" I gasped.

"If that's her name — yes. I doubt he'll go after her, but if you don't want to run the risk, my advice is to call and tell her to—"

I was hitting buttons before he finished. Debbie's phone rang four times. Five. Six. Seven. I was about to dash to her rescue, regardless of my bad leg, when she picked up and said, "Hello?"

"It's me."

"Darren? What are—"

"Debbie — do you trust me?"

There was a startled pause. "Is this a joke?"

"Do you trust me?" I growled.

"Of course," she answered, sensing my seriousness.

"Then get out now. Throw some gear into a bag and scram. Find a hotel for the weekend. Stay there."

"Darren, what's going on? Have you lost your—"

"Do you want to die?" I interrupted.

A silent beat. Then, quietly, "No."

"Then get out." I hit the disconnect button and prayed she'd heed my warning. "Does the vampaneze know where I'm staying?" I asked, thinking of Harkat.

"I doubt it," Steve said. "If he did, he'd have attacked you there. From what I saw, he stumbled upon you earlier tonight by chance. He was casing a crowd, selecting his next victim, when he saw you and picked up your trail. He followed you to your friend's house, waited, trailed after you when you left, and..."

I knew the rest.

Steve fetched a first-aid kit from a shelf behind the couch. He told me to lean forward, then examined the back of my head. "Is it cut?" I asked.

"Yes, but not badly. It doesn't need stitches. I'll clean it up and apply a dressing." With my head seen to, he focused on my leg. It was deeply gashed and the material of my trousers was soaked through with blood. Steve snipped it away with a sharp pair of scissors, exposing the flesh beneath, then swabbed at the wound with cotton wool. When it was clean, he studied it momentarily, then left and came back with a reel of catgut and a needle. "This'll hurt," he said.

"It won't be the first time I've been stitched back together," I grinned. He went to work on the cut, and did a neat job on it. I'd only have a small scar when it was fully healed. "You've done this before," I noted as he tucked the catgut away.

"I took first-aid classes," he said. "Figured they'd come in handy. Never guessed who my first patient would be." He asked if I wanted something to drink.

"Just some water."

He pulled a bottle of mineral water out of a bag by the sink and filled a couple of glasses. "Sorry it's not cold. The fridge won't work without electricity."

"No problem," I said, taking a long drink. Then I nodded at the sink. "Has the water been cut off too?"

"No, but you wouldn't want to drink any — fine for washing, but you'd be on a toilet for days if you swallowed."

We smiled at each other over the rims of our glasses.

"So," I said, "mind telling me what you've been up to these last fifteen years?"

"You first," Steve said.

"Nuh-uh. You're the host. It's your place to start."

"Toss you for it?" he suggested.

"OK."

He produced a coin and told me to call. "Heads."

He flipped the coin, caught it and slapped it over. When he took his hand away he grimaced. "I never did have much luck," he sighed, then started to talk. It was a long story, and we were down to the bottom of the bottle of water and on to a second candle before he finished.

Steve hated Mr Crepsley and me for a long, long time. He'd sit up late into the night, plotting his future, dreaming of the day he'd track us down and stake us through the heart. "I was crazy with rage," he muttered. "I couldn't think about anything else. In woodwork classes I made stakes. In geography I committed the maps of the world to memory, so I'd know my way around whichever country I traced you to."

He found out everything there was to know about vampires. He'd had a large collection of horror books when I knew him, but he'd doubled, then trebled that in the space of a year. He learnt what climates we favoured, where we preferred to make our homes, how best to kill us. "I got in contact with people on the Internet," he said. "You'd be surprised how many vampire hunters there are. We exchanged notes, stories, opinions. Most were crackpots, but a few knew what they were talking about."

When he turned sixteen he left school and home, and went out into the world. He supported himself through a series of odd jobs, working in hotels, restaurants and factories. Sometimes he stole, or broke into empty houses and squatted. They were rough, lean, lonely years. He had very few scruples, hardly any friends, and no real interests except learning how to become a killer of vampires.

"To begin with, I thought I'd pretend to befriend them," he explained. "I went in search of vampires, acting as if I wanted to become one. Most of what I'd read in books or gleaned through the Internet was rubbish. I decided the best way to rid myself of my enemies was to get to know them."

Of course, when he eventually tracked a few vampires down and worked himself into their good books, he realized we weren't monsters. He discovered our respect for life, that we didn't kill humans when we drank and that we were people of honour. "It made me take a long, hard look at myself," he sighed, his face dark and sad by the light of the candle. "I saw that *I* was the monster, like Captain Ahab in *Moby Dick*, chasing a pair of killer whales — except these whales weren't killers!"

Gradually his hatred subsided. He still resented me for going off with Mr Crepsley, but accepted the fact that I hadn't done it to spite him. When he looked back at the past, he saw that I'd given up my family and home to save his life, and hadn't tricked or plotted against him.

That's when he dropped his crazy quest. He stopped searching for us, put all thoughts of revenge from his mind, and sat down to work out what he was going to do with the rest of his life. "I could have gone back," he said. "My mother's still alive. I could have returned home, finished my education, found a normal job, carved out an ordinary life for myself. But the night has a way of claiming those who embrace it. I'd found out the truth about vampires — but also about vampaneze."

Steve couldn't stop thinking about the vampaneze. He thought it was incredible that creatures like that could exist, roaming and killing as they pleased. It angered him. He wanted to put a stop to their murderous ways. "But I couldn't go to the police," he smiled ruefully. "I'd have had to capture a live vampaneze to prove they existed, but taking a vampaneze alive is almost impossible, as I'm sure you know.

Even if they believed me, what could they have done? Vampaneze move in, kill, then move on. By the time I'd convinced the police of the danger they were in, the vampaneze would have vanished, and the danger with him. There was only one thing for it — I had to take them on myself!"

Applying the knowledge he'd gathered when studying to be a vampire hunter, Steve set himself the task of tracking down and killing as many vampaneze as he could. It wasn't easy — vampaneze hide their tracks (and the bodies of their victims) expertly, leaving little evidence of their existence — but in time he found people who knew something of their ways, and he built up a picture of vampaneze habits, traits and routes, and eventually stumbled upon one.

"Killing him was the hardest thing I'd ever done," Steve said grimly. "I knew he was a killer, and would kill again if I let him go, but as I stood there, studying him while he slept..." He shivered.

"How did you do it?" I asked quietly. "A stake?"

He nodded bitterly. "Fool that I was — yes."

"I don't understand," I frowned. "Isn't a stake the best way to kill a vampaneze, like with vampires?"

He stared coldly at me. "Ever kill anybody with a stake?"

"No."

"Don't!" he snorted. "Driving it in is simple enough, but blood gushes up into your face, over your arms and chest, and the vampaneze doesn't die straightaway like vampires do in movies. The one I killed lived for the better part of a minute, thrashing and screaming. He crawled out of the coffin and came after me. He was slow, but I slipped on his blood, and before I knew what was happening, he was on top of me."

"What did you do?" I gasped.

"I punched and kicked him and tried to knock him off. Fortunately he'd lost too much blood and hadn't the strength to kill me. But he died on top of me, his blood drenching me, his face next to mine as he shuddered and sobbed and..."

Steve looked away. I didn't press him for further details.

"Since then I've learnt to use those." He nodded at the arrow guns. "They're the best there is. An axe is good too – if you have a good aim and the strength to chop a head clean off — but stay away from ordinary guns — they're not reliable where the extra tough bones and muscles of the vampaneze are concerned."

"I'll bear that in mind," I said, grinning sickly, then asked how many vampaneze Steve had killed.

"Six, though two of those were mad and would have died before long anyway."

I was impressed. "That's more than most vampires kill."

"Humans have an advantage over vampires," Steve said. "We can move about and strike by day. In a fair contest, a vampaneze would wipe the floor with me. But if you catch them in the day, while they're sleeping...

"Although," he added, "that's changing. The last few I've tracked have been accompanied by humans. I wasn't able to get close enough to kill them. It's the first time I've heard of vampaneze travelling with human assistants."

"They're called vampets," I told him.

He frowned. "How do you know? I thought the families of the night had nothing to do with one another."

"We hadn't until recently," I said grimly, then glanced at my watch. Steve's story wasn't complete — he still hadn't explained how he'd wound up here — but it was time I made a move. It was getting late and I didn't want Harkat to worry. "Will you come to my hotel with me? You can finish telling me about yourself there. Besides, there's someone I'd like you to share your story with."

"Mr Crepsley?" Steve guessed.

"No. He's away on ... business. This is somebody else."

"Who?"

"It would take too long to explain. Will you come?"

He hesitated a moment, then said he would. But he stopped to grab his arrow guns before we left — I had a feeling Steve didn't even go to the toilet without his weapons!

CHAPTER TWELVE

DURING THE walk to the hotel, I filled Steve in on what I'd been up to. It was a greatly condensed version, but I covered most of the bases, and told him about the War of the Scars and how it started.

"The Lord of the Vampaneze," he muttered. "I thought it was strange, how they were organizing."

I asked Steve about my family and friends, but he hadn't been home since he was sixteen, and knew nothing about them.

At the hotel he clambered on to my back and I scaled the outside wall. The stitches in my leg strained with the effort, but held. I rapped on the window and Harkat quickly appeared and let us in. He stared suspiciously at Steve but said nothing until I'd made the introductions.

"Steve Leopard," he mused. "I've heard much ... about you."

"None of it good, I bet," Steve laughed, rubbing his hands together — he hadn't taken off his gloves, although he'd loosened his scarf slightly. There was a strong medicinal smell coming from him, which I only noticed now that we were in a warm, normal room.

"What's he doing here?" Harkat asked me, green eyes pinned on Steve. I gave him a quick run-down. Harkat relaxed slightly when he heard that Steve had saved my life, but remained on guard. "You think it was wise to bring ... him here?"

"He's my friend," I said shortly. "He saved my life."

"But he knows where we are now."

"So?" I snapped.

"Harkat's right," Steve said. "I'm human. If I fell into the hands of the vampaneze, they could torture the name of this place out of me. You should move on to somewhere new in the morning, and not tell me about it."

"I don't think that will be necessary," I said stiffly, angry with Harkat for not trusting Steve.

There was an uncomfortable silence. "Well!" Steve laughed, breaking it. "It's rude to ask, but I have to. What on earth *are* you, Harkat Mulds?"

The Little Person grinned at the directness of the question and warmed to Steve a bit. Asking Steve to sit, he told him about himself, how he was a ghost who'd been brought back to life by Mr Tiny. Steve was astounded. "I've never heard anything like this before!" he exclaimed. "I was interested in the small people in the blue robes when I saw them at the Cirque Du Freak — I sensed there was something weird about them. But with all that's happened since, they'd slipped my mind entirely."

Harkat's revelation – that he'd been a ghost – unnerved Steve. "Something wrong?" I asked.

"Kind of," he muttered. "I never believed in life after death. When I killed, I thought that was the end of the matter. Knowing that people have souls, that they can survive death and even come back... It's not the most welcome news."

"Afraid the vampaneze you killed will come after you?" I smirked.

"Something like that." Shaking his head, Steve settled down and finished telling the story he'd started earlier that night in his apartment. "I came here two months ago, when I heard reports of what appeared to be a vampaneze presence. I thought the killer must be a mad vampaneze, since normally only the crazy ones leave bodies where they can be found. But what I discovered was far more disturbing."

Steve was a highly resourceful investigator. He'd managed to examine three of the victims, and found minor differences in the ways they'd been killed. "Vampaneze – even the crazy ones – have highly developed drinking patterns. No two kill and drain a victim exactly alike, and no vampaneze varies his method. There had to be more than one of them at work."

And since mad vampaneze were by their nature loners, Steve concluded that the killers must be sane.

"But it doesn't make sense," he sighed. "Sane vampaneze shouldn't leave bodies where they can be found. As far as I can figure, they're setting a trap for someone, though I've no idea who."

I glanced questioningly at Harkat. He hesitated, then nodded. "Tell him," he said, and I told Steve about the fake forms which had been sent to Mahler's.

"They're after *you*?" Steve asked incredulously.

"Possibly," I said. "Or Mr Crepsley. But we're not entirely sure. Somebody else might be behind it, someone who wants to pit us against the vampaneze."

Steve thought about that in silence.

"You still haven't told us how you were ... there to save Darren tonight," Harkat said, interrupting Steve's reverie.

Steve shrugged. "Luck. I've been turning this city upside-down, searching for vampaneze. The killers aren't in any of their usual hiding places — abandoned factories or buildings, crypts, old theatres. Eight nights ago, I spotted a large man with hooks for hands emerging from an underground tunnel."

"That's the guy who attacked me," I told Harkat. "He has three hooks on either arm. One hand's made of gold, the other of silver."

"I've been following him every night since," Steve continued. "It isn't easy for a human to trail a vampaneze – their senses are much more acute – but I've had plenty of practice. Sometimes I lose him, but I always pick him up again exiting the tunnels at dusk."

"He comes out the same way every night?" I asked.

"Of course not," Steve snorted. "Even a crazy vampaneze wouldn't do that."

"Then how do you find him?"

"By wiring manhole covers." Steve beamed proudly. "Vampaneze won't use the same exit night after night, but they tend to stick to a strictly defined area when they set up base. I wired every manhole cover within a two hundred metre radius — I've extended that to half a kilometre since. Whenever one of them opens, a light flashes on a kit I have, and it's a simple matter to track the vampaneze down.

"At least, it *was*." He paused unhappily. "After tonight, he'll probably move on to somewhere new. He won't know how much I know about him, but he'll expect the worst. I don't think he'll use those tunnels again."

"Did you know it was Darren you were saving?" Harkat asked.

Steve nodded seriously. "I wouldn't have come to his rescue otherwise."

"What do you mean?" I frowned.

"I could have taken Hooky out ages ago," Steve said, "but I knew he wasn't working alone. I wanted to track down his companions. I've been exploring the tunnels by day, hoping to trail him to his base. By interfering tonight, I've blown that chance. I wouldn't have done that for anyone but you."

"If he'd attacked an ordinary human, you'd have let him kill?" I gasped.

"Yes." Steve's eyes were hard. "If sacrificing one person means saving many more, I will. If I hadn't caught a glimpse of your face as you left your lady friend's, I'd have let Hooky kill you."

That was a harsh way of looking at the world, but it was a way I understood. Vampires knew the needs of the group had to be put before those of the individual. It surprised me that Steve was able to think that way – most humans can't – but I suppose you have to learn to be ruthless if you dedicate yourself to the hunting and killing of ruthless creatures.

"That's about the bones of it," Steve said, pulling his dark overcoat a notch tighter around his shoulders, suppressing a shiver. "There's plenty I haven't mentioned, but I've covered most of the major stuff."

"Are you cold?" Harkat asked, noting Steve's shivers. "I can turn up the heat."

"Wouldn't do any good," Steve said. "I picked up some kind of germ when Mr Crepsley *tested* me all those years ago. I catch colds simply by looking at someone with a runny nose." He plucked at the scarf around his throat, then wiggled his gloved fingers. "That's why I wrap up so much. If I don't, I wind up confined to bed for days on ends, coughing and spluttering."

"Is that why you smell?" I asked.

Steve laughed. "Yeah. It's a special herbal mix. I rub it in all over before I get dressed every morning. It works wonders. The only drawback is the stench. I have to be careful to keep downwind of the vampaneze when I'm tracking them — one whiff of this and they'd have me pegged."

We discussed the past some more – Steve wanted to know what life in the Cirque Du Freak had been like; I wanted to know where he'd been and what he'd got up to when he wasn't hunting – then talk returned to the present and what we were going to do about the vampaneze.

"If Hooky was acting alone," Steve said, "my attack would have driven him off. The vampaneze don't take chances when they're alone. If they think they've been discovered, they flee. But since he's part of a gang, I doubt he'll run."

"I agree," I said. "They've gone to too much trouble preparing this trap to walk away the first time something goes wrong."

"Do you think the vampaneze will know it was … you who saved Darren?" Harkat asked.

"I don't see how," Steve replied. "They know nothing about me. They'll probably think it was you or Mr Crepsley. I was careful not to reveal myself to Hooky."

"Then we might still get the better of them," Harkat said. "We haven't gone hunting for them since … Mr Crepsley left. It would be too dangerous, just the … two of us."

"But if you had *me* to go with you," Steve said, reading Harkat's thoughts, "it would be different. I'm accustomed to vampaneze hunts. I know where to look and how to track them."

"And with us to back you up," I added, "you could work faster than normal and cover more ground."

We gazed silently around at one another.

"You'd be taking a big risk, getting involved ... with us," Harkat warned him. "Whoever set us up knows all ... about us. You might tip them off to your presence by ... pitching in with us."

"It'd be risky for you too," Steve countered. "You're safe up here. Underground, it's their turf, and if we go down, we're inviting an attack. Remember — though vampaneze usually sleep by day, they don't need to when they're sheltered from the sun. They could be awake and waiting."

We thought about it some more. Then I stretched forth my right hand and held it out in front of me, palm downwards. "I'm up for it if you are," I said.

Steve immediately laid his left hand – the one with the scarred palm – on top of mine and said, "I've nothing to lose. I'm with you."

Harkat was slower to react. "I wish Mr Crepsley was here," he mumbled.

"Me too," I said. "But he's not. And the longer we wait for him, the more time the vampaneze have to plan an attack. If Steve's right, and they panic and switch base, it'll take them a while to settle. They'll be vulnerable. This could be our best chance to strike."

Harkat sighed unhappily. "It could also be our best chance to walk ... straight into a trap. But," he added, laying a large grey hand on top of ours, "the rewards justify the risks. If we can find and kill them, we'll save ... many lives. I'm with you."

Smiling at Harkat, I proposed a vow. "To the death?" I suggested.

"To the death," Steve agreed.

"To the death," Harkat nodded, then added pointedly, "but not, I hope, *ours!*"

CHAPTER THIRTEEN

WE SPENT Saturday and Sunday exploring the tunnels. Harkat and Steve carried arrow guns. They were simple to use — load an arrow, point and fire. Deadly up to a range of twenty metres. As a vampire, I'd sworn not to use such weapons, so I had to make do with my usual short sword and knives.

We started with the area where Steve had first spotted 'Hooky', in the hope of finding some trace of him or his companions. We took the tunnels one at a time, examining the walls for marks of vampaneze nails or hooks, listening carefully for sounds of life, keeping within sight of each other. We moved swiftly at first – Steve knew these tunnels – but when our search extended to new, unfamiliar sections, we advanced more cautiously.

We found nothing.

That night, after a long wash and simple meal together, we talked some more. Steve hadn't changed much. He was as lively and funny as ever, although he'd sometimes get a faraway look in his eyes and fall silent, perhaps thinking about the vampaneze he'd killed or the path in life he'd chosen. He got nervous whenever talk swung round to Mr Crepsley. Steve had never forgotten the vampire's reason for rejecting him – Mr Crepsley said Steve had bad blood and was evil – and didn't think the vampire would be glad to see him.

"I don't know why he thought I was evil," Steve grumbled. "I was wild as a kid, sure, but never evil — was I, Darren?"

"Of course not," I said.

"Maybe he mistook determination for evil," Steve mused. "When I believe in a cause, I'll commit to it wholeheartedly. Like my quest to kill vampaneze. Most humans couldn't kill another living being, even a killer. They'd rather turn them over to the law. But I'll go on killing vampaneze until I die. Maybe Mr Crepsley saw my *ability* to kill and confused it with a *desire* to kill."

We had lots of dark conversations like that, talking about the human soul and the nature of good and evil. Steve had devoted many long hours to Mr Crepsley's cruel judgement. He was almost obsessed with it. "I can't wait to prove him wrong," he smiled. "When he learns I'm on his side, helping the vampires in spite of his rejecting me... That's something I'm looking forward to."

When the weekend drew to a close, I had a decision to make regarding school. I didn't want to bother with Mahler's – it seemed a waste of time – but there was Debbie and Mr

Blaws to consider. If I dropped out suddenly, without a reason, the inspector would come looking for me. Steve said this wasn't a problem, that we could switch to another hotel, but I didn't want to leave until Mr Crepsley returned. The Debbie situation was even more complicated. The vampaneze now knew she was connected to me, and where she lived. Somehow I had to convince her to move to a new apartment — but how? What sort of a story could I concoct to persuade her to leave home?

I decided to go to school that Monday morning, mostly to sort things out with Debbie. With my other teachers, I'd pretend I was coming down with a virus, so they wouldn't suspect anything was amiss when I didn't turn up the next day. I didn't think Mr Blaws would be sent to investigate before the weekend — missing three or four days was hardly unusual — and by the time he did, Mr Crepsley would have hopefully returned. When he was back, we could sit down and establish a definite plan.

Steve and Harkat were going to continue hunting for the vampaneze when I was at school, but agreed to be careful, and promised not to engage them by themselves if they found any.

At Mahler's, I looked for Debbie before classes began. I was going to tell her that an enemy from my past had found out I was seeing her, and I feared he planned to hurt her, to get at me. I'd say he didn't know where she worked, just where she lived, so if she found somewhere new for a few weeks and didn't go back to her old apartment, she'd be fine.

It was a weak story, but I could think of nothing better. I'd plead with her if I had to, and do all in my power to persuade her to heed my warning. If that failed, I'd have to consider kidnapping her and locking her up to protect her.

But there was no sign of Debbie at school. I went to the staffroom during the break, but she hadn't turned up for work and nobody knew where she was. Mr Chivers was with the teachers and he was furious. He couldn't stand it when people — teachers or students — didn't call in before going absent.

I returned to class with a sinking feeling in my gut. I wished I'd asked Debbie to contact me with her new address, but hadn't thought of that when I'd told her to move. Now there was no way for me to check on her.

The two hours of classes and first forty minutes of lunch were some of the most miserable moments of my life. I wanted to flee the school and dash round to Debbie's old apartment, to see if there was any sign of her there. But I realized that it would be better not to act at all than to act in panic. It was tearing me apart, but it would be for the best if I waited for my head to clear before I went investigating.

Then, at ten to two, something wonderful happened — Debbie arrived! I was moping about in the computer room — Richard had sensed my dark mood and left me alone — when I saw her pulling up outside the back of the school in a car accompanied by two men and a woman — all three dressed in police uniforms! Getting out, she entered the building with the woman and one of the men.

Hurrying, I caught up with her on her way to Mr Chivers' office. "Miss Hemlock!" I shouted, alarming the policeman, who turned quickly, hand going for a weapon on his belt. He stopped when he saw my school uniform and relaxed. I raised a shaking hand. "Could I talk to you for a minute, Miss?"

Debbie asked the officers if she could have a few words with me. They nodded, but kept a close watch on us. "What's going on?" I whispered.

"You don't know?" She'd been crying and her face was a mess. I shook my head. "Why did you tell me to leave?" she asked, and there was surprising bitterness in her voice.

"It's complicated."

"Did you know what was going to happen? If you did, I'll hate you forever!"

"Debbie, I don't know what you're talking about. Honestly."

She studied my face for a hint of a lie. Finding none, her expression softened. "You'll hear about it on the news soon," she muttered, "so I guess it doesn't matter if I break it to you now, but don't tell anyone else." She took a deep breath. "I left on Friday when you told me. Booked into a hotel, even though I thought you were crazy."

She paused. "*And?*" I prompted her.

"Somebody attacked the people in the apartments next to mine," she said. "Mr and Mrs Andrews, and Mr Hugon. You never met them, did you?"

"I saw Mrs Andrews once." I licked my lips nervously. "Were they killed?" Debbie nodded. Fresh tears sprung to her eyes. "And drained of blood?" I croaked, dreading the answer.

"Yes."

I looked away, ashamed. I never thought the vampaneze would go after Debbie's neighbours. I'd had only her welfare in mind, not anybody else's. I should have staked out her building, anticipating the worst. Three people were dead because I hadn't.

"When did it happen?" I asked sickly.

"Late Saturday night or early Sunday morning. The bodies were discovered yesterday afternoon, but the police didn't track me down until today. They've kept it quiet, but I think the news is breaking. There were news teams swarming around the building when I passed on my way over here."

"Why did the police want to track you down?" I asked.

She glared at me. "If the people either side of the apartment where *you* lived were killed, and you were nowhere to be found, don't you think the police would look for you too?" she snapped.

"Sorry. Dumb question. I wasn't thinking straight."

Lowering her head, she asked very quietly, "Do you know who did it?"

I hesitated before replying. "Yes and no. I don't know their names, but I know what they are and why they did it."

"You must tell the police," she said.

"It wouldn't help. This is beyond them."

Looking at me through her tears, she said, "I'll be released later this evening. They've taken my statement, but they want to run me through it a few more times. When they release me, I'm coming to put some hard questions to *you*. If I'm not happy with your answers, I'll turn you over to them."

"Thank–" She swivelled sharply and stormed off, joining the police officers and proceeding on to Mr Chivers' office "–you," I finished to myself, then slowly headed back for class. The bell rang, signalling the end of lunch — but to me it sounded like a death knell.

CHAPTER FOURTEEN

THE TIME had come to fill Debbie in on the truth, but Steve and Harkat weren't keen on the idea. "What if she informs the police?" Steve screeched.

"It's dangerous," Harkat warned. "Humans are unpredictable at ... the best of times. You can't know how she'll act or what ... she'll do."

"I don't care," I said stubbornly. "The vampaneze aren't toying with us any longer. They know we know about them. They went to kill Debbie. When they couldn't find her, they slaughtered the people living next door. The stakes have risen. We're in deep now. Debbie has to be told how serious this is."

"And if she betrays us to the police?" Steve asked quietly.

"It's a risk we have to take," I sniffed.

"A risk *you* have to take," Steve said pointedly.

"I thought we were in this together," I sighed. "If I was wrong, leave. I won't stop you."

Steve fidgeted in his chair and traced the cross on his bare left palm with the gloved fingers of his right hand. He did that often, like Mr Crepsley stroking his scar when he was thinking. "There's no need to snap," Steve said sullenly. "I'm with you to the end, like I vowed. But you're making a decision that affects all of us. That isn't right. We should vote on this."

I shook my head. "No votes. I can't sacrifice Debbie, any more than you could let Hooky kill me in the alley. I know I'm putting Debbie before our mission, but I can't help that."

"You feel that strongly about her?" Steve asked.

"Yes."

"Then I won't argue any more. Tell her the truth."

"Thanks." I looked to Harkat for his approval.

The Little Person dropped his gaze. "This is wrong. I can't stop you, so I won't try, but ... I don't approve. The group should *always* come before the ... individual." Pulling his mask — the one he needed to filter out the air, which was poisonous to him — up around his mouth, he turned his back on us and brooded in sullen silence.

Debbie turned up shortly before seven. She'd showered and changed clothes — the police had fetched some of her personal items from her apartment — but still looked terrible. "There's a police officer in the lobby," she said as she entered. "They asked if I wanted a personal guard and I said I did. He thinks I came up here to tutor you. I gave him your name. If you object to that — tough!"

"Nice to see you too," I smiled, holding out my hands to

take her coat. She ignored me and walked into the apartment, stopping short when she caught sight of Steve and Harkat (who was facing away from her).

"You didn't say we'd have company," she said stiffly.

"They have to be here," I replied. "They're part of what I have to tell you."

"Who are they?" she asked.

"This is Steve Leopard." Steve took a quick bow. "And that's Harkat Mulds."

For a moment I didn't think Harkat was going to face her. Then he slowly turned around. "Oh, my lord!" Debbie gasped, shocked by his grey, scarred, unnatural features.

"Guess you don't get many like ... *me* in school," Harkat smiled nervously.

"Is..." Debbie licked her lips. "Is he from that institute you told me about? Where you and Evra Von lived?"

"There is no institute. That was a lie."

She eyed me coldly. "What else have you lied about?"

"Everything, more or less," I grinned guiltily. "But the lies stop here. Tonight I'll tell you the truth. By the end you'll either think I'm crazy or wish I'd never told you, but you have to hear me out — your life depends on it."

"Is it a long story?" she asked.

"One of the longest you'll ever hear," Steve answered with a laugh.

"Then I'd better take a pew," she said. She chose a chair, shrugged off her coat, laid it across her lap, and nodded curtly to let me know I could begin.

I started with the Cirque Du Freak and Madam Octa, and took it from there. I quickly covered my years as Mr Crepsley's assistant and my time in Vampire Mountain. I told her about Harkat and the Lord of the Vampaneze. Then I explained why we'd come here, how fake forms had been submitted to Mahler's, how I'd run into Steve and what role he played in this. I finished with the events of the weekend.

There was a long pause at the end.

"It's insane," Debbie finally said. "You can't be serious."

"He is," Steve chuckled.

"Vampires ... ghosts ... vampaneze... It's ludicrous."

"It's true," I said softly. "I can prove it." I raised my fingers to show her the scars on my fingertips.

"Scars don't prove anything," she sneered.

I walked to the window. "Go to the door and face me," I said. Debbie didn't respond. I could see the doubt in her eyes. "Go on," I said. "I won't hurt you." Holding her coat in front of her, she went to the door and stood opposite me. "Keep your eyes open," I said. "Don't even blink if you can help it."

"What are you going to do?" she asked.

"You'll see — or, rather, you won't."

When she was watching carefully, I tensed the muscles in my legs, then dashed forward, drawing up just in front of her. I moved as quickly as I could, quicker than a human eye could follow. To Debbie it must have seemed that I simply disappeared and reappeared before her. Her eyes shot wide and she leant against the door. Turning, I darted back, again faster than she could follow, stopping by the window.

"Ta-da!" Steve said, clapping dryly.

"How did you do that?" Debbie asked, voice trembling. "You just ... you were there ... then you were here ... then..."

"I can move at tremendously fast speeds. I'm strong, too — I could put a fist through any of these walls and not tear the skin on my knuckles. I can leap higher and further than any human. Hold my breath for longer. Live for centuries." I shrugged. "I'm a half-vampire."

"But it isn't possible! Vampires don't..." Debbie took a few steps towards me, then stopped. She was torn between wanting to disbelieve me and knowing in her heart that I was telling the truth.

"I can spend all night proving it to you," I said. "And you can spend all night pretending there's some other logical explanation. The truth's the truth, Debbie. Accept it or don't — it's your call."

"I don't ... I can't..." She studied my eyes for a long, searching moment. Then she nodded and sank back into her chair. "I believe you," she moaned. "Yesterday I wouldn't have, but I saw photos of the Andrews and Mr Hugon after they'd been killed. I don't think anyone human could have done that."

"You see now why I had to tell you?" I asked. "We don't know why the vampaneze lured us here or why they're playing with us, but their plan is surely to kill us. The attack on your neighbours was only the start of the bloodshed. They won't stop with that. You'll be next if they find you."

"But why?" she asked weakly. "If it's you and this Mr Crepsley they want, why come after me?"

"I don't know. It doesn't make sense. That's what's so frightening."

"What are you doing to stop them?" she asked.

"Tracking them by day. Hopefully we'll find them. If we do, we'll fight. With luck, we'll win."

"You've got to tell the police," she insisted. "And the army. They can—"

"No," I said firmly. "The vampaneze are *our* concern. We'll deal with them."

"How can you say that when it's humans they're killing?" She was angry now. "The police have struggled to find the killers because they don't know anything about them. If you'd told them what they should be looking for, they might have put an end to these creatures months ago."

"It doesn't work that way," I said. "It can't."

"It can!" she snapped. "And it will! I'm going to tell the officer in the lobby about this. We'll see what—"

"How will you convince him?" Steve interrupted.

"I'll..." She drew up short.

"He wouldn't believe you," Steve pressed. "He'd think you were mad. He'd call a doctor and they'd take you away to—" he grinned "—*cure* you."

"I could take Darren with me," she said unconvincingly. "He—"

"—would smile sweetly and ask the kind policeman why his teacher was acting so strangely," Steve chortled.

"You're wrong," Debbie said shakily. "I *could* convince people."

"Then go ahead," Steve smirked. "You know where the door is. Best of luck. Send us a postcard to let us know how you got on."

"I don't like you," Debbie snarled. "You're cocky and arrogant."

"You don't have to like me," Steve retorted. "This isn't a popularity contest. It's a matter of life and death. I've studied the vampaneze and killed six of them. Darren and Harkat have fought and killed them too. We know what we have to do to put a stop to them. Do you honestly think you have the right to stand there and tell us our business? You hadn't even *heard* of the vampaneze until a few hours ago!"

Debbie opened her mouth to argue, then closed it. "You're right," she admitted sullenly. "You've risked your lives for the sake of others, and you know more about this than me. I shouldn't be lecturing you. I guess it's the teacher in me." She managed a very feeble smile.

"Then you trust us to deal with it?" I asked. "You'll find a new apartment, maybe move out of the city for a few weeks, until it's over?"

"I trust you," she said, "but if you think I'm running away, you're deluding yourself. I'm staying to fight."

"What are you talking about?" I frowned.

"I'll help you find and kill the vampaneze."

I stared at her, astonished by the simple way she'd put it, as though we were in search of a lost puppy. "Debbie!" I gasped. "Haven't you been listening? These are creatures that can move at super-fast speeds and flick you into the middle of next week with a snap of a finger. What can you — an ordinary human — hope to accomplish?"

"I can explore the tunnels with you," she said, "provide an extra pair of legs, eyes, ears. With me we can split into pairs and cover twice the ground."

"You couldn't keep up." I protested. "We move too fast."

"Through dark tunnels, with the threat of the vampaneze ever present?" She smiled. "I doubt it."

"OK," I agreed, "you could probably match us for pace, but not endurance. We go all day, hour after hour, without pause. You'd tire and fall behind."

"Steve keeps up," she noted.

"Steve's trained himself to track them. Besides," I added, "Steve doesn't have to report to school every day."

"Neither do I," she said. "I'm on compassionate leave. They don't expect me back until the start of next week at the earliest."

"Debbie ... you ... it's..." I sputtered, then turned appealingly to Steve. "Tell her she's out of her mind," I pleaded.

"Actually, I think it's a good idea," he said.

"*What?*" I roared.

"We could do with another pair of legs down there. If she has the guts for it, I say we give her a go."

"And if we run into the vampaneze?" I challenged him. "Do you see Debbie going face to face with Hooky or his pals?"

"I do, as a matter of fact," he smiled. "From what I've seen, she's got a spine of steel."

"Thank you," Debbie said.

"Don't mention it," he laughed, then grew serious. "I can kit her out with an arrow gun. In a scrape we might be glad of an extra body. At least she'd give the vampaneze another target to worry about."

"I won't stand for it," I growled. "Harkat — tell them."

The Little Person's green eyes were thoughtful. "Tell them what, Darren?"

"That it's madness! Lunacy! Stupidity!"

"Is it?" he asked quietly. "If Debbie was any other person, would you be so ... quick to turn down her offer? The odds are against us. We need allies if we are to triumph."

"But—" I began.

"*You* got her into this," Harkat interrupted. "I told you not to. You ignored me. You can't control people once ... you involve them. She knows the danger and she ... accepts it. What excuse have you to reject her offer ... other than you're fond of her and ... don't want to see her harmed?"

Put like that, there was nothing I could say. "Very well," I sighed. "I don't like this, but if you want to pitch in, I guess we have to let you."

"He's so gallant, isn't he?" Steve observed.

"He certainly knows how to make a girl feel welcome," Debbie grinned, then dropped her coat and leant forward. "Now," she said, "let's quit with the time-wasting and get down to business. I want to know everything there is to know about these monsters. What do they look like? Describe their smell. What sort of tracks do they leave? Where do—"

"Quiet!" I snapped, cutting her short.

She stared at me, offended. "What did I—"

"Hush," I said, quieter this time, laying a finger to my lips. I advanced to the door and pressed my ear against it.

"Trouble?" Harkat asked, stepping up beside me.

"I heard soft footsteps in the hallway a minute ago — but no door has opened."

We retreated, communicating with our eyes. Harkat found his arrow gun, then went to check on the window.

"What's happening?" Debbie asked. I could hear the fast, hard beat of her heart.

"Maybe nothing — maybe an attack."

"Vampaneze?" Steve asked grimly.

"I don't know. It could just be an inquisitive maid. But somebody's out there. Maybe they've been eavesdropping, maybe they haven't. Best not to take chances."

Steve swung his arrow gun around and slid an arrow into it.

"Anyone outside?" I asked Harkat.

"No. I think the way's clear if we have to make a ... break for it."

I drew my sword and tested the blade while considering our next move. If we left now, it would be safer – especially for Debbie – but once you start running, it's hard to stop.

"Up for a scrap?" I asked Steve.

He let out an uneven breath. "I've never fought a vampaneze on its feet," he said. "I've always struck by day, while they were sleeping. I don't know how much use I'd be."

"Harkat?" I asked.

"I think you and I should go see ... what's going on," he said. "Steve and Debbie can wait by the window. If they hear sounds of fighting, they ... should leave."

"How?" I asked. "There's no fire escape and they can't scale walls."

"No problem," Steve said. Reaching inside his jacket, he unwrapped a thin rope from around his waist. "I always come prepared," he winked.

"Will that hold two of you?" Harkat asked.

Steve nodded and tied one end of the rope to a radiator. Going to the window, he swung it open and threw the other end of the rope down. "Over here," he said to Debbie, and she went to him without objecting. He got her to climb on to the window sill and back out over it, holding on to the rope, so she was ready to descend in a hurry. "You two do what you have to," Steve said, covering the door with his arrow gun. "We'll get out if things look bad."

I checked with Harkat, then tiptoed to the door and took hold of the handle. "I'll go first," I said, "and drop low. You come straight after me. If you see anyone who looks like they don't belong — scalp them. We'll stop to ask for their credentials later."

I opened the door and dived into the hall, not bothering with a count. Harkat stepped out after me, arrow gun raised. Nobody to my left. I spun right — no one there either. I paused, ears cocked.

Long, tense moments passed. We didn't move. The silence gnawed at our nerves but we ignored it and concentrated —

when you're fighting vampaneze, a second of distraction is all they need.

Then someone coughed overhead.

Dropping to the floor, I twisted on to my back and brought my sword upright, while Harkat swung his arrow gun up.

The figure clinging to the ceiling dropped before Harkat could fire, knocked him across the hallway, then kicked my sword from my hands. I scrambled after it, then stopped at a familiar chuckle. "Game, set and match to me, I think."

Turning, I was greeted with the sight of a chunky man dressed in purple animal skins, with bare feet and dyed green hair. It was my fellow Vampire Prince — Vancha March!

"*Vancha!*" I gasped, as he grabbed me by the scruff of the neck and helped me to my feet. Harkat had risen by himself and was rubbing the back of his head, where Vancha had struck him.

"Darren," Vancha said. "Harkat." He wagged a finger at us. "You should always check the shadows overhead when scanning for danger. If I'd meant to harm you, the two of you would be dead now."

"When did you get back?" I cried excitedly. "Why did you sneak up on us? Where's Mr Crepsley?"

"Larten's on the roof. We got back about fifteen minutes ago. We heard unfamiliar voices in the room, which is why we moved cautiously. Who's in there with you?"

"Come in and I'll introduce you," I grinned, then led him into the room. I told Steve and Debbie that we were safe, and went to the window to call down a wary, wind-bitten, very welcome Mr Crepsley.

CHAPTER FIFTEEN

MR CREPSLEY was every bit as suspicious of Steve as Steve had predicted. Even after I'd told him about the attack and Steve saving my life, he regarded the human with ill-concealed contempt and remained at a distance. "Blood does not change," he growled. "When I tested Steve Leonard's blood, it was the taste of pure evil. Time cannot have diluted that."

"I'm not evil," Steve growled in return. "*You're* the cruel one, making horrible, unfounded accusations. Do you realize how low an opinion I had of myself after you'd dismissed me as a monster? Your ugly rejection almost drove me to evil!"

"It would not, I think, have been a lengthy drive," Mr Crepsley said smoothly.

"You could have been wrong, Larten," Vancha said. The Prince was lying on the couch, feet propped on the TV set, which he'd dragged closer. His skin wasn't as red as it had been when I last saw him (Vancha was convinced he could train himself to survive sunlight, and often strolled about by day for an hour or so, allowing himself to be badly burnt, building up his body's defences). I guessed he must have spent the past few months walled-up inside Vampire Mountain.

"I was not wrong," Mr Crepsley insisted. "I know the taste of evil."

"I wouldn't bet on that," Vancha said, scratching an armpit. A bug fell out and landed on the floor. He guided it away with his right foot. "Blood's not as easy to divine as certain vampires think. I've found traces of 'evil' blood in several people over the decades, and kept tabs on them. Three went bad, so I killed them. The others led normal lives."

"Not all who are *born* evil *commit* evil," Mr Crepsley said, "but I do not believe in taking chances. I cannot trust him."

"That's stupid," I snapped. "You have to judge people by what they do, not by what you believe they might do. Steve's my friend. I'll vouch for him."

"Me too," Harkat said. "I was cautious at first, but I'm confident now that ... he's on our side. It's not just Darren he saved — he also warned him ... to ring Debbie and tell her to get out. She'd be dead otherwise."

Mr Crepsley shook his head stubbornly. "I say we should test his blood again. Vancha can do it. He will see that I am telling the truth."

"There's no point," Vancha said. "If you say there are traces of evil in his blood, I'm sure there are. But people can overcome their natural defects. I know nothing of this man, but I know Darren and Harkat, and I place more faith in their judgement than in the quality of Steve's blood."

Mr Crepsley muttered something under his breath, but he knew he was outnumbered. "Very well," he said mechanically. "I will speak no more of it. But I will keep a *very* close watch on you," he warned Steve.

"Watch away," Steve sniffed in reply.

To clear the air, I asked Vancha why he'd been absent so long. He said he'd reported to Mika Ver Leth and Paris Skyle and told them about the Vampaneze Lord. He would have left immediately, but he saw how close to death Paris was, and decided to see out the Prince's last few months beside him.

"He died well," Vancha said. "When he knew he was no longer able to play his part, he slipped away in secret. We found his body a few nights later, locked in a death embrace with a bear."

"That's horrible!" Debbie gasped, and everybody in the room smiled at her typical human reaction.

"Trust me," I told her, "there's no worse way for a vampire to die than in a bed, peacefully. Paris had more than eight hundred years under his belt. I doubt he left this world with any complaints."

"Still..." she said, troubled.

"That's the vampire way," Vancha said, leaning across to give her hand a comforting squeeze. "I'll take you aside some night and explain it to you," he added, leaving his hand on hers a few seconds longer than necessary.

If Mr Crepsley was going to keep a close eye on Steve, *I* was going to keep an even closer one on Vancha! I could see that he fancied Debbie. I didn't think she'd be attracted to the ill-mannered, mud-stained, smelly Prince — but I wouldn't leave him alone with her to find out!

"Any news of the Vampaneze Lord or Gannen Harst?" I asked, to distract him.

"No," he said. "I told the Generals that Gannen was my brother and gave them a full description of him, but none had seen him recently."

"What of events here?" Mr Crepsley asked. "Has anybody been murdered, apart from Miss Hemlock's neighbours?"

"Please," Debbie smiled. "Call me Debbie."

"If he won't, I certainly will," Vancha grinned and leant across to pat her hand again. I felt like saying something rude, but constrained myself. Vancha saw me puffing up and winked suggestively.

We told Mr Crepsley and Vancha how quiet things had been before 'Hooky' attacked me in the alley. "I don't like the sound of this Hooky," Vancha grumbled. "I've never heard of a hook-handed vampaneze before. By tradition, a vampaneze would rather do without a lost leg or arm than replace it with an artificial limb. It's strange."

"What is stranger is that he has not attacked since," Mr Crepsley said. "If this vampaneze is in league with those who sent Darren's particulars to Mahler's, he knows the address of this hotel — so why not attack him here?"

"You think there might be two bands of vampaneze at work?" Vancha asked.

"Possibly. Or it could be that the vampaneze are responsible for the murders, while another — perhaps Desmond Tiny — set up Darren at school. Mr Tiny could also have arranged for the hook-handed vampaneze to cross paths with Darren."

"But how did Hooky recognize Darren?" Harkat asked.

"Maybe by the scent of Darren's blood," Mr Crepsley said.

"I don't like this," Vancha grumbled. "Too many 'ifs' and 'buts'. Too twisted by far. I say we get out and leave the humans to fend for themselves."

"I am inclined to agree with you," Mr Crepsley said. "It pains me to say it, but perhaps our purposes would be best served by retreat."

"Then retreat and be damned!" Debbie snapped, and we all stared at her as she got to her feet and faced Mr Crepsley and Vancha, hands bunched into fists, eyes on fire. "What sort of monsters are you?" she snarled. "You talk of people as if we're inferior beings who don't matter!"

"May I remind you, madam," Mr Crepsley replied stiffly, "that we came here to fight the vampaneze and protect you and your kind?"

"Should we be grateful?" she sneered. "You did what anyone with even a trace of humanity would have done. And before you come back with that 'We aren't human' crud, you don't have to be human to be humane!"

"She's a fiery wench, isn't she?" Vancha remarked to me in a stage-whisper. "I could easily fall in love with a woman like this."

"Fall somewhere else," I responded quickly.

Debbie paid no attention to our brief bit of interplay. Her eyes were fixed on Mr Crepsley, who was gazing coolly back at her. "Would you ask us to stay and sacrifice our lives?" he said quietly.

"I'm asking nothing," she retorted. "But if you leave and the killing continues, will you be able to live with yourselves? Can you turn a deaf ear to the cries of those who'll die?"

Mr Crepsley maintained eye contact with Debbie a few beats more, then averted his gaze and muttered softly, "No." Debbie sat, satisfied. "But we cannot chase shadows indefinitely," Mr Crepsley said. "Darren, Vancha and I are on a mission, which has been deferred too long already. We must think about moving on."

He faced Vancha. "I suggest we remain one more week, until the end of next weekend. We will do all in our power to engage the vampaneze, but if they continue to evade us, we should concede defeat and withdraw."

Vancha nodded slowly. "I'd rather get out now, but that's acceptable. Darren?"

"A week," I agreed, then caught Debbie's eye and shrugged. "It's the best we can do," I whispered.

"*I* can do more," Harkat said. "I am not tied to the mission as you ... three are. I will stay beyond the deadline, if matters ... are not resolved by then."

"Me too," Steve said. "I won't quit until the end."

"Thank you," Debbie said softly. "Thank you all." Then she grinned weakly at me and said, "All for one and one for all?"

I grinned back. "All for one and one for all," I agreed, and then everyone in the room repeated it, unbidden, one at a time — although Mr Crepsley did glance at Steve and grunt ironically when it was his turn to make the vow!

CHAPTER SIXTEEN

IT WAS almost dawn before we got to bed (Debbie dismissed her police guard earlier in the night). Everyone crammed into the two hotel rooms. Harkat, Vancha and I slept on the floor, Mr Crepsley in his bed, Steve on the couch, and Debbie in the bed in the other room. Vancha had offered to share Debbie's bed if she wanted someone to keep her warm.

"Thanks," she'd said coyly, "but I'd rather sleep with an orang-utan."

"She likes me!" Vancha declared as she left. "They always play hard to get when they like me!"

At dusk, Mr Crepsley and I checked out of the hotel. Now that Vancha, Steve and Debbie had joined us, we needed to find somewhere quieter. Steve's almost deserted apartment block was ideal. We took over the two apartments next to his and moved straight in. A quick spot of tidying-up and the rooms were ready to inhabit. They weren't comfortable — they were cold and damp — but they'd suffice.

Then it was time to go vampaneze hunting.

We paired off into three teams. I wanted to go with Debbie, but Mr Crepsley said it would be better if she accompanied one of the full-vampires. Vancha immediately offered to be her partner, but I put a quick stop to that idea. In the end we agreed that Debbie would go with Mr Crepsley, Steve with Vancha, and Harkat with me.

Along with our weapons, each of us carried a mobile phone. Vancha didn't like phones — a tom-tom drum was the closest he'd got to modern telecommunications — but we convinced him that it made sense — this way, if one of us found the vampaneze, we'd be able to summon the others swiftly.

Disregarding the tunnels we'd already examined, and those that were used regularly by humans, we divided up the city's underground terrain into three sectors, assigned one per team, and descended into darkness.

A long, disappointing night lay ahead of us. Nobody found any trace of the vampaneze, although Vancha and Steve discovered a human corpse that had been stashed away by the blood-suckers many weeks earlier. They made a note of where it was, and Steve said he'd inform the authorities later, when we'd finished searching, so the body could be claimed and buried.

Debbie looked like a ghost when we met at Steve's apartment the following morning. Her hair was wet and scraggly, her clothes torn, her cheeks scratched, her hands cut by sharp stones and old pipes. While I cleaned out her cuts and bandaged her hands, she stared ahead at the wall, dark rims around her eyes.

"How do you do it, night after night?" she asked in a weak voice.

"We're stronger than humans," I replied. "Fitter and faster. I tried telling you that before, but you wouldn't listen."

"But Steve isn't a vampire."

"He works out. And he's had years of practice." I paused and studied her weary brown eyes. "You don't have to come with us," I said. "You could co-ordinate the search from here. You'd be more use up here than—"

"No," she interrupted firmly. "I said I'd do it and I will."

"OK," I sighed. I finished dressing her wounds and helped her hobble to bed. We'd said nothing about our argument on Friday — this wasn't the time for personal problems.

Mr Crepsley was smiling when I returned. "She will make it," he said.

"You think so?" I asked.

He nodded. "I made no allowances. I held to a steady pace. Yet she kept up and did not complain. It has taken its toll — that is natural — but she will be stronger after a good day's sleep. She will not let us down."

Debbie looked no better when she woke late that evening, but perked up after a hot meal and shower, and was first out the door, nipping down to the shops to buy a strong pair of gloves, water-resistant boots and new clothes. She also tied her hair back and wore a baseball cap, and when we parted that night, I couldn't help admiring how fierce (but beautiful) she looked. I was glad it wasn't *me* she was coming after with the arrow gun she'd borrowed from Steve!

Wednesday was another wash-out, as was Thursday. We knew the vampaneze were down here, but the system of tunnels was vast, and it seemed as if we were never going to find them. Early Friday morning, as Harkat and I were making our way back to base, I stopped at a newspaper stand to buy some papers and catch up with the news. This was the first time since the weekend that I'd paused to check on the state of the world, and as I thumbed through the uppermost paper, a small article caught my eye and I came to a stop.

"What's wrong?" Harkat asked.

I didn't answer. I was too busy reading. The article was about a boy the police were looking for. He was missing, a presumed victim of the killers who'd struck again on Tuesday, murdering a young girl. The wanted boy's name? *Darren Horston!*

I discussed the article with Mr Crepsley and Vancha after Debbie had gone to bed (I didn't want to alarm her). It said simply that I'd been at school on Monday and hadn't been seen since. The police had checked up on me, as they were checking on all students who'd gone absent without contacting their schools (I forgot to phone in to say that I was sick). When they couldn't find me, they'd issued a general description and a plea for anyone who knew anything about me to come forward. They were also 'interested in talking to' my 'father — Vur Horston'.

I suggested ringing Mahler's to say I was OK, but Mr Crepsley thought it would be better if I went in personally. "If you call, they may want to send someone to interview you. And if we ignore the problem, someone might spot you and alert the police."

We agreed I should go in, pretend I'd been sick and that my father moved me to my uncle's house for the good of my health. I'd stay for a few classes – just long enough to assure everyone that I was OK – then say I felt sick again and ask one of my teachers to call my 'uncle' Steve to collect me. He'd remark to the teacher that my father had gone for a job interview, which would be the excuse we'd use on Monday — my father got the job, had to start straightaway, and had sent for me to join him in another city.

It was an unwelcome distraction, but I wanted to be free to throw my weight behind the search for the vampaneze this weekend, so I dressed up in my school uniform and headed in. I reported to Mr Chivers' office twenty minutes before the start of class, thinking I'd have to wait for the perennial late-bird, but was surprised to find him in residence. I knocked and entered at his call. "Darren!" he gasped when he saw me. He jumped up and grasped my shoulders. "Where have you been? What happened? Why didn't you call?"

I ran through my story and apologized for not contacting him. I said I'd only found out that people were looking for me this morning. I also told him I hadn't been keeping up with the news, and that my father was away on business. Mr Chivers scolded me for not letting them know where I was, but was too relieved to find me safe and well to bear me a grudge.

"I'd almost given up on you," he sighed, running a hand through hair that hadn't been washed lately. He looked old and shaken. "Wouldn't it have been awful if you'd been taken as well? Two in a week... It doesn't bear thinking about."

"Two, sir?" I asked.

"Yes. Losing Tara was terrible, but if we'd—"

"Tara?" I interrupted sharply.

"Tara Williams. The girl who was killed last Tuesday." He stared at me incredulously. "Surely you heard."

"I read the name in the papers. Was she a student at Mahler's?"

"Great heavens, boy, don't you know?" he boomed.

"Know what?"

"Tara Williams was a classmate of yours! That's why we were so worried — we thought maybe the two of you had been together when the killer struck."

I ran the name through my memory banks but couldn't match it to a face. I'd met lots of people since coming to Mahler's, but hadn't got to know many, and hardly any of the few I knew were girls.

"You must know her," Mr Chivers insisted. "You sat next to her in English!"

I froze, her face suddenly clicking into place. A small girl, light brown hair, silver braces on her teeth, very quiet. She'd sat to the left of me in English. She let me share her poetry book one day when I left mine in the hotel by accident.

"Oh, no," I moaned, certain this was no coincidence.

"Are you all right?" Mr Chivers asked. "Would you care for something to drink?"

I shook my head numbly. "Tara Williams," I muttered weakly, feeling a chill spread through my body from the inside out. First Debbie's neighbours. Now one of my classmates. Who would be next...?

"Oh, no!" I moaned again, but louder this time. Because I'd just remembered who sat to my right in English — *Richard!*

CHAPTER SEVENTEEN

I ASKED Mr Chivers if I could take the day off. I said I hadn't been feeling well to begin with, and couldn't face classes with the thought of Tara on my mind. He agreed that I'd be better off at home. "Darren," he said as I was leaving, "will you stay in this weekend and take care?"

"Yes, sir," I lied, then hurried downstairs to look for Richard.

Smickey Martin and a couple of his friends were lounging by the entrance as I hit the ground floor. He'd said nothing to me since our run-in on the stairs — he'd shown his true yellow colours by fleeing — but he called out jeeringly when he saw me. "Look what the cat's dragged in! Shame — I thought the vampires had done for you, like they did for Ta-ta Williams." Pausing, I stomped across to face him. He looked wary. "Watch yourself, Horsty," he growled. "If you get in my face, I'll—"

I grabbed the front of his jumper, lifted him off the ground and held him high above my head. He shrieked like a little child and slapped and kicked at me, but I didn't let go, only shook him roughly until he was quiet. "I'm looking for Richard Montrose," I said. "Have you seen him?" Smickey glared at me and said nothing. With my left fingers and thumb, I caught his nose and squeezed until he wailed. "Have you seen him?" I asked again.

"Yuhs!" he squealed.

I let go of his nose. "When? Where?"

"A few minutes ago," he mumbled. "Heading for the computer room."

I sighed, relieved, and gently lowered Smickey. "Thanks," I said. Smickey told me what I could do with my thanks. Smiling, I waved a sarcastic goodbye to the humbled bully, then left the building, satisfied that Richard was safe — at least until night...

At Steve's I woke the sleeping vampires and humans — Harkat was already awake — and discussed the latest twist with them. This was the first Debbie had heard about the murdered girl — she hadn't seen the papers — and the news struck her hard. "Tara," she whispered, tears in her eyes. "What sort of a beast would pick on an innocent young child like Tara?"

I told them about Richard, and put forward the proposal that he was next on the vampaneze hit list. "Not necessarily," Mr Crepsley said. "I think they *will* go after another of your classmates — just as they executed those living to either side of Debbie — but they might go for the boy or girl sitting in front of or behind you."

"But Richard's my friend," I pointed out. "I barely know the others."

"I do not think the vampaneze are aware of that," he said. "If they were, they would have targeted Richard first."

"We need to stake out all three," Vancha said. "Do we know where they live?"

"I can find out," Debbie said, wiping tears from her cheeks. Vancha tossed her a dirty scrap of cloth, which she accepted gratefully. "The student files are accessible by remote computer. I know the password. I'll go to an Internet café, tap into the files and get their addresses."

"What do we do when — if — they attack?" Steve asked.

"We do to them what they did to Tara," Debbie growled before any of the rest of us could answer.

"You think that's wise?" Steve responded. "We know there's more than one of them in operation, but I doubt they'll all turn out to kill a child. Wouldn't it be wiser to trace the attacker back to—"

"Hold on," Debbie interrupted. "Are you saying we let them kill Richard or one of the others?"

"It makes sense. Our primary aim is to—"

Debbie slapped his face before he got any further. "Animal!" she hissed.

Steve stared at her emotionlessly. "I am what I have to be," he said. "We won't stop the vampaneze by being civilized."

"You ... you..." She couldn't think of anything dreadful enough to call him.

"He's got a point," Vancha interceded. Debbie turned on him, appalled. "Well, he *has*," Vancha grumbled, dropping his gaze. "I don't like the idea of letting them kill another child, but if it means saving others..."

"No," Debbie said. "No sacrifices. I won't allow it."

"Me neither," I said.

"Have you an alternative suggestion?" Steve asked.

"Injury," Mr Crepsley answered when the rest of us were silent. "We stake out the houses, wait for a vampaneze, then shoot him with an arrow before he strikes. But we do not kill him — we target his legs or arms. Then we follow and, if we are lucky, he will lead us back to his companions."

"I dunno," Vancha muttered. "You, me and Darren can't use those guns — it's not the vampire way — which means we'll have to rely upon the aim of Steve, Harkat and Debbie."

"I won't miss," Steve vowed.

"I won't either," Debbie said.

"Nor me," Harkat added.

"Maybe you won't," Vancha agreed, "but if there are two or more of them, you won't have time to target a second — the arrow guns are single-shooters."

"It is a risk we must take," Mr Crepsley said. "Now, Debbie, you should go to one of these *inferno net* cafés and find the addresses as soon as possible, then get to bed and sleep. We must be ready for action when night comes."

Mr Crepsley and Debbie staked out the house of Derek Barry, the boy who sat in front of me in English. Vancha and Steve took responsibility for Gretchen Kelton (Gretch the Wretch, as Smickey Martin called her), who sat behind me. Harkat and I covered the Montrose household.

Friday was a dark, cold, wet night. Richard lived in a big house with his parents and several brothers and sisters. There were lots of upper windows the vampaneze could use to get in. We couldn't cover them all. But vampaneze almost never kill people in their homes — it was how the myth that vampires can't cross a threshold without being invited started — and although Debbie's neighbours had been killed in their apartments, all the others had been attacked in the open.

Nothing happened that night. Richard stayed indoors the whole time. I caught glimpses of him and his family through the curtains every now and then, and envied them their simple lives — none of the Montroses would ever have to stake out a house, anticipating an attack by dark-souled monsters of the night.

When the family was all in bed and the lights went off, Harkat and I took to the roof of the building, where we remained the rest of the night, hidden in the shadows, keeping guard. We left with the rising sun and met the others back at the apartments. They'd had a quiet night too. Nobody had seen any vampaneze.

"The army are back," Vancha noted, referring to the soldiers who'd returned to guard the streets following the murder of Tara Williams. "We'll have to take care not to get in their way — they could mistake us for the killers and open fire."

After Debbie had gone to bed, the rest of us discussed our post-weekend plans. Although Mr Crepsley, Vancha and I had agreed to leave on Monday if we hadn't run down the vampaneze, I thought we should reconsider — things had changed with the murder of Tara and the threat to Richard.

The vampires were having none of it. "A vow's a vow," Vancha insisted. "We set a deadline and must stick to it. If we postpone leaving once, we'll postpone again."

"Vancha is right," Mr Crepsley agreed. "Whether we sight our opponents or not, on Monday we leave. It will not be pleasant, but our quest takes priority. We must do what is best for the clan."

I had to go along with them. Indecision is the source of chaos, as Paris Skyle used to say. This wasn't the time to risk a rift with my two closest allies.

As things worked out, I needn't have worried, because late that Saturday, with heavy clouds masking an almost full moon, the vampaneze finally struck — and all bloody hell broke loose!

CHAPTER EIGHTEEN

HARKAT SAW him first. It was a quarter past eight. Richard and one of his brothers had left the house to go to a nearby shop and were returning with bags full of shopping. We'd shadowed them every step of the way. Richard was laughing at some joke his brother had cracked, when Harkat put a hand on my shoulder and pointed to the skyline. It took me no more than a second to spot the figure crossing the roof of a large apartment store, trailing the boys below.

"Is it Hooky?" Harkat asked.

"I don't know," I said, straining my eyes. "He's not close enough to the edge. I can't see."

The brothers were approaching the mouth of an alley that they had to walk through to get home. That was the logical place for the vampaneze to strike, so Harkat and I hurried after the boys, until we were only a few metres behind when they turned off the main street. We hung back as they started down the alley. Harkat produced his arrow gun (he'd removed the trigger-guard, to accommodate his large finger) and loaded it. I took a couple of throwing knives (courtesy of Vancha) from my belt, ready to back Harkat up if he missed.

Richard and his brother were halfway down the alley when the vampaneze appeared. I saw his gold and silver hooks first — it *was* Hooky! — then his head came into view, masked by a balaclava as it had been before. He would have seen us if he'd checked, but he had eyes only for the humans.

Hooky advanced to the edge of the wall, then skulked along after the brothers, stealthy as a cat. He presented a perfect target, and I was tempted to tell Harkat to shoot to kill. But there were other fish in the vampaneze sea, and if we didn't use this one as bait, we'd never catch them. "His left leg," I whispered. "Below the knee. That'll slow him down."

Harkat nodded without taking his eyes off the vampaneze. I could see Hooky preparing to leap. I wanted to ask Harkat what he was waiting for, but that would have distracted him. Then, as Hooky crouched low to jump, Harkat squeezed the trigger and sent his arrow flying through the darkness. It struck Hooky exactly where I'd suggested. The vampaneze howled with pain and toppled clumsily from the wall. Richard and his brother jumped and dropped their bags. They stared at the person writhing on the floor, not sure whether to flee or go to his aid.

"Get out of here!" I roared, stepping forward, covering my face with my hands so that Richard couldn't identify me.

"Run now if you want to live!" That decided them. Leaving the bags, they bolted. For a couple of humans, it was amazing how fast they could run.

Hooky, meanwhile, was back on his feet. "My leg!" he roared, tugging at the arrow. But Steve was a cunning designer and it wouldn't come loose. Hooky pulled again, harder, and it snapped off in his hand, leaving the head embedded in the muscles of his lower leg. "*Aiiiieeee!*" Hooky screamed, throwing the useless shaft at us.

"Move in," I said to Harkat, deliberately louder than necessary. "We'll trap him and finish him off."

Hooky stiffened when he heard that, the whimpers dying on his lips. Realizing the danger he was in, he tried leaping back up on to the wall. But his left leg was no good and he couldn't manage the jump. Cursing, he pulled a knife out of his belt and propelled it towards us. We had to duck sharply to avoid it, which gave Hooky the time he needed to turn and flee — exactly what we wanted!

As we started after the vampaneze, Harkat phoned the others and told them what was happening. It was his job to keep them informed of developments — I had to focus on Hooky and make sure we didn't lose him.

He'd disappeared from sight when I reached the end of the alley, and for an awful moment I thought he'd escaped. But then I saw drops of blood on the pavement and followed them to the mouth of another alley, where I found him scaling a low wall. I let him get up, and then on to the roof of a neighbouring house, before going after him. It suited my purposes far better to have him up above the streets for the duration of the chase, illuminated by the glow of street lamps, out of the way of police and soldiers.

Hooky was waiting for me on the roof. He'd torn tiles loose and launched them at me, howling like a rabid dog. I dodged one, but had to use my hands to protect myself from the other. It shattered over my knuckles, but caused no real damage. The hook-handed vampaneze advanced, snarling. I was momentarily confused when I noticed that one of his eyes no longer glowed red – it was an ordinary blue or green colour – but I'd no time to mull it over. Bringing my knives up, I prepared to meet the killer's challenge. I didn't want to kill him before he'd had a chance to lead us back to his companions, but if I had to, I would.

Before he could test me, Vancha and Steve appeared. Steve fired an arrow at the vampaneze – missing on purpose – and Vancha leapt on to the wall. Hooky howled again, sent another few tiles flying towards us, then scrambled up the roof and down the other side.

"Are you OK?" Vancha asked, stopping beside me.

"Yes. We got him in the leg. He's bleeding."

"I noticed."

There was a small pool of blood nearby. I dipped a finger into it and sniffed. It smelt of vampaneze blood, but I still asked Vancha to test it. "It's vampaneze," he said, tasting it. "Why wouldn't it be?" I explained about Hooky's eyes. "Strange," he grunted, but said no more. Helping me to my feet, he scuttled to the top of the roof, checked to make sure

Hooky wasn't lying in wait for us, then beckoned me to follow. The chase was on!

While Vancha and I trailed the vampaneze across the rooftops, Harkat and Steve kept abreast of us on the ground, slowing only to negotiate their way around roadblocks or police patrols. About five minutes into the chase, Mr Crepsley and Debbie connected with us, Debbie joining those below, the vampire taking to the roofs.

We could have closed in on Hooky – he was having a hard time, slowed by his injured leg, the pain and loss of blood – but we allowed him to remain ahead of us. There was no way he could ditch us up here. If we'd wanted to kill him, it would have been a simple matter to reel him in. But we didn't want to kill him — yet!

"We mustn't let him grow suspicious," Vancha said after several minutes of silence. "If we hang back too long, he'll guess something's up. Time to drive him to earth." Vancha moved ahead of us, until he was within shuriken-throwing range of the vampaneze. He took a throwing star from the belts looped around his chest, aimed carefully and sent it skimming off a chimney just above Hooky's head.

Whirling, the vampaneze shouted something unintelligible back at us and angrily shook a golden hook. Vancha silenced him with another shuriken, which flew even closer to its mark than the first. Dropping to his belly, Hooky slid to the edge of the roof, where he grabbed on to the guttering with his hooks, halting his fall. He hung over open space a moment, checked the area underneath, jerked his hooks clear of the guttering and then dropped. It was a four-storey fall, but that was nothing to a vampaneze.

"Here we go," Mr Crepsley muttered, making for a nearby fire escape. "Call the others and warn them — we do not want them running into him on the streets."

I did that while jogging down the steps of the fire escape. They were a block and a half behind us. I told them to hold position until further notice. While Mr Crepsley and I followed the vampaneze on the ground, Vancha kept sight of him from the rooftops, making sure he couldn't take to the roofs again, narrowing his options so that he had to choose between the streets and the tunnels.

After three minutes of frenzied running, he chose the tunnels.

We found a discarded manhole cover and a trail of blood leading down into the darkness. "This is it," I sighed nervously as we stood waiting for Vancha. I hit the redial button on my mobile and summoned the others. When they arrived, we paired off into our regular teams, and climbed down into the tunnels. Each of us knew what we had to do and no words were exchanged.

Vancha and Steve led the pursuit. The rest of us trailed behind, covering adjacent tunnels, so Hooky couldn't double back. It wasn't easy tracking Hooky down here. The water in the tunnels had washed much of his blood away, and the darkness made it hard to see very far ahead. But we'd become accustomed to these tight, dark spaces, and we moved quickly and efficiently, keeping close, picking up on the slightest identifying marks.

Hooky led us deeper into the tunnels than we'd ever been. Even the mad vampaneze, Murlough, hadn't delved this deeply into the underbelly of the city. Was Hooky heading for his companions and help, or simply trying to lose us?

"We must be nearing the city limits," Harkat remarked as we rested a moment. "The tunnels must run out soon, or else..."

"What?" I asked when he didn't continue.

"They could open up," he said. "Perhaps he is making a break ... for freedom. If he reaches open countryside and ... has a clear run, he can flit to safety."

"Won't his wounds stop him doing that?" I asked.

"Perhaps. But if he is desperate enough ... perhaps not."

We resumed the chase and caught up with Vancha and Steve. Harkat told Vancha what he thought Hooky was planning. Vancha replied that he'd already thought of that, and was gradually closing in on the fleeing vampaneze — if Hooky angled for the surface, Vancha would head him off and make an end of him.

But, to our surprise, instead of heading upwards, the vampaneze led us ever further down. I'd no idea the tunnels ran this deep, and couldn't imagine what they were for — they were modern in design, and showed no signs of having been used. As I was pondering it, Vancha came to a standstill and I almost walked into him.

"What is it?" I asked.

"He's stopped," Vancha whispered. "There's a room or cave up ahead and he's come to a halt."

"Waiting for us, to make a final stand?" I suggested.

"Perhaps," Vancha replied uneasily. "He's lost a lot of blood and the pace of the chase must be sapping his energy. But why stop now? Why here?" He shook his head. "I don't like it."

As Mr Crepsley and Debbie arrived, Steve unstrapped his arrow gun and loaded it by torchlight.

"Careful!" I hissed. "He'll see the light."

Steve shrugged. "So? He knows we're here. We might as well operate by light as in darkness."

That made sense, so we all lit the torches we'd brought, keeping the lights dim so as not to create too many distracting shadows.

"Do we go after him," Steve asked, "or stay here and wait for him to attack?"

"We go in," Mr Crepsley answered after the briefest of pauses.

"Aye," Vancha said. "In."

I studied Debbie. She was trembling and looked ready to collapse. "You can wait out here if you like," I told her.

"No," she said. "I'm coming." She stopped trembling. "For Tara."

"Steve and Debbie will keep to the back," Vancha said, loosening a few of his shurikens. "Larten and I will lead. Darren and Harkat in the middle." Everybody nodded obediently. "If he's alone, I'll take him," Vancha went on. "An even fight, one-on-one. If he has *company*—" he grinned humourlessly "—it's everyone for themselves."

One final check to make sure we were ready and he advanced, Mr Crepsley to his right, Harkat and I close behind, Steve and Debbie bringing up the rear.

We found ourselves in a large, domed room, modern like the tunnels. A handful of candles jutted from the walls, casting a gloomy, flickering light. There was another way into the room directly across from us, but it was barred by a heavy, round, metal door, like those used for walk-in safes in banks. Hooky had squatted a few metres in front of the door. His knees were drawn up to cover his face, and his hands were busy trying to pry the arrow head from his leg.

We fanned out, Vancha in front, the rest of us forming a protective semi-circle behind him. "The game's over," Vancha said, holding back, examining the shadows for traces of other vampaneze.

"Think so?" Hooky snorted and looked up at us with his one red eye and one blue-green. "*I* think it's only beginning." The vampaneze clashed his hooks together. Once. Twice. Three times.

And someone dropped from the ceiling.

The someone landed beside Hooky. Stood and faced us. His face was purple and his eyes were blood-red — a vampaneze. Someone else dropped. Another. More. I felt sick inside as I watched vampaneze drop. There were human vampets among them too, dressed in brown shirts and black trousers, with skinned heads, a tattooed 'V' above either ear, and red circles painted around their eyes, carrying rifles, pistols and crossbows.

I counted nine vampaneze and fourteen vampets, not including Hooky. We'd walked into a trap, and as I stared around at the armed, grim-faced warriors, I knew we'd need all the luck of the vampires just to scrape out of this alive.

CHAPTER NINETEEN

As POOR as the odds were, they were about to get even worse. As we stood awaiting the onslaught, the huge door behind Hooky opened and four more vampaneze stepped through to join the others. That made it twenty-eight to six. We hadn't a hope.

"Not so pleased with yourselves now, are you?" Hooky jeered, hobbling forward a few gleeful paces.

"I don't know about that," Vancha sniffed. "This just means more of you for us to kill."

Hooky's smile vanished. "Are you arrogant or ignorant?" he snapped.

"Neither," Vancha said, gazing calmly at our foes. "I'm a vampire."

"You really think you stand a chance against us?" Hooky sneered.

"Yes," Vancha answered softly. "Were we fighting honest, noble vampaneze, I'd think otherwise. But a vampaneze who sends armed humans to fight his battles is a coward, without honour. I have nothing to fear from such pitiable beasts."

"Be careful what you say," the vampaneze to the left of Hooky growled. "We don't take kindly to insults."

"*We're* the ones who've been insulted," Vancha replied. "There's honour in dying at the hands of a worthy foe. If you'd sent your best warriors against us and killed us, we'd have died with smiles on our lips. But to send these ... these..." He spat into the dust of the floor. "There's no word low enough to describe them."

The vampets bristled at that, but the vampaneze looked uneasy, almost ashamed, and I realized they were no fonder of the vampets than we were. Vancha noticed this too and slowly loosened his belts of shurikens. "Drop your arrow guns," he said to Steve, Harkat and Debbie. They stared at him dumbly. "Do it!" he insisted gruffly and they complied. Vancha held up his bare hands. "We've put our long-range weapons aside. Will you order your pets to do the same and engage us honourably — or will you have us shot down in cold blood like the curs I think you are?"

"Shoot them!" Hooky screamed, his voice laced with hatred. "Shoot them all!"

The vampets raised their weapons and took aim.

"No!" the vampaneze to Hooky's left bellowed and the vampets paused. "By all the shadows of the night, I say no!"

Hooky whirled on him. "Are you crazy?"

"Beware," the vampaneze warned him. "If you cross me on this, I'll kill you where you stand."

Hooky stepped back, stunned. The vampaneze faced the vampets. "Drop your guns," he commanded. "We'll fight with our traditional weapons. With *honour*."

The vampets obeyed the order. Vancha turned and winked at us while they were laying their weapons aside. Then he faced the vampaneze again. "Before we start," he said, "I'd like to know what manner of creature this thing with the hooks is."

"I'm a vampaneze!" Hooky replied indignantly.

"Really?" Vancha smirked. "I've never seen one with mismatched eyes before."

Hooky's eyes twitched exploratively. "Damn!" he shouted. "It must have slipped out when I fell."

"What slipped out?" Vancha asked.

"A contact lens," I answered softly. "He's wearing red contact lenses."

"No I'm not!" Hooky yelled. "That's a lie! Tell them, Bargen. My eyes are as red as yours and my skin's as purple."

The vampaneze to Hooky's left shuffled his feet with embarrassment. "He *is* a vampaneze," he said, "but he's only been recently blooded. He wanted to look like the rest of us, so he wears contacts and..." Bargen coughed into a fist. "He paints his face and body purple."

"Traitor!" Hooky howled.

Bargen looked up at him, disgusted, then spat into the dust of the floor as Vancha had moments before.

"What has the world come to when the vampaneze blood maniacs like this and recruit humans to fight for them?"

Vancha asked quietly and there was no mockery in his voice — it was a genuine, puzzled query.

"Times change," Bargen answered. "We don't like the changes, but we accept them. Our Lord has said it must be so."

"This is what the great Lord of the Vampaneze has brought to his people?" Vancha barked. "Human thugs and crazy, hook-handed monsters?"

"I'm not crazy!" Hooky shouted. "Except crazy with rage!" He pointed at me and snarled. "And it's all *his* fault."

Vancha turned and stared at me, as did everybody else in the room.

"Darren?" Mr Crepsley asked quietly.

"I don't know what he's talking about," I said.

"Liar!" Hooky laughed and started dancing. "Liar, liar, pants on fire!"

"Do you know this *creature*?" Mr Crepsley enquired.

"No," I insisted. "The first time I saw him was when he attacked me in the alley. I never—"

"Lies!" Hooky screamed, then stopped dancing and glared at me. "Pretend all you like, man, but you know who I am. And you know what you did to drive me to this." He held up his arms, so the hooks glinted in the light of the candles.

"Honestly," I swore, "I haven't a clue what you're on about."

"No?" he sneered. "It's easy to lie to a mask. Let's see if you can stick to your lie when faced with—" he removed the balaclava with one quick sweep of his left hooks, revealing his face "—*this!*"

It was a round, heavy, bearded face, smeared with purple paint. For a few seconds I couldn't place it. Then, putting it together with the missing hands, and the familiarity of the voice that I'd previously noted, I nailed him. *"Reggie Veggie?"* I gasped.

"Don't call me that!" he shrieked. "It's *R.V.* — and it stands for Righteous Vampaneze!"

I didn't know whether to laugh or cry. R.V. was a man I'd run into not long after joining the Cirque Du Freak, an eco-warrior who'd devoted his life to the protection of the countryside. We'd been friends until he found me killing animals to feed the Little People. He set out to free the Wolf Man — he thought we were mistreating him — but the savage beast bit his arms off. The last time I'd seen him, he'd been fleeing into the night, screaming loudly, "My hands! My hands!"

Now he was here. With the vampaneze. And I began to understand why I'd been set up and who was behind it. *"You* sent those forms to Mahler's!" I accused him.

He grinned slyly, then shook his head. "With hands like these?" He waved the hooks at me. "They're good for chopping and slicing and gutting, but not for writing. I played my part to get you down here, but it was one with a lot more cunning than me who dreamt the plan up."

"I don't understand," Vancha interrupted. "Who is this lunatic?"

"It's a long story," I said. "I'll tell you later."

"Optimistic to the last," Vancha chuckled.

I stepped closer to R.V., ignoring the threat of the vampaneze and vampets, until I was only a metre or so away. I studied his face silently. He fidgeted but didn't back off. "What happened to you?" I asked, appalled. "You loved life. You were gentle and kind. You were a vegetarian!"

"Not any more," R.V. chuckled. "I eat plenty of meat now and I like it *bloody*!" His smile faded. "*You* happened to me, you and your band of freaks. You ruined my life, man. I wandered the world, alone, frightened, defenceless, until the vampaneze took me in. They gave me strength. They equipped me with new hands. In turn, I helped give them *you*."

I shook my head sadly. "You're wrong. They haven't made you strong. They've turned you into an abomination."

His face darkened. "Take that back! Take that back or I'll—"

"Before this goes any further," Vancha interrupted dryly, "could I ask one more question? It's my final one." R.V. stared at him in silence. "If *you* didn't set us up, who did?" R.V. said nothing. Nor did the other vampaneze. "Come on!" Vancha shouted. "Don't be shy. Who's the clever boy?"

The silence held a few moments more. Then, from behind us, somebody said in a soft, wicked voice, "*I* am."

I whirled around to see who'd spoken. So did Vancha, Harkat and Mr Crepsley. But Debbie didn't whirl, because she was standing still, a knife pressed to the soft flesh of her throat. And Steve Leopard didn't whirl either, because he was standing beside her — *holding the knife!*

We gawped wordlessly at the pair. I blinked twice, slowly,

thinking maybe that would restore sanity to the world. But it didn't. Steve was still there, holding his knife on Debbie, grinning darkly.

"Take off your gloves," Mr Crepsley said, his voice strained. "Take them off and show us your hands."

Steve smiled knowingly, then put the fingertips of his left hand — which was wrapped around Debbie's throat — to his mouth, gripped the ends of the glove with his teeth, and pulled his hand free. The first thing my eyes went to was the cross carved into the flesh of his palm, the cross he'd made the night he vowed to track me down and kill me. Then my eyes slid from his palm to the end of his fingers, and I understood why Mr Crepsley had asked him to remove the glove.

There were five small scars running along his fingertips — the sign that he was a creature of the night. But Steve hadn't been blooded by a vampire. He'd been blooded by one of the others. *He was a half-vampaneze!*

CHAPTER TWENTY

As the initial shock faded, a cold, dark hatred grew in the pit of my stomach. I forgot about the vampaneze and vampets and focused entirely on Steve. My best friend. The boy whose life I'd saved. The man I'd welcomed back with open arms. I'd vouched for him. Trusted him. Included him in our plans.

And all along he'd been plotting against us.

I would have gone for him there and then, and ripped him to pieces, except he was using Debbie as a shield. Fast as I was, I wouldn't be able to stop him slashing the knife across her throat. If I attacked, Debbie would die.

"I knew we could not trust him," Mr Crepsley said, looking only slightly less wrathful than I felt. "Blood does not change. I should have killed him years ago."

"Don't be a sore loser," Steve laughed, pulling Debbie even tighter in to him.

"It was all a ploy, wasn't it?" Vancha noted. "The hooked one's attack and your rescue of Darren was staged."

"Of course," Steve smirked. "I knew where they were all along. *I* suckered them in, sending R.V. to this city to spread panic among the humans, knowing it would draw Creepy Crepsley back."

"How did you know?" Mr Crepsley asked, astonished.

"Research," Steve said. "I found out all I could about you. I made you my life's work. It wasn't easy, but I traced you in the end. Found your birth certificate. Connected you to this place. I teamed up with my good friends, the vampaneze, during the course of my travels. They didn't reject me like you did. Through them I learnt that one of their brethren — poor, deranged Murlough — had gone missing here some years ago. Knowing what I did about you and your movements, it wasn't difficult to join the dots.

"What *did* happen with Murlough?" Steve asked. "Did you kill him or merely scare him off?"

Mr Crepsley didn't answer. Nor did I.

"No matter," Steve said. "It's not important. But I figured that if you came back to help these people once, you'd do it again."

"Very clever," Mr Crepsley snarled. His fingers were twitching like spider legs by his sides, and I knew he was itching to wrap them around Steve's throat.

"What I don't understand," Vancha remarked, "is what this lot are doing here." He nodded at Bargen and the other vampaneze and vampets. "Surely they're not here to assist you in your insane quest for revenge."

"Of course not," Steve said. "I'm just a humble half-vampaneze. It's not for me to command my betters. I told them about Murlough, which interested them, but they're here for other reasons, on someone else's say-so."

"Whose?" Vancha asked.

"That would be telling. And we aren't here to tell — we're here to kill!"

Behind us, the vampaneze and vampets advanced. Vancha, Mr Crepsley and Harkat spun to face their challenge. I didn't. I couldn't tear my eyes away from Steve and Debbie. She was weeping, but holding herself steady, looking appealingly in my direction.

"*Why?*" I croaked.

"Why what?" Steve replied.

"Why do you hate us? We did nothing to hurt you."

"*He* said I was evil!" Steve howled, nodding at Mr Crepsley, who didn't turn to remonstrate with him. "And *you* chose his side over mine. You set that spider on me and tried to kill me."

"No! I saved you. I gave up everything so that you could live."

"Nonsense," he snorted. "I know what really happened. You plotted with him against me, so you could take my rightful place among the vampires. You were jealous of me."

"No, Steve," I groaned. "That's madness. You don't know what—"

"Save it!" Steve interrupted. "I'm not interested. Besides, here comes the guest of honour — a man I'm sure you're all just *dying* to meet."

I didn't want to turn away from Steve, but I had to see what he was talking about. Looking over my shoulder, I saw two vague shapes behind the massed vampaneze and vampets. Vancha, Mr Crepsley and Harkat were ignoring Steve's jibes and the pair at the back, concentrating instead on the foes directly in front of them, warding off their early testing jabs. Then the vampaneze parted slightly and I had a clear view of the two behind them.

"Vancha!" I shouted.

"What?" he snapped.

"At the rear — it's..." I licked my lips. The taller of the pair had spotted me and was gazing at me with a neutral, inquisitive expression. The other was dressed in dark green robes, his face covered by a hood.

"Who?" Vancha shouted, knocking aside a vampet's blade with his bare hands.

"It's your brother, Gannen Harst," I said quietly and Vancha stopped fighting. So did Mr Crepsley and Harkat. And so, puzzled, did the vampaneze.

Vancha stood to his fullest height and stared over the heads of those in front of him. Gannen Harst's eyes left mine and locked on Vancha's. The brothers stared at each other. Then Vancha's gaze switched to the person in the robes and hood — the Lord of the Vampaneze!

"*Him! Here!*" Vancha gasped.

"You've met before, I take it," Steve commented snidely.

Vancha ignored the half-vampaneze. *"Here!"* he gasped again, eyes pinned on the leader of the vampaneze, the man we'd sworn to kill. Then he did the last thing the vampaneze had been expecting — with a roar of pure adrenaline, he *charged!*

It was lunacy, one unarmed vampire taking on twenty-eight armed and able opponents, but that lunacy worked in his favour. Before the vampaneze and vampets had time to come to terms with the craziness of Vancha's charge, he'd barrelled through nine or ten of them, knocking them to the ground or into the way of others, and was almost upon Gannen Harst and the Vampaneze Lord before they knew what was happening.

Seizing the moment, Mr Crepsley reacted quicker than anyone else and darted after Vancha. He dived among the vampaneze and vampets, knives outstretched in his extended hands like a pair of talons at the end of a bat's wings, and three of our foes fell, throats or chests slit open.

As Harkat swung in behind the vampires, burying the head of his axe in the skull of a vampet, the last in the line of vampaneze closed ranks on Vancha and blocked his path to their Lord. The Prince lashed at them with his blade-like hands, but they knew what they were doing now, and although he killed one of them, the others surged forward and forced him to a halt.

I should have gone after my companions — killing the Vampaneze Lord meant more than anything else — but my senses were screaming one name only, and it was a name I reacted to impulsively: *"Debbie!"* Swivelling away from the battle, praying that Steve had been distracted by the sudden outbreak, I sent a knife flying towards him. It wasn't intended to hit — I couldn't risk striking Debbie — just to make him duck.

It worked. Startled by the swiftness of my move, Steve jerked his head behind Debbie's for protection. His left arm loosened around her throat, and his right hand — holding the knife — dropped a fraction. As I raced forward, I knew the momentary swing of fortune wasn't enough — he'd still have time to recover and kill Debbie before I reached him. But then Debbie, acting like a trained warrior, dug her left elbow sharply back into Steve's ribs, and broke free of his hold, throwing herself to the floor.

Before Steve could dive after her, I was on him. I grabbed him around the waist and propelled him backwards into the wall. He connected harshly and cried out. Stepping away from him, I sent my right fist smashing into the side of his face. The force of the blow knocked him down. It also nearly broke a couple of small bones in my fingers, but that didn't bother me. Falling upon him, I grabbed his ears, pulled his head up, then smashed it down on the hard concrete floor. He grunted and the lights went out in his eyes. He was dazed and defenceless — mine for the taking.

My hand went for the hilt of my sword. Then I saw Steve's own knife lying close beside his head, and decided it would be more fitting to kill him with that. Picking it up, I positioned it above his dark, monstrous heart and prodded through the material of his shirt to make sure he wasn't protected by a breastplate or some other such armour. Then I raised the knife high above my head and brought it down slowly, determined to strike the mark and put an end to the life of the man I'd once counted as my dearest friend.

CHAPTER TWENTY-ONE

"STOP!" R.V. screamed as my blade descended, and something in his voice made me pause and look back. My heart sank — he had Debbie! He was holding her as Steve had, the hooks of his golden right hand pressed up into the flesh of her jaw. A couple of hooks had lightly punctured the skin and thin streams of blood trickled down the golden blades. "Drop the knife or I slit her like a pig!" R.V. hissed.

If I dropped the knife, Debbie would die anyway, along with the rest of us. There was only one thing for it — I had to try and force a stand-off. Grabbing Steve by his long grey hair, I jammed my knife against the flesh of his throat. "If she dies, he dies," I growled and I saw doubt fill R.V.'s eyes.

"Don't play games with me," the hook-handed vampaneze warned. "Let him go or I kill her."

"If she dies, he dies," I said again.

R.V. cursed, then glanced over his shoulder for help. The

battle was going the way of the vampaneze. Those who'd stumbled in the first few seconds of the fight had regained their feet, and now encircled Vancha, Mr Crepsley and Harkat, who fought back to back, protecting each other, unable to advance or retreat. Beyond the crush, Gannen Harst and the Lord of the Vampaneze looked on.

"Forget about them," I said. "This is between you and me. It's got nothing to do with anybody else." I managed a weak smile. "Or are you afraid to face me on your own?"

R.V. sneered. "I'm afraid of nothing, man. Except..." He stopped.

Guessing what he'd been about to say, I put my head back and howled like a wolf. R.V.'s eyes widened with fear at the sound, but then he collected himself and stood firm. "Howling won't save your tasty little girlfriend," he taunted me.

I had a strange sense of *déjà vu* — Murlough used to speak that way about Debbie, and for a moment it was as though the spirit of the dead vampaneze was alive inside R.V. Then I put such macabre thoughts behind me and concentrated.

"Let's stop wasting each other's time," I said. "You put Debbie aside, I'll put Steve aside, and we'll settle this man to man, winner takes all."

R.V. grinned and shook his head. "No deal. I don't have to risk my neck. I'm holding all the cards."

Keeping Debbie in front of him, he edged towards the exit at the opposite side of the room, skirting the vampaneze.

"What are you doing?" I shouted, moving to block him.

"Stay back!" he roared, digging his hooks deeper into Debbie's jaw, causing her to gasp with pain.

I stopped uncertainly. "Let her go," I said quietly, desperately.

"No," he replied. "I'm taking her. If you try to stop me, I'll kill her."

"I'll kill Steve if you do."

He laughed. "I don't care for Steve as much as you care for precious little Debbie. I'll sacrifice my friend if you'll sacrifice yours. How about it, Shan?" I studied Debbie's round, terrified eyes, then took a step back, clearing the way for R.V. to pass. "Wise move," he grunted, easing past, not turning his back on me.

"If you harm her..." I sobbed.

"I won't," he said. "Not for the time being. I want to see you squirm before I do. But if you kill Steve or come after me..." His cold, mismatched eyes told me what would happen.

Laughing, the hook-handed monster slipped past the vampaneze, then past Gannen Harst and his Lord, vanishing into the gloomy darkness of the tunnel beyond, taking Debbie with him, leaving me and the others to the mercy of the vampaneze.

Now that Debbie was beyond saving, my choices were clear. I could try to help my friends, who were trapped by the vampaneze, or go after the Vampaneze Lord. It took me no time to choose. I couldn't rescue my friends – there were just too many vampaneze and vampets – and even if I could, I wouldn't have — the Vampaneze Lord came first. I'd momentarily forgotten that when Steve seized Debbie, but now my training reasserted itself. Across the way, Steve was still unconscious. No time to finish him off — I'd do it later, if possible. Sneaking around the vampaneze, drawing my sword, meaning to take on Gannen Harst and the figure he guarded.

Harst spotted me, put his fingers to his mouth and whistled loudly. Four of the vampaneze at the rear of the group looked to him, then followed the direction of his finger as he pointed towards me. Turning away from the ruckus, they blocked my path, then advanced.

I might have tried to fight my way through them, hopeless as it was, but then I saw Gannen Harst call another two vampaneze away from the fighting. He gave the Vampaneze Lord to them and they exited down the tunnel that R.V. had fled through. Gannen Harst swung the huge door shut after them and spun a large, circular lock at the centre of it. Without the combination, it would be impossible to get through a door as thick as that.

Gannen Harst stepped up behind the four vampaneze who were converging on me. He clicked his tongue against the roof of his mouth and the vampaneze came to a standstill. Harst looked into my eyes, then made the death's touch sign by pressing his middle finger to the centre of his forehead, the two adjacent fingers over his eyes, and spreading his thumb and little finger out wide. "Even in death, may you be triumphant," he said.

I glanced around swiftly, taking in the state of play. Close to my right, the battle still raged. Mr Crepsley, Vancha and Harkat were cut in many places, bleeding liberally, yet none had sustained fatal wounds. They were on their feet, weapons in hand — except Vancha, whose weapons *were* his hands — keeping the circle of vampaneze and vampets at bay.

I couldn't understand it. Given our foes' superior numbers, they should have overwhelmed and dispatched the trio by now. The longer the fighting progressed, the more damage we were inflicting — at least six vampets and three vampaneze were dead, and several more nursed life-threatening injuries. Yet still they fought warily, judging their blows with care, almost as though they didn't want to kill us.

I reached a snap decision and knew what I had to do. I faced Gannen Harst and screamed, "I'll be triumphant in life!" in defiance, then whipped out a knife and launched it at the vampaneze, throwing it deliberately high. As the five vampaneze ahead of me ducked to avoid the knife, I swivelled and swung with my sword at the vampaneze and vampets packed tightly around Mr Crepsley, Vancha and Harkat. Now that the Lord of the Vampaneze was beyond reach, I was free to help or perish with my friends. A few moments earlier, we'd surely have perished, but the pendulum had swung round slightly in our favour. The pack had been whittled down by half a dozen members — two had left with their Lord, and four more were standing with Gannen Harst. The remaining vampaneze and vampets had spread themselves out to cover for their missing clansmen.

My sword connected with the vampaneze to my right, and narrowly missed the throat of a vampet to my left. The vampaneze and vampet both stepped aside at the same moment, instinctively, in opposite directions, creating a gap. "To me!" I cried at the trio trapped in the middle of the mayhem.

Before the gap could be filled, Harkat burst through, chopping with his axe. More vampaneze and vampets drew back, and Mr Crepsley and Vancha hurried after Harkat, fanning out around him, turning so that they were all facing the same way, instead of having to fight back to back.

We retreated swiftly towards the tunnel leading out of the cavern.

"Quick — block the exit!" one of the four vampaneze with Gannen Harst yelled, moving forward to bar our way.

"Hold," Gannen Harst responded quietly and the vampaneze stopped. He looked back at Harst, puzzled, but Harst only shook his head grimly.

I wasn't sure why Harst had prevented his men from blocking our one route of escape, but I didn't stop to ponder it. As we backed up towards the exit, lashing out at the vampaneze and vampets who pushed forward after us, we passed Steve. He was regaining his senses and was half sitting up. I paused as we came abreast of him, grabbed him by his hair and hauled him to his feet. He yelped and struggled, but then I stuck the edge of my sword to his throat and he went quiet. "You're coming with us!" I hissed in his ear. "If we die, so do you." I'd have killed him then and there, except I remembered what R.V. had said — if I killed Steve, he'd kill Debbie.

As we came to the mouth of the tunnel, a vampet swung a short length of chain at Vancha. The vampire grabbed the chain, yanked the vampet in, caught him by the head, and made to twist it sharply to the right, meaning to snap his neck and kill him.

"Enough!" Gannen Harst bellowed and the vampaneze and vampets closing upon us instantly stopped fighting and dropped back two paces.

Vancha relaxed his lock, but didn't release the vampet, and glared around suspiciously. "What now?" he muttered.

"I do not know," Mr Crepsley said, wiping sweat and blood from his brow. "But they fight most bizarrely. Nothing they do would surprise me."

Gannen Harst pushed through the vampaneze until he was standing in front of his brother. The two didn't look alike – where Vancha was burly, gruff and rough, Gannen was slim, cultured and smooth – but there was a certain way they had of standing and inclining their heads that was very similar.

"Vancha," Gannen greeted his estranged brother.

"Gannen," Vancha replied, not letting go of the vampet, watching the other vampaneze like a hawk in case they made any sudden moves.

Gannen looked at Mr Crepsley, Harkat and me. "We meet again," he said, "as was destined. Last time, you had the beating of me. Now the tables have turned." He paused and gazed around the room at the silent vampaneze and vampets, then at their dead and dying colleagues. Then he glanced at the tunnel behind us. "We could kill you here, in this tunnel, but you would take many of us with you," he sighed. "I tire of needless bloodshed. Shall we strike a deal?"

"What sort of a deal?" Vancha grunted, trying to hide his bewilderment.

"It would be easier for us to slaughter you in the larger tunnels beyond this one. We could pick you off, in our own time, possibly without losing more of our men."

"You want us to make your job easier for you?" Vancha laughed.

"Let me finish," Gannen continued. "As things stand, you have no hope of making it back to the surface alive. If we attack you here, our losses will be great, but all four of you will certainly die. If, on the other hand, we were to give you a head start..." He trailed off into silence, then spoke again. "Fifteen minutes, Vancha. Leave your hostages — you can move more quickly without them — and flee. For fifteen minutes, nobody will follow. You have my word."

"This is a trick," Vancha snarled. "You wouldn't let us go, not like this."

"I don't lie," Gannen said stiffly. "The odds are still in our favour — we know these tunnels better than you do, and will probably catch you before you make it to freedom. But this way you have hope — and I won't have to bury any more of my friends."

Vancha exchanged a furtive glance with Mr Crepsley.

"What about Debbie?" I shouted before either vampire could speak. "I want to take her too!"

Gannen Harst shook his head. "I command those in this room," he said, "but not he of the hooks. She is his now."

"Not good enough," I snorted. "If Debbie doesn't leave, I don't either. I'll stay here and kill as many of you as I can."

"Darren—" Vancha began to protest.

"Do not argue," Mr Crepsley intervened. "I know Darren — your words would be wasted. He will not leave without her. And if he will not leave, nor will I."

Vancha cursed, then looked his brother clean in the eye. "There you have it. If they won't go, I won't either."

Harkat cleared his throat. "These fools don't speak ... for me. *I'll* go." Then he smiled to show he was joking.

Gannen spat between his feet, disgusted. In my arms, Steve stirred and groaned. Gannen studied him for a moment, then looked at his brother again. "Let's try this then," Gannen said. "R.V. and Steve Leonard are close friends. Leonard designed R.V.'s hooks and persuaded us to blood him. I don't think R.V. would kill the woman if it meant Leonard's death, despite his threats. When you leave, you can take Leonard with you. If you escape, perhaps you'll be able to use him to bargain for the woman's life at a later time." He squinted at me warningly. "That is the best I can do — and it's more than you have a right to expect."

I thought it over, realized this was Debbie's only real hope, and nodded imperceptibly.

"Is that a yes?" Gannen asked.

"Yes," I croaked.

"Then go now!" he snapped. "From the moment you start to walk, the clock begins to tick. In fifteen minutes, we come — and if we catch you, you die."

At a signal from Gannen, the vampaneze and vampets drew back and regrouped around him. Gannen stood in front of them all, hands folded across his chest, waiting for us to leave.

I shuffled forward to my three friends, pushing Steve ahead of me. Vancha still had hold of his captured vampet and was gripping him as I gripped Steve. "Is he serious?" I asked in a whisper.

"It seems so," Vancha replied, though I could tell he hardly believed it either.

"Why is he doing this?" Mr Crepsley asked. "He knows it is our mission to kill the Lord of the Vampaneze. By offering us this opportunity, he frees us to perhaps recover and strike again."

"It's crazy," Vancha agreed, "but we'd be just as crazy to look this gift horse in the mouth. Let's get out before he changes his mind. We can debate it later — if we survive."

Keeping his vampet in front of him, as a shield, Vancha retreated. I followed, an arm wrapped around Steve, who was fully conscious now, but too groggy to make a break for freedom. Mr Crepsley and Harkat came after us. The vampaneze and vampets watched us leave. Many of the red or red-rimmed eyes were filled with loathing and disgust — but none pursued us.

We backed up through the tunnel for a while, until we were certain we weren't being followed. Then we stopped and exchanged uncertain looks. I opened my mouth to say something, but Vancha silenced me before I spoke. "Let's not waste time." Turning, he pushed his vampet ahead of him and began jogging. Harkat took off after him, shrugging helplessly at me as he passed. Mr Crepsley pointed at me to go next, with Steve. Shoving Steve in front, I poked him in the back with the tip of my sword, and roughly encouraged him forward at a brisk pace.

Up through the long, dark tunnels we padded, the hunters and their prisoners, beaten, bloodied, bruised and bewildered. I thought about the Vampaneze Lord, the insane R.V. and his hapless prisoner — Debbie. It tore me up inside to leave her behind, but I had no choice. Later, if I lived, I'd return for her. Right now I had to think only of my own life.

With a great effort, I thrust all thoughts of Debbie from my head and concentrated on the path ahead. At the back of my mind, unbidden, a clock formed, and with every footstep I could hear the hands ticking down the seconds, cutting away at our period of grace, bringing us relentlessly closer to the moment when Gannen Harst would set the vampaneze and vampets after us — freeing the hounds of hell.

TO BE CONTINUED....

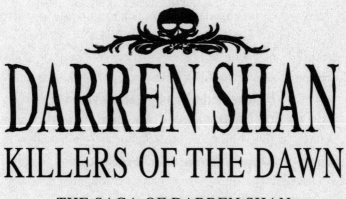

DARREN SHAN

KILLERS OF THE DAWN

THE SAGA OF DARREN SHAN
BOOK 9

For:

Bas – my dawn bird

OBE's

(Order of the Bloody Entrails) to:
Maiko "minder" Enomoto
&
Megumi "fault-finder" Hashimoto
✻

Gillie Russell & Zoë Clarke – the Sisters Grimm
✻

the Christopher Little Clan – troll-masters

PROLOGUE

IT WAS an age of deceit. Everyone was suspicious of everyone else — and with good reason! You never knew when a trusted ally would turn, bare his fangs and rip you to pieces.

The vampires and vampaneze were at war — the War of the Scars — and the result hinged upon finding and killing the Lord of the Vampaneze. If the vampires did that, victory would be theirs. Otherwise, the night would belong to their purple-skinned blood-cousins, who would drive the vampires to extinction.

Three vampires were sent by Mr Desmond Tiny to hunt the Vampaneze Lord — Vancha March, Larten Crepsley and me, Darren Shan. I'm a half-vampire.

Mr Tiny told us that other vampires couldn't assist us in our hunt, but non-vampires could. Thus, the only one to accompany us was a Little Person called Harkat Mulds, though a witch known as Lady Evanna also travelled with us for a short time during our quest.

After unwittingly letting the Vampaneze Lord slip through our fingers in the first of four predicted encounters, we travelled to the city of Mr Crepsley's birth. We didn't expect to find the Lord of the Vampaneze there — we came to track down and stop a gang of vampaneze who were murdering humans.

We attracted two more companions in the city — my ex-girlfriend, Debbie Hemlock, and Steve Leopard. Steve used to be my best friend. He said he'd become a vampaneze-hunter, and swore he'd help us put an end to the killer vampaneze. Mr Crepsley was suspicious of Steve – he believed Steve had evil blood – but I persuaded him to grant my old friend the benefit of the doubt.

Our target was an insane, hook-handed vampaneze. It turned out he was another of my ex-associates — R.V., which originally stood for Reggie Veggie, though he now claimed it was short for Righteous Vampaneze. He was once an eco-warrior, until his hands had been bitten off by the Wolf Man at the Cirque Du Freak. He blamed me for the accident, and had teamed up with the vampaneze in order to exact revenge.

We could have killed R.V., but we knew he was in league with other vampaneze, and we chose instead to trick him into leading us to them. What we didn't know was that we were actually the flies in the trap, not the spiders. Deep beneath the streets of the city, dozens of vampaneze were waiting for us. Among them stood the Lord of the Vampaneze and his protector, Gannen Harst — Vancha March's estranged brother.

In an underground cavern, Steve Leopard revealed his true colours. He was a half-vampaneze and had plotted with R.V. and the Vampaneze Lord to lure us to our doom. But Steve underestimated us, and I overcame him and would have killed him — except R.V. captured Debbie and threatened to murder her in retaliation.

While this was happening, my allies pursued the Vampaneze Lord, but the odds were stacked against them and he escaped. The vampaneze could have slaughtered us all, but we would have killed many of them in the process. To avoid the bloodshed, Gannen Harst let us go and gave us a fifteen-minute head start — it would be easier for the vampaneze to kill us in the tunnels.

With me holding Steve Leopard hostage, and Vancha clutching a vampet – a human who'd been trained in the ways of the vampaneze – we retreated, leaving R.V. free to do all the terrible things he wanted to Debbie. Through the tunnels we hurried, exhausted and distraught, knowing the vampaneze would soon swarm after us and cut us down dead if they caught up...

CHAPTER ONE

WE SCURRIED through the tunnels, Mr Crepsley leading the way, Vancha and I in the middle with our prisoners, Harkat bringing up the rear. We said as little as possible, and I cuffed Steve into silence whenever he started to speak — I wasn't in the mood to listen to his threats or insults.

I didn't have a watch, but I'd been ticking off the seconds inside my head. About ten minutes or so had passed by my reckoning. We'd moved out of the modern tunnels and were back in the warren of old, damp tunnels. There was still a long way to go — plenty of time for the vampaneze to run us down.

We came to a junction and Mr Crepsley took the left turn. Vancha started to follow him, then stopped. "Larten," he called him back. When Mr Crepsley returned, Vancha crouched low. He was almost invisible in the darkness of the tunnels. "We have to try and shake them off," he said. "If we make straight for the surface, they'll be upon us before we're halfway there."

"But we could lose ourselves if we detour," Mr Crepsley said. "We do not know this area. We might run into a dead end."

"Aye," Vancha sighed, "but it's a chance we'll have to take. I'll act as a decoy and go back the way we came. The rest of you try and find an alternative route out. I'll work my way back to you later, if the luck of the vampires is with me."

Mr Crepsley thought about that a moment, then nodded quickly. "Luck, Sire," he said, but Vancha was already gone, disappearing into the gloom in an instant, moving with the almost perfect silence of the vampires.

We rested a moment, then took the right tunnel and pressed on, Harkat now in charge of the vampet Vancha had kidnapped. We moved quickly but carefully, trying not to leave any signs that we'd passed this way. At the end of the tunnel, we branched off, again to the right. As we entered a fresh stretch of tunnel, Steve coughed loudly. Mr Crepsley was on him in a flash. "Do that again and you die!" he snapped, and I sensed the blade of his knife pressing against Steve's throat.

"It was a real cough — not a signal," Steve snarled in reply.

"It matters not!" Mr Crepsley hissed. "The next time, I will kill you."

Steve was silent after that, as was the vampet. We marched steadily upwards, instinctively navigating the tunnels, wading through water and waste. I felt terrible, tired and drawn, but I didn't slow down. It must be daylight above ground, or very close to it. Our only hope was to get clear of the tunnels before the vampaneze found us — the sunlight should prevent them from pursuing us any further.

A short while later, we heard the vampaneze and vampets. They were coming up the tunnels at great speed, not having to worry about stealth. Mr Crepsley dropped back a bit, to check if they were following us, but they didn't seem to have found our trail — all of them appeared to have gone after Vancha.

We continued to climb, working our way closer to the surface. Our pursuers kept passing in and out of earshot. By the sounds they made, they'd realized we weren't following the shortest route back, and had stopped and fanned out in search of us. I guessed that we were at least half an hour from ground level. If they located us any time soon, we were certainly doomed. The tunnels were as tight as they were dark — a lone, well-placed vampet would have no difficulty mowing us down with a rifle or arrow-gun.

We were picking our way over a heap of rubble in a crumbling tunnel when we were eventually spotted. A vampet with a torch entered the tunnel at the far end, picked us out with a strong beam of light, and roared triumphantly. "I've found them! They're here! They—"

He got no further. A figure stepped out of the shadows behind him, grabbed his head and twisted sharply, left then right. The vampet dropped to the ground. His assailant paused just long enough to turn off the torch, then hurried over. I knew without having to see him that it was Vancha.

"Good timing," Harkat muttered as the scraggly Prince joined us.

"I've been shadowing you for a while," Vancha said. "He's not the first one I've picked off. He just got a bit closer to you than the others."

"Any idea how far we are from the surface?" I asked.

"No," Vancha said. "I was ahead of you earlier, but I've been bringing up the rear for the last quarter of an hour, covering you and laying a few false trails."

"What about the vampaneze?" Mr Crepsley said. "Are they close?"

"Aye," came Vancha's reply, and then he slipped away again, to provide more cover.

Slightly further ahead, we found ourselves in familiar tunnels. We'd explored a vast slice of the city's infrastructure when hunting for the vampaneze, and had been in this section three or four times. We were no more than six or seven minutes from safety. Mr Crepsley whistled loudly, signalling to Vancha. The Prince swiftly joined us and we pushed on vigorously, finding a new lease of life.

"There they go!"

The shout came from a tunnel to our left. We didn't stop to check how many were nearby — putting our heads down, we pushed Steve and the vampet in front and ran.

The vampaneze weren't long surging after us. Vancha dropped back and kept them at bay with his shurikens — sharp, multi-edged throwing stars which were lethal when thrown by one as experienced as Vancha March. By the hysterical voices, I knew most — if not all — of the vampaneze and vampets had now converged behind us, but the tunnel we were in ran straight ahead, with hardly any side-tunnels opening out of it. Our enemies weren't able to sneak around and attack us from the sides or in front — they were forced to follow behind.

As we got closer to street level, the tunnels grew brighter, and my half-vampire eyes quickly adjusted to the dim light. I was now able to see the vampaneze and vampets trailing behind — and they were able to see us! The vampaneze, like vampires, had sworn not to use any missile-firing weapons such as guns or bows, but the vampets weren't limited by that oath. They began firing as soon as they had a clear line of sight, and we had to run doubled-over. If we'd had to cover a long distance in that uncomfortable crouch, they'd have surely picked us off one by one, but within a minute of them opening fire, we arrived at a steel ladder leading up to a manhole.

"Go!" Vancha barked, unleashing a hail of shurikens at the vampets.

Mr Crepsley grabbed me and shoved me up the ladder. I didn't protest at being first. It made the most sense — if the vampaneze pressed forward, Mr Crepsley was better equipped to fight them off.

At the top of the ladder I braced myself, then heaved against the manhole cover with my shoulders. It flew off, clearing the way up. I hauled myself out and quickly checked my surroundings. I was in the middle of a small street; it was early in the morning and nobody was about. Leaning back over the manhole, I yelled, "It's clear!"

Seconds later, Steve Leopard crawled out of the manhole, grimacing in the sunlight (almost blinding after being down the tunnels so long). Then Harkat came, followed by the vampet. There was a short delay after that. The tunnel underneath echoed with angry gun retorts. Fearing the worst, I was about to climb back down the ladder to check on Mr Crepsley and Vancha, when the orange-haired vampire burst out of the manhole, gasping wildly. Almost immediately, Vancha shot out after him. The pair must have jumped, one directly after the other.

As soon as Vancha was clear of the manhole, I stumbled across the street, picked up the cover, shuffled back with it and set it in place. Then all four of us gathered around it, Vancha grasping several shurikens, Mr Crepsley his knives, Harkat his axe, and me my sword. We waited ten seconds. Twenty. Half a minute. A minute passed. Mr Crepsley and Vancha were sweating stingingly beneath the wan glare of the morning sun.

Nobody came.

Vancha cocked an eyebrow at Mr Crepsley. "Think they've given up?"

"For the moment," Mr Crepsley nodded, backing off warily, switching his attention to Steve and the vampet, making sure they didn't make a break for freedom.

"We should get out of … this city," Harkat said, wiping a layer of dried blood from around his stitched-together grey face. Like Mr Crepsley and Vancha, he was nicked in many places after his battle with the vampaneze, but the cuts weren't serious. "It would be suicide to remain."

"Run, rabbits, run," Steve murmured, and I cuffed him around the ears again, shutting him up.

"I'm not leaving Debbie," I said. "R.V.'s a crazed killer. I'm not going to abandon her to him."

"What did you do to that maniac to madden him so much?" Vancha asked, peeking down one of the small holes in the manhole cover, still not entirely convinced that we were in the clear. The purple animal hides he dressed in were hanging from his frame in shreds, and his dyed green hair was flecked with blood.

"Nothing," I sighed. "There was an accident at the Cirque Du Freak. He—"

"We have no time for recollections," Mr Crepsley interrupted, tearing off the left sleeve of his red shirt, which had been slashed in as many places as Vancha's hides. He squinted up at the sun. "In our state, we cannot bear to stay in the sun very long. Whatever our choice, we must choose soon."

"Darren's right," Vancha said. "We can't leave. Not because of Debbie – much as I like her, I wouldn't sacrifice myself for her — but the Lord of the Vampaneze. We know he's down there. We have to go after him."

"But he's too well protected," Harkat protested. "Those tunnels are full of vampaneze … and vampets. We'd perish for certain if we went … down again. I say we flee and come back … later, with help."

"You've forgotten Mr Tiny's warning," Vancha said. "We can't ask other vampires for help. I don't care how poor the odds are — we must try to breach their defences and kill their Lord."

"I agree," Mr Crepsley said. "But now is not the time. We are wounded and exhausted. We should rest and form a plan of action. The question is, where do we retire to — the apartments we have been using, or elsewhere?"

"Elsewhere," Harkat said instantly. "The vampaneze know where … we've been living. If we stay, we'd be crazy to go where … they can attack any time they like."

"I don't know," I muttered. "It was weird, the way they let us leave. I know Gannen said it was to spare the lives of his companions, but if they'd killed us, they were guaranteed victory in the War of the Scars. I think there's more to it than he was letting on. Having spared us when they had us trapped on their own turf, I doubt they'll come all the way up here to fight on our territory."

My companions mused on that in silence.

"I think we should return to our base and try to make sense of this," I said. "Even if we can't, we can get some rest and tend to our wounds. Then, come night, we'll attack."

"Sounds good to me," Vancha said.

"As good a plan as any," Mr Crepsley sighed.

"Harkat?" I asked the Little Person.

His round green eyes were full of doubt, but he grimaced and nodded. "I think we're fools to stay, but if … we're going to, I guess at least we have weapons and … provisions there."

"Besides," Vancha added grimly, "most of the apartments are empty. It's quiet." He ran a menacing finger along the neck of his captured vampet, a shaven-headed man with the dark 'V' of the vampets tattooed above either ear. "There are some questions I want answered, but the asking won't be pleasant. It'll be for the best if there's nobody around to hear."

The vampet sneered at Vancha as though unimpressed, but I could see fear in his blood-rimmed eyes. Vampaneze had the strength to withstand horrible torture, but vampets were human. A vampire could do terrible things to a human.

Mr Crepsley and Vancha wrapped their robes and hides around their heads and shoulders, to protect them from the worst of the sun. Then, pushing Steve and the vampet ahead of us, we climbed to roof level, got our bearings, and wearily headed for base.

CHAPTER TWO

"Base" was the fifth floor of an ancient, largely abandoned block of apartments. It was where Steve had set up camp. We'd moved in when we teamed up with him. We occupied three apartments on the floor. While Mr Crepsley, Harkat and I bundled Steve into the middle apartment, Vancha grabbed the vampet by his ears and hauled him off to the apartment on the right.

"Will he torture him?" I asked Mr Crepsley, pausing at the door.

"Yes," the vampire answered bluntly.

I didn't like the thought of that, but the circumstances called for swift, true answers. Vancha was only doing what had to be done. In war there's sometimes no room for compassion or humanity.

Entering our apartment, I hurried to the fridge. It didn't work – the apartment had no electricity – but we stored our drinks and food there.

"Anyone hungry or thirsty?" I asked.

"I'll have a *steak* — extra bloody — fries and a Coke to go," Steve quipped. He'd made himself comfortable on the couch, and was smiling around at us as though we were one big happy family.

I ignored him. "Mr Crepsley? Harkat?"

"Water, please," Mr Crepsley said, shrugging off his tattered red cloak, so he could examine his wounds. "And bandages," he added.

"Are you hurt?" Harkat asked.

"Not really. But the tunnels we crawled through were unhygienic. We should all clean out our wounds to prevent infection."

I washed my hands, then threw some food together. I wasn't hungry but I felt I should eat — my body was working solely on excess adrenaline; it needed feeding. Harkat and Mr Crepsley also tucked into the food and soon we were finishing off the last of the crumbs.

We offered none to Steve.

While we were tending to our wounds, I stared hatefully at Steve, who grinned back mockingly. "How long did it take to set this up?" I asked. "Getting us here, arranging those false papers for me and sending me to school, luring us down the tunnels — how long?"

"Years," Steve replied proudly. "It wasn't easy. You don't know the half of it. That cavern where the trap was set — we built that from scratch, along with the tunnels leading in and out of it. We built other caverns too. There's one I'm especially proud of. I hope I have the chance to show it to you some time."

"You went to all this trouble just for us?" Mr Crepsley asked, startled.

"Yes," Steve replied smugly.

"Why?" I asked. "Wouldn't it have been easier to fight us in the old, existing tunnels?"

"Easier," Steve agreed, "but not as much fun. I've developed a love of the dramatic over the years — a bit like Mr Tiny. You should appreciate that, having worked for a circus for so long."

"What *I* don't understand," Harkat mused, "is what the … Vampaneze Lord was doing there, or why the other vampaneze … aided you in your insane plans."

"Not as insane as you might think," Steve retorted. "The Vampaneze Lord knew you'd be coming. Mr Tiny told him all about the hunters who would dog his footsteps. He also said that running away or hiding wasn't an option — if our Lord didn't make a stand and face those who hunted him, the War of the Scars would be lost.

"When he learnt of my interest in you – and R.V.'s – he consulted us and together we hatched this plan. Gannen Harst cautioned against it – he's old school and would have preferred a direct confrontation – but the Vampaneze Lord shares my theatrical tastes."

"This Lord of yours," Mr Crepsley said. "What does he look like?"

Steve laughed and shook a finger at the vampire. "Now, now, Larten. You don't honestly expect me to describe him, do you? He's been very careful not to show his face, even to most of those who follow him."

"We could torture it out of you," I growled.

"I doubt it," Steve smirked. "I'm half-vampaneze. I can take anything you can dish out. I'd let you kill me before I betrayed the clan." He shrugged off the heavy jacket he'd been wearing since we met. Strong chemical odours wafted off him.

"He's not shivering any more," Harkat said suddenly. Steve had told us he suffered from colds, which was why he had to wear lots of clothes and smear on lotions to protect himself.

"Of course not," Steve said. "That was all for show."

"You have the slyness of a demon," Mr Crepsley grunted. "By claiming to be susceptible to colds, you were able to wear gloves to hide your fingertip scars, and douse yourself in sickly-smelling lotions to mask your vampaneze stench."

"The smell was the difficult bit," Steve laughed. "I knew your sensitive noses would sniff my blood out, so I had to distract them." He pulled a face. "But it hasn't been easy. My sense of smell is also highly developed, so the fumes have played havoc with my sinuses. The headaches are awful."

"My heart bleeds for you," I snarled sarcastically, and Steve laughed with delight. He was having a great time, even though he was our prisoner. His eyes were alight with evil glee.

"You won't be grinning if R.V. refuses to trade Debbie for you," I told him.

"True enough," he admitted. "But I live only to see you and Creepy Crepsley suffer. I could die happy knowing the torment you'll endure if R.V. carves up your darling teacher girlfriend."

I shook my head, appalled. "How did you get so twisted?" I asked. "We were friends, almost like brothers. You weren't evil then. What happened to you?"

Steve's face darkened. "I was betrayed," he said quietly.

"That isn't true," I replied. "I saved your life. I gave up everything so that you could live. I didn't want to become a half-vampire. I—"

"Shut it!" Steve snapped. "Torture me if you wish, but don't insult me with lies. I know you plotted with Creepy Crepsley to spite me. I could have been a vampire, powerful, long-living, majestic. But you left me as a human, to shuffle through a pitifully short life, weak and afraid like everybody else. Well, guess what? I outsmarted you! I tracked down those in the other camp and gained my rightful powers and privileges anyway!"

"For all the good it has done you," Mr Crepsley snorted.

"What do you mean?" Steve snapped.

"You have wasted your life on hatred and revenge," Mr Crepsley said. "What good is life if there is no joy or creative purpose? You would have been better off living five years as a human than five hundred as a monster."

"I'm no monster!" Steve snarled. "I'm..." He stopped and growled something to himself. "Enough of this crap," he declared aloud. "You're boring me. If you haven't anything more intelligent to say, keep your mouths shut."

"Impudent cur!" Mr Crepsley roared, and swung the back of his hand across Steve's cheek, drawing blood. Steve sneered at the vampire, wiped the blood off with his fingers, then put them to his lips.

"One night soon, it'll be *your* blood I dine on," he whispered, then lapsed into silence.

Exasperated and weary, Mr Crepsley, Harkat and I also fell silent. We finished cleaning our wounds, then lay back and relaxed. If we'd been alone, we'd have dozed off — but none of us dared shut our eyes with a destructive beast like Steve Leopard in the room.

More than an hour after Vancha had taken his captive vampet aside, he returned. His face was dark and although he'd washed his hands before coming in, he hadn't been able to remove all the traces of blood. Some of it was his own, from wounds received in the tunnels, but most had come from the vampet.

Vancha found a bottle of warm beer in the out-of-order fridge, yanked the top off and downed it hungrily. He normally never drank anything other than fresh water, milk and blood — but these were hardly normal times.

He wiped around his mouth with the back of a hand when he was done, then stared at the faint red stains on his flesh. "He was a brave man," Vancha said quietly. "He resisted longer than I thought possible. I had to do bad things to make him talk. I..." He shivered and opened another bottle. There were bitter tears in his eyes as he drank.

"Is he dead?" I asked, my voice trembling.

Vancha sighed and looked away. "We're at war. We cannot afford to spare our enemies' lives. Besides, by the time I'd finished, it seemed cruel to let him live. Killing him was a mercy in the end."

"Praise the gods of the vampires for small mercies," Steve laughed, then flinched as Vancha spun, drew a shuriken and sent it flying at him. The sharp throwing star buried itself in the material of the couch, less than a centimetre beneath Steve's right ear.

"I won't miss with the next," Vancha swore, and at last the smile slipped from Steve's face, as he realized how serious the Prince was.

Mr Crepsley got up and laid a calming hand on Vancha's shoulder, directing him to a chair. "Was the interrogation worthwhile?" he asked. "Had the vampet anything new to reveal?"

Vancha didn't answer immediately. He was still glaring at Steve. Then the question sunk in and he wiped around his large eyes with the ends of one of his animal hides. "He'd plenty to say," Vancha grunted, then lapsed into silence and stared down at the bottle of beer in his hands, as though he didn't know how it got there.

"The vampet!" he said loudly after a minute of quiet, head snapping up, eyes clicking into focus. "Yes. I found out, for starters, why Gannen didn't kill us, and why the others fought so cagily." Leaning forward, he lobbed the empty beer bottle at Steve, who swatted it aside, then stared arrogantly back at the Prince. "Only the Vampaneze Lord can kill us," Vancha said softly.

"What do you mean?" I frowned.

"He's bound by Mr Tiny's rules, the same as us," Vancha explained. "Just as *we* can't call upon others for help in tracking and fighting him, *he* can't ask his underlings to kill us. Mr Tiny said he had to kill us himself to ensure victory. He can call upon all the vampaneze he likes to fight us, but if one should strike too deeply and inflict a fatal wound, they're destined to lose the war."

That was exciting news and we discussed it eagerly. Until now, we thought we stood no chance against the Vampaneze Lord's minions — there were simply too many of them for us to cut a path through. But if they weren't allowed to kill us…

"Let's not get carried away," Harkat cautioned. "Even if they can't kill us, they can … stall and subdue us. If they capture us and give us to … their Lord, it will be a simple matter for him to … drive a stake through our hearts."

"How come they didn't kill *you*?" I asked Harkat. "You're not one of the three hunters."

"Maybe they don't know that," Harkat said.

Steve muttered something beneath his breath.

"What was that?" Vancha shouted, prodding him sharply with his left foot.

"I said we didn't know before, but we do now!" Steve jeered. "At least," he added sulkily, "*I* know."

"You did not know who the hunters were?" Mr Crepsley asked.

Steve shook his head. "We knew there were three of you, and Mr Tiny told us that one would be a child, so we had Darren pegged straight off. But when five of you turned up — you three, Harkat and Debbie — we weren't sure about the others. We guessed the hunters would be vampires, but we didn't want to take unnecessary chances."

"Is that why you pretended to be our ally?" I asked. "You wanted to get close to us, to figure out who the hunters were?"

"That was part of it," Steve nodded, "although mostly I just wanted to toy with you. It was fun, getting so close that I could kill you whenever I wished, delaying the fatal blow until the time was right."

"He's a fool," Vancha snorted. "Anyone who wouldn't strike his foe dead at the first opportunity is asking for trouble."

"Steve Leonard is many things," Mr Crepsley said, "but not foolish." He rubbed the long scar on the left side of his face, thinking deeply. "You thought this plan through most thoroughly, did you not?" he asked Steve.

"I sure did," Steve smirked.

"You accounted for every possible twist and turn?"

"As many as I could imagine."

Mr Crepsley stopped stroking his scar and his eyes narrowed. "Then you must have considered what would happen if we escaped."

Steve's smile widened but he said nothing.

"What was the back-up plan?" Mr Crepsley asked, his voice strained.

"'Back-up plan'?" Steve echoed innocently.

"Do not play games with me!" Mr Crepsley hissed. "You must have discussed alternate plans with R.V. and Gannen Harst. Once you had revealed your location to us, you could not afford to sit back and wait. Time is precious now that we know where your Lord is hiding, and how those with him cannot take our lives."

Mr Crepsley stopped speaking and snapped to his feet. Vancha was only a second behind him. Their eyes locked and, as one, they exclaimed, "A trap!"

"I knew he came too quietly up the tunnels," Vancha growled, hurrying to the apartment door, opening it and checking the corridor outside. "Deserted."

"I will try the window," Mr Crepsley said, starting towards it.

"No point," Vancha said. "Vampaneze wouldn't attack in the open by day."

"No," Mr Crepsley agreed, "but vampets would." He reached the window and drew back the heavy blind which was blocking the harmful rays of the sun. His breath caught in his throat. "Charna's guts!" he gasped.

Vancha, Harkat and I rushed over to see what had upset him (Vancha grabbed hold of Steve on the way). What we saw caused us all to curse, except Steve, who laughed deliriously.

The street outside was teeming with police cars, army vans, policemen and soldiers. They were lined up in front of the building, and stretched around the sides. Many carried rifles. In the building opposite, we glimpsed figures in the windows, also armed. As we watched, a helicopter buzzed down from overhead and hung in the air a couple of floors above us. There was a soldier in the helicopter with a rifle so big it could have been used to shoot elephants.

But the marksman wasn't interested in elephants. He was aiming at the same target as those in the building and on the ground — *us!*

CHAPTER THREE

As A strong spotlight was trained on the window to dazzle us, we all turned to one side and let the blind fall back into place. Retreating, Vancha cursed at his loudest and vilest, while the rest of us glanced uneasily at one another, waiting for someone to propose a plan.

"How did they sneak up without ... us hearing?" Harkat asked.

"We weren't paying attention to what was happening outside," I said.

"Even so," Harkat insisted, "we should have ... picked up on the sirens."

"They didn't use sirens," Steve laughed. "They were warned to tread quietly. And, before you waste time checking, they've got the rear of the building and roof covered as well as the front." As we stared at him questioningly, he said, "I wasn't distracted. *I* heard them coming."

Vancha bellowed madly at Steve, then made a dive for him. Mr Crepsley stepped into his path to reason with him, but Vancha shoved him aside without regard and charged towards Steve, murder in his eyes.

A voice from outside, amplified by a megaphone, stopped him.

"You in there!" it bellowed. "*Killers!*"

Vancha hesitated, fingers balled into fists, then pointed at Steve and snarled, "Later!" Spinning, he hurried to the window and nudged the blind aside a fraction. Light from the sun and spotlight flooded the room.

Letting the blind fall back into place, Vancha roared, "Turn off the light!"

"No chance!" the person with the megaphone laughed in reply.

Vancha stood there a moment, thinking, then nodded at Mr Crepsley and Harkat. "Check the corridors above and below. Find out if they're inside the building. Don't clash with them — if that lot outside start firing, they'll cut us to ribbons."

Mr Crepsley and Harkat obeyed without question.

"Bring that sorry excuse for a dog over here," Vancha said to me, and I dragged Steve to the window. Vancha wrapped a hand around Steve's throat and growled in his ear, "Why are they here?"

"They think you're the killers," Steve chuckled. "The ones who killed all those humans."

"You son of a mongrel!" Vancha snarled.

"Please," Steve replied smugly. "Let's not get personal."

Mr Crepsley and Harkat returned.

"They're packed tight two floors … above," Harkat reported.

"The same two floors below," Mr Crepsley said grimly.

Vancha cursed again, then thought quickly. "We'll break through the floorboards," he decided. "The humans will be in the halls. They won't expect us to go straight down through the apartments."

"Yes they will," Steve disagreed. "They've been warned to fill every room below, above and adjoining."

Vancha stared at Steve, looking for the slightest hint of a bluff. When he found none, his features softened and the ghostly traces of defeat welled in his eyes. Then he shook his head and put self-pity behind him.

"We have to talk to them," he said. "Find out where we stand and maybe buy some time to think this through. Anyone want to volunteer?" When nobody replied, he grunted. "Guess that means I'm the negotiator. Just don't blame me if it all goes wrong." Leaving the blind over the window, he smashed a pane of glass, then leant close and shouted at the humans below. "Who's down there and what the hell do you want?"

There was a pause, then the same voice as before spoke to us via a megaphone. "Who am I talking to?" the person asked. Now that I concentrated on the voice, I realized it was a woman's.

"None of your business!" Vancha roared.

Another pause. Then, "We know your names. Larten Crepsley, Vancha March, Darren Shan and Harkat Mulds. I just want to know which one of you I'm in contact with."

Vancha's jaw dropped.

Steve doubled over with laughter.

"Tell them who you are," Harkat whispered. "They know too much. Best to act like we're … co-operating."

Vancha nodded, then shouted through the covered hole in the window, "Vancha March."

As he did that, I peeked through a gap at the side of the blind, looking for weak points in the defences below. I didn't find any, but I did get a fix on the woman who was speaking to us — tall and broad, with short white hair.

"Listen, March," the woman called as I stepped away from the window. "I'm Chief Inspector Alice Burgess. I'm running this freak show." An ironic choice of words, though none of us commented on it. "If you want to negotiate a deal, you'll be negotiating with me. One warning — I'm not here to play games. I've more than two hundred men and women out here and inside your building, just dying to put a round of bullets through your black excuse for a heart. At the first sign that you're messing with us, I'll give the order and they'll open fire. Understand?"

Vancha bared his teeth and snarled, "I understand." Then he repeated it, louder, so she could hear. "I understand!"

"Good," Chief Inspector Burgess responded. "First of all — are your hostages alive and unharmed?"

"'Hostages'?" Vancha replied.

"Steve Leonard and Mark Ryter. We know you have them, so don't act the innocent."

"Mark Ryter must have been the vampet," I remarked.

"You're soooooo observant," Steve laughed, then pushed Vancha aside and put his face up close to the window. "This is Steve Leonard!" he yelled, mimicking terror. "They haven't killed me yet, but they killed Mark. They tortured him first. It was horrible. They—"

He stopped, as though we'd cut him off mid-sentence, and stepped back, taking a self-indulgent bow.

"Sons of..." the officer cursed over the megaphone, then collected her wits and addressed us calmly and dryly. "OK — this is how it works. Release your remaining hostage. When he's safely in our custody, come down after him, one at a time. Any sign of a weapon, or any unexpected moves, and you're history."

"Let's talk about this," Vancha shouted.

"No talking," Burgess snapped.

"We're not going to release him," Vancha roared. "You don't know what he is, what he's done. Let me—"

A rifle fired and a volley of bullets tore up the outside of the building. We fell to the floor, cursing and yelping, although there was no cause for concern — the marksmen were aiming deliberately high.

When the scream of bullets died away, the Chief Inspector addressed us again. "That was a warning — your last. Next time we shoot to kill. No bargaining. No tradeoffs. No talking. You've terrorized this city for most of a year, but it stops here. You're through.

"Two minutes," she said. "Then we come in after you."

A troubled silence descended.

"That's that," Harkat muttered after a handful of slow-ticking seconds. "We're finished."

"Maybe," Vancha sighed. Then his gaze fell on Steve and he grinned. "But we won't die alone."

Vancha brought the fingers of his right hand together and held them out straight so they formed a blade of flesh and bone. He raised the hand above his head like a knife and advanced.

Steve closed his eyes and waited for death with a smile on his face.

"Wait," Mr Crepsley said softly, halting him. "There *is* a way out."

Vancha paused. "How?" he asked suspiciously.

"The window," Mr Crepsley said. "We jump. They will not expect that."

Vancha considered the plan. "The drop's no problem," he mused. "Not for us, anyway. How about you, Harkat?"

"Five storeys?" Harkat smiled. "I could do that ... in my sleep."

"But what do we do once down there?" Vancha asked. "The place is crawling with police and soldiers."

"We flit," Mr Crepsley said. "I will carry Darren. You carry Harkat. It will not be easy — they might shoot us before we can work up to flitting speed — but it can be done. With luck."

"It's crazy," Vancha growled, then winked at us. "I like it!" He pointed at Steve. "But we kill him before we leave."

"One minute!" Alice Burgess shouted through her megaphone.

Steve hadn't moved. His eyes were still closed. He was still smiling.

I didn't want Vancha to kill Steve. Although he'd betrayed us, he'd been my friend once, and the thought of him being killed in cold blood disturbed me. Also, there was Debbie to think about — if we killed Steve, R.V. would certainly kill Debbie in retaliation. It was crazy to worry about her, considering the trouble we were in, but I couldn't help it.

I was about to ask Vancha to spare Steve's life — although I didn't think he'd listen to me — when Mr Crepsley beat me to the punch.

"We cannot kill him," he said, sounding disgusted.

"Come again?" Vancha blinked.

"It is not the end of the world if we are captured," Mr Crepsley said.

"Thirty seconds!" Burgess screamed tensely.

Mr Crepsley ignored the interruption. "If we are captured and taken alive, there may be chances to escape later. But if we kill Steve Leonard, I do not think they will spare us. These humans are ready to butcher us at the drop of a pin."

Vancha shook his head uncertainly. "I don't like it. I'd rather kill him and take our chances."

"I would too," Mr Crepsley agreed. "But there is the Vampaneze Lord to consider. We must put the hunt before our personal wishes. Sparing Steve Leonard is—"

"Ten seconds!" Burgess bellowed.

Vancha glowered over Steve a few seconds more, undecided, then cursed, twisted his hand, and whacked him over the back of the head with the flat of his palm. Steve toppled to the floor. I thought Vancha had killed him, but the Prince had only knocked him out.

"That should shut him up for a while," Vancha grunted, checking his shuriken belts and wrapping his animal hides tight around him. "If we get the chance later, we'll track him down and finish him off."

"Time's up!" Alice Burgess warned us. "Come out immediately or we open fire!"

"Ready?" Vancha asked.

"Ready," Mr Crepsley said, drawing his knives.

"Ready," Harkat said, testing the head of his axe with a large, grey finger.

"Ready," I said, taking out my sword and holding it across my chest.

"Harkat jumps with me," Vancha said. "Larten and Darren — you come next. Give us a second or two to roll out of your way."

"Luck, Vancha," Mr Crepsley said.

"Luck," Vancha replied, then grinned savagely, slapped Harkat on the back, and leapt through the window, shattering the blind and glass, Harkat not far behind.

Mr Crepsley and I waited the agreed seconds, then jumped through the jagged remains of the window after our friends, and dropped swiftly to the ground like a couple of wingless bats, into the hellish cauldron which awaited us below.

CHAPTER FOUR

AS THE ground rushed up to meet me, I brought my legs together, hunched my upper body, spread my hands and landed in a crouch. My extra-strong bones absorbed the shock without breaking, although the force of the contact sent me rolling forward and I almost impaled myself on my sword (which would have been an embarrassing way to die).

There was a sharp yell of pain to my left, and as I bounced on to my feet I saw Mr Crepsley lying on the ground, nursing his right ankle, unable to stand. Ignoring my injured friend, I brought up my sword defensively and looked for Vancha and Harkat.

Our leap through the window had taken the police and soldiers by surprise. They were falling over one another and getting in each other's way, making it impossible for anyone to take a clean shot.

Harkat had grabbed a young soldier in the midst of the confusion and was holding him close to his chest, spinning quickly in circles so nobody had time to shoot him in the back. Vancha, meanwhile, had set his sights on the big cheese. As I watched, he charged through several officers and soldiers, leapt over a car, and brought Chief Inspector Alice Burgess crashing to the ground with a perfectly timed tackle.

While all human eyes fixed on Vancha and the Chief Inspector, I hurried to Mr Crepsley's side and helped him up. His teeth were gritted in pain and I could tell instantly that his ankle wouldn't support him.

"Is it broken?" I shouted, dragging him behind a car for cover before someone snapped to his senses and took a shot at us.

"I do not think so," he gasped, "but the pain is intense." He collapsed behind the car and rubbed the flesh around his ankle, trying to massage out the pain.

Across the way, Vancha was on his feet, Alice Burgess' throat clutched in one hand, her megaphone in the other. "Hear this!" he roared through the megaphone at the police and soldiers. "If you shoot, your Chief dies!"

Above us, the blades of the helicopter hummed like the wings of a thousand angry bees. Otherwise — total silence.

Burgess broke it. "Forget about me!" she roared. "Take these creeps out now!"

Several marksmen raised their weapons obediently.

Vancha tightened his fingers around the police chief's throat. Her eyes bulged worryingly. The marksmen hesitated, then lowered their weapons slightly. Vancha loosened his grip, but didn't let go completely. Holding the white-haired woman in front of him, he shuffled over to where Harkat was standing with his human shield. The two got back to back, then slowly crossed to where Mr Crepsley and I were sheltering. They resembled a large and clumsy crab as they moved, but it worked. Nobody fired.

"How bad is it?" Vancha asked, crouching beside us, dragging Burgess down with him. Harkat did likewise with his soldier.

"Bad," Mr Crepsley said soberly, locking gazes with Vancha.

"You can't flit?" Vancha asked softly.

"Not like this."

They stared at each other silently.

"Then we'll have to leave you behind," Vancha said.

"Aye." Mr Crepsley smiled thinly.

"I'm staying with him," I said instantly.

"This is no time for false heroics," Vancha growled. "You're coming — end of story."

I shook my head. "The hell with false heroics — I'm being practical. You can't flit with both me and Harkat on your back. It would take too long to work up the speed. We'd be shot dead before we got to the end of the street."

Vancha opened his mouth to object, realized my argument was valid, and closed it.

"I'm staying too," Harkat said.

Vancha groaned. "We don't have time for this rubbish!"

"It's not rubbish," Harkat said calmly. "I travel with Darren. Where he goes, I go. Where he stays, I stay. Besides, you'll stand a better chance … without me."

"How do you figure that?" Vancha asked.

Harkat pointed at Alice Burgess, still gasping from the tightness of Vancha's grip. "Alone, you can carry her and use her as a … shield until you flit."

Vancha sighed downheartedly. "You're all too clever for me. I'm not going to sit here and try to talk you round." He stuck his head up over the bonnet of the car to check on the surrounding troops, squinting hard against the daylight. "Stay back," he warned, "or these two die!"

"You'll … never get … away," Burgess croaked, her pale blue eyes filled with hate, her ghostly white skin flushed a deep, angry red. "The first … clear shot they have … they'll take you out!"

"Then we'll have to make sure we don't give them one," Vancha laughed, covering her mouth with a hand before she could reply. His smile faded. "I can't come back for you," he said to us. "If you stay, you're on your own."

"We know," Mr Crepsley said.

Vancha glanced up at the sun. "You'd better surrender straightaway and pray to the gods that they bundle you into a cell without windows."

"Aye." Mr Crepsley's teeth were chattering, partly from the pain in his ankle, partly from fear of the deadly rays of the sun.

Leaning forward, Vancha whispered so that Burgess and the soldier couldn't hear. "If I escape, I'll return for the Vampaneze Lord. I'll wait in the cavern where we fought last night. I'll give you until midnight. If you aren't there by then, I'll go after him alone."

Mr Crepsley nodded. "We will do our best to break out. If I cannot walk, Darren and Harkat will escape without me." He stared searchingly at us. "*Yes?*"

"Yes," Harkat said.

I stared back silently a moment longer, then dropped my gaze. "Yes," I muttered reluctantly.

Vancha grunted, then stuck out his free hand. We all joined a hand to his. "Luck," he said, and each of us repeated it in turn.

Then, without waiting, Vancha stood and walked away, Burgess held stiffly in front of him. He'd dropped the megaphone on his way over. Now he stopped to pick it up and address the troops again. "I'm making a break for it!" he bellowed pleasantly. "I know it's your job to stop me, but if you fire, your boss dies too. If you're wise, you'll wait for me to make an error. After all," he chuckled, "you've got cars and helicopters. I'm on foot.

I'm sure you can keep pace with me until the time's right to pounce."

Tossing aside the megaphone, Vancha lifted the Chief Inspector off the ground, held her in front of him like a doll, and ran.

A senior officer darted for the megaphone, snatched it up and issued orders. "Hold your fire!" he shouted. "Don't break ranks. Wait for him to stumble or drop her. He can't escape. Train your sights on him, wait for a clean shot, then let him have it in the—"

He stopped abruptly. He'd been watching Vancha race towards a blockade at the end of the street as he was talking, but in the blink of an eye the vampire had disappeared. Vancha had hit flitting speed, and to the humans it seemed as if he'd simply vanished into thin air.

As the police and soldiers crowded forward in disbelief, guns cocked, staring at the ground as though they thought Vancha and their Chief had sunk into it, Mr Crepsley, Harkat and I grinned at each other.

"At least one of us is in the clear," Mr Crepsley said.

"We would have been too, if you weren't such a clumsy ox," I grunted.

Mr Crepsley glanced up at the sun and his smile slipped. "If they leave me in a cell which is open to the sun," he said quietly, "I will not wait to burn to death. I will escape or die trying."

I nodded grimly. "We all will."

Harkat pulled his soldier around so that he was facing us. The young man's face was green with terror and he was incapable of speech.

"Do we leave him or … try to use him as a bargaining chip?" Harkat asked.

"Leave him," I said. "They're less likely to shoot if we give ourselves up freely. If we try bargaining now, after Vancha has escaped with their boss, I think they'll mow us down."

"We must leave our weapons too," Mr Crepsley said, laying his knives aside.

I didn't want to part with my sword, but common sense prevailed and I left it in a heap with Mr Crepsley's knives, Harkat's axe, and the other bits and pieces we'd been carrying. Then we rolled up the arms of our sleeves, raised our hands above our heads, shouted that we were surrendering, and walked out – Mr Crepsley hopping on one leg – to be arrested and imprisoned by the dark-faced, trigger-itchy officers of the law, who handcuffed us, cursed us, bundled us into vans and drove us away — to prison.

CHAPTER FIVE

I WAS in a cell no more than four metres by four, with a ceiling maybe three metres high. There were no windows – apart from a small one set in the door – and no two-way mirrors. There were two surveillance cameras in the corners above the door, a long table with a tape recorder on it, three chairs, me — and three grim-looking police officers.

One of the officers was standing by the door, a rifle cradled tightly across his chest, eyes sharp. He hadn't told me his name – he hadn't spoken a word – but I could read it from his badge: William McKay.

The other two weren't wearing badges, but had told me their names: Con and Ivan. Con was tall, dark-faced and very lean, with a gruff manner and ready sneer. Ivan was older and thinner, with grey hair. He looked tired and spoke softly, as though the questions were exhausting him.

"Is Darren Shan your real name, like we've been told?" Ivan enquired for about the twentieth time since I'd been admitted to the holding cell. They'd been asking the same questions over and over, and showed no signs of letting up.

I didn't answer. So far I hadn't said anything.

"Or is it Darren Horston — the name you've been using recently?" Ivan asked after a few seconds of silence.

No answer.

"How about your travelling companion — Larten Crepsley or Vur Horston?"

I looked down at my hands, which were handcuffed, and said nothing. I examined the chain linking the handcuffs: steel, short, thick. I thought I'd be able to snap it if I had to, but I wasn't sure.

My ankles were cuffed as well. The chain linking my ankles had been short when I was arrested. The police left the short chain on while I was being fingerprinted and photographed, but took it off and replaced it with a longer chain soon after they locked me away securely in the cell.

"What about the freak?" the officer called Con asked. "That grey-skinned monster. What's—"

"He isn't a monster!" I snapped, breaking my code of silence.

"Oh?" Con sneered. "What is he then?"

I shook my head. "You wouldn't believe me if I told you."

"Try us," Ivan encouraged me, but I only shook my head again.

"What about the other two?" Con asked. "Vancha March and Larten Crepsley. Our informants told us they were vampires. What do you have to say about that?"

I smiled humourlessly. "Vampires don't exist," I said. "Everyone knows that."

"That's right," Ivan said. "They don't." He leant across the table, as though to tell me a secret. "But those two aren't entirely normal, Darren, as I'm sure you already know. March disappeared like a magician, while Crepsley..." He coughed. "Well, we haven't been able to photograph him."

I smiled when he said that, and looked up at the video cameras. Full-vampires have peculiar atoms, which make it impossible for them to be captured on film. The police could take snaps of Mr Crepsley from every angle they could dream of, with the best cameras available — to no visible effect.

"Look at the grin on him!" Con snapped. "He thinks this is funny!"

"No," I said, wiping the smile from my face. "I don't."

"Then why are you laughing?"

I shrugged. "I was thinking of something else."

Ivan slumped back in his chair, disappointed by my answers. "We've taken a blood sample from Crepsley," he said. "From the thing called Harkat Mulds too. We'll find out what they are when the results come back. It would be to your advantage to tell us now."

I didn't reply. Ivan waited a moment, then ran a hand through his grey hair. He sighed despondently, and began with the questions again. "What's your real name? What's your relationship to the others? Where…"

More time passed. I wasn't able to judge exactly how long I'd been imprisoned. It felt like a day or more, but realistically it was probably only four or five hours, maybe less. The sun was most likely still shining outside.

I thought about Mr Crepsley and wondered how he was faring. If he was in a cell like mine, he'd nothing to worry about. But if they'd put him in a cell with windows…

"Where are my friends?" I asked.

Con and Ivan had been discussing something under their breath. Now they looked at me, expressions guarded.

"You'd like to see them?" Ivan asked.

"I just want to know where they are," I said.

"If you answer our questions, a meeting can be arranged," Ivan promised.

"I just want to know where they are," I repeated.

"They're close," Con grunted. "Locked away nice and tight like you."

"In cells like this?" I asked.

"Exactly the same," Con said, then looked around at the walls and smiled as he realized why I was concerned. "Cells without windows," he chuckled, then nudged his partner in the ribs. "But that can be changed, can't it, Ivan? What say we move the 'vampire' to a cell with lovely round windows? A cell with a view of the outside … the sky … the *sun*."

I said nothing, but locked gazes with Con and stared back angrily.

"You don't like the sound of that, do you?" Con hissed. "The thought of us sticking Crepsley in a room with windows terrifies you, doesn't it?"

I shrugged indifferently and averted my eyes. "I want to speak to a lawyer," I said.

Con burst out laughing. Ivan hid a smile behind a hand. Even the guard with the rifle smirked, as though I'd cracked the best joke ever.

"What's so funny?" I snapped. "I know my rights. I'm entitled to a phonecall and a lawyer."

"Of course," Con crowed. "Even killers have rights." He rapped the table with his knuckles, then turned off the tape recorder. "But guess what — we're withholding those rights. We'll catch hell for it later, but we don't care. We've got you walled up here and we won't let you take advantage of your rights until you give with some answers."

"That's illegal," I growled. "You can't do that."

"Normally, no," he agreed. "Normally our Chief Inspector would barge in and kick up a storm if she heard about something like this. But our Chief isn't here, is she? She's been abducted by your fellow killer, Vancha March."

I went white-lipped when I heard that and realized what it meant. With their Chief out of the way, they'd taken the law into their own hands, and were prepared to do whatever it took to find out where she was and get her back. It might cost them their careers, but they didn't care. This was personal.

"You'll have to torture me to make me talk," I said stiffly, testing them to see how far they were willing to go.

"Torture's not our way," Ivan said immediately. "We don't do things like that."

"Unlike some people we could mention," Con added, then tossed a photo across the table at me. I tried to ignore it, but my eyes flicked automatically to the figure in it. I saw that it was the vampet we'd taken hostage earlier that morning in the tunnels, the one called Mark Ryter — the one Vancha had tortured and killed.

"We're not evil," I said quietly. But I could see things from their point of view and understood how monstrous we must look. "There are sides to this you don't know about. We're not the killers you seek. We're trying to stop them, the same as you."

Con barked a laugh.

"It's true," I insisted. "Mark Ryter was one of the bad guys. We had to hurt him to find out about the others. We're not your enemies. You and I are on the same side."

"That's the weakest lie I've ever heard," Con snapped. "How dumb do you think we are?"

"I don't think you're dumb at all," I said. "But you're misguided. You've been tricked. You..." I leant forward eagerly. "Who told you where to find us? Who told you our names, that we were vampires, that we were your killers?"

The policemen shared an uneasy glance, then Ivan said, "It was an anonymous tip-off. The caller rang from a public phone booth, left no name, and was gone when we arrived."

"Doesn't that sound fishy to you?" I asked.

"We receive anonymous tips all the time," Ivan said, but he looked fidgety and I knew he had his doubts. If he'd been alone, maybe I could have talked him round to my way of thinking, and persuaded him to grant me the benefit of the doubt. But before I could say anything more, Con tossed another photo across the table at me, then another. Close-ups of Mark Ryter, capturing even more of the grisly details than the first.

"People on *our* side don't kill other people," he said coldly. "Even when they'd like to," he added meaningfully, pointing a finger at me.

I sighed and let it drop, knowing I couldn't convince them of my innocence. A few seconds of silence passed, while they settled down after the exchange and composed themselves. Then they switched the tape recorder on and the questions started again. Who was I? Where had I come from? Where did Vancha March go? How many people had we killed? On and on and on and...

The police were getting nowhere with me, and it was frustrating them. Ivan and Con had been joined by another officer called Morgan, who had pinpoint eyes and dark brown hair. He sat stiff-backed, his hands flat on the table, subjecting me to a cool, unbreaking gaze. I had the feeling that Morgan was here to get nasty, although so far he'd made no violent moves against me.

"How old are you?" Con was asking. "Where are you from? How long have you been here? Why pick this city? How many others have you murdered? Where are the bodies? What have—"

He stopped at a knock on the door. Turning away, he went to see who was there. Ivan's eyes followed Con as he went, but Morgan's stayed on me. He blinked once every four seconds, no more, no less, like a robot.

Con had a murmured conversation with the person outside the door, then stood back and motioned the guard with the rifle away. The guard sidestepped over to the wall and trained his weapon on me, making sure I wouldn't try anything funny.

I was expecting another police officer, or maybe a soldier – I hadn't seen anyone from the army since I'd been arrested – but the meek little man who entered took me by complete surprise.

"*Mr Blaws?*" I gasped.

The school inspector who'd forced me to go to Mahler's looked nervous. He was carrying the same huge briefcase as before, and wearing the same old-fashioned bowler hat. He advanced half a metre, then stopped, reluctant to come any closer.

"Thank you for coming, Walter," Ivan said, rising to shake the visitor's hand.

Mr Blaws nodded feebly and squeaked, "Glad to be of assistance."

"Would you like a chair?" Ivan asked.

Mr Blaws shook his head quickly. "No thanks. I'd rather not stop any longer than necessary. Rounds to do. Places to be. You know how it is."

Ivan nodded sympathetically. "That's fine. You brought the papers?"

Mr Blaws nodded. "The forms he filled in, all the files we have on him. Yes. I left them with a man at the front desk. He's photocopying them and giving the originals back to me before I leave. I have to hang on to the originals for the school records."

"Fine," Ivan said again, then stepped aside and jerked his head at me. "Can you identify this boy?" he asked officiously.

"Yes," Mr Blaws said. "He's Darren Horston. He enrolled with Mahler's on the..." He paused and frowned. "I've forgotten the exact date. I should know it, because I was looking at it on the way in."

"That's OK," Ivan smiled. "We'll get it from the photocopies. But this is definitely the boy who called himself Darren Horston? You're sure?"

Mr Blaws nodded firmly. "Oh yes," he said. "I never forget the face of a pupil, especially one who's played truant."

"Thank you, Walter," Ivan said, taking the school inspector's arm. "If we need you again, we'll..."

He stopped. Mr Blaws hadn't moved. He was staring at me with wide eyes and a trembling lip. "Is it true?" Mr Blaws asked. "What the media are saying — he and his friends are the killers?"

Ivan hesitated. "We can't really say right now, but as soon as we—"

"How could you?" Mr Blaws shouted at me. "How could you kill all those people? And poor little Tara Williams — your own classmate!"

"I didn't kill Tara," I said tiredly. "I didn't kill anybody. I'm not a killer. The police have arrested the wrong people."

"Hah!" Con snorted.

"You're a beast," Mr Blaws growled, raising his briefcase high in the air, as though he meant to throw it at me. "You should be ... you should ... should..."

He couldn't say any more. His lips tightened and his jaw clenched shut. Turning his back on me, he started out of the door. As he was stepping through, I reacted to a childish impulse and called him back.

"Mr Blaws?" I shouted. He paused and looked over his shoulder questioningly. I adopted an innocent, dismayed expression. "This won't harm my grades, will it, sir?" I enquired sweetly.

The school inspector gawped at me, then glared furiously when he realized I was teasing him, turned up his nose, showed me a clean pair of heels and clacked away down the corridor.

I laughed aloud as Mr Blaws departed, taking absurd comfort in the annoying little man's irate expression. Con, Ivan and the guard with the gun smiled too, despite themselves, but Morgan didn't. He remained as steely-faced as ever, a terrible, unspoken menace in his sharp, mechanical eyes.

CHAPTER SIX

IVAN WAS replaced by a burly police officer called Dave shortly after Mr Blaws had departed. Dave acted friendly — the first thing he did when he came in was ask me if I'd like anything to eat or drink — but I wasn't fooled. I'd watched enough TV shows to know all about the good cop/bad cop routine.

"We're here to help you, Darren," Dave assured me, tearing open a sachet of sugar and pouring it into a plastic cup filled with steaming coffee. Some of the sugar spilt over the side, on to the table. I was ninety per cent certain the spill was deliberate — Dave wanted me to think he was a bumbler.

"Taking off these handcuffs and setting me free would be a big help," I quipped, watching Dave cautiously as he tore open another sachet of sugar. Morgan worried me the most — Con might knock me around a bit, if things got

414

rough, but I believed Morgan was capable of worse – but I'd have to be extra careful with Dave, or he'd worm my secrets out of me. I'd been awake a long time. I was drained and light-headed. Prone to slips.

"Take off your handcuffs and set you free," Dave smirked, winking at me. "Good one. Of course, we both know that isn't going to happen, but there are things I *can* do. Get you a lawyer for one. A bath. A change of clothes. A nice bunk for the night. You're going to be with us a long time, I fear, but it doesn't have to be an unpleasant stay."

"What do I have to do to make it *pleasant*?" I asked cagily.

Dave shrugged and sipped the coffee. "Ouch! Too hot!" Fanning his lips with a hand to cool them down, he smiled. "Not much," he said in answer to my question. "Tell us your real name, where you're from, what you're doing here. That kind of stuff."

I shook my head wryly — new face, same old questions.

Dave saw I wasn't going to answer, so he changed tack. "That routine's stale, right? Let's try something else. Your friend, Harkat Mulds, says he needs his mask to survive, that he'll die if exposed to air for more than ten or twelve hours. Is that true?"

I nodded cautiously. "Yes."

Dave looked glum. "This is bad," he muttered. "Very, very bad."

"What do you mean?" I asked.

"This is a prison, Darren. You and your friends are murder suspects. There are rules … guidelines … things we must do. Taking objects like belts, ties and *masks* from possible killers when they're admitted is one of the rules."

I stiffened in my chair. "You've taken away Harkat's mask?" I snapped.

"We had to," Dave said.

"But he'll die without it!"

Dave rolled his shoulders carelessly. "We've only your word for that. It's not enough. But if you tell us what he is and why normal air is deadly for him … and if you tell us about your other friends, Crepsley and March … maybe we can help."

I glared hatefully at the policeman. "So it's rat on my friends or you'll let Harkat die?" I sneered.

"That's a horrible way to put it," Dave protested warmly. "We don't intend to let any of you die. If your short, unusual friend takes a turn for the worse, we'll hurry him down to the medical wing and patch him up, like we're doing for the man you took hostage. But—"

"Steve's here?" I interrupted. "You've got Steve Leopard in the medical wing?"

"Steve *Leonard*," he corrected me, unaware of Steve's nickname. "We brought him here to recover. Easier to guard him from the media."

That was great news. I thought we'd lost Steve. If we could get to him when we were escaping and take him with us, we could use him when it came to trying to save Debbie's life.

I stretched my chained hands above my head and yawned. "What's the time?" I asked casually.

"Sorry," Dave smiled. "That's classified information."

I lowered my arms. "You know you asked me earlier if there was anything I wanted?"

"Uh-huh," Dave replied, eyes narrowing hopefully.

"Would it be OK if I walked around for a few minutes? My legs are cramping up."

Dave looked disappointed — he'd been anticipating a more involved request. "You can't leave this room," he said.

"I'm not asking to. A couple of minutes pacing from one side to the other will be fine."

Dave checked with Con and Morgan to see what they thought.

"Let him," Con said, "as long as he stays on his own side of the table."

Morgan didn't say anything, just nodded once to show it was OK.

Pushing my chair back, I stood, stepped away from the table, jangled the chain linking my ankles together, loosening it, then walked from one wall to the other, stretching my legs, working the tension out of my muscles, formulating an escape plan.

After a while I stopped at one of the walls and rested my forehead against it. I began lightly kicking the lower part of the wall with my left foot, as if I was nervous and claustrophobic. In reality I was testing it. I wanted to know how thick the wall was and if I could break through.

The results of the test were unpromising. By the feel of the wall, and the dull echoes from my kicks, it was made of solid concrete, two or three blocks thick. I could bust through eventually, but it would take a lot of work and – more crucially – time. The guard by the door would have ample opportunity to raise his weapon and fire.

Levering myself away from the wall, I started walking again, eyes flicking from the door to the wall at the front of the cell. The door looked pretty solid – steel – but maybe the wall it was set in wasn't as thick as the others. Perhaps I could break through it quicker than through the sides or back. Wait until it was definitely night, hope the police left me alone in the cell, then smash through and...

No. Even if the police left me, the video cameras set in the corners above the door wouldn't. Someone would be watching all the time. The alarm would sound as soon as I attacked the wall, and the corridor outside would fill with police within seconds.

It had to be the ceiling. From where I stood, I'd no idea whether it was reinforced or normal, if I could punch a way through or not. But it was the only logical escape route. If I was left alone, I could knock out the cameras, take to the rafters, and hopefully lose my pursuers along the way. I wouldn't have time to search for Harkat and Mr Crepsley, so I'd just have to hope they made it out by themselves.

It wasn't much of a plan — I still hadn't figured out how I was going to get the policemen to leave; I didn't think they'd withdraw for the night to let me catch up on my beauty sleep — but at least it was the beginning of one. The rest would fall into place along the way.

I hoped!

I walked for a few minutes more, then Dave asked me to sit again, and we were back to the questions. This time they came quicker than before, more urgently. I got the sense that their patience was nearing its end. Violence couldn't be far off.

The police were increasing the pressure. The offers of food and drinks were no longer being made, and Dave's smile was a slim shadow of its former self. The large officer had loosened his collar button and was sweating freely as he pounded me with question after question. He'd given up asking about my name and background. Now he wanted to know how many people I'd killed, where the bodies were, and if I was just an accomplice or an active member of the murderous gang.

In reply to his questions I kept saying, "I didn't kill anyone. I'm not your enemy. You have the wrong person."

Con wasn't as polite as Dave. He'd started slamming the table with his fists and leaning forward menacingly every time he addressed me. I believed he was only minutes away from setting about me with his fists, and steeled myself against the blows which seemed sure to come.

Morgan hadn't changed. He sat quiet and still, staring relentlessly, blinking once every four seconds.

"Are there others?" Dave growled. "Is it just the four of you, or are there more killers in the gang that we don't know about?"

"We're not killers," I sighed, rubbing my eyes, trying to stay alert.

"Did you kill them first, then drink from them, or was it the other way round?" Dave pressed.

I shook my head and didn't reply.

"Do you really believe you're vampires, or is that a cover story, or some sick game you like to indulge in?"

"Leave me alone," I whispered, dropping my gaze. "You've got it all wrong. We're not your enemies."

"How many have you killed?" Dave roared. Where are—"

He stopped. People had poured into the corridor outside during the last few seconds, and now it was teeming with police and staff, all shouting wildly.

"What the hell's going on?" Dave snapped.

"Want me to check?" William McKay — the guard with the rifle — asked.

"No," Con responded. "I'll do it. You keep a watch on the boy."

Going to the door, Con banged on it and called for it to be opened. There was no immediate response, so he called again, louder, and this time it swung open. Stepping out, the dark-faced officer grabbed a woman who was rushing past and quickly shook a few answers out of her.

Con had to lean in close to the woman to hear what she was saying. When he had it straight, he let go of her and rushed back into my cell, eyes wide. "It's a breakout!" Con shouted.

"Which one?" Dave yelled, jumping up. "Crepsley? Mulds?"

"Neither," Con gasped. "It's the hostage — Steve Leonard!"

"*Leonard?*" Dave repeated uncertainly. "But he's not a prisoner. Why should he want to break—"

"I don't know!" Con shouted. "Apparently, he regained consciousness a few minutes ago, took stock of the situation, then murdered a guard and two nurses."

The colour drained from Dave's face, and William McKay almost dropped his rifle.

"A guard and two..." Dave murmured.

"That's not all," Con said. "He's killed or wounded another three on his way out. They think he's still in the building."

Dave's face hardened. He started for the door, then remembered me, paused, and looked back over his shoulder.

"I'm not a killer," I said quietly, staring him straight in the eye. "I'm not the one you want. I'm on your side."

This time, I think he half-believed me.

"What about me?" William McKay asked as the two officers filed out. "Do I stay or go?"

"Come with us," Con snapped.

"What about the boy?"

"I'll take care of him," Morgan said softly. His eyes hadn't strayed from my face, even while Con was telling Dave about Steve. The guard hurried out after the others, slamming the door shut behind him.

I was alone at last — with Morgan.

The officer with the tiny, watchful eyes sat staring at me. Four seconds — blink. Eight seconds — blink. Twelve seconds — blink.

He leant forward, turned off the tape recorder, then stood and stretched. "I thought we'd never get rid of them," he said. Strolling to the door, he glanced out of the small window set high in it, and spoke softly, his face hidden from the cameras overhead. "You'll have to go through the ceiling, but you had figured that out already, hadn't you?"

"Excuse me?" I said, startled.

"I saw you casing the room while you were 'exercising'," he smiled. "The walls are too thick. You don't have time to break through."

I said nothing, but stared hard at the brown-haired officer, wondering what he was up to.

"I'm going to attack you in a minute," Morgan said. "I'll put on a show for the cameras, pretend to lose my rag and go for your throat. Slam me over the head with your fists, hard, and I'll go down for the count. After that it's up to you. I've no key for your chains, so you'll have to snap out of them yourself. If you can't — tough. Nor can I guarantee how much time you'll have, but with all the panic in the halls outside, there should be plenty."

"Why are you doing this?" I asked, stunned by the unexpected turn of events.

"You'll see," Morgan said, spinning to face me, then advancing in what would appear on camera to be a violent, threatening manner. "I'll be helpless when I hit the floor," Morgan said, waving his arms about wildly. "If you decide to kill me, I won't be able to stop you. But from what I've heard, you're not the sort to kill a defenceless opponent."

"Why should I want to kill you when you're helping me escape?" I asked, bewildered.

Morgan grinned nastily. "You'll see," he said again, then dived over the table at me.

I was so amazed by what was happening, that when he wrapped his hands around my throat, I didn't do anything, just stared back at him uncertainly. Then he squeezed tightly and self-preservation kicked in. Jerking my head backwards, I brought up my chained hands and shoved him away. He slapped at my hands, then came at me again. Lurching to my feet, I pushed his head down, held it between my knees, raised my arms, brought my hands together and smashed him over the back of his head.

With a grunt, Morgan slid off the table, dropped to the floor and lay there motionless. I was worried that I'd really hurt him. Hurrying around the table, I bent to check his pulse. As I leant down, I got close enough to his head to see through his thin layer of hair to the scalp beneath. What I saw sent a flash chill racing down my spine. Underneath the hair, tattooed into the flesh, was a large, rough 'V' — the mark of the vampets!

"Yuh-yuh-yuh-you're..." I stuttered.

"Yes," Morgan said softly. He'd landed with his left arm thrown over his face, hiding his mouth and eyes from the lens of the camera. "And proud to serve the rightful rulers of the night."

I reeled away from the police vampet, more unnerved than ever. I'd thought the vampets served alongside their masters. It never occurred to me that some could be working undercover as ordinary humans.

Morgan opened his left eye and glanced up at me without moving. "You'd better get moving," he hissed, "before the cavalry arrives."

Remembering where I was and what was at stake, I got to my feet and tried not to dwell on the shock of finding a vampet here among the police. I wanted to leap on to the table and make my escape via the ceiling, but first there were the cameras to take care of. Bending, I picked up the tape recorder, quickly crossed the room and used the base of the recorder to shatter the video cameras, rendering them useless.

"Very good," Morgan whispered as I retraced my steps. "Very clever. Now fly, little bat. Fly like the devil is after you."

Pausing over the vampet, I glared down at him, drew back my right foot as far as my chains would allow, and kicked him hard in the side of the head. He grunted, rolled over and lay still. I didn't know if he was really unconscious or if this was part of his act, and I didn't stay to find out.

Jumping on to the table, I stuck my hands together, paused, then wrenched my wrists apart as sharply as possible, using all of my vampiric powers. I almost dislocated my lower arms, and roared aloud with pain, but it worked — the chain joining my handcuffs snapped in the middle, freeing my hands.

I stood on the ends of the chain linking my ankles, grabbed it in the middle and pulled upwards quickly. *Too* quickly — I rolled back off the table and collapsed in a heap on the floor!

Groaning, I rolled over, got up, stood on the chain again, braced my back against a wall, and made a second stab at the chain. This time I was successful and it snapped in two. I wrapped the twin lengths of chain around my ankles, to prevent them snagging on corners, then did the same thing with the chains dangling from my wrists.

I was ready. Hopping on to the table again, I crouched, took a deep breath, then leapt, the fingers of both hands held out flat and straight.

The ceiling, thankfully, was made of ordinary plaster tiles, and my fingers burst through with only the barest of resistance. Sweeping my hands apart while hovering in midair, my forearms connected with rafters on either side. Splaying my fingers, I caught hold of the lengths of wood as gravity dragged me back to earth, and held firm, halting my fall.

I hung there a moment, until I stopped swinging, then hauled my legs and body out of the cell, up into darkness and the freedom it promised.

CHAPTER SEVEN

THERE WAS a gap of half a metre between the rafters I was
lying on and those overhead. It wasn't much, and it made
life very uncomfortable, but it was more than I'd expected.

Stretching out flat, I listened for sounds of pursuit in
the cell below. There weren't any. I could hear people
colliding with each other and barking out orders in the
corridor, so either the police weren't aware I'd broken out,
or had found their way blocked by the panicked crowds.

Whatever the answer, I had time on my side; time I
hadn't bargained for, which I could put to good use. I'd
planned to flee as swiftly as possible, leaving Mr Crepsley
and Harkat behind, but now I was in a position to go and
look for them.

But where to look? The light was pretty good up here –
there were many cracks between the plaster tiles, and light
seeped up from the rooms and corridors below – and I

could see for ten or twelve metres whichever way I looked. This was a big building, and if my friends were being held on another floor, I hadn't a hope in hell of finding them. But if they were nearby, and I hurried...

Scuttling over the rafters, I reached the ceiling of the cell next to mine, paused and cocked my ears. My sharp sense of hearing would detect any sound above that of a heartbeat. I waited a few seconds, but heard nothing. I moved on.

The next two cells were empty. In the third I heard someone scratching himself. I thought about calling out Mr Crepsley and Harkat's names, but if there were police in the cell, they would raise the alarm. There was only one thing for it. Taking a deep breath, I gripped the rafters on either side with my hands and feet, then punched through the thin material of the ceiling with my head.

I blew dust from my lips and blinked it out of my eyes, then focused on the scene below. I was ready to drop through the ceiling if either of my friends was within, but the only occupant was a bearded old man who stared up at me, mouth agape, blinking rapidly.

"Sorry," I said, forcing a quick smile. "Wrong room."

Withdrawing, I scurried forward, leaving the startled prisoner behind.

Three more empty cells. The next was occupied, but by two loud-talking men who'd been captured trying to rob a corner shop. I didn't stop to check on them — the police were hardly likely to lump a potential killer in with a couple of burglars.

Another empty cell. I thought the next was empty too, and had almost moved on when my ears picked up on the faint rustling of fabric. I came to a halt and listened intently, but there were no further sounds. Crawling backwards, skin itching from the insulating flakes which littered the ceiling tiles like snow, I got into position, took another deep breath, then head-butted through the tiles.

A wary Harkat Mulds jumped out of the chair he'd been sitting in and brought his arms up defensively as my head broke through and clouds of dust descended. Then the Little Person saw who it was, reached up, tore loose his mask (Dave had obviously been lying when he said they'd taken it away) and shouted my name with unconstrained delight. "*Darren!*"

"Howdy, pardner," I grinned, using my hands to widen the hole. I shook the dust from my hair and eyebrows.

"What are you doing ... up there?" Harkat asked.

I groaned at the dumb question. "Sightseeing!" I snapped, then lowered a hand. "C'mon — we haven't much time, and we have to find Mr Crepsley."

I'm sure Harkat had a thousand questions – I had too, like how come he was all alone, and why wasn't he handcuffed? – but he realized how perilous our position was, grabbed the offered hand and let me drag him up, saying nothing.

He had a harder time squeezing on to the rafters than

429

me – his body was a lot rounder than mine – but finally he was lying out flat beside me and we crawled forward, side by side, without discussing our plight.

The next eight or nine cells were empty or occupied by humans. I was growing anxious about the amount of time that had passed. Regardless of what was happening with Steve Leopard, my escape was bound to be noticed sooner rather than later, and pursuit would be fierce when it came. I was wondering whether it would be wiser to quit while we were ahead, when someone spoke from a spot in the cell underneath, just ahead of me.

"I am ready to make a statement now," said the voice, and by the second syllable I had the speaker pegged — Mr Crepsley!

I held up a hand for Harkat to stop, but he'd heard it too and had already come to a standstill (or rather, a *crawl*still).

"About time," a policeman said. "Let me check that our recorder's working…"

"Never mind your infernal recording device," Mr Crepsley sniffed. "I do not address myself to inanimate machines. Nor do I waste words on buffoons. I will speak to neither you nor your partner on my left. As for that cretin by the door with the rifle…"

I had to stifle a giggle. The sly old fox! He must have heard us crawling about up here and was letting us know exactly how things stood in the cell, how many police were present and where they were.

"You'd better watch yourself," the policeman snapped.

"I've a good mind to—"

"You have no sort of mind at all," Mr Crepsley interrupted. "You are a fool. The officer who was here earlier, on the other hand — Matt — struck me as a sensible man. Fetch him and I will confess. Otherwise my lips remain sealed."

The officer cursed, then shuffled to his feet and started for the door. "Keep an eye on him," he told the other two. "The first sign of a twitch — hit him hard! Remember who and what he is. Take no chances."

"Find out what the fuss is about while you're out there," one of the other officers said as his colleague was leaving. "The way people are rushing about, there must be some emergency."

"Will do," the officer said, then called for the door to be opened and let himself out.

I pointed Harkat off to the left, where the guard by the door would be. He slid forward silently, stopping when he got a fix on the policeman. I listened for sounds of the officer closer to Mr Crepsley, tuned into his heavy breathing, shifted back a metre or so, then held my left hand up, the thumb and first two fingers spread. I counted to two and lowered my middle finger. Another couple of seconds and I bent down my index finger. Finally, nodding swiftly at Harkat, I lowered my thumb.

At the signal, Harkat let go of the rafters and dropped through the plaster tiles of the ceiling, smashing them to pieces in the process. I followed almost instantly, bringing my legs down first, howling like a wolf for added effect.

The policemen didn't know what to make of our sudden appearance. The guard by the door tried to bring his rifle up, but Harkat's plummeting body collided with his arms and knocked it free of his grip. My officer, meanwhile, only gawped at me, making no move to protect himself.

While Harkat clambered to his feet and threw punches at the guard, I drew a fist back to let the officer have a bunch of fives in the face. Mr Crepsley stopped me. "Please," he said politely, getting to his feet and tapping the officer on the shoulder. "Let me."

The officer turned as though hypnotized. Mr Crepsley opened his mouth and breathed the special knockout gas of the vampires over him. One whiff of it and the officer's eyes were rolling in their sockets. I caught him as he fell, and gently lowered him to the floor.

"I was not expecting you so soon," Mr Crepsley said conversationally, picking at the lock of his left handcuff with the fingers of his right.

"We didn't want to keep you waiting," I said tightly, eager to be out of there, but not wanting to appear any less composed than my old friend and mentor, who looked entirely untroubled.

"You should not have rushed on my account," Mr Crepsley said, his handcuffs snapping free with a click. He bent to work on the chains around his ankles. "I was perfectly content. These are old-style handcuffs. I was wriggling out of their kind before the officers holding me were even born. It was never a question of *if* I was going to escape, but rather *when*."

"He can be an annoying … know-it-all sometimes," Harkat commented dryly. He'd knocked the guard out and had shuffled over to the table, to make his way back up to the safety of the ceiling.

"We can leave you behind and return for you later," I suggested to the vampire as he stepped out of his leg restraints.

"No," he said. "I might as well depart now that you are here." He winced as he took a step forward. "But, seriously, a few extra hours would not have been unwelcome. My ankle has healed considerably, but is not yet one hundred per cent. Further rest would have been beneficial."

"Will you be able to walk?" I asked.

He nodded. "I will win no races, but nor shall I be a hindrance. I am more worried about the sun — I have over two and a half hours of it to deal with."

"We'll cross that bridge when we come to it," I snapped. "Now, are you ready to continue, or do you want to stand here and shoot the breeze all day until the police come back?"

"Nervous?" Mr Crepsley asked, a glint in his eye.

"Yes," I said.

"Do not be," he told me. "The worst the humans can do is kill us." He got up on the table and paused. "By the end of the coming night, death may seem a blessing."

With that cheerless comment, he followed Harkat up

into the gloomy half-world of the rafters. I waited for him to pull his legs clear, then jumped up after him. We spread out so we weren't in one another's way, then Mr Crepsley asked which direction we should take.

"Right," I replied. "That leads to the rear of the building, I think."

"Very well," Mr Crepsley said, wriggling ahead of us. "Crawl slowly," he whispered over his shoulder, "and try not to pick up any splinters."

Harkat and I shared a rueful look – the phrase "cool as a cucumber" could have been invented with Mr Crepsley in mind – then hurried after the departing vampire before he got too far ahead and left us behind.

CHAPTER EIGHT

WE KICKED our way through the wall at the back of the building and found ourselves on the second floor, above a deserted alley.

"Can you jump?" I asked Mr Crepsley.

"No," he said, "but I can climb."

While Mr Crepsley swung out over the edge of the hole in the wall and dug his nails into the bricks, Harkat and I dropped to the ground and crouched low, scanning the shadows for signs of life. When Mr Crepsley joined us, we hurried to the end of the alley, where we paused to scout the terrain.

Mr Crepsley glanced up at the sun. It wasn't very strong — a weak, autumnal, afternoon glow — but two hours of exposure could be fatal for the vampire. If he'd been wearing his cloak, he could have pulled it up over his head and sheltered beneath it, but he'd taken it off in the apartment and left it there.

"What do we do now?" Harkat asked, gazing around uncertainly.

"Find a manhole and get underground," I replied. "They won't be able to track us through the tunnels, and Mr Crepsley won't have to worry about the sun."

"A worthy plan," Mr Crepsley said, rubbing his sore right ankle and looking for a manhole cover. There weren't any in the immediate vicinity, so we pressed on, Harkat and I supporting the vampire, sticking close to the walls of the alley.

The alley forked at the end. The left turn led towards a busy main street, the right on to another dark alley. I'd turned right on impulse and was starting towards the alley when Harkat stopped me.

"Wait," he hissed. "I see a way down."

I looked back and saw a cat picking through a mound of rubbish which had spilt out of a toppled bin and half-obscured a round manhole cover. Hurrying over, we shooed the cat away – cats aren't great lovers of vampires, and it hissed angrily at us before fleeing – and kicked the rubbish from the cover. Then Harkat and I pulled the cover off and laid it to one side.

"I'll go first," I said, starting down the ladder into the welcome darkness. "Mr Crepsley next. Harkat last."

They didn't question my orders. As a Vampire Prince, it was my place to take control. Mr Crepsley would have objected if he disagreed with my decision, but in the normal run of things he was satisfied to follow my command.

I climbed down the ladder. The rungs were cold and my fingers tingled from the contact. As I neared the bottom, I stretched out my left leg to step off the ladder—

—then snatched it back quickly when a gun fired and a bullet tore a chunk out of the wall close to the side of my shin!

Heart pounding, I clung to the ladder, ears ringing from the echoes of the bullet, wondering how the police got down here so quickly, and how they knew which way we'd take.

Then someone chuckled in the darkness and said, "Greetings, vampire. We've been expecting you."

My eyes narrowed. That was no policeman — it was a vampet! Despite the danger, I squatted low on the ladder and peered up the tunnel. There was a large man standing in the shadows, too far away for me to identify.

"Who are you?" I snapped.

"One who follows the Lord of the Vampaneze," he answered.

"What are you doing here?"

"Blocking your passage," he chuckled.

"How did you know we'd come this way?"

"We didn't. But we guessed you'd escape and make for the tunnels. Our Lord doesn't want you down here yet — the day is long, and it amuses him to think of you and your vampire friend struggling through it — so we've blocked off all entrances to the underworld. When night falls, we'll retreat, but until then these tunnels are off limits."

With that, he fired at me again. It was a warning shot, like the first, but I didn't stick around to test his aim any further. Climbing the ladder, I shot out of the manhole as though propelled, and cursed loudly as I kicked a large empty tin across the alley.

"Police?" Mr Crepsley asked sullenly.

"No — vampets. They've blocked off all entrances to the tunnels until nightfall. They want us to suffer."

"They can't have covered *every* … entrance, can they?" Harkat asked.

"Enough of them," Mr Crepsley responded. "The tunnels this close to the surface are carefully linked. By choosing the right spot, one man can block the paths of six or seven entrances. If we had time, we might find a way past, but we do not. We must abandon the tunnels."

"Where do we go instead?" I asked.

"We run," the vampire said simply. "Or hobble, as the case may be. We try to avoid the police, find somewhere to hole up, and wait for night."

"That won't be easy," I noted.

Mr Crepsley shrugged. "If you had held tight for sunset to make your break, it would have been easier. You did not, so we must make the best of things. Come," he said, turning his back on the manhole. "Let us make tracks."

I paused to spit bitterly down the hole, then took off after Mr Crepsley and Harkat, putting the disappointment of the blocked-off tunnels behind, focusing on the flight ahead.

Less than three minutes later, the police were hot on our trail.

We heard them spilling out of the station, shouting at each other, piling into cars, honking horns, turning blaring sirens on full. We'd been moving steadily but hadn't drifted far away from the station — we'd been avoiding main streets, sticking to back alleys, which had an annoying habit of doubling back on themselves. We'd have taken to the rooftops, except that would have meant exposing Mr Crepsley more fully to the rays of the sun.

"This is useless," the vampire said as we drew up beside a building overlooking a busy shopping street. "We are making no progress. We must ascend."

"But the sun..." I said.

"Forget it," he snapped. "If I burn, I burn. It will not kill me immediately — but the police will if they catch up!"

Nodding, I looked for a way up to the roofs. Then a thought struck. I gazed at the teeming street, then studied my clothes. I was dishevelled and dirty, but didn't look a whole lot worse than any average teenager going through a grunge or heavy metal phase.

"Have we money?" I asked, rubbing the worst of the dirt from my face and slicking back my hair with a handful of spit. Then I tucked the chains of the cuffs in under my shirt ends and trouser legs, masking them from view.

"The time he picks to go shopping!" Harkat groaned.

"I know what I'm doing," I grinned. "Have we money or not?"

"I had some notes, but the police took them," Mr Crepsley said. "I am … how do the humans put it … *skinned*?"

"*Skint*," I laughed. "No matter. I'll do without."

"Wait!" Harkat said as I started forward. "Where are you going? We can't split up … now. We must stay together."

"I won't be long," I said. "And I won't take any stupid chances. Wait here for me. If I'm not back in five minutes, leave without me and I'll catch up with you later, in the tunnels."

"Where are you—" Mr Crepsley began, but I didn't have time for a debate, so I slid out of the alley before he finished and walked swiftly along the street, looking for a minimarket.

I kept one eye peeled for police or soldiers, but there were none about. After a few seconds, I spotted a shop across the street, waited for the light to turn green, then strolled across and entered. A middle-aged woman and a young man with long hair were serving behind the counter. The shop was quite busy — there were six or seven customers — which was good. It meant I wouldn't stick out. A TV on the left of the doorway was tuned to a news channel, but the sound was down low. There was a security camera above the TV, scanning and recording, but that didn't bother me — with all the crimes I'd been charged with, I wasn't going to sweat about being booked for petty theft!

I walked slowly up and down the aisles, looking for sun-wear items. It wasn't the right time of year for sunglasses and sun hats, but I was sure they'd have a few knick-knacks lying around somewhere.

Next to a row of baby-care products, I found them — several bottles of suntan lotion, standing forlornly on a battered old shelf. The choice wasn't great, but they'd do. I quickly read the labels, looking for the strongest sun block I could find. Factor ten ... twelve ... fifteen. I chose the bottle with the highest number (it was for fair-skinned babies, but I wouldn't tell Mr Crepsley that!), then stood uncertainly with it in my hand, wondering what to do next.

I wasn't an experienced shoplifter. I'd stolen a few sweets with friends when I was very young, and once swiped a load of golf balls with a cousin of mine, but I'd never enjoyed it and hadn't taken it any further. I was sure my face would give me away if I just pocketed the bottle and tried walking straight out of the shop.

I thought about it for a few seconds, then slyly slipped the bottle inside the waist of my trousers, draped the hem of my shirt over it, grabbed another bottle, turned and marched up to the counter.

"Excuse me," I said to the female assistant as she was serving one of the other customers, "but do you have any

Sun Undone lotion?" I'd made the name up, and hoped there wasn't a real brand by that name available.

"Only what's on the shelves," the woman snapped irritably.

"Oh," I smiled. "That's OK. Thanks. I'll put this back."

I was turning when the young, long-haired man said, "Hey! Hold on!" Stomach sinking, I looked back questioningly, getting ready to run. "It wasn't Sunnydun you wanted, was it?" he asked. "We've got a crate of those somewhere in the back. I could get a bottle if you—"

"No," I interrupted, relaxing. "It was Sun Undone. My mum won't use anything else."

"Suit yourself," he shrugged, no longer interested, turning to deal with another customer.

I walked back to the shelf, laid the bottle on it, and made for the door as casually as I could. I nodded amiably at the young man as I was passing, and he half-waved at me in reply. I had one foot out the door, delighted with myself, when I caught sight of a familiar face on the TV and stopped, dumbstruck.

It was *me!*

The photograph must have been taken this morning, while I was being arrested. I looked pale, haggard and frightened, my hands cuffed, eyes wary, policemen on either side of me.

Stepping back into the store, I reached up and turned up the volume.

"Hey!" the male attendant grunted. "You can't..."

I ignored him and concentrated on what the newsreader was saying.

"—might look harmless, but police are urging the public not to be taken in by his appearance. Darren Shan — or Darren Horston, as he is also known — is a teenager, but he consorts with brutal killers, and may be a killer himself."

My photograph faded, to be replaced by a female newsreader with a grim expression. After a couple of seconds, my photo appeared again, smaller this time, in the upper right hand corner of the screen. Harkat's appeared to the left, and accurate artist's impressions of Mr Crepsley and Vancha March between us.

"To repeat our incredible breaking story," said the newsreader. "Three alleged members of the gang of killers known as the Vampires were cornered and apprehended by the police this morning. One, Vancha March—" the lines around the drawing of Vancha flashed "—escaped, taking Chief Inspector Alice Burgess hostage. The other two were detained for questioning, but made a violent break for freedom less than twenty minutes ago, killing or seriously wounding an unspecified number of officers and nurses. They are considered armed and exceedingly dangerous. If spotted, they should not be approached. Instead, call one of the following numbers..."

I turned away from the TV, stunned. I should have known the media would go into overdrive about a story this big, but I'd innocently assumed that we had only the police and army to worry about. I'd never stopped to think of city-wide alerts and how they'd affect us.

As I stood, digesting this new turn of events, brooding on the news that we'd been blamed for Steve's murders in the station, the middle-aged lady behind the counter pointed at me and gasped in a high voice, "It's him! The boy! The *killer!*"

Startled, I looked up and saw that every person in the shop was staring at me, their faces twisted with fear and horror.

"It's the one called Darren Shan!" a customer yelled. "They say he killed that girl, Tara Williams — that he drank her blood and ate her!"

"He's a vampire!" a wrinkly old man shrieked. "Someone get a stake! We have to kill him!"

That might have been funny if I'd seen it in a film — the thought of this little old man driving a stake through a vampire's hardened heart was ludicrous — but I hadn't time to see the funny side of things. Raising my hands to show I wasn't armed, I backed out of the door.

"Derek!" the female assistant shouted at the young man. "Grab the gun and shoot him!"

That was enough for me. Pivoting sharply, I dived out of the door and raced across the road, not stopping for traffic, darting out of the way of cars as they screeched to a halt, ignoring the drivers as they pounded on their horns and yelled abuse after me.

I came to a halt in the mouth of the alley, where a worried Harkat and Mr Crepsley were waiting. Digging out the bottle of suntan lotion, I tossed it to the vampire. "Spread that on yourself, quick," I gasped, bending over for breath.

"What—" he began to ask.

"Don't argue!" I shouted. "Do it!"

The vampire yanked the top off the bottle and poured half the contents out into his hands, then smeared it over his face and scalp and other exposed areas. He rubbed the lotion in, poured the rest out, rubbed that in too, then tossed the bottle away into the gutter.

"Done," he said.

"We certainly are," I muttered, standing up. "You're not going to believe—"

"There they are!" someone bellowed, cutting me short. "That's them — the Vampires!"

The three of us looked around and I saw the little old wrinkly man from the shop wrestling a large rifle from the long-haired attendant. "Give me that!" he shouted. "I hunted deer when I was younger!"

Tossing his walking stick to one side, the pensioner turned, lifted the rifle with remarkable speed, and fired.

We fell to the ground as the wall above our heads exploded into fragments. The old man fired again, even closer this time. But then he had to pause to reload. While he was doing that, we jumped to our feet, about-faced and fled, Mr Crepsley swinging his injured leg forward and backward like a demented Long John Silver.

The crowd behind us paused a moment, torn between fear and excitement. Then, with roars of rage, they grabbed sticks and iron bars and the lids off rubbish bins, and surged after us. No longer a mere crowd, but a bloodthirsty *mob*.

CHAPTER NINE

WE TORE ahead of the mob to begin with — humans can't match vampires or Little People for speed — but then Mr Crepsley's right ankle swelled up and his pace dropped steadily.

"No ... good," he gasped, as we stopped at a corner and rested. "Cannot ... continue. You must go ... on without me."

"No," I said instantly. "We're taking you with us."

"I cannot ... keep up," he snarled, teeth gritted against the pain.

"Then we'll stand and fight," I told him. "But we stick together. That's an order."

The vampire forced a weak smile. "Careful, Darren," he said. "You might be a Prince, but you are still my assistant. I can slap sense into you if I have to."

"That's why I have to keep you with me," I grinned.

"You stop me from getting a big head."

Mr Crepsley sighed and bent to rub the purple flesh around his ankle.

"Here!" Harkat said, and we looked up. The Little Person had pulled down the ladder of an overhead fire escape. "They'll find it hard to follow if ... we take to the roofs. We must go up."

Mr Crepsley nodded. "Harkat is correct."

"Will the lotion protect you from the sun?" I asked.

"From the worst of it," he said. "I will be red by sunset, but it should prevent severe burning."

"Then let's go!"

I was first up the ladder, Mr Crepsley next, Harkat last. The mob poured into the alley as Harkat was drawing his legs up, and those to the fore almost grabbed him. He had to kick hard at their hands to break free, then hurried up after us.

"Let me shoot!" the little old man with the rifle was shouting. "Out of my way! I can take them!" But there were too many people in the alley. It was packed tight and he couldn't raise his rifle to aim.

While the humans squabbled over who would get the ladder, we scrambled up the stairs. Mr Crepsley moved faster now that he had a railing to lean on for support. He winced as we moved out of the shadows and into direct sunlight, but didn't slow down.

I paused at the top of the fire escape and waited for Mr Crepsley. As I stood there, feeling more confident than I had a couple of minutes earlier, a helicopter dropped from the sky and someone yelled at me through a megaphone, "Stop where you are or we'll shoot!"

Cursing, I called down to Mr Crepsley, "Quick! We have to go now or—"

I got no further. Above, a marksman opened fire. The air around me whizzed with bullets, which zinged piercingly off the bars of the fire escape. Screaming wildly, I threw myself down the stairs and collided with Mr Crepsley and Harkat. If Mr Crepsley hadn't been holding on so tightly to the rail to ease the pressure on his injured ankle, we might all have gone over the side!

We hurried down a couple of flights, where the marksman couldn't see us, then huddled on a landing, frightened ... miserable ... *trapped*.

"They might have to leave ... to refuel," Harkat said hopefully.

"Sure," I snorted, "in an hour or two!"

"How are the humans below faring?" Mr Crepsley asked.

I stuck my head over the side and looked down. "The first few have made it to the top of the ladder. They'll be on us in a minute or less."

"We are in a good position to defend ourselves here," the vampire mused. "They will have to attack in small groups. We should be able to push them back."

"Sure," I snorted again, "but what good will that do? A few more minutes and the police and soldiers will arrive. It won't take them long to climb the building opposite and pick us off with their rifles."

"Damned above and damned below," Harkat said, wiping a few beads of green sweat from his round, bald head. "That leaves…" He pointed to the window behind us, leading into the building.

"Another trap," I complained. "All the police have to do is surround the building, enter in armed teams, flush us out — and we're finished."

"True," Mr Crepsley agreed thoughtfully, "but what if they have to fight to get in? And what if we are not there when they arrive?"

We stared at Mr Crepsley questioningly. "Follow me," he said, sliding the window open and crawling inside. "I have a plan!"

Turning our backs on the advancing humans beneath and the hovering helicopter above, Harkat and I dived through the window and into the hall, where Mr Crepsley was on his feet and calmly brushing flecks of dirt from his shirt, as though waiting for a bus on a slow Sunday morning.

"Ready?" he asked when we were standing beside him.

"Ready for *what*?" I replied, exasperated.

"Ready to set the cat among the pigeons," he laughed. Striding to the nearest door, he paused a moment, then slammed on it with the flat of his palm. "Vampires!" he bellowed. "Vampires in the building! Everybody out!"

He stepped away, faced us, and started counting. "One. Two. Three. Fo–"

The door burst open and a woman wearing a skimpy nightdress and no shoes raced out into the hallway, screeching and waving her hands above her head.

"Quick!" Mr Crepsley shouted, taking her arm and pointing her towards the stairs. "Head for the ground floor! We have to get out! We will die if we stay! The vampires are here!"

"Aiiieeee!" she screamed, then ran with astonishing speed for the stairs.

"See?" Mr Crepsley beamed.

"I see," I smirked.

"Me too," Harkat said.

"Then get busy," Mr Crepsley said, hopping to the next door, pounding upon it, roaring, "Vampires! Vampires! Beware the living dead!"

Harkat and I ran ahead of him, mimicking his knocks and cries, and within seconds the hallway was jammed with terrified humans, running about directionlessly, knocking one another over, almost flying down the stairs to safety.

As we reached the end of the corridor, I glanced over the railing of the stairway and saw those rushing down the stairs colliding with members of the mob, who'd stormed the building in an attempt to track us through it. Those fleeing couldn't get out, and those chasing us couldn't get in.

Wicked!

"Hurry," Harkat said, slapping my back. "They're coming in by the ... fire escape."

Looking back, I saw the first of our pursuers poking his head through the window. I turned left and raced up the next corridor with Harkat and Mr Crepsley, raising a false alarm, emptying the apartments of their human inhabitants, clogging the hallway behind us.

While the mob vanguard clashed with the panicked residents, we turned down another corridor, fled to a fire escape on the opposite side of the building, crawled out, and leapt across to the neighbouring block of apartments. We darted through this one, spreading the same warning message, banging on doors, yelling about vampires, causing havoc.

Making our way to the rear of the building, we jumped across to a third apartment block, and again set the humans running in fear for their lives. But when we got to the end of this one, we paused and gazed on the alley below and the sky overhead. There was no sign of the mob, and the helicopter was hovering over the two buildings behind us. We could hear police sirens closing in.

"Now is the time to lose ourselves," Mr Crepsley said. "The chaos behind us will last a handful of minutes at most. We must make good use of that time."

"Which way do we go?" I asked, scanning the surrounding buildings.

Mr Crepsley's eyes darted from one building to another, settling on a low-built structure to our right. "There," he pointed. "That looks deserted. We will try it and pray that the luck of the vampires is with us."

There was no fire escape where we were, so we hurried down the stairs at the back of the building and out into the alley. Sticking close to the walls, we crept to the building we'd set our sights on, broke a window to gain entry – no alarms sounded – and found ourselves in an old, abandoned factory.

We stumbled up a couple of floors, then ran as fast as we could to the back. There we discovered the shell of a decrepit apartment building due for demolition. Tearing through the lower floor, we emerged at the far side on to a maze of tight, dark, unpopulated alleys. We paused, ears open for sounds of pursuit. There weren't any.

We shared quick, shaky grins, then Harkat and I wrapped an arm around Mr Crepsley. He raised his painful right foot and we hobbled forward at a slower pace than before, enjoying our period of respite, but experienced enough to know that we weren't out of the frying pan yet. Not by a long shot.

Through the alleys we fled. We passed a few people, but none paid any attention to us — the afternoon was darkening with heavy clouds, casting the already gloomy alleys into pools of murky shadows. We could see clearly with our advanced eyesight, but to humans we appeared as nothing more than vaguely defined figures in the half-light.

Neither the mob nor the police followed. We could still hear the ruckus they were creating, but it hadn't moved on from the three apartment blocks we'd terrorized. For the time being, we were in the clear.

We stopped outside the back of a supermarket to catch our breath. Mr Crepsley's right leg was purple up to his knee now and he must have been in immense pain. "We need ice for that," I said. "I could slip into the supermarket and—"

"No!" the vampire barked. "You have already inspired one mob with your shopping antics. We can do very nicely without inciting another."

"I was only trying to help," I grumbled.

"I know," he sighed, "but reckless risks only make matters worse. My injury is not as serious as it looks. A few hours' rest and I will be fine."

"How about these bins?" Harkat asked, tapping a couple of large, black rubbish bins. "We could crawl inside and wait ... for night."

"No," I said. "People use bins like this all the time. We'd be discovered."

"Then where?" Harkat enquired.

"I don't know," I snapped. "Maybe we can find an empty apartment or an abandoned building. We could duck into Debbie's if we were close enough, but we're too far..."

I stopped, eyes settling on a street sign across from the supermarket. "Baker's Lane," I muttered, rubbing the bridge of my nose. "I know this place. We've been here before, when we were searching for the vampaneze killers, before we knew about R.V. and Steve."

"We travelled almost everywhere in our search for the killers," Mr Crepsley commented.

"Yes, but I remember this place because ... because..."

I frowned, and then it came to me and I snapped my fingers. "Because Richard lives close by!"

"Richard?" Mr Crepsley frowned. "Your friend from school?"

"Yes," I said, excited. "His house is only three or four minutes away."

"You think he'd shelter us?" Harkat asked.

"Maybe, if I explain things to him." The others looked uncertain. "Have you any better ideas?" I challenged them. "Richard's a friend. I trust him. The worst he can do is turn us away."

Mr Crepsley thought about it a moment, then nodded. "Very well. We will ask him for help. As you say, we have nothing to lose."

Leaving the supermarket, we struck for Richard's house, and this time I walked with a bounce in my step. I was sure Richard would help. After all, hadn't I saved him on the stairs at Mahler's?

We made it to Richard's in just over four minutes. Wasting no time, we climbed on to the roof and hid in the shadows of a large chimney. I'd seen a light in Richard's room from the ground, so once I was sure that Harkat and Mr Crepsley were settled, I crept to the edge of the roof and lowered myself over it.

"Wait," Mr Crepsley whispered, sliding up beside me. "I will come with you."

"No," I whispered back. "The sight of you might scare him. Let me go alone."

"Very well," he said, "but I will wait outside the window, in case you run into trouble."

I didn't see what sort of trouble I could run into, but Mr Crepsley had a stubborn look in his eyes, so I simply nodded and swung out over the roof, got a toehold, drove my fingernails into the stone of the wall, then climbed down to Richard's room like a spider.

The curtains were drawn, but not all the way, and I was able to see directly into my friend's bedroom. Richard was lying on his bed, a packet of popcorn and a glass of orange juice propped on his chest, watching a rerun of the *Addams Family* on a portable TV set.

Richard was laughing at the antics of the TV freaks, and I had to smile at how oddly fitting it was that he should be watching this when three real freaks of the night had just turned up. Fate has a strange sense of humour.

I thought about knocking on the window, but that might startle him. I studied the simple latch inside the glass, then pointed it out to Mr Crepsley (who'd scaled down the wall beside me) and raised my eyebrows in a silent question: "Can you open it?"

The vampire rubbed the thumb, index and middle fingers of his right hand together very, *very* swiftly. When he'd produced a strong static charge, he lowered his hand, pointed his fingers at the latch, and made a gentle uplifting motion.

Nothing happened.

The vampire frowned, leant forward for a closer look, then snorted. "It is made of plastic!" I turned aside to hide a smile. "No matter," Mr Crepsley said, and cut a small hole in the glass with the nail of his right index finger. It made only a tiny squeaking noise, which Richard didn't hear over the sound of the TV. Mr Crepsley popped the glass inwards, crooked the latch up with his finger, then swung out of the way and motioned me forward.

Taking a deep breath to steady myself, I pushed the window open and stepped into the room as casually as possible. "Hi, Richard," I said.

Richard's head jerked around. When he realized who it was, his jaw dropped and he began to quiver.

"It's OK," I said, taking a step closer to the bed, raising my hands in a gesture of friendship. "I'm not going to hurt you. I'm in trouble, Richard, and I need your help. I've a cheek to ask, but could you put me and a couple of my friends up for a few hours? We'll hide in the wardrobe or under the bed. We won't be any bother, honest."

"Vuh-vuh-vuh," Richard stuttered, eyes wide with terror.

"Richard?" I asked, concerned. "Are you OK?"

"Vuh-vuh-*vampire!*" he croaked, pointing a trembling finger at me.

"Oh," I said. "You've heard. Yes, I'm a half-vampire, but it's not what you think. I'm not evil or a killer. Let me call my friends, we'll get comfy, then I'll tell you all about—"

"*Vampire!*" Richard screamed, loudly this time, then turned to face the door of his room and bellowed at the top of his lungs: "Mum! Dad! Vampires! Vampires! Vampires! Vam—"

His cries were cut short by Mr Crepsley, who swung into the room, darted ahead of me, grabbed the boy by his throat, and breathed sharply over his face. Gas shot up Richard's nose and into his mouth. For a second he struggled, terrified. Then his features relaxed, his eyes closed, and he slumped back on the bed.

"Check the door!" Mr Crepsley hissed, rolling off the bed, crouching on the floor defensively.

I obeyed immediately, even though Richard's reaction had left me sick to my stomach. Opening the door a crack, I listened for sounds of Richard's family rushing to investigate his cry. They didn't come. The larger TV set in the living room was turned on and the noise must have masked Richard's shouts.

"It's OK," I said, closing the door. "We're safe."

"So much for friendship," Mr Crepsley snapped, brushing a few popcorn crumbs from his clothes.

"He was scared witless," I said miserably, staring down at Richard. "We were friends ... he knew me ... I saved his life ... and for all that, he still thought I was here to kill him."

"He believes you are a blood-crazed monster," Mr Crepsley said. "Humans do not understand vampires. His reaction was predictable. We would have anticipated it and left him alone if we had been thinking clearly."

Mr Crepsley turned slowly and examined the room.

"This would be a good place to hide," he said. "The boy's family will probably not bother him when they see that he is sleeping. There is plenty of space in the wardrobe. I think all three of us could fit."

"No," I said firmly. "I won't take advantage of him. If he'd offered his help — great. But he didn't. He was afraid of me. It'd be wrong to stay."

Mr Crepsley's expression showed what he thought of that, but he respected my wishes and made for the window without any argument. I was heading after him when I saw that during the brief struggle the popcorn had spilled over the bedsheets, and the glass of orange juice had been knocked over. Stopping to shovel the popcorn back into its packet, I found a box of tissues, ripped several free and used them to mop up the worst of the orange juice. I made sure Richard was OK, set the TV to stand-by, bid my friend a silent goodbye, and left quietly, to run once again from the misguided humans who wished to kill me.

CHAPTER TEN

WE TOOK to the rooftops. There were no helicopters nearby, and the shadows of the gloomy afternoon masked us from general view, so it seemed safer to carry on up high, where we could make good time.

Moving carefully but quickly, we aimed for areas far beyond the chaos behind us, where we could hole up until night. For fifteen minutes we leapt and slid from one rooftop to another, unseen by anyone, getting further and further away from the humans who were hunting us.

Finally, we came to a crumbling old silo — a building in which grain was once stored. A spiral staircase still ran up the outside, though the lowest section had rotted and crumbled away. Leaping on to the upper half of the stairs from a roof, we climbed to the top, kicked down the locked door and let ourselves in.

Closing the door, we edged further into the silo along

a narrow ledge, until we reached a semi-circular platform, where we lay down. There were holes and cracks in the roof overhead and the dim light was strong enough for us to see by.

"Do you think we'll be ... safe here?" Harkat asked, lowering his mask. Streams of green sweat were flooding the scars and stitches of his grey face.

"Yes," Mr Crepsley said confidently. "They will have to organize a complete search. They dare leave no stone unturned. That will slow them down. It will be morning or later before they make it this far across the city." The vampire shut his eyes and massaged his eyelids. Even doused in suntan lotion, his skin had turned a dark pink colour.

"How are you bearing up?" I asked.

"Better than I dared hope," he said, still rubbing his eyelids. "I have the start of an excruciating headache, but now that I am out of the sunlight, perhaps it will subside." He lowered his fingers, opened his eyes, stretched his right leg out and stared grimly at the swollen flesh rising from his ankle to his knee. He'd taken his shoes off earlier, which was a good thing, as I doubt he'd have been able to pry the right shoe loose now. "I only hope *that* subsides too," he muttered.

"Do you think it will?" I asked, studying the ugly bruise.

"Hopefully," he said, rubbing his lower leg gingerly. "If not, we may have to bleed it."

"You mean cut into it to let the blood out?" I asked.

"Yes," he said. "Desperate times call for desperate measures. But we will wait and see — with luck it will improve of its own accord."

While Mr Crepsley was tending to his ankle, I unwrapped the chains around my wrists and legs and tried picking the locks. Mr Crepsley had taught me the fundamentals of lock-picking, but I'd never quite got the knack of it.

"Here," he said after a couple of minutes, when he saw I wasn't getting anywhere.

The vampire made quick work of the locks, and seconds later the cuffs and chains were lying in heaps on the floor. I rubbed my freed flesh gratefully, then glanced at Harkat, who was using the hem of his robes to wipe green sweat from his face. "How come they didn't put handcuffs on you?" I asked.

"They did," he replied, "but they took them off ... once I was inside my cell."

"Why?"

The Little Person's wide mouth split into a hideous smirk. "They didn't know what I was or ... what to make of me. They asked if I was in ... pain, so I said I was. They asked if the handcuffs ... hurt, so I said they did. So they took them off."

"Just like that?" I asked.

"Yes," he chuckled.

"Lucky beggar," I sniffed.

"Looking like something Dr Frankenstein ... threw

together has its advantages sometimes," Harkat informed me. "That's also why I was … alone. I could see they were uneasy … around me, so shortly after they began interviewing … me, I told them not to touch me — said I had an … infectious disease. You should have seen them … run!"

All three of us laughed aloud.

"You should've told them you were a resurrected corpse," I chuckled. "That would have put their minds at rest!"

We relaxed after that and lay back against the wall of the silo, saying little, eyes half-closed, ruminating on the day's events and the night to come. I was thirsty, so after a while I climbed down the interior stairs and went looking for water. I didn't find any, but I did find a few cans of beans on a shelf in one of the front offices. Carrying them up, I cut them open with my nails and Mr Crepsley and I tucked in. Harkat wasn't hungry — he could go for days on end without food if he had to.

The beans settled nicely in my stomach – cold as they were — and I lay back for an hour, quiet and thoughtful. We weren't in any rush. We had until midnight to rendezvous with Vancha (assuming he made it) and it would take us no more than a couple of hours to march through the tunnels to the cavern where we'd fought the vampaneze.

"Do you think Steve escaped?" I asked eventually.

"I am sure of it," Mr Crepsley replied. "That one has

the luck of a demon, and the cunning to match."

"He killed people — police and nurses — while he was escaping," I said.

Mr Crepsley sighed. "I did not think he would attack those who helped him. I would have killed him before we were taken into custody if I had known what he was planning."

"How do you think he got to be so vicious?" I asked. "He wasn't like this when I knew him."

"Yes, he was," Mr Crepsley disagreed. "He just had not grown into his true evil self yet. He was born bad, as certain people are. Humans will tell you that everybody can be helped, that everyone has a choice. In my experience, that is not so. Good people can sometimes choose badness, but bad people cannot choose good."

"I don't believe that," Harkat said softly. "I think good and evil exist ... in all of us. We might be born leaning more towards ... one than the other, but the choice is there. It *has* to be. Otherwise, we're mere ... puppets of fate."

"Perhaps," Mr Crepsley grunted. "Many see it as you do. But I do not think so. Most are born with the freedom of choice. But there are those who defy the rules, who are wicked from the beginning. Maybe they *are* puppets of fate, born that way for a reason, to test the rest of us. I do not know. But natural monsters do exist. On that point, nothing you say can shake me. And Steve Leonard is one of them."

"But then it isn't his fault," I said, frowning. "If he was born bad, he isn't to blame for growing up evil."

"No more than a lion is to blame for being a predator," Mr Crepsley agreed.

I thought about that. "If that's the case, we shouldn't hate him — we should pity him."

Mr Crepsley shook his head. "No, Darren. You should neither hate nor pity a monster — merely fear it, and do all in your power to make an end of it before it destroys you." Leaning forward, he rapped on the hard platform with his knuckles. "But remember," he said sternly. "When we venture down the tunnels tonight, Steve Leonard is not our primary enemy — the Lord of the Vampaneze is. If the chance to kill Leonard arises, by all means seize it. But if you have to choose between him and the Lord he serves, strike first for the latter. We must put our personal feelings aside and focus on our mission."

Harkat and I nodded in agreement with the vampire, but he wasn't finished. Pointing at me with a long, bony finger, he said, "That also applies to Miss Hemlock."

"What do you mean?" I asked.

"The vampaneze might taunt you with her," he said. "We know they cannot kill us — only their Lord dare cut us down. So they may try to split us up, making it easier for them to capture us. It will hurt, but you must put all thoughts of Debbie aside until the quest to kill the Vampaneze Lord has been settled."

"I don't know if I can do that," I said, eyes downcast.

Mr Crepsley stared hard at me, then dropped his gaze. "You are a Prince," he said quietly. "I cannot command you. If your heart leads you to Debbie, and it proves impossible to resist its call, you must follow. But I ask you to remember the vampires you serve, and what will happen to our clan if we fail."

I nodded soberly. "I haven't forgotten. I'm just not sure, in the heat of the moment, if I'll be able to abandon her."

"But you know that you should?" he pressed. "You understand how important your choice is?"

"Yes," I whispered.

"That is enough," he said. "I trust you to make the right choice."

I cocked an eyebrow. "You sound more like Seba Nile with every passing year," I commented dryly. Seba was the vampire who'd taught Mr Crepsley the ways of the clan.

"I will take that as a compliment," he smiled, then lay back, closed his eyes, and rested in silence, leaving me to think about Debbie and the Lord of the Vampaneze, and contemplate the desperate choice I might be called upon to make.

CHAPTER ELEVEN

MR CREPSLEY'S ankle had improved vastly by the time we left the silo to face our destiny. His flesh was still a nasty shade of purple, but the worst of the swelling had died down. He tested the ankle as little as possible during our trek through the tunnels, but was able to stand unassisted when he had to.

There was no fuss about our descent into the menacing darkness. When the time came, we simply walked down the stairs of the silo, broke out through a boarded-up door, found a manhole, slipped beneath the streets and advanced. We didn't encounter any vampaneze or traps.

We said nothing during the journey. Each of us knew how serious this was, and the odds stacked against us. Victory was unlikely, and even if it came, escape seemed impossible. If we managed to kill the Lord of the Vampaneze, his followers would surely cut us down in revenge, their hands no longer tied by the prophecies of Mr Tiny. We were marching to our doom, and tongues have a tendency to seize up at such times, regardless of how brave you might be.

After a long, uneventful journey, we reached the newly built tunnels, dry and warm in comparison to the older links, and from there it was only a short walk to the cavern where we'd faced the vampaneze less than twenty-four hours ago.

Twenty-four hours... It felt like years!

Several burning candles were set in nooks around the walls, and their light revealed an apparently deserted cavern. The bodies of the vampaneze we'd killed the night before had been dragged away, though drying pools of their blood remained. The huge door at the other side of the cavern was closed.

"Tread carefully," Mr Crepsley said, pausing at the entrance. "Hold your weapons low and—"

He stopped abruptly and his face fell. Clearing his throat, he said in a surprisingly meek voice, "Did either of you bring a weapon?"

"Of course—" I began, then stopped as suddenly as Mr Crepsley had, my hand flying to my waist, where my sword would normally be nesting. But not now. I'd abandoned it when I was arrested, and with all that had happened since then, it had never occurred to me to replace it.

"Um ... you're not going to believe this..." I mumbled.

"You forgot too?" Mr Crepsley groaned.

We looked appealingly at Harkat.

The Little Person shook his neckless grey head. "Sorry."

"Brilliant!" Mr Crepsley snapped. "The most important fight of our lives, and we come unarmed. What manner of fools are we?"

"The greatest who ever stalked the shadows of the night," said someone from within the cavern.

Freezing, we stared into the gloom, our fingers twitching helplessly by our sides. Then a head popped into view from above the doorway and our hearts sank back in our chests. "*Vancha!*" we cheered.

"The one and only," grinned the Prince. He swung around from where he'd been hanging from the ceiling. Landing on his feet, he turned to greet us. Harkat and I hurried forward and embraced the scruffy, smelly man with the dyed green hair and animal hides. Vancha's huge eyes widened with surprise. Then his small mouth split into a smile. "Sappy idiots," he chuckled, hugging us back. He stuck his arms out to Mr Crepsley. "Haven't *you* got a hug for me, Larten, old buddy?" he croaked.

"You know where you can insert your hug," Mr Crepsley retorted.

"Oh, the ingratitude," Vancha moaned, then let us go and took a step back, beckoning us forward into the cavern. "Is it true what I overheard?" he asked. "You came without weapons?"

"We have had a difficult afternoon," Mr Crepsley sniffed, ears reddening.

"It must have been the most bloody awful afternoon in history if you forgot to come armed to the scrap of the century," Vancha chuckled, then grew serious. "Did you get away OK? Any unpleasantness?"

"Our breakout was relatively easy," Mr Crepsley said. "There were some sticky moments along the way – it has been a long time since I had to flee a wrathful mob – but all things considered, we fared rather splendidly. Our captors, however, were not so fortunate…"

He told Vancha about Steve and the guards and nurses he'd killed. Vancha's red face – he'd been engaged in a private duel with the sun for many decades – darkened when he heard the news. "That one is aptly nicknamed," he growled. "If ever a human was bonded at the soul with a leopard, it's him. I just pray to the gods that I have a chance to slit his throat tonight."

"You'll have to get in line," I said. Nobody laughed — they knew I wasn't joking.

"Anyway," Vancha boomed, "one point of order at a time. I don't mind taking the vampaneze on empty-handed – it's my preferred method of fighting – but you three will need more than your fists and feet if we're to stand any chance of getting out of this alive. Luckily, Uncle Vancha has been busy. Follow me."

Vancha led us to one of the darker corners of the cavern, where a small pile of weapons lay stacked next to a large, motionless figure.

"Where did you get these?" Harkat asked, jumping on the

weapons before Mr Crepsley and I had a chance. Rooting through them, he found a jagged knife and a small double-headed axe, which he swung over his head, delighted.

"The vampaneze left them when they were clearing their dead away," Vancha explained. "I imagine they assumed we'd come armed. If they knew how empty-headed you lot were, they'd have taken more care."

Ignoring the Prince's jibes, Mr Crepsley and I picked through the pile. He took a couple of long knives and a few shorter ones for throwing. I found a small curved sword I liked the feel of. I tucked a knife into the back of my trousers, for back-up, and then I was ready.

"What's that?" Harkat asked, nodding at the large figure on the ground.

"My guest," Vancha said, and rolled the figure over.

The pale white face of a bound, gagged, enraged Chief Inspector Alice Burgess came into view. "Urfl guffle snurf!" she shouted into the folds of her gag, and I'm certain she wasn't saying hello or wishing us well!

"What's she doing here?" I snapped.

"She was company for me," Vancha smirked. "Besides, I didn't know what to expect when I returned. If the police had taken to the tunnels and sewers, I might have needed her to trade my way past."

"What do you plan to do with her now?" Mr Crepsley asked coolly.

"I'm not sure," Vancha frowned, crouching to study the Chief Inspector. "I tried explaining things to her while we were passing the day away in a forest a few miles outside the city, but I don't think she believed me. In fact, by what she told me to do with my tales of vampires and vampaneze, I *know* she didn't!" The Prince paused. "Having said that, she'd be a great one to have on our side. We may have need of an extra pair of hands in the battle ahead."

"Could we trust her?" I asked.

"I don't know," Vancha said. "But there's one way to find out."

Vancha started to undo the knots of the Chief Inspector's gag. He stopped on the final knot and addressed her sternly. "I'm only going to say this once, so pay attention. I'm sure your first impulse when I free you will be to scream and curse and tell us what trouble we're in. And when you're on your feet, weapon in hand, you might feel like taking a stab at us and setting off by yourself.

"*Don't!*" His eyes were grim. "I know what you think of us, but you're wrong. We didn't kill your people. We're out to stop the killers. If you want to put an end to the torment, come with us and fight. You've nothing to gain by attacking us. Even if you don't believe that, act as if you do. Otherwise, I'll leave you here, trussed up like a turkey."

"Animal!" the Chief Inspector spat, as Vancha removed her gag. "I'll see you hang for this, all of you. I'll have you shaved bald, smeared with tar, covered with feathers, then set alight as you dangle!"

"Isn't she magnificent?" Vancha beamed, freeing her legs and arms. "She's been like that all afternoon. I think I'm falling in love."

"Savage!" she shouted, and struck out at him.

Vancha caught her arm and held it in mid air, his expression grave. "Remember what I said, Alice? I don't want to leave you here, at the mercy of our enemies, but I will if you force me to."

The Chief Inspector glared at him, then turned her head aside, disgusted, and held her tongue.

"Better," Vancha said, letting go. "Now, pick a weapon — two or three if you'd prefer — and get ready. We've an army of darkness to deal with."

The Chief Inspector gazed around at us uncertainly. "You guys are crazy," she muttered. "You really expect me to believe you're vampires, but not killers? That you're here to take on a bunch of ... what did you call them?"

"Vampaneze," Vancha said cheerfully.

"That these vampaneze are the bad guys and you're here to sort them out, even though there's dozens of them and only four of you?"

"That's about the sum of it," Vancha smirked, "except there's five of us now, which should make all the difference."

"Crazy," she growled, but bent and picked up a long hunting knife, tested it, and gathered together another few knives. "OK," she said, standing. "I don't believe your story, but I'll tag along for the time being. If we run into these vampaneze, and they're all that you say, I'll throw my lot in with you. If we don't…" She pointed at Vancha's throat with the largest of her knives and jerked it sharply to one side.

"I love it when you talk threateningly," Vancha laughed, then checked that we were all prepared, pulled his belts of shurikens tight around his chest, and led us forward in search of the vampaneze lair.

CHAPTER TWELVE

WE DIDN'T get very far before running into our first obstacle. The huge door leading out of the cavern was bolted shut and wouldn't open. It was the type of door you find on walk-in safes in banks. There was a long row of combination locks running across the middle, beneath a circular handle.

"I wrestled with this for more than an hour," Vancha said, tapping the row of small lock windows. "Couldn't make head nor tail of it."

"Let me have a look," Mr Crepsley said, stepping forward. "I am not adept at locks such as these, but I have broken into safes before. I may be able to…" He trailed off, studied the locks a minute, then cursed foully and kicked the door.

"Something wrong?" I asked lightly.

"We cannot go this way," he snapped. "It is too intricately coded. We must find a way around."

"Easier said than done," Vancha replied. "I've scoured the cavern for hidden passages and tunnels — didn't find any. This place has been purpose-built. I think this is the only way ahead."

"What about the ceiling?" I asked. "The vampaneze came that way the last time we were down here."

"There are removable panels in the roof of the cavern," Vancha said, "but the space above them is only accessible from down here, not through the tunnel."

"Couldn't we break through the wall … around the door?" Harkat asked.

"I tried," Vancha said, nodding at a hole he'd punched out a few metres to our left. "It's steel-lined. *Thick* steel. Even vampires have their limits."

"This doesn't make sense," I grumbled. "They knew we'd come. They *want* us to come. Why strand us here? There must be a way through." I knelt and examined the rows of tiny windows, each of which contained two numbers. "Explain this lock to me," I said to Mr Crepsley.

"It is a combination lock. Quite straightforward. The dials are down there." He pointed to a series of thin dials beneath the windows. "You twist them clockwise for a higher number, anti-clockwise for a lower number. When the correct numbers have been entered in all fifteen windows, the door will open."

"And each number's different?" I asked.

"I assume so." He sighed. "Fifteen different locks,

fifteen different numbers. I could crack the code eventually, but it would take several nights and days."

"It doesn't make sense," I said again, staring at the meaningless numbers in the windows. "Steve helped design this trap. He wouldn't have built something we couldn't get past. There must be..." I stopped. The last three windows were blank. I pointed them out to Mr Crepsley and asked why.

"They must not form part of the code," he said.

"So we've only twelve numbers to worry about?"

He smiled ruefully. "That should save us half a night or so."

"Why twelve?" I thought aloud, then closed my eyes and tried to think as Steve might (not a pleasant experience!). He'd exercised great patience in tricking us and setting us up for a fall, but now that we were close to the end, I couldn't picture him placing a boulder in our path which would take a week to remove. He'd be eager to get at us. The code he picked must be one we'd be able to crack pretty quickly, so it had to be simple, something which looked impossible, but in reality was as plain as...

I groaned, then began counting. "Try these numbers as I call them out," I said to Mr Crepsley, eyes still closed. "Nineteen ... Twenty ... Five..."

I carried on until I got to "Eighteen ... Four." I stopped and opened my eyes. Mr Crepsley spun the last counter anti-clockwise to four. There was a click and the circular handle popped out. Startled, the vampire grabbed it and twisted. It turned easily at his touch and the round door swung open.

Mr Crepsley, Harkat and Vancha stared at me, awed.

"How…?" Vancha gasped.

"Oh, please!" Alice Burgess snorted. "Isn't it obvious? He just converted the alphabet into numbers, starting with one and finishing with twenty-six. It's the most simplistic code in operation. A child could work it out."

"Oh," Harkat said. "I get it now. A was 1, B was … 2, and so on."

"Right," I smiled. "Using that code, I dialled in 'Steve Leopard'. I knew it had to be something easy like that."

"Isn't education wonderful, Larten?" Vancha smirked. "We'll have to attend night classes when this is over."

"Quiet!" Mr Crepsley snapped, not amused. He was gazing into the darkness of the tunnel beyond. "Remember where we are and who we are facing."

"You can't talk to a Prince like that," Vancha grumbled, but straightened up and focused on the stretch of tunnel ahead. "Get in line," he said, moving to take the lead. "I'll go first, Harkat second, Alice in the middle, Darren behind, Larten at the rear."

Nobody argued with him. Though I was of equal rank, Vancha was far more experienced, and there was no doubt as to who was in charge.

Entering the tunnel, we advanced. Though the ceiling wasn't high, the tunnel was wide, and we were able to walk quite comfortably. Torches were set in the walls at regular intervals. I looked for tunnels leading off this one, but couldn't see any. We pressed on straight ahead.

We'd gone maybe forty metres when a sharp, clanging noise behind made us jump. Turning swiftly, we saw someone standing by the door we'd just come through. When he stepped forward into the light of the closest torch, hooks held up above his head, we knew instantly who it was — *R.V.!*

"Lady and gentlemen!" he boomed. "Welcome! The proprietors of the Cavern of Retribution wish you well and hope you enjoy your stay. If you've any complaints, please don't hesitate to—"

"Where's Debbie, you monster?" I screamed, trying to shove past Mr Crepsley. The vampire held me back with a firm arm and shook his head tautly.

"Remember what we discussed in the silo," he hissed.

I struggled a moment, then stepped back and glared at the insane vampaneze, who was jumping about from foot to foot, laughing crazily.

"Where is she?" I snarled.

"Not far from here," he chuckled, his voice carrying in the close confines of the tunnel. "Quite close as the crow flies. Closer still as the crow *dies*."

"That's a lousy pun," Harkat shouted.

"I ain't a poet but I don't know it," R.V. tossed back in reply. Then he stopped dancing and stared at us coldly. "Debbie's close, man," he hissed. "And she's alive. But she won't be much longer, not if you don't come with me now,

Shan. Leave your rotten friends and surrender yourself to me — I'll let her go. Stay with them and pursue your hateful quest — I'll kill her!"

"If you do..." I growled.

"What?" he jeered. "You'll kill me too? You'll have to catch me first, Shanny boy, and that's a lot easier said than done. R.V.'s quick on his feet, yes indeedy, quick as a gazelle."

"He sounds so much like Murlough," Mr Crepsley whispered, referring to a mad vampaneze we'd killed many years earlier. "It is as if his spirit has survived and found a home inside R.V."

I'd no time to worry about spirits of the past. As I thought over the offer, R.V. darted to a hole on his left – it had been covered by a panel when we passed it – ducked into it, then stuck his head out, grinning wildly. "How about it, Shanny? Your life for Debbie's. Is it a deal or do I make her squeal?"

This was my moment of truth. I'd have given my life gladly if it meant sparing Debbie's. But if the Lord of the Vampaneze got the better of us, he'd lead his people to victory over the vampires. My duty was to those who'd placed their faith in me. I had more than myself to think about. And though it pained me intensely, I lowered my head in response to R.V.'s offer and said softly, "No."

"What was that?" R.V. shouted. "Speak up — I can't hear you."

"*NO!*" I roared, whipping out my knife and launching it at him, although I knew I couldn't hit him from where I was standing.

R.V.'s face twisted with hate. "Cretin!" he snarled. "The others said you wouldn't trade for her, but I was sure you would. Very well. Have it your way, man. It's Debbie stew for breakfast!"

Laughing at me, he withdrew and slammed the panel shut on the passageway. I wanted to run after him, pound on the panel and scream for him to bring Debbie back. But I knew he wouldn't, so I restrained myself — just.

"You did well, Darren," Mr Crepsley said, laying a hand on my shoulder.

"I did what had to be done," I sighed, taking no pleasure from his compliment.

"Was that one of those vampaneze you've been talking about?" Burgess asked, visibly shaken.

"That's one of our ruby-lipped boys, sure enough," Vancha replied chirpily.

"Are they all like that?" she asked, eyes wide, white hair frizzy with fright.

"Oh, no," Vancha said, faking an innocent look. "Most are far worse!"

Then the Prince winked, faced front, and moved on, leading us further down the throat-like tunnel, into the stomach of the vampaneze's monstrous trap, where destiny and death were lying in wait.

CHAPTER THIRTEEN

THE TUNNEL ran straight and downwards for five or six hundred metres, before opening out on to a huge, man-made cavern with smooth walls and an extremely high ceiling. Three heavy silver chandeliers hung from the ceiling, each adorned with dozens of thick, red, burning candles.

As we entered the cavern I saw that it was oval in shape, wide across the middle, narrowing at either end. There was a platform set close in front of the wall across from us, suspended on sturdy steel pillars, fifteen metres high. We drifted towards it, weapons poised, spreading out to form an orderly line, Vancha slightly in front, his eyes flicking left, right, upwards, searching for vampaneze.

"Hold it," Vancha said as we approached the platform. We stopped instantly. I thought he'd seen a vampaneze, but he was gazing down at the ground, puzzled but not alarmed. "Have a look at this," he murmured, beckoning us forward.

Stepping up beside him, I felt my insides turn to ice. We were standing on the edge of a pit – oval like the cavern – which was filled with steel-tipped stakes two or three metres tall. It reminded me of the pit in the Hall of Death in Vampire Mountain, only this was much bigger.

"A trap for us to fall ... into?" Harkat asked.

"I doubt it," Vancha said. "The vampaneze would have covered it over if they wanted us to walk into it." He looked up. The platform was built directly over the pit, the support pillars rising from among the stakes. Now that we were close, we could see a long plank connecting the rear right of the platform to a hole in the wall behind it. There was also a thick rope running from the front left side of the platform to our side of the pit, where it was tied to a large holding stake.

"Looks like that's the only way forward," I noted, not liking the set-up one little bit.

"We could skirt the pit and climb the wall," Mr Crepsley suggested.

Vancha shook his head. "Look again," he said.

I peered closely at the wall, as did Mr Crepsley. He saw what we were looking for just before I did and growled something foul beneath his breath.

"What is it?" Harkat asked, his round green eyes not as sharp as ours.

"There are scores of tiny holes in the wall," I said. "Ideal for firing darts or bullets through."

"They'd cut us down in seconds if we tried climbing it," Vancha said.

"That's dumb," Chief Inspector Burgess muttered. We looked back at her. "Why lay a trap here and not in the tunnel?" she asked. "The walls of the tunnel could have been peppered with holes like that one. We had nowhere to turn, nowhere to run. We were sitting ducks. Why leave it till now?"

"Because it isn't a trap," Vancha told her. "It's a warning. They don't want us going that way. They want us to use the platform."

The police chief frowned. "I thought they wanted to kill you."

"They do," Vancha said, "but they want to play with us first."

"Dumb," she muttered again, clutching her knife close to her chest, turning slowly to survey the whole of the cavern, as though she expected demons to dart from the walls and floor.

"You smell that?" Mr Crepsley asked, his nose wrinkling.

"Petrol," I nodded. "It's coming from the pit."

"Perhaps we should move back," Vancha suggested, and we quickly withdrew without need of further prompting.

We examined the rope tethered to the stake. It was thickly woven and taut, professionally tied. Vancha tested it by crawling a few metres along, while we stood with our weapons drawn, covering him.

The Prince looked thoughtful when he returned. "It's strong," he said. "I think it would support all of us at the same time. But we won't chance it. We'll cross one at a time, the same order as we came through the tunnel."

"What about the platform?" Harkat asked. "It could be rigged to … collapse when we are on it."

Vancha nodded. "When I get up, I'll hurry to the opening across the plank. Don't come up until I'm safe. When you do, make straight for the tunnel. The same goes for the rest of you. If they take the platform down while we're crossing, only one of us will die."

"Great," the Chief Inspector snorted. "So I've a one in five chance of making it across alive."

"Those are good odds," Vancha said. "Much better than those we'll be facing when the vampaneze make their move."

Vancha made sure his shurikens were strapped tight, grabbed hold of the rope, shimmied up it a few metres, then swung over on to his back, so he was hanging upside-down. He started across, hand over hand, foot over foot. The rope cut up at a steep angle, but the Prince was strong and his pace didn't falter.

He was almost halfway across, dangling over the pit of deadly stakes, when a figure appeared in the mouth of the tunnel. Burgess spotted it first. "Hey!" she shouted, raising a hand to point. "Someone's up there!"

Our eyes — and Vancha's — snapped to the tunnel entrance. The light was poor, and it was impossible to tell if the figure was big or small, male or female. Then it stepped forward on to the plank and the mystery was solved.

"*Steve!*" I hissed, eyes filling with hatred.

"Howdy, boys!" the half-vampaneze boomed, striding across the plank, not in the least bit afraid of falling and impaling himself on the stakes beneath. "Find your way here OK? I was expecting you ages ago. Thought you might have got lost. I was preparing a search party to send after you."

Steve reached the platform and walked to the waist-high railing which ran around the sides. He peered down at Vancha and beamed as though welcoming an old friend. "We meet again, Mr March," he chuckled, waving sarcastically.

Vancha snarled like an animal and began crawling faster than before. Steve watched, amused, then reached into a pocket, produced a match and held it up for our eyes to fix on. He winked, bent and struck the match on the floor of the platform. He cupped it close to his face a moment, while it flared into life, then casually tossed it over the railing — into the petrol-soaked pit.

There was an explosive roar which almost burst my ear drums. Flames shot up out of the pit like huge, fiery fingers. They billowed over the edges of the platform, but didn't threaten Steve — he laughed through the red and yellow wall of fire. The flames scorched the roof and wall to the rear — and completely consumed the rope and Vancha, swallowing the Prince whole in the blink of a flame-filled eye.

CHAPTER FOURTEEN

I DARTED forward impulsively when I saw Vancha disappear amidst the flames, but was quickly forced back by the waves of fire which rolled down towards me. As they broke upon the floor of the cavern, or spat themselves out in the air above our heads, the sound of Steve Leopard's laughter filled my ears. Shielding my eyes with my hands, I glanced up at the platform and saw him leaping about, a heavy sword held high above his head, cheering and whooping with wicked glee. "Bye-bye, Vancha!" he hollered. "So long, Mr March! Adios, Princey! Farewell, vam—"

"Don't write my death-notices yet, Leonard!" a voice roared from within the blanket of fire, and as Steve's face dropped, the flames died down slightly, revealing a singed, blackened, but very much alive Vancha March, hanging by one hand from the rope, furiously slapping out flames in his hair and animal hides with the other.

"Vancha!" I yelled, delighted. "You're alive!"

"Of course I am," he replied, grinning painfully as he extinguished the last of the flames.

"You're a tough old badger, aren't you?" Steve remarked sourly, glaring down at the Prince.

"Aye," Vancha growled, a gleam in his eye. "And you haven't seen anything yet — just wait till I get my hands on your scrawny, evil neck!"

"I'm *soooo* scared," Steve snorted. Then, as Vancha began climbing again, he hurried to the end of the platform where the rope was tied and tapped it with his sword. "No you don't," he chortled. "One more centimetre and I'll send you crashing to your doom."

Vancha stopped and studied Steve and the stretch of rope left to cross, calculating the odds. Steve chuckled dryly. "Come off it, March. Even an oaf like you knows when he's beaten. I don't want to cut this rope — not yet — but if I set my mind to it, there's nothing you can do to stop me."

"We'll see about that," Vancha growled, then ripped a throwing star loose and sent it flying at the half-vampaneze.

Steve didn't flinch as the shuriken buried itself harmlessly in the underbelly of the steel platform. "The angle isn't right," he yawned, unimpressed. "You can't hit me from there, no matter how fine a shot you are. Now, will you slide down and join your friends on the ground, or do I have to get nasty?"

Vancha spat at Steve — his spit falling long short of its target — then tucked his arms and legs around the rope and quickly slid over the heads of the flames, away from the platform, to where we were waiting.

"Wise move," Steve said as Vancha steadied himself on his feet and we checked his back and hair for smouldering embers.

"If I had a gun," Burgess muttered, "I could take that wiseass out."

"You're starting to see things from our point of view," Vancha noted wryly.

"I'm still undecided about you lot," the Chief Inspector replied, "but I know out-and-out evil when I see it."

"Now then," Steve announced loudly, "if we're all good and ready, let's get this show on the road." Sticking two fingers between his lips, he whistled loudly three times. Above us, panels in the ceiling were ripped free, and vampaneze and vampets descended on ropes. Similar panels were removed in the walls of the cavern and more of our enemies stepped through and advanced. I counted twenty … thirty … forty … more. Most were armed with swords, axes and clubs, but a few of the vampets carried rifles, handguns and crossbows.

We backed up to the edge of the pit as the vampaneze and vampets closed on us, so they couldn't attack us from behind. We stared at the ranks of grim-faced soldiers, counting silently, hopes fading as we realized how hopelessly overwhelmed we were.

Vancha cleared his throat. "I make it about ten or twelve for each of us," he commented. "Does anybody have any favourites, or will we divide them up at random?"

"You can take as many as you want," I said, spotting a familiar face in the middle of the crowd to my left, "but leave that guy over there for me."

Chief Inspector Burgess gasped when she saw who I was pointing at. "*Morgan James?*"

"Evening, ma'am," the sharp-eyed policeman/vampet saluted her mockingly. He'd changed out of his uniform. He was now wearing the brown shirt and black trousers of the vampets, and he'd daubed red circles of blood around his eyes.

"Morgan's one of *them?*" the Chief Inspector asked, shocked.

"Yes," I said. "He helped me escape. He knew that Steve would murder his colleagues — and he let him."

Her face darkened. "Shan," she growled, "if you want him, you'll have to fight me for him — that bastard's *mine!*"

I turned to argue with her, saw the fierce glow in her eyes, and relented with a nod.

The vampaneze and vampets stopped about three metres short of us and stood, swinging their weapons, eyes alert, awaiting the order to attack. On the platform, Steve grunted happily, then clapped his hands. Out of the corner of my eye I saw somebody appear in the mouth of the tunnel behind us. Glancing over my shoulder, I realized two people had emerged and were crossing the plank to the platform. Both were familiar — Gannen Harst and the Lord of the Vampaneze!

"Look!" I hissed at my companions.

Vancha moaned aloud when he saw the pair, turned quickly, drew three of his shurikens, took aim and fired. The range wasn't a problem, but the angle – as when he was on the rope and firing at Steve – wasn't favourable, and the stars struck and bounced off the underside of the platform.

"Greetings, brother," Gannen Harst said, nodding at Vancha.

"We've got to get up there!" Vancha snapped, looking for a way forward.

"If you can lead, I will gladly follow," Mr Crepsley said.

"The rope…" Vancha began, but stopped when he saw a group of vampaneze standing between us and the stake where the rope was tied. Even the wild, ever optimistic Prince knew there was no way through so many foes. If the element of surprise had been on our side, we might have battled through them, but after our last encounter they were prepared for mindless, lightning attacks.

"Even if we made the … rope," Harkat said, "those on the platform could cut it before … we got across."

"So what do we do?" Vancha growled, frustrated.

"*Die?*" Mr Crepsley suggested.

Vancha winced. "I don't fear death," he said, "but I won't rush to embrace it. We aren't finished yet. We wouldn't be standing here talking if we were — they'd have rushed us by now. Cover me." So saying, he turned to address the trio on the platform, who were now standing side by side, close to the plank.

"Gannen!" Vancha shouted. "What's going on? Why haven't your men attacked us yet?"

"You know why," Harst responded. "They're afraid they might kill you in the heat of battle. According to Desmond Tiny, only our Lord is supposed to kill the hunters."

"Does that mean they won't defend themselves if we attack?" Vancha asked.

Steve barked a laugh. "Dream on, you stupid old—"

"Enough!" Gannen Harst shouted, silencing the half-vampaneze. "You will not interrupt when I am speaking with my brother." Steve glowered at the protector of the Vampaneze Lord, then lowered his head and held his tongue.

"Of course they'll defend themselves," Harst said, facing Vancha again, "but we hope to avoid such a scene. Apart from the risk of killing you, we've lost too many good men already and don't wish to sacrifice any more. It might be possible to agree a compromise."

"I'm listening," Vancha said.

Gannen Harst gave Steve a quick look. Steve cupped his hands to his mouth and shouted at the ceiling, "Lower away, R.V.!"

There was a pause, then a panel in the ceiling was thrown back and somebody was lowered through the gap on a rope — *Debbie!*

My heart lurched at the sight of her, and I raised my arms, as though I could reach across the great divide and grab her. She didn't appear to have suffered at the hands (*hooks*) of the insane R.V., though her forehead was gashed, her clothes were ripped, and she looked incredibly weary. Her hands were tied behind her back, but her legs were free, and she kicked out at Steve and the others as she came level with the platform. They only laughed, and R.V. lowered her another metre, so she was too low to aim at them.

"Debbie!" I shouted desperately.

"Darren!" she screamed. "Get out! Don't trust them! They let Steve and R.V. do as they please. They even take orders from them. Flee quick before—"

"If you don't shut up," Steve snarled, "I'll shut you up." He stretched the flat of his sword out and touched it to the thin rope tied around her middle — which was all that lay between Debbie and a deadly drop into the pit.

Debbie saw the peril she was in and bit down on her tongue.

"Good," Gannen Harst said when silence had returned. "Now — our offer. We are interested only in the hunters. Debbie Hemlock, Alice Burgess and the Little Person don't matter. We have you outnumbered, Vancha. Our victory is assured. You cannot win, only injure us, and perhaps foil us by dying at the hands of one who isn't our Lord."

"That'll be good enough for me," Vancha sniffed.

"Perhaps," Harst nodded. "And I'm sure Larten Crepsley and Darren Shan feel the same. But what of the others? Will they give their lives so freely, for the sake of the vampire clan?"

"I will!" Harkat boomed.

Gannen Harst smiled. "I expect you would, grey one. But you don't have to. Nor do the women. If Vancha, Larten and Darren lay down their weapons and surrender, we'll free the rest of you. You can walk away, lives intact."

"No way!" Vancha shouted immediately. "I wouldn't roll over and die at the best of times — I'm certainly not doing it now, when so much is at stake."

"Nor shall I agree to such a deal," Mr Crepsley said.

"What of Darren Shan?" Harst asked. "Will he agree to our deal, or will he condemn his friends to die with the rest of you?"

All eyes fixed on me. I gazed up at Debbie, dangling on the rope, frightened, bloodied, desolate. I had it in my power to set her free. Cut a deal with the vampaneze, face a quick death instead of perhaps a slow, painful one, and save the life of the woman I loved. It would have been inhuman of me to reject such a deal...

...but I *wasn't* human. I was a half-vampire. More — a Vampire Prince. And Princes don't cut deals, not when the fate of their people is at stake. "No," I said miserably. "We fight and we die. All for one and one for all."

Gannen Harst nodded understandingly. "I expected that, but one should always open with a weak offer. Very well — let me put another proposal to you. Same basic outline as the first. Drop your weapons, surrender, and we let the humans walk. Only this time, Darren Shan gets to go head to head with our Lord and Steve Leonard."

Vancha's face creased suspiciously. "What are you talking about?"

"If you and Larten turn yourselves over to us without a fight," Harst said, "we will allow Darren to duel with our Lord and Steve Leonard. It will be two on one, but he'll be equipped with weapons. If Darren wins, we free all three of you along with the others. If he loses, we execute you and Larten, but the humans and Harkat Mulds go free.

"Think it over," he urged us. "It's a good, honest deal, more than you could have reasonably hoped for."

Vancha turned away from the platform, troubled, and looked to Mr Crepsley for advice. The vampire, for once, didn't know what to say, and merely shook his head mutely.

"What do *you* think?" Vancha asked me.

"There has to be a catch," I muttered. "Why risk their Lord's life if they don't have to?"

"Gannen wouldn't lie," Vancha said. His face hardened. "But he mightn't tell us the whole truth. Gannen!" he roared. "What guarantee do you give that it'll be a fair fight? How do we know that R.V. or the others won't join in?"

"I give my word," Gannen Harst said softly. "Only the pair on the platform with me will fight Darren Shan. Nobody else will interfere. I'll kill any who seeks to swing the balance one way or the other."

"That's good enough for me," Vancha said. "I believe him. But is this the way we want to go? We've never seen their Lord fight, so we don't know what he's capable of — but we know Leonard's a sly, dangerous opponent. The two of them together..." He grimaced.

"If we agree to Gannen's deal," Mr Crepsley said, "and send Darren up to face them, we place all our eggs in one basket. If Darren wins — wonderful. But if he loses..."

Mr Crepsley and Vancha gazed long and hard at me.

"Well, Darren?" Mr Crepsley asked. "It is an enormous burden to take upon yourself. Are you prepared to shoulder such a solemn responsibility?"

"I don't know," I sighed. "I still think there's a catch. If the odds were fifty-fifty, I'd jump at it. But I don't think they are. I believe..." I stopped. "But that doesn't matter. If this is our best chance, we have to grab it. If you two trust me, I'll accept the challenge — and the blame if I fail."

"He said that like a true vampire," Vancha noted warmly.

"He *is* a true vampire," Mr Crepsley replied, and I felt pride bloom burningly within me.

"Very well," Vancha shouted. "We accept. But first you have to set the humans and Harkat free. After that, Darren fights your Lord and Steve. Only then, if the fight is fair and he loses, will Larten and I lay down our arms."

"That's not the deal," Harst replied stiffly. "You must lay your weapons to one side and surrender before–"

"No," Vancha interrupted. "We do it this way or not at all. You have my word that we'll let your people take us if Darren loses — assuming he loses fairly. If my word's not good enough, we have a problem."

Gannen Harst hesitated, then nodded curtly. "Your word is good," he said, then told R.V. to haul Debbie up and escort her down.

"No!" R.V. howled. "Steve said I could kill her! He said I could cut her up into tiny little pieces and—"

"Now I'm saying different!" Steve roared. "Don't cross me on this. There'll be other nights and humans – plenty of them – but there's only one Darren Shan."

We heard R.V. grumbling, but then he pulled on the rope and Debbie ascended in a series of short, uncomfortable jerks.

While waiting for Debbie to be returned to us, I got ready for my fight with the pair on the platform, wiping my hands clean, checking my weapons, clearing my mind of all thoughts except those of battle.

"How do you feel?" Vancha asked.

"Fine."

"Remember," he said, "all that matters is the result. Fight dirty if you have to. Kick and spit, scratch and pinch, hit below the belt."

"I will," I grinned. Lowering my voice, I asked, "Will you really surrender if I lose?"

"I gave my word, didn't I?" Vancha said, then winked and whispered in a voice even lower than mine. "I promised we'd drop our weapons and let them take us. And so we will. But I said nothing about letting them keep us or not picking our weapons up again!"

The vampaneze ahead of us parted ranks as R.V. marched through, dragging Debbie behind him by her hair.

"Stop that!" I shouted angrily. "You're hurting her!"

R.V. bared his teeth and laughed. He was still wearing one red contact lens and hadn't replaced the one he'd lost the night before. His bushy beard was flecked with bits of moss, twigs, dirt and blood. It would have been easy to feel sorry for him — he'd been a decent man before he lost his hands to the jaws of the Wolf Man at the Cirque Du Freak — but I had no time for sympathy. I reminded myself that he was the enemy and erased all traces of pity from my mind.

R.V. tossed Debbie down in front of me. She cried out in pain, then lunged to her knees and flew into my arms. I clutched her close as she sobbed and tried to speak. "Shhh," I said. "Take it easy. You're safe. Don't say anything."

"I ... must," she wept. "So much ... to say. I ... I love you, Darren."

"Of course you do," I smiled, my eyes filling with tears.

"Such a touching scene," Steve sneered. "Someone pass me a hankie."

I ignored him and held Debbie's face away from me. I kissed her quickly, then smiled. "You look awful," I said.

"Charming!" she half-laughed, then stared at me

appealingly. "I don't want to leave," she croaked. "Not until after the fight."

"No," I said quickly. "You have to go. I don't want you to stay and watch."

"In case you are killed?" she asked.

I nodded, and her lips thinned almost to nothing.

"I want to stay too," Harkat said, stepping up beside us, his green eyes filled with determination.

"It's your right to," I agreed. "I won't stop you. But I'd rather you didn't. If you value our friendship, you'll take Debbie and the Chief Inspector, lead them to the surface, and make sure they get away safely. I don't trust these monsters — they might go on a rampage and kill us all if I win."

"Then I should stay to fight ... with you," Harkat said.

"No," I said softly. "Not this time. Please, for my sake and Debbie's, will you leave?"

Harkat didn't like it, but he nodded reluctantly.

"Come on then," someone snapped behind us. "Let's get them out if they're going."

I looked up and saw the treacherous police officer called Morgan James striding towards us. He was carrying a slim rifle, the butt of which he poked into his Chief Inspector's ribs.

"Get the hell away from me!" she snapped, turning on him furiously.

"Easy, Chief," he drawled, grinning like a jackal, bringing up the rifle. "I'd hate to have to shoot you."

"When we get back, you're history," she snarled.

"I won't be coming back," he smirked. "I'll guide you lot to the cavern at the end of the tunnel, lock you out to make sure you can't create a disturbance, then take off with the others when the fighting's over."

"You won't escape that easy," Burgess snorted. "I'll track you down and make you pay for this, even if I have to travel halfway round the world."

"Sure you will," Morgan laughed, then nudged her in the ribs again, harder this time.

The Chief Inspector spat at her ex-officer, then pushed him away and crouched next to Vancha to tie her laces. As she was doing that, she whispered to him out of the side of her mouth. "The guy in the hood and cloak — that's the one you have to kill, right?" Vancha nodded wordlessly, guarding his expression. "I don't like the idea of sending the kid up to fight them," Burgess said. "If I can create a bit of space, and provide firing cover, d'you reckon you or Crepsley could get up there?"

"Maybe," Vancha said, lips barely moving.

"Then I'll see what I can do." Burgess finished tying her laces, stood and winked. "Come on," she said aloud to Harkat and Debbie. "The air stinks here. The sooner we're out, the better."

The Chief Inspector started walking, shoving ahead of Morgan, purpose in her stride. The rows of vampaneze ahead of her parted, clearing a path. Only a few now stood between us and the stake the rope was tied to.

Harkat and Debbie looked back at me sorrowfully. Debbie opened her mouth to say something, but words wouldn't come. Crying, she shook her head and turned her back on me, shoulders shaking miserably. Harkat put his arms around her and led her away, following the Chief Inspector.

Burgess was almost at the mouth of the tunnel leading out of the cavern when she paused and glanced over her shoulder. Morgan was close to her, cradling his rifle. Harkat and Debbie were several metres behind, progressing slowly.

"Hurry up!" Burgess snapped at the dawdling pair. "This isn't a funeral procession!"

Morgan smiled and looked back automatically at Harkat and Debbie. As he did, the Chief Inspector swung into action. Throwing herself at him, she grabbed the butt of the rifle and dug it into the soft flesh of his stomach, fast and hard, winding him. Morgan yelled in pain and surprise, then snatched the rifle back as she tried to pull it away. He almost wrenched it from her grasp, but not quite, and the pair rolled over on the ground, wrestling for the gun. Behind them, the vampaneze and vampets moved to intercept them.

Before the advancing troops reached her, Burgess got a finger on the trigger of the rifle and squeezed off a shot. It could have been pointing anywhere – she didn't have time to aim – but as luck had it, it was pointing at the jaw of the vampet she was struggling with — Morgan James!

There was a flash and a roar of gunfire. Then Morgan

was falling away from the Chief Inspector, shrieking with agony, the left side of his face a bloody, shredded mess.

As Morgan surged to his feet, hands clutching the remains of his face, Burgess slammed him over the back of his head with the butt of the rifle, knocking him unconscious. Then, as vampaneze and vampets swarmed towards her, she leant a knee on the ex-officer's back, swung her rifle up, took careful aim, and fired off a volley of shots at the platform — at Steve, Gannen Harst ... and the Lord of the Vampaneze!

CHAPTER FIFTEEN

BULLETS POUNDED the platform, railing, wall and ceiling. The three men caught in the line of fire ducked backwards quickly, but not quickly enough — one of the bullets struck the Vampaneze Lord high in his right shoulder, drawing an arc of blood and a sharp cry of pain!

At their Lord's cry, the vampaneze and vampets exploded with rage. Screaming and howling like mad animals, they launched themselves *en masse* at the Chief Inspector, who was still firing. Barrelling over one another in their haste to be first upon her, they descended upon Burgess in a vicious, churning wave, breaking over Harkat and Debbie along the way.

My first instinct was to rush to Debbie and pull her from the crush, but Vancha grabbed me before I could move and pointed to the rope — it was no longer guarded.

I knew immediately that this was our first priority. Debbie would have to fend for herself.

"Who goes?" I gasped, as we hurried to the stake.

"Me," Vancha said, grabbing the rope.

"No," Mr Crepsley disagreed, laying a hand on the Prince's shoulder. "It must be me."

"We don't have time to—" Vancha started.

"That is true," Mr Crepsley interrupted. "We do not have time. So let me pass without any arguments."

"Larten..." Vancha growled.

"He's right," I said softly. "It has to be him."

Vancha gawped at me. "Why?"

"Because Steve was my best friend and Gannen's your brother," I explained. "Mr Crepsley's the only one who can concentrate wholly on the Vampaneze Lord. You or I would have one eye on Steve or Gannen, no matter how hard we tried to ignore them."

Vancha thought about that, nodded and let go of the rope, clearing the way for Mr Crepsley. "Give them hell, Larten," he said.

"I will," Mr Crepsley smiled. He took hold of the rope and started across.

"We must cover him from this side," Vancha said, drawing a handful of shurikens and squinting up at the platform.

"I know," I said, eyes on the thrashing vampaneze ahead of me, ready to combat them when they awoke to the threat of Mr Crepsley's challenge.

One of the trio on the platform must have spotted Mr Crepsley, because Vancha suddenly let fly with a couple of throwing stars – he had a clear shot at them from where we were standing – and I heard a curse above as whoever it was jumped back out of the way of the shurikens.

There was a pause, then a roar which filled the cavern and cut through the cries and mayhem of the battling vampaneze. "Servants of the night!" Gannen Harst bellowed. "Look to your Lord! Danger approaches!"

Heads turned and eyes fixed, first on the platform, then on the rope and Mr Crepsley. With fresh yelps and gasps, the vampaneze and vampets spun and rushed towards the spot where Vancha and I were standing.

If there hadn't been quite so many, they'd have mown us down, but their numbers worked against them. Too many attacked at the same time, resulting in confusion and chaos. So, instead of facing a solid wall of warriors, we were able to pick off individuals.

As I swung my sword wildly and Vancha lashed out with his hands, I spotted Gannen Harst stealing towards the end of the platform where the rope was tied, a sharp dagger in his right hand. It didn't take a genius to work out his intentions. I roared at Vancha, warning him, but there was no room for him to turn and throw. I shouted at Mr Crepsley to hurry up, but he was still a long way from safety and could go no faster than he was already going.

As Harst reached the rope and prepared to cut it, someone fired at him. He ducked low and rolled back out of the way as bullets turned the air red around him.

Standing on my toes, I spotted a bruised, battered, but still living Alice Burgess, on her feet, rifle in hand, quickly reloading it with bullets she'd snatched from Morgan James. Just ahead of her stood Harkat Mulds and Debbie Hemlock; Harkat wielding his axe, Debbie awkwardly swinging a short sword, both of them protecting the Chief Inspector from the handful of vampaneze and vampets who hadn't been drawn away to deal with the rope.

I felt like cheering aloud at the sight, and would have if a vampaneze hadn't crashed into my back and knocked me to the ground. As I rolled away from stomping feet, the vampaneze dived after me. Pinning me to the floor, he wrapped his fingers around my neck and squeezed. I lashed out at him but he had the beating of me — I was finished!

But the luck of the vampires was on my side. Before his fingers could close and crush my throat, one of his own men was punched by Vancha, fell back, collided with the vampaneze on top of me, and knocked him off. As he yelled, frustrated, I leapt to my feet, grabbed a mace which someone had dropped in the fighting, and let him have it full in the face. The vampaneze dropped, screaming, and I was back in the thick of the fighting.

I saw a vampet swing an axe at the rope tied to the stake. Roaring, I threw the mace at him, but too late — the head of the axe cut clean through the strands of the rope, severing it entirely.

My eyes darted to where Mr Crepsley was hanging, and my insides clenched as he swung down underneath the platform, through the red flames of the pit, which still burnt brightly.

It seemed to take an age for the rope to reach the length of its arc and swing back towards me. When it did, the vampire was no longer in sight, and my heart dropped. Then my eyes slid down and I realized he was still clinging to the rope, but had slipped a few metres. As flames licked the undersides of his feet, he began climbing again, and within a couple of seconds was clear of the fire and back on course for the platform.

A quick-minded vampet broke clear of the mêlée, raised a crossbow and fired at Mr Crepsley. He missed. Before he could fire again, I found a spear and sent it soaring. It struck him in the upper right arm and he fell to his knees, moaning.

I glanced to where Burgess was firing again, covering Mr Crepsley as he climbed. Debbie was struggling with a vampet twice her size. She'd thrown her arms around him so he couldn't use his sword and had buried a knife in the small of his back. She was raking his face with her nails, and putting her left knee to very naughty use. Not bad for an English teacher!

Harkat, meanwhile, was chopping vampaneze and vampets to pieces. The Little Person was an experienced, lethal fighter, much stronger and faster than he looked. Many vampaneze charged him, expecting to swat him to one side — none lived to write their memoirs.

Then, as Harkat dispatched another vampet with an almost casual swing of his axe, there was a loud, animal-like cry, and a furious R.V. entered the fray. He'd been trapped in the middle of a crowd of vampaneze, unable to join the fighting. Now at last he broke free, fixed on Harkat, and bore down upon him, hooks glinting and teeth gnashing. Tears of rage trickled from his mismatched eyes. "Kill you!" he roared. "Kill you! Kill you! Kill!"

He brought the hooks on his left hand down on Harkat's head, but the Little Person ducked out of the way and clubbed the hooks aside with the flat of his axe. R.V. swung his other set of hooks towards Harkat's stomach. Harkat brought his free hand down in the nick of time and caught R.V.'s arm above the elbow, stopping the tips of the hooks less than a centimetre from the flesh of his midriff. As R.V. screamed and spat at Harkat, the Little Person calmly grabbed the straps attaching the hooks to R.V.'s arm, ripped them loose and tossed the hook-hand away.

R.V. shrieked as though stabbed, and punched Harkat with the stump at the end of his elbow. Harkat took no notice, only reached up, caught hold of R.V.'s other hook-hand, and ripped that off too.

"*NO!!!*" R.V. screeched, diving after the hooks. "My hands! My hands!"

R.V. recovered the hooks, but couldn't strap them back on without help. He yelled at his comrades to assist him, but they had troubles of their own. He was still screaming when Alice Burgess lowered her rifle and stared at the platform. Turning to see what she was looking at, I saw Mr Crepsley climb over the railing, and I too relaxed.

All eyes gradually drifted to the platform and the battle died down. When people saw Mr Crepsley standing on the platform, they stopped fighting and fixed upon the scene, sensing as I did that our squabbles were no longer relevant — the only fight that mattered was the one about to take place overhead.

When everyone was still, a strange silence settled on us, which lasted a minute or more. Mr Crepsley stood at his end of the platform, impassive, while his three opponents stood just as sentry-like at theirs.

Finally, as the hairs on the back of my neck were beginning to lie down — they'd been standing up stiff since the start of the battle — the Lord of the Vampaneze stepped forward to the railing, lowered his hood, faced those of us on the ground, and spoke.

CHAPTER SIXTEEN

"LET THE fighting cease," the Lord of the Vampaneze said in a low, unmelodramatic voice. "There's no need for it now."

It was the first time I'd seen the Vampaneze Lord's face and I was surprised by how ordinary he looked. I'd built up a picture in my mind of a fierce, fiery, wild-eyed tyrant, whose gaze could turn water to steam. But this was just a man in his twenties or early thirties, normal build, light brown hair and rather sad eyes. The wound he'd received to his shoulder was minor — the blood had already dried — and he ignored it as he spoke.

"I knew this was coming," the Lord of the Vampaneze said softly, turning his head to gaze at Mr Crepsley. "Des Tiny predicted it. He said I'd have to fight one of the hunters here, above the flames, and that it would most likely be Larten Crepsley. We tried to turn his prophecy on its head and lure the boy up instead. For a while I thought we'd succeeded. But in my heart I knew it was you I'd have to face."

Mr Crepsley raised a sceptical eyebrow. "Did Mr Tiny say which of us would triumph?" he asked.

A thin smile broke across the Vampaneze Lord's lips. "No. He said it could swing either way."

"That is encouraging," Mr Crepsley said dryly.

Mr Crepsley held one of his knives up to catch the light of the chandelier high above his head, studying the blade. The instant he did that, Gannen Harst stepped in front of his Lord, defensively.

"The deal's off," Harst said gruffly. "The two to one ratio no longer applies. If you'd sent Darren Shan as agreed, we'd have kept our side of the bargain. Since you've come in his place, you can't expect us to offer the same generous odds."

"I expect nothing of madmen and traitors," Mr Crepsley said archly, causing the vampaneze and vampets in the cavern to mutter darkly.

"Take heed," Gannen Harst snarled, "or I'll–"

"Peace, Gannen," said the Lord of the Vampaneze. "The time for threats has passed. Let us lock weapons and wits without any further rancour."

The Vampaneze Lord stepped out from behind Gannen Harst and produced a barbed short sword. Harst drew a longer, straight sword, while Steve whistled merrily and dug out a gold dagger and long length of spiked chain.

"Are you ready, Larten Crepsley?" the Vampaneze Lord asked. "Have you made your peace with the gods?"

"I did that long ago," Mr Crepsley said, both knives in his hands, his eyes alert. "But, before we begin, I would like to know what happens after. If I win, will my allies be set free, or must they—"

"No bargains!" the Lord of the Vampaneze snapped. "We're not here to make deals. We're here to fight. The fate of the others — my people and yours — can be settled after we lock blades. Only we matter now. All else is meaningless."

"Very well," Mr Crepsley grunted, then stepped away from the rail, crouched low and edged towards his foes.

On the ground, nobody moved. Vancha, Harkat, Debbie, Burgess and I had lowered our weapons and were oblivious to all around us. It would have been a simple task for the vampaneze to capture us, but they were as captivated by events on the platform as we were.

As Mr Crepsley advanced, the three vampaneze assumed a 'V' formation and shuffled forward a few metres. The Vampaneze Lord was in the middle, Gannen Harst a metre ahead of him on his left, Steve Leopard the same distance ahead on his right. It was a cautiously effective strategy. Mr Crepsley would have to attack through the centre — he had to kill the Vampaneze Lord; the others didn't matter. When he attacked, Harst and Steve would be able to strike from both sides at once.

Mr Crepsley stopped short of the three, arms outstretched to protect against darting attacks from either side. His eyes were focused on the Vampaneze Lord and he didn't blink once while I was watching.

Several strained seconds passed. Then Steve lashed out at Mr Crepsley with his chain. I saw spikes glitter as it snaked towards Mr Crepsley's head — they'd cause serious damage if they connected. But the vampire was faster than the half-vampaneze. Twisting his head ever so slightly to the left, he avoided the chain and spikes by a centimetre, then stabbed sharply at Steve's stomach with the knife in his left hand.

As Mr Crepsley attacked Steve, Gannen Harst swung at the vampire with his sword. My mouth opened to shout a warning, but then I saw I needn't bother — the vampire had been expecting the counter-measure and pivoted sweetly away from the sword, gliding inside the range of its sweep, coming within striking distance of the Vampaneze Lord.

Mr Crepsley used the knife in his right hand to slash forward, seeking to open the Vampaneze Lord's stomach. But the leader of the vampaneze was swift and blocked the blow with his barbed sword. The tip of Mr Crepsley's knife bit into the Lord's waist but only drew a thin trickle of blood.

Before the vampire could strike again, Steve struck at him with his dagger. He chopped wildly at Mr Crepsley — too wild for accuracy — and forced him back. Then Gannen Harst stepped in and let fly with his sword, and Mr Crepsley had to drop to the floor and roll backwards to escape.

They were on him before he got to his feet, blades flashing, Steve's chain whipping. It took all Mr Crepsley's speed, strength and skill to turn the swords aside, duck out of the way of the chain, and retreat on his knees before they overwhelmed him.

As the vampaneze hastened after the vampire, I feared they had the beating of him — the swords and chain were sneaking through Mr Crepsley's desperate defences, nicking him here, slicing him there. The wounds weren't life-threatening, but it was only a matter of time before a blade cut deeply into his stomach or chest, or the spikes of the chain snagged on his nose or eyes.

Mr Crepsley must have known the danger he was in, but he continued to fight a rearguard action, no longer taking the battle to the enemy, merely retreating and protecting himself as best he could, giving ground steadily, letting them push him towards the rail at the end of the platform, where he'd be cornered.

"He can't keep this up," I muttered to Vancha, who was standing close by, his eyes glued to the platform. "He's got to take a risk, and soon, before they trap him."

"You think he's unaware of that?" Vancha replied tersely.

"Then why doesn't he—"

"Hush, boy," the scruffy Prince said softly. "Larten knows what he's doing."

I wasn't so sure. Mr Crepsley was an expert fighter, but I felt he was in over his head this time. One to one, he could handle any vampaneze. Even in a two to one situation, I'd fancy him to walk away victorious. But three to one...

I looked for some way up to the platform — if I could join him, I might be able to turn the tide of battle. But just then, the fight took a terminal turn.

Mr Crepsley was almost backed up against the rail, no more than half a metre away from a dead end. The vampaneze knew the difficult position he was in, and pushed forward with renewed eagerness, sensing the end. Steve sent his chain flicking at Mr Crepsley's face again, for the umpteenth time, but on this occasion the vampire didn't dodge the deadly spikes or duck out of their way. Instead, dropping the knife in his left hand, he reached up and grabbed the chain mid air. His fingers closed on spikes, and his mouth tightened with pain, but he didn't let go. Yanking sharply on the chain, he brought Steve crashing towards him. At the last possible instant he lowered his chin, so that Steve's face connected bone-crunchingly with the vampire's forehead.

Steve's nose popped and gushed blood. He shrieked loudly, falling to the floor. As he fell, Mr Crepsley sent the knife in his right hand flying at Gannen Harst, leaving himself weaponless. As Harst instinctively pulled out of the path of the knife, the Vampaneze Lord drove at Mr Crepsley with his sword.

Mr Crepsley threw himself away from the incoming sword tip. Crashing into the railing, he spun around so he was facing away from his opponents, grabbed the rail with his hands, swung his legs and body up with ferocious speed, and ended up doing a handstand on the rail.

While those of us on the ground gawped, stunned by the unexpected manoeuvre, Mr Crepsley lowered himself to chin level with the rail, then thrust away from it with all his strength. The vampire sailed, full stretch, through the air, soaring over the Vampaneze Lord and Gannen Harst – who'd stepped in front of his Lord to protect him, as he'd done many times during the fight – and Steve Leopard, who was still lying on the platform.

Mr Crepsley landed on his feet like a cat, behind the unprotected back of the Vampaneze Lord. Before the half-vampaneze or Gannen Harst could react, Mr Crepsley seized the Lord by the scruff of his shirt with his left hand, grabbed the waist of his trousers with his right, lifted him off the floor, spun to the edge of the platform — and tossed him head-first over the side, into the pit of stakes below!

There was time for the Lord of the Vampaneze to scream – once – then he hit the stakes with a thud which made me wince. The stakes impaled him in a dozen different places, including through the heart and head. His body twitched a couple of times, then went still, and flames caught in his hair and clothes.

It happened so fast, at first I couldn't take it all in. But as the seconds passed, and the vampaneze stared, bewildered and distraught, into the pit at the flaming corpse of their leader, the full truth struck home. Mr

Crepsley had killed the Lord of the Vampaneze …
without their leader, they faced destined defeat … the War
of the Scars was over … the future was ours … we'd *WON!*

CHAPTER SEVENTEEN

IT WAS incredible. It was wonderful. It was almost beyond belief.

As the spirit of the vampaneze blew apart like the chains of smoke rising from their burning Lord's dead body, mine soared and I felt as though my chest would burst with relief and delight. In our darkest hour, despite the odds, against all expectations, we'd taken the fight to our foes and put their destructive designs to the sword. In my wildest dreams, I couldn't have imagined anything sweeter.

My eyes rose as Mr Crepsley stepped to the edge of the platform. The vampire was bloodied, sweating and exhausted, but a light shone in his eyes which could have illuminated the entire cavern. Spotting me among the shaken vampaneze, he smiled, raised a hand in salute, and opened his mouth to call something down.

That's when Steve Leopard screamed wildly and threw himself firmly into the back of the vampire.

Mr Crepsley pitched forward, arms flailing, clutching for the rail. It looked for a split second as if he was going to grab hold and haul himself up, but then gravity dragged him down with sickening speed, over the rail, out of safety's reach ... into the pit after the Lord of the Vampaneze!

CHAPTER EIGHTEEN

THOUGH STEVE had sent Mr Crepsley plummeting to his doom, he also accidentally threw the vampire a slender lifeline. Because as Mr Crepsley toppled, Steve leant over the railing, eager to watch the vampire hit the stakes and die. As he did, the length of chain he'd used as a weapon — which he still clutched in his right hand — unfurled and dropped beside Mr Crepsley like a rope.

Throwing out a desperate hand, the vampire grabbed the chain, once again ignoring the pain as spikes buried themselves deep in the flesh of his palm. The chain reached its limit and snapped taut, halting Mr Crepsley's fall.

On the platform, Steve wailed as the weight of Mr Crepsley caused the chain to tighten around the flesh of his right hand. He tried shaking it loose, but couldn't. As he stood, leaning half over the rail, struggling with the chain, Mr Crepsley reached up, grabbed the sleeve of

Steve's shirt, and pulled him over further, caring nothing for his own life, intent only on taking Steve's.

As the pair fell – Steve screaming, Mr Crepsley laughing – Gannen Harst thrust a hand out and caught Steve's flailing left hand. The vampaneze groaned painfully as the weight of the two men dragged on the muscles and tendons in his arm, but braced himself against an upright support post and held tight.

"Let go!" Steve screamed, kicking out at Mr Crepsley, trying to knock him off. "You'll kill us both!"

"That is what I mean to do!" Mr Crepsley roared. He didn't seem in the least bit bothered by the threat of death. Maybe it was the rush of adrenaline pumping through his veins, having killed the Lord of the Vampaneze — or perhaps he didn't care about his own life if it meant killing Steve. Either way, he'd accepted his fate and made no attempt to climb Steve's body to safety. In fact, he started tugging on the chain, trying to break Gannen Harst's hold.

"Stop!" Gannen Harst roared. "Stop and we'll let you go!"

"Too late!" Mr Crepsley howled. "I swore two things to myself when I came down here. One — I would kill the Lord of the Vampaneze. Two — I would kill Steve Leonard! I am not a man for leaving a job half done, so..."

He tugged even harder than before. Above him, Gannen Harst gasped and shut his eyes against the pain. "I can't ... hold on ... much longer!" he moaned.

"Larten!" Vancha shouted. "Don't do it! Trade your life for his. We'll track him down later and finish him off!"

"By the black blood of Harnon Oan — no!" Mr Crepsley roared. "I have him now, so I will kill him. Let that be the end of it!"

"And what ... about your ... allies?" Gannen Harst shouted, and as the words penetrated Mr Crepsley's skull, he stopped struggling and gazed up warily at the ex-protector of the Vampaneze Lord.

"As *you* hold the life of Steve Leonard in your hands," Harst said quickly, "*I* hold the lives of your friends. If you kill Steve, I'll order their deaths too!"

"No," Mr Crepsley said quietly. "Leonard is a madman. His life must not be spared. Let me—"

"*No!*" Gannen Harst yelled. "Spare Steve and I'll spare the others. That's the deal. Agree to it, quick, before I lose my grip and the bloodshed continues."

Mr Crepsley paused thoughtfully.

"His life too!" I shouted. "Spare Mr Crepsley, or—"

"No!" Steve snarled. "Creepy Crepsley dies. I won't let him go."

"Don't be stupid!" Gannen Harst bellowed. "You'll die too if we don't release him!"

"Then I'll die," Steve sneered.

"You don't know what you're saying!" Harst hissed.

"I do," Steve replied softly. "I'll let the others go, but Crepsley dies now, because he said I was evil." Steve glared down at the silent Mr Crepsley. "And if I have to die with him, I will — consequences be damned!"

While Gannen Harst stared at Steve, mouth agape, Mr

Crepsley looked to where Vancha and I were standing. As our eyes locked in grim understanding, Debbie rushed up beside us. "Darren!" she shouted. "We have to save him! We can't let him die! We—"

"Shhh," I whispered, kissing her forehead, holding her close.

"But—" she sobbed.

"We can't do anything," I sighed.

While Debbie moaned and buried her face in my chest, Mr Crepsley addressed Vancha. "It seems our paths must part, Sire."

"Aye," Vancha croaked bitterly.

"We shared some good times," Mr Crepsley said.

"Great times," Vancha corrected him.

"Will you sing my praises in the Halls of Vampire Mountain when you return, and drink a toast to me, even if it is only a glass of water?"

"I'll drink a crate of ale to your name," Vancha vowed, "and sing death songs till my voice cracks."

"You always did take things to extremes," Mr Crepsley laughed. Then his gaze settled on me. "Darren," he said.

"Larten," I replied, smiling awkwardly. I felt like crying, but couldn't. There was an awful emptiness inside of me and my emotions wouldn't respond.

"Hurry!" Gannen Harst shouted. "My grip is slipping. A few more seconds and I'll—"

"A few seconds will suffice," Mr Crepsley said, not one to be rushed, even when death was beckoning. Smiling sadly at me, he said, "Do not let hatred rule your life. My death does not need to be avenged. Live as a free vampire, not as a twisted, revenge-driven creature of despair. Do not become like Steve Leonard or R.V. My spirit will not rest easy in Paradise if you do."

"You don't want me to kill Steve?" I asked uncertainly.

"By all means kill him!" Mr Crepsley boomed. "But do not devote yourself to the task. Do not—"

"I can't … hold … any longer!" Gannen Harst wheezed. He was trembling and sweating from the strain.

"Nor shall you have to," Mr Crepsley responded. His eyes passed from me to Vancha and back again, then up to the ceiling. He stared as though he could see through the layers of rock, concrete and earth above to the sky beyond. "Gods of the vampires!" he bellowed. "Even in death, may I be triumphant!"

Then, as the echoes of his final cry reverberated around the walls of the cavern, Mr Crepsley let go of the chain. He hung in the air an impossible moment, almost as though he could fly … then dropped like a stone towards the steel-tipped stakes beneath.

CHAPTER NINETEEN

AT THE last possible moment, when all seemed lost, someone on a rope swung from the ceiling, streaked through the air, grabbed Mr Crepsley around the waist, and rose with him to the safety of the platform, where they landed on their feet. As I stared, amazed, mouth hanging open, Mr Crepsley's rescuer turned — it was Mika Ver Leth, one of my fellow Vampire Princes!

"Now!" Mika roared, and at his cry an army of vampires climbed through the holes in the ceiling and dropped to the floor, landing among the flabbergasted vampaneze and vampets. Before our foes had a chance to defend themselves, our troops were upon them, swords swinging, knives darting, axes chopping.

On the platform, Gannen Harst howled miserably — "*No!*" — then threw himself at Mr Crepsley and Mika. As Harst lunged, Mika calmly stepped in front of Mr

Crepsley, drew his sword, and swung it broadly at the advancing vampaneze, cutting his head clean off at the neck, sending it sailing through the air like a misdirected bowling ball.

As Gannen Harst's lifeless, headless body toppled over the side of the platform, Steve Leopard yelped, turned, and dashed for the safety of the tunnel. He'd made it almost to the end of the plank when Mr Crepsley borrowed one of Mika's knives, took careful aim, and sent it flashing through the air at the half-vampaneze.

The knife buried itself between Steve's shoulder blades. He gasped, stopped, spun around slowly, face white, eyes bulging, hands grasping for the hilt of the knife, unable to draw it out. Coughing up blood, he collapsed on to the plank, spasmed briefly and fell still.

Around us, the vampires were finishing off their opponents. Harkat and Vancha had joined the fighting and were cheerfully dispatching vampaneze and vampets. Behind them, Chief Inspector Alice Burgess was gazing upon the bloodshed, unsure of who these new warriors were. She sensed they were on our side, but she held on to her rifle, just in case.

Debbie was still sobbing into my chest — she hadn't looked up and realized what was happening! "It's OK," I told her, tilting her head up. "Mr Crepsley's safe. He's alive. The cavalry arrived."

"*Cavalry?*" she echoed, gazing around, wiping tears from her eyes. "I don't understand. What…? How…?"

"I don't know!" I chortled, then grabbed Vancha's arm as he came within range. "What's going on?" I roared in his ear. "Where did this lot come from?"

"I fetched them!" he shouted gleefully. "When I left yesterday, I flitted to Vampire Mountain and told them what was going on. They flitted back with me. They had to tread cautiously – I told them not to interfere until we'd killed the Vampaneze Lord – but they've been here all along, waiting."

"But ... I don't ... it's..."

I stopped before my babbling got the better of me. I couldn't understand how they'd crept up so quietly, or how Vancha had reached Vampire Mountain and got back so quickly – even flitting, it should have taken him a few nights – but what did that matter? They were here, they were kicking ass, Mr Crepsley was alive and Steve Leopard and the Lord of the Vampaneze were dead. Why question it?

As I spun around like a child on Christmas Day surrounded by a room full of the most amazing presents, I saw a fabulously familiar figure pushing through the fighting, orange hair flecked with blood, a few new scars to add to the long one which carved up the left side of his face, limping on his sore ankle, but otherwise unbowed.

"Mr Crepsley!" I roared, throwing myself into his arms.

"Master Shan!" he laughed, hugging me tight to his chest. "Did you think I was finished?"

"Yes!" I sobbed.

"Hah!" he chuckled. "You do not get rid of me that easily! You still have much to learn about our ways and customs. Who but I would have the patience to teach you?"

"Vain old git!" I snuffled.

"Rude young brat!" he retorted, then pushed me back to study my face. Raising a hand, he thumbed tears and dirt away from my cheeks and then … then … then…

CHAPTER TWENTY

NO. THAT'S not how it happened.

I wish it was. With all my heart and soul, I wish he'd been rescued and our foes defeated. In that terrible, impossibly long moment of his fall, I imagined half a dozen fantastic scenarios, where Mika or Arrow or Mr Tall intervened to divert the course of fate, and we all walked away smiling. But it wasn't to be. There was no last-minute cavalry charge. No miraculous rescue. Vancha hadn't flitted to Vampire Mountain. We were alone, as we had to be, as destiny willed it.

Mr Crepsley dropped. He was impaled on the stakes. He died.

And it was *awful*.

I can't even say that it was quick and merciful, as it was for the Lord of the Vampaneze, because he didn't die straightaway. The stakes didn't kill him instantly, and though his soul didn't linger long, his cries while he writhed there, bleeding and dying, burning and screaming, will stay with me till I die. Maybe I'll even carry them with me when I go.

Debbie wept bitterly. Vancha howled like a wolf. Green tears trickled from Harkat's round green eyes. Even the Chief Inspector turned away from the scene and sniffed miserably.

Not me. I couldn't. My eyes stayed dry.

Stumbling forward, I stopped at the edge of the pit and stared down at the stakes and the two bodies being quickly stripped bare of their flesh by the flames. I stood as though on guard, not budging or looking away, paying no attention as the vampaneze and vampets filed silently out of the cavern. They could have executed us, but their leader was dead, their dreams had been dashed, and they were no longer interested in battle – not even in revenge.

I was barely aware of Vancha, Debbie, Harkat and Alice Burgess as they came to stand by my side.

"We should go now," Vancha muttered after a while.

"No," I replied dully. "I'm taking him with us, to bury him properly."

"It'll be hours before the fire dies out," Vancha said.

"I'm in no rush. The hunt's over. We've all the time in the world."

Vancha sighed deeply, then nodded. "Very well. We'll wait."

"Not me," Debbie sobbed. "I can't. It's too horrible. I can't stay and..." She broke down in tears. I wanted to comfort her, but couldn't. There was nothing I could think to say to make her feel better.

"I'll look after her," Burgess said, taking charge. "We'll walk up the tunnel and wait for you in the smaller cavern."

"Thanks, Alice," Vancha said.

Burgess paused before leaving. "I'm still not sure about you guys," she said, "if you're really vampires or not. And I haven't a clue what I'm going to tell my people about this. But I know evil when I see it, and I like to think I know good too. I won't stand in your way when it's time for you to leave. And if you need any help, you only have to call."

"Thanks," Vancha said again, and this time he managed a thin, grateful smile.

The women left, Debbie crying, Burgess supporting her. They pushed through the departing ranks of vampaneze and vampets, who gave way meekly to the pair who'd helped bring about the downfall of their Lord.

Minutes passed. The flames flickered on. Mr Crepsley and the Lord of the Vampaneze burned.

Then a strange-looking pair hobbled up to confront us. One had no hands, although he carried a pair of hook-hands slung around his neck. The other had only half a face and was moaning piteously. R.V. and Morgan James.

"We'll get you swine!" R.V. snarled, pointing threateningly with his left stump. "Gannen gave his word that he'd let you go, so we can't harm you now, but we'll hunt you down later and make you sorry you were born."

"You'd better come well prepared, Hooky," Vancha commented dryly. "You'll find us a real *hand*ful."

R.V. hissed at the joke and made to attack the Prince. Morgan held him back, mumbling through teeth — half of which had been shattered by Burgess' bullet — "Curhm awahy! Thuy ahn't wurth iht!"

"Hah," Vancha chuckled spitefully. "That's easy for you to say!"

This time R.V. had to push Morgan James back as he struggled to get his hands on Vancha. Cursing and fighting with each other, they backed off, joined the ranks of their numbed colleagues, and drifted away to patch themselves up and plot mean-spirited revenge.

Again we were alone at the pit. The cavern was quieter now. Almost all the vampaneze and vampets had exited. Only a last few stragglers remained. Among them were Gannen Harst and a grinning Steve Leopard, who couldn't resist ambling over for one last mocking laugh.

"What's that cooking on the fire, boys?" he asked, putting up his hands as if to warm them.

"Go away," I said blankly, "or I'll kill you."

Steve's face dropped and he glared at me. "It's your own fault," he pouted. "If you hadn't betrayed me—"

I swung my sword up, meaning to cut him in two.

Vancha swatted it aside with the flat of his hand before I drew blood. "No," he said, stepping between us. "If you kill him, the others will return and kill us. Let it drop. We'll get him later."

"Wise words, brother," Gannen Harst said, stepping up beside Vancha. His face was drawn. "There's been enough killing. We—"

"Get lost!" Vancha snapped.

Harst's expression darkened. "Don't speak to me like—"

"I won't warn you again," Vancha growled.

The ex-protector of the Vampaneze Lord bristled angrily, then raised his hands peacefully and backed away from his brother.

Steve didn't follow.

"I want to tell him," the half-vampaneze said, eyes pinned on me.

"No!" Gannen Harst hissed. "You mustn't! Not now! You—"

"I *want* to *tell* him," Steve said again, more forcefully this time.

Harst cursed beneath his breath, glanced from one of us to the other, then nodded tensely. "Very well. But over to one side, where nobody else can hear."

"What are you up to now?" Vancha asked suspiciously.

"You'll find out," Steve giggled, taking hold of my left elbow.

I shrugged him off. "Keep away from me, monster!" I spat.

"Now, now," he said. "Don't be hasty. I've news I'm bursting to tell you."

"I don't want to hear it."

"Oh, but you do," he insisted. "You'll kick yourself from here to the moon if you don't come and listen."

I wanted to tell him what he could do with his news, but there was something in his wicked eyes which made me pause. I hesitated a moment, then stomped away out of earshot of the others. Steve followed me, Gannen Harst hot on his heels.

"If you hurt him..." Vancha warned them.

"We won't," Harst promised, then stopped and shielded us with his body from the view of the rest.

"Well?" I asked, as Steve stood smirking at me.

"We've come a long way, haven't we, Darren?" he remarked. "From the classroom at home to this Cavern of Retribution. From humanity to vampirism and vampanizm. From the day to the night."

"Tell me something I don't know," I grunted.

"I used to think it could have been different," he said softly, eyes distant. "But now I think it was always meant to be this way. It was your destiny to betray me and form an alliance with the vampires, your fate to become a Vampire Prince and lead the hunt for the Vampaneze Lord. Just as it was my destiny to find my own path into the night and..."

He stopped and a sly expression crept over his face. "Hold him," he grunted, and Gannen Harst grabbed my arms and held me rooted to the spot. "Are you ready to send him sleepy-byes?"

"Yes," Harst said. "But hurry, before the others intervene."

"Your wish is my command," Steve smiled, then put his lips close to my right ear and whispered something terrible … something dreadful … something that turned my world on its head and would haunt my every waking and sleeping moment from that instant on.

As he drew away, having tormented me with his devastating secret, I opened my mouth wide to shout the news to Vancha. Before I could utter a syllable, Gannen Harst breathed over me, the knockout gas of the vampires and vampaneze. As the fumes filled my lungs, the world around me faded, and then I was falling, unconscious, into the tortured sleep of the damned.

The last thing I heard before I blacked out was Steve, laughing hysterically — the sound of a victorious demon cackling.

CHAPTER TWENTY-ONE

I DIDN'T know where I was when I awoke. I opened my eyes and saw a ceiling high above me, with lots of panels ripped out of it, three chandeliers burning dimly now that their candles were mere waxen stumps. I couldn't think where I might be. I sat up, groaning, and looked for Mr Crepsley, to ask him what was going on.

That's when I remembered.

Moaning as the painful memories returned, I clambered to my feet and looked around in desperation. The fire in the pit of stakes had almost burnt itself out. Mr Crepsley and the half-vampaneze were charred, unrecognizable collections of brittle, blackened bones. Vancha and Harkat were sitting by the edge of the pit, faces glum, silently mourning.

"How long was I out?" I shouted, lurching towards the tunnel leading out of the cavern, falling clumsily to my knees in my frenzied haste.

"Take it easy," Vancha said, helping me back to my feet.

I swiped his hands away and spun fiercely on him. "*How long?*" I roared.

Vancha eyeballed me, bemused, then shrugged. "Three hours, maybe more."

My eyelids closed hopelessly and I let myself collapse again. Too long. They'd be halfway to the other side of the world by now.

"What happened?" I asked. "The gas should have only knocked me out for fifteen or twenty minutes."

"You were exhausted," Vancha said. "It's been a long night. I'm surprised you woke this soon. It's dawn outside. We didn't expect you to stir until dusk."

I shook my head mutely, disgusted.

"Are you OK, Darren?" Harkat asked, hobbling over to join us.

"No!" I snapped. "I'm not OK. None of us is."

Rising, I brushed past the puzzled-looking pair, and made my slow, painful way to the pit, where I gazed once more upon the smouldering remains of my dearest friend and mentor.

"He's in a state of shock," I heard Vancha mutter softly to Harkat. "Go easy on him. It'll take him a while to recover."

"*Recover!*" I shrieked, sitting down and laughing maniacally.

Vancha and Harkat sat beside me, Vancha to my left, Harkat to my right. Each laid a hand on mine in a silent show of support. My throat grew tight and I thought I was going to cry at last. But after a few seconds the tears still wouldn't come, so I let my gaze drift back to the pit, while my thoughts returned to Steve's chilling revelation.

The flames grew lower and the cavern cooled. It also darkened, as the candles overhead quenched themselves one by one.

"We'd better get up there and ... relight the candles," Harkat said, "or else we won't be able to ... see clearly when we go down to ... collect Mr Crepsley's bones."

"Leave him there," I said sullenly. "This is as good a resting place as any."

Harkat and Vancha stared at me uncertainly.

"But you were the one who wanted to bury him," Vancha reminded me.

"That was before Steve took me aside," I sighed. "It doesn't matter where we leave him now. Nothing matters any more."

"How can you say that?" Vancha snapped angrily. "We won, Darren! We killed the Lord of the Vampaneze! The price we paid was high, but it was worth it."

"You think so?" I asked bitterly.

"Of course!" he shouted. "What's one life judged against thousands? We knew the odds coming into this. We'd have sacrificed all our lives if we had to. I feel Larten's loss as much as you — he was my friend long before he was yours. But he died honourably, and gave his life for a cause that was just. If his spirit's looking down on us, he'll be willing us to celebrate his great victory, not bemoan his—"

"You remember our first run-in with the Vampaneze Lord?" I interrupted. "You recall how he masqueraded as a servant, so we paid no notice to him and attacked the others, allowing him to escape?"

Vancha nodded warily. "Aye. What of it?"

"They tricked us then, Vancha," I said, "and they've done it again. We've won nothing. Mr Crepsley died in vain."

Vancha and Harkat gawped at me.

"What...? I don't... Are you saying...? *What?*" Harkat gasped eventually.

"The cloaked half-vampaneze on the platform was a decoy," I sighed. "He wasn't the same person we saw in the glade. Steve told me the truth before he left. That was his parting present."

"No!" Vancha wheezed, his face ashen. "He lied! That was their Lord. The look of despair on their faces when we killed him—"

"—was genuine," I said. "Most of the vampaneze and vampets in the cavern believed he was their Lord. They were tricked just like we were. Only Gannen Harst and a handful of others knew the truth."

"Then we're back where we were at the start?" Vancha moaned. "He's alive? We've no idea what he looks like? No way of knowing where he'll turn next?"

"Not exactly," I said with a crooked half-smile. "There are only two hunters left now. That much has changed." I let out a long, disparaging breath, and gazed down into the pit again. I didn't want to tell them the rest, not coming so hot on the heels of Mr Crepsley's death and news of the Vampaneze Lord's escape. I'd have spared them this extra blow if I could.

But they had to be warned. In case something happened to me, they had to be told, so they could spread the word and carry on without me if necessary.

"I know who he is," I whispered emotionlessly. "Steve told me. He broke the big secret. Harst didn't want him to, but he did it anyway, to hurt me that little bit more, as if Mr Crepsley's death wasn't bad enough."

"He told you who the ... Vampaneze Lord is?" Harkat gasped.

I nodded.

"Who?" Vancha shouted, leaping to his feet. "Which one of those scum sends others to do his dirty work for him? Tell me and I'll—"

"It's Steve," I said, and Vancha's strength deserted him. Slumping to the floor, he gazed at me in horror. Harkat too. "It's Steve," I said again, feeling empty and scared inside, knowing I'd never feel any different until – unless – he was killed, even if I lived to be a thousand. Wetting my lips, focusing on the flames, I said the whole terrible truth out loud. *"Steve Leopard is the Lord of the Vampaneze."*

After that there was only silence, burning and despair.

TO BE CONTINUED...

RAT GUTS

→ Double history on a Wednesday afternoon — total nightmare! A few minutes ago, I would have said that I couldn't imagine anything worse. But when there's a knock at the door, and it opens, and I spot my Mum outside, I realise — life can always get worse.

When a parent turns up at school, unexpected, it means one of two things. Either somebody close to you has been seriously injured or died, or you're in trouble.

My immediate reaction — please don't let anybody be dead! I think of Dad, Gret, uncles, aunts, cousins. It could be any of them. Alive and kicking this morning. Now stiff and cold, tongue sticking out, a slab of dead meat just waiting to be cremated or buried. I remember Gran's funeral. The open coffin. Her shining flesh, having to kiss her forehead, the pain, the tears. Please don't let anyone be dead! Please! Please! Please! Ple—

Then I see Mum's face, white with rage, and I know she's here to punish, not comfort.

I groan, roll my eyes and mutter under my breath, "Bring on the corpses!"

→ The head's office. Me, Mum and Mr Donnellan. Mum's ranting and raving about cigarettes. I've been seen smoking behind the bike shed (the oldest cliché in the book!). She wants to know if the head's aware of this, of what the pupils in his school are getting up to.

I feel a bit sorry for Mr Donnellan. He has to sit there, looking like a schoolboy himself, shuffling his feet and saying he didn't know this was going on and he'll launch an investigation and put a quick end to it. Liar! Of course he knew. Every school has a smoking area. That's life. Teachers don't approve, but they turn a blind eye most of the time. Certain kids smoke — fact. Safer to have them smoking at school than sneaking off the grounds during breaks and at lunch.

Mum knows that too. She must! She was young once, like she's always reminding me. Kids were no different in Mum's time. If she stopped for a minute and thought back, she'd see what a bloody embarrassment she's being. I wouldn't mind her having a go at me at home, but you don't march into school and start laying down the law in the headmaster's office. She's out of order — big time.

But it's not like I can tell her, is it? I can't pipe up with, "Oi! Mother! You're disgracing us both, so shut yer trap!"

I smirk at the thought, and of course that's when Mum pauses for the briefest of moments and catches me. "What are you grinning at?" she roars, and then she's off again — I'm smoking myself into an early grave, the school's responsible, what sort of a freak show is Mr Donnellan running, la-di-la-di-la-di-bloody-la!

BAWR*ing!*

➜ Her rant at school's nothing compared to the one I get at home. Screaming at the top of her lungs, blue bloody murder.

She's going to send me off to boarding school — no, military school! See how I like that, having to get up at dawn each morning and do a hundred press-ups before breakfast. How does *that* sound?

"Is breakfast a fry-up or some cereally, yoghurty crap?" is my response, and I know the second it's out of my stupid mouth that it's the wrong thing to say. This isn't the time for the famed Grubbs Grady brand of cutting-edge humour.

Cue the enraged Mum fireworks. Who do I think I am? Do I *know* how much they spend on me? What if I get kicked out of school? Then the clincher, the one Mum doesn't pull too often, which I know means there'll be hell to pay when she does: "Just wait till your father gets home!"

→ Dad's not as freaked out as Mum, but he's not happy. He tells me how disappointed he is. They've warned me so many times about the dangers of smoking, how it destroys people's lungs and gives them cancer.

"Smoking's dumb," he says. We're in the kitchen (I haven't been out of it since Mum dragged me home from school early, except to go to the toilet). "It's disgusting, antisocial and lethal. Why do it, Grubbs? I thought you had more sense."

I shrug wordlessly. What's there to say? They're being unfair. *Of course* smoking's dumb. *Of course* it gives you cancer. *Of course* I shouldn't be doing it. But my friends smoke. It's cool. You get to hang out with cool people at lunch and talk about cool things. But only if you smoke. You can't be *in* if you're *out*. And they know that. Yet here they stand, acting all Gestapo, asking me to account for my actions.

"How long has he been smoking? That's what I want to know!" Mum's started referring to me in the third person since Dad arrived. I'm beneath direct mention.

"Yes," Dad says. "How long, Grubbs?"

"I dunno."

"Weeks? Months? Longer?"

"A few months maybe. But only a couple a day."

"If he says a couple, he means at least five or six," Mum snorts.

"No, I don't!" I shout. "I mean a couple!"

"Don't raise your voice to me!" Mum roars back.

"Easy," Dad begins, but Mum goes on as if he isn't there.

"Do you think it's clever? Filling your lungs with rubbish, killing yourself? We didn't bring you up to watch you give yourself cancer! We don't need this, certainly not at this time, not when —"

"Enough!" Dad shouts, and we both jump. Dad almost never shouts. He usually gets very quiet when he's angry. Now his face is red and he's glaring — but at both of us, not just me.

Mum coughs, as if she's ashamed of herself. She sits, brushes her hair back off her face and looks at me with wounded eyes. I hate it when she pulls a face like this. It's impossible to look at her straight or argue back.

"I want you to stop, Grubbs," Dad says, back in control now. "We're not going to punish you—" Mum starts to object, but Dad silences her with a curt wave of his hand "—but I want your word that you'll stop. I know it won't be easy. I know your friends will give you a hard time. But this is important. Some things matter more than looking cool. Will you promise, Grubbs?" He pauses. "Of course, that's if you're *able* to quit…"

"Of course I'm able," I mutter. "I'm not addicted or anything."

"Then will you? For *your* sake — not ours?"

I shrug, trying to act like it's no big thing, like I was planning to stop anyway. "Sure, if you're going to make that much of a fuss about it," I yawn.

Dad smiles. Mum smiles. I smile.

Then Gret walks in the back door and she's smiling too — but it's an evil, big-sister-superior smile. "Have we sorted all our little problems out yet?" she asks, voice high and fake-innocent.

And I know instantly — Gret grassed me up to Mum! She found out that I was smoking and she told. The cow!

As she swishes past, beaming like an angel, I burn fiery holes in the back of her head with my eyes, and a single word echoes through my head like the sound of ungodly thunder…

Revenge!

→ I love rubbish dumps. You can find all sorts of disgusting stuff there. The perfect place to go browsing if you want to get even with your annoying traitor of a sister.

I climb over mounds of garbage and root through black bags and soggy cardboard boxes. I'm not sure exactly what I'm going to use, or in what fashion, so I wait for inspiration to strike. Then, in a small plastic bag, I find six dead rats, necks broken, just starting to rot. *Excellent!*

Look out, Gret — here I come!

→ Eating breakfast at the kitchen table. Radio turned down low. Listening to the noises upstairs. Trying not to giggle. Waiting for the outburst.

Gret's in her shower. She showers all the time, at least twice a day, before she goes to school and when she gets back. Sometimes she has one before going to bed too. I don't know why anybody would bother to keep themselves so clean. I reckon it's a form of madness.

Because she's so obsessed with showering, Mum and Dad gave her the *en suite* bedroom. They figured I wouldn't mind. And I don't. In fact, it's perfect. I wouldn't have been able to pull my trick if Gret didn't have her own shower, with its very own towel rack.

The shower goes off. Splatters, then drips, then silence. I tense with excitement. I know Gret's routines inside out. She always pulls her towel down off its rack *after* she's showered, not before. I can't hear her footsteps, but I imagine her taking the three or four steps to the towel rack. Reaching up. Pulling it down. Aaaaaaaaannndddd...

On cue — screams galore. A shocked, single scream to start. Then a volley of them, one running into another. I push my bowl of soggy cornflakes aside and prepare myself for the biggest laugh of the year.

Mum and Dad are by the sink, discussing the day ahead. They go stiff when they hear the screams, then dash towards the stairs, which I can see from where I'm sitting.

Gret appears before they reach the stairs. Crashes out of her room, screaming, slapping bloody shreds from her arms, tearing them from her hair. She's covered in red. Towel clutched with one hand over her front — even terrified out of her wits, there's no way she's going to come down naked!

"What's wrong?" Mum shouts. "What's happening?"

"Blood!" Gret screams. "I'm covered in blood! I pulled the towel down! I…"

She stops. She's spotted me laughing. I'm doubled over. It's the funniest thing I've ever seen.

Mum turns and looks at me. Dad does too. They're speechless.

Gret picks a sticky, pink chunk out of her hair, slowly this time, and studies it. "What did you put on my towel?" she asks quietly.

"Rat guts!" I howl, pounding the table, crying with laughter. "I got… rats at the rubbish dump… chopped them up… and…" I almost get sick, I'm laughing so much.

Mum stares at me. Dad stares at me. Gret stares at me.

Then —

"You lousy son of a–!"

I don't catch the rest of the insult — Gret flies down the

stairs ahead of it. She drops her towel on the way. I don't have time to react to that before she's on me, slapping and scratching at my face.

"What's wrong, *Gretelda*?" I giggle, fending her off, calling her by the name she hates. She normally calls me Grubitsch in response, but she's too mad to think of it now.

"Scum!" she shrieks. Then she lunges at me sharply, grabs my jaw, jerks my mouth open and tries her hardest to stuff a handful of rat guts down my throat.

I stop laughing instantly — a mouthful of rotten rat guts wasn't part of the grand über-joke! "Get off!" I roar, lashing out wildly. Mum and Dad suddenly recover and shout at exactly the same time.

"Stop that!"

"Don't hit your sister!"

"She's a lunatic!" I gasp, pushing myself away from the steaming Gret, falling off my chair.

"He's an animal!" Gret sobs, picking more chunks of guts from her hair, wiping rat blood from her face. I realise she's crying — serious waterworks — and her face is as red as her long, straight hair. Not red from the blood — red from anger, shame and... *fear*?

Mum picks up the dropped towel, takes it to Gret, wraps it around her. Dad's just behind them, face as dark as death. Gret picks more strands and loops of rat guts from her hair, then howls with anguish.

"They're all over me!" she yells, then throws some of the guts at me. "You bloody little monster!"

"*You're* the one who's *bloody!*" I cackle. Gret dives for my throat.

"No more!" Dad doesn't raise his voice but his tone stops us dead.

Mum's staring at me with open disgust. Dad's shooting daggers. I sense that I'm the only one who sees the funny side of this.

"It was just a joke," I mutter defensively before the accusations fly.

"I hate you!" Gret hisses, then bursts into fresh tears and flees dramatically.

"Cal," Mum says to Dad, freezing me with an ice-cold glare. "Take Grubitsch in hand. I'm going up to try and comfort Gretelda." Mum always calls us by our given names. She's the one who picked them, and is the only person in the world who doesn't see how shudderingly awful they are.

Mum heads upstairs. Dad sighs, walks to the counter, tears off several sheets of kitchen paper and mops up some of the guts and streaks of blood from the floor. After a couple of silent minutes of this, as I lie uncertainly by my upturned chair, he turns his steely gaze on me. Lots of sharp lines around his mouth and eyes — the sign that he's *really* angry, even angrier than he was about me smoking.

"You shouldn't have done that," he says.

"It was funny," I mutter.

"No," he barks. "It wasn't."

"I didn't mean anything by it!" I cry. "She's done worse to me! She told Mum about me smoking — I know it was her!

And remember the time she melted my lead soldiers? And cut up my comics? And—"

"There are some things you should never do," Dad interrupts softly. "This was *wrong*. You invaded your sister's privacy, humiliated her, terrified her senseless. And the timing! You…" He pauses and ends with a fairly weak "…upset her greatly." He checks his watch. "Get ready for school. We'll discuss your punishment later."

I trudge upstairs miserably, unable to see what all the aggro is about. It was a great joke. I laughed for hours when I thought of it. And all that hard work — chopping the rats up, mixing in some water to keep them fresh and make them gooey, getting up early, sneaking into her bathroom while she was asleep, carefully putting the guts in place — wasted!

I pass Gret's bedroom and hear her crying pitifully. Mum's whispering softly to her. My stomach gets hard, the way it does when I know I've done something bad. I ignore it. "I don't care what they say," I grumble, kicking open the door to my room and tearing off my pyjamas. "It was a brilliant joke!"

→ Purgatory. Confined to my room after school for a month. A whole bloody *MONTH*! No TV, no computer, no comics, no books — except schoolbooks. Dad leaves my chess set in the room too — no fear my chess-mad parents would take *that* away from me! Chess is almost a religion in this house. Gret and I were reared on it. While other toddlers were being taught how to put jigsaws together, we were busy learning the ridiculous rules of chess.

I can come downstairs for meals, and bathroom visits are allowed, but otherwise I'm a prisoner. I can't even go out at the weekends.

In solitude, I call Gret every name under the moon the first night. Mum and Dad bear the brunt of my curses the next. After that I'm too miserable to blame anyone, so I sulk in moody silence and play chess against myself to pass the time.

They don't talk to me at meals. The three of them act like I'm not not there. Gret doesn't even glance at me spitefully and sneer, the way she usually does when I'm getting the doghouse treatment.

But what have I done that's so bad? OK, it was a crude joke and I knew I'd get into trouble — but their reactions are waaaaaaay over the top. If I'd done something to embarrass Gret in public, fair enough, I'd take what was coming. But this was a private joke, just between us. They shouldn't be making such a song and dance about it.

Dad's words echo back to me — "And the timing!" I think about them a lot. And Mum's, when she was having a go at me about smoking, just before Dad cut her short — "We don't need this, certainly not at this time, not when—"

What did they mean? What were they talking about? What does the timing have to do with anything?

Something stinks here — and it's not just rat guts.

DARREN SHAN
VAMPIRE BLOOD TRILOGY

THE SAGA OF DARREN SHAN

No one expects to pay for
their mistakes in blood

But for Darren Shan, life as an ordinary schoolboy is over.
In *Cirque Du Freak*, Darren strikes a deal with
a creature of the night that will change his life for ever.
In *The Vampire's Assistant*, Darren joins the vampire ranks,
but fights the urge to drink human blood.
And in *Tunnels of Blood*, Darren will need all the luck of
the vampires to defeat a savage enemy.

Become a half-vampire
Explore the night
Feed

ISBN 0 00 714374-5

www.harpercollinschildrensbooks.co.uk

DARREN SHAN

VAMPIRE RITES TRILOGY

THE SAGA OF DARREN SHAN

In *Vampire Mountain*, Darren Shan and Mr Crepsley
embark on a dangerous trek to the very heart
of the vampire world. In *Trials of Death*, Darren has to
pass five Trials to prove himself to the vampire clan.
And in *The Vampire Prince*, can Darren outwit
a Vampire Prince, or is this the end of thousands
of years of vampire rule…?

Become a half-vampire
Explore the night
Feed

ISBN 0 00 714375-3

www.harpercollinschildrensbooks.co.uk

DARREN SHAN
VAMPIRE DESTINY TRILOGY

THE SAGA OF DARREN SHAN

In *The Lake of Souls*, there's a deadly new challenge
for Darren Shan, the Vampire Prince. What awaits
Darren and Harkat in the murky waters of the dead?
Who will rule the night in *Lord of the Shadows* — Darren or
his deadly enemy, Steve Leopard? And in *Sons of Destiny*,
the Saga of Darren Shan comes to its final,
bloody conclusion.

Become a half-vampire
Explore the night
Feed

ISBN 0 00 717959-6

www.harpercollinschildrensbooks.co.uk

Order Form

To order direct from the publishers, just make a list of the titles you want and fill in the form below:

Name ....

Address ....

....

....

Send to: Dept 6, HarperCollins Publishers Ltd, Westerhill Road, Bishopbriggs, Glasgow G64 2QT.

Please enclose a cheque or postal order to the value of the cover price, plus:

UK & BFPO: Add £1.00 for the first book, and 25p per copy for each additional book ordered.

Overseas and Eire: Add £2.95 service charge. Books will be sent by surface mail but quotes for airmail despatch will be given on request.

A 24-hour telephone ordering service is available to holders of Visa, MasterCard, Amex or Switch cards on 0141- 772 2281.

HarperCollins *Children's Books*